LAND OF MILK
AND MONEY

Anthony Barcellos

LAND OF MILK
AND MONEY

A Novel

Tagus Press at UMass Dartmouth ⋄ *Dartmouth, Massachusetts*

Tagus Press at UMass Dartmouth

www.portstudies.umassd.edu

© 2012 Anthony Barcellos

All rights reserved

Manufactured in the United States of America

General Editor: Frank F. Sousa

Managing Editor: Mario Pereira

Manuscript Editor: Richard J. Larschan

Designed by Mindy Basinger Hill

Typeset in 11/14 Adobe Jenson Pro

Money image © Vitalik-sv | Dreamstime.com

Cow image by E. Dronkert,

www.flickr.com/photos/dnet/5977968089

Tagus Press books are produced and
distributed for Tagus Press by University Press
of New England, which is a member of the Green
Press Initiative. The paper used in this book meets
their minimum requirement for recycled paper.

For all inquiries, please contact:

Tagus Press at UMass Dartmouth

Center for Portuguese Studies and Culture

285 Old Westport Road

North Dartmouth MA 02747-2300

Tel. 508-999-8255

Fax 508-999-9272

www.portstudies.umassd.edu

Library of Congress Cataloging-
in-Publication Data

Barcellos, Anthony.

Land of milk and money:

a novel / Anthony Barcellos.

          p.   cm.—

(Portuguese in the Americas series; 18)

ISBN 978-1-933227-40-5 (pbk.: alk. paper)

1. Azorean Americans—California—Fiction.

2. Immigrant families—Fiction.

3. Inheritance and succession—Fiction.

4. Right ofproperty—Fiction.

5. Dairy farmers—California—Central Valley
(Valley)—Fiction.

6. Tulare County (Calif.)—Fiction.

7. Domestic fiction. I. Title.

PS3602.A7695L36 2012

813'.6—dc22   2011053100

5   4   3   2   1

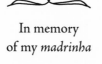

In memory
of my *madrinha*

Contents

PART VI

PART VII

PART VIII

Author's Note

A helpful glossary of Portuguese words
and phrases can be found at the back of the book,
along with a cast of characters.

Preface

When I was a boy, I had a tree house made of twine. The twine came from the remains of hay bales used to feed cattle on our family dairy farm. I braided the twine into ropes that I stretched among the branches of a tree in our backyard to anchor the space occupied by my tree house. Individual strands were then woven back and forth among the anchor ropes, creating a taut mesh that formed the floor and walls. The result was a sisal-fiber penthouse in the treetops, perfect for long, comfortable hours of reading or the occasional gently swaying nap. I was probably one of the few boys who read Tolkien's account of Lothlórien ensconced in a woven aerie in an *Ailanthus* tree.

I wrote *Land of Milk and Money* in the same way I created my tree house. The trial scenes framing the structure occur in chronological order at regular intervals beginning each major division throughout the book, while flashbacks to other incidents in the lives of the principals are woven about them, finally knotted together in the resolution of the family battle.

Residents of Tulare County may fancy they recognize individuals and incidents depicted here, but this narrative interweaves fictional people and events with bygone memories of farm life that are essentially imaginary, not autobiographical.

ANTHONY BARCELLOS

THE FRANCISCO-SALAZAR FAMILIES

Paulo Candido "Chico" Francisco {1894} + Teresa Maria Machado {1894}

Fatima Lourdes Francisco {1919} + Louis Manuel Salazar {1916}

Candido Gabriel "Candy" Francisco {1922} + Odile Marie Avila {1928}

Paulo Agosto "Paulinho" Francisco {1925} + Carmina Maria Soares {1931}

Antonio Louis "Tony" Salazar {1941}

Manuel Paulo "Manny" Salazar {1944} + Linda Maria Fonseca {1945}

Otelo Candido Salazar {1947}

Leonel Gabriel "Leo" Salazar {1948}

Catarina "Cat" Salazar {1954} + Kevin Lineman {1953}

Elvino "Elvis" Salazar {1956}

Randall "Randy" Salazar {1960}

Candido Gabriel "Junior" Francisco, Jr. {1949} + Sofia Silveira {1952}

João José "Jojo" Francisco {1951} + Rita Branco {1951}

Ferdinando Alberto "Ferdie" Francisco {1952}

Paul Francisco {1951}

Mary Carmen Francisco {1954} + Gerry Chamberlain {1953}

Henry "Hank" Francisco {1955} + Magdalena Maria Fontes {1955}

Alexander "Alex" Francisco {1970}

PART I

The Gambit

"Greetings! We who are about to lose salute you!"

The strangely cheerful salutation disturbed the members of the Francisco family. They exchanged nervous glances, concerned that their attorneys were talking about losing.

"Harold, I think you owe our clients an explanation."

The speaker was the eldest of the three-man legal team. Ryan Bowman was tall and spare. He spoke with measured tones and held himself with dignity — diminished somewhat by the obvious hairpiece that covered his bald pate.

Bowman had addressed the shortest member of the team. Harold Widener was energetic and compact, with black hair and a feral glint in his eye.

"Sorry, folks. It's a strategic move. Today I guarantee that the judge is going to rule against us. No question."

"No question at all," added Dennis Ramos, the third and youngest member of the team. Ramos was round-faced and blond. As usual, there was a smile on his face. He often used it to good effect in the courtroom.

"We're going to ask for the moon," added Ramos, "and there's no way the judge will give it to us."

Bowman was the lead attorney for the team, so he offered a summation.

"Today we confront directly the claim that Teresa Francisco's will was forged. One by one we've knocked down the petitioners' claims and it's down to this last key item. The other side is going to bring in a big-city expert to explain to us simple country folk that Mrs. Francisco's signature is not authentic. I will make a motion that the expert witness be barred from testifying. The judge will deny the motion and we'll move on from there."

Despite their differences in size and age, the Franciscos all bore the stamp of their Azorean heritage — variations on the theme of brown eyes and dark hair (if it hadn't gone gray or disappeared). The eldest was close to sixty, while the youngest was not yet in his teens. They murmured among themselves for several seconds, then one of the Franciscos raised his voice to ask a question.

"Why will we ask to have the witness barred if we already know we're going to lose?" asked Paul.

The attorneys grinned at the naïveté of the young man's question. Bowman answered.

"First of all, it is just barely possible we could get lucky and win the motion. You never know unless you try. Second, though, you have to keep the pressure on. By making a motion in front of the jury that a witness is not competent to testify, you plant a seed in their minds that maybe they shouldn't take her too seriously. And in this case we can plant a really big seed."

"The biggest seed ever," said Widener. "Things are going to get rough. Ryan did the legwork in investigating the 'expert' witness and today he's going after her. I'm going to make all the objections when the opposing counsel sets her foot wrong. We've tangled before and she hates me, so it'll get her back up if I'm the one who offers the objections. Dennis here will do any sweet and gentle follow-ups we need, because he's got a knack for being the nice guy and the jury will like him."

Widener looked at his co-counsels. "Did I leave anything out, guys?"

Bowman slowly shook his head in solemn negation, doing his elder statesman routine for the benefit of their clients. "No, it was a good summation."

Ramos flashed his patented jury-pleasing grin. "Right on the money, Hare."

Widener turned back to the family and singled out Candido Francisco, the balding, long-faced senior member of the clan. The small attorney was a study in contrasts with the tall and corpulent Candido.

"Okay, Mr. Francisco, I'm on your side for now and we'll all do the best we can. But once we win the lawsuit over your mother's will, rest assured I'll get every cent of your winnings for your wife in the divorce case."

"Just a second, Hare. I might have a claim on some of that in the boys' lawsuit over the dissolution of the family business," said Ramos, the smile still on his face.

The lawyers' observations reminded the Francisco family of the deep divisions that had split them into factions, and people suddenly shuffled about to give themselves more space.

Candido found himself standing alone.

Orphaned

The candy-striper who worked the reception desk looked up as a tall, long-faced man rushed into the hospital. He came directly to her and leaned his beefy body over the counter.

"I just got a message telling me that Dr. Schein wanted to see me. Can you tell him Candido Francisco is here?"

"Just a moment, sir."

As the young woman paged the doctor, Candido realized that he had forgotten to read her nametag. It said "Jennifer." Normally he would have taken care to look for the tag before speaking so that he could call her by name. He thought of it as a friendly gesture, but most of the recipients of his overt familiarity regarded him as slightly smarmy. Candido was imperviously unaware of how others reacted to him, but today he was also off his game and flustered.

"Mr. Francisco, please take a seat. I paged Dr. Schein and he'll see you as soon as he can."

"Thanks — uh — Jennifer. Thanks."

Candido sat down and rubbed his palms across the thighs of his jeans. The dampness of his hands and the dust on his pants left streaks on his palms, but he didn't notice. He had been stringing barbed wire on the fence posts of the new holding pen when his youngest son Ferdinando had barreled up in a Jeep to tell him that he had a phone message from the hospital.

"Was it Dr. Schein? What did he say?"

"I don't know, Dad. I didn't take the message."

"Who did? When did it come in?"

"It was in Mom's handwriting. She left it on the kitchen table. I saw it when I went in for a snack."

"*Damn!* Did it have a time written on it? Did you bring it with you, Ferdie?"

"Uh. Sorry. No. I mean, I didn't bring it. And I don't know if it had a time on it. Mom's not home. I don't know when she took the call."

Candido dropped the wire snips from his hand.

"Clean up here. I have to go."

He dashed past his son and jumped into the Jeep. Twenty minutes later he burst into the hospital's main reception area. It was only another twenty minutes, though it seemed longer, before the doctor appeared.

Candido jumped to his feet. The doctor solemnly gave his hand a brief shake, his slender fingers vanishing entirely into Candido's huge grip. He extricated himself, took Candido by the arm and steered him out of the reception area and into the garden courtyard. He led the anxious man to an isolated bench in the midst of the foliage and sat him down. The doctor sat down next to Candido, giving him a level gaze.

"I'm sorry, Mr. Francisco. It happened this morning."

Candido let out an inarticulate moan. The doctor continued.

"Her condition took a serious turn for the worse as we were prepping her for the hip replacement. We never even began the procedure. That's when I called you and your brother. We made her comfortable, as comfortable as we could, and waited to see if she would stabilize. But she just kept getting weaker. Your mother passed away" — the doctor paused to glance at his wristwatch — "about two hours ago."

When Candido found his voice it was hoarse.

"Was anyone with her?"

"Your brother and sister-in-law got here in time. And their daughter, too."

"But I'm her eldest and I wasn't here."

"Mr. Francisco, your mother did not regain consciousness. She wouldn't have known."

"She knows *now*," said Candido, his eyes darting around the courtyard as if he expected his mother's shade to be lurking behind the bushes. The doctor maintained a diplomatic silence for several seconds.

Candido sucked in a huge breath and exhaled slowly. And again. He got control over himself and stood up. The doctor rose, too.

"Thank you, doctor. Thank you for everything you did for my mother. The whole family thanks you. I guess it was just her time." He trailed off. "She lived a long time and I guess it was enough. It was her time."

Candido thrust out his paw and gave the doctor's hand another squeeze. With an audible sniff he turned and marched back into the reception area, across the room, and out the main entrance.

His mother's death left him both bereaved and freed. She had been one of the great constants in his life, but he had chafed under her quiet disapproval. With conflicting emotions gnawing at him, Candido made a decision.

He found the bank of pay phones under the breezeway next to the parking lot. He scrambled in his pocket for change and found none. Cursing softly, he picked up the phone and placed a collect call. Candido waited impatiently as the operator made the connection and verified that the recipient was willing to accept the charges.

"Will you accept a collect call from Candido Francisco?"

"Of course, operator. Thank you. Candy, is that you?"

"It's me, honey. It's me. I'm sorry to be bothering you, but I have to talk to someone."

"No bother. Are you okay?"

Candido paused before answering. Then he blurted it out.

"My mom. She died this morning. Two hours ago. She's gone."

He started sobbing.

"Oh, Candy! I'm so sorry! Is there anything I can do to help? Do you need help? What can I do for you and Odile?"

Candido stiffened at the mention of his wife's name.

"Odile doesn't need anything. Or she needs too much. You know. The usual with her. She didn't even take the trouble to tell me when the hospital called. She just left a note and then went off to town. I think I have to go off, too."

"What do you mean? I don't understand. Go off where?"

"You asked if I need anything. I need *you*. I'm going home to pack a bag and then I'm coming up there. I need to be with someone I love and that sure as hell isn't Odile."

Candido held his breath waiting for the answer.

"Candy, are you really, really sure? You're distraught right now and you might want to think about it some more."

"I already know what I want. What I need. I need to get out of here. I need to get away from here. I need to be with you. Can I be with you?"

"Okay, Candy. Okay. I'll be here waiting for you."

"Two hours. I'll be there in two hours."

Candido hung up the phone and stood there biting his lip. He realized that his face was wet. The tears had started at the beginning of the phone call and had been streaming down his face the entire time. The pockets he had searched unsuccessfully for change contained one of his big red handkerchiefs. Pulling it out and deciding it was clean enough, he wiped his face.

Candido walked over to where he had parked the Jeep and started it up. He drove out of the parking lot and toward what would soon be his ex-home.

MARCH 1940

Dear Dairy

The sun was low on the horizon as Paulo "Chico" Candido Francisco gazed across the field with a sharp eye. He was looking for shadows indicating depressions or bright spots revealing high points. Chico smiled because he wasn't seeing any. He and his sons had done good work in leveling their new parcel of land.

Chico squatted down and dug his fingers into the soil, squeezing the clumps of earth, still slightly damp with the morning's dew. He breathed in the wine-rich tang of living matter. It would bear good crops when brought under cultivation. He stood up and dusted off his hands.

The land would bear good crops when the water came. California's Central Valley was arid. The morning dew and the occasional rain could support nothing more than nondescript scrub. This field had been second-rate grazing land, sufficient to keep alive some scrawny heifers as they wandered about, cropping the sparse grass and nibbling at whatever brush they could find. Chico was not interested in scrawny livestock. When he and his sons made the field bloom with alfalfa or oats, they would harvest a bounty that would fatten up his herd and produce gallon upon gallon of creamy milk.

When the water came. Chico cast his eyes over to the property line, where thin wooden stakes bore brightly colored flags. He grinned. Chico remembered when the men from Sacramento had come to Tulare County, hauling their surveying equipment with them. While many of the locals had eyed them with suspicion before turning away and ignoring them, Chico had grabbed his younger son and gone over to talk to them. The boy had grown up in California and spoke English like a native. He helped his father communicate with the survey team.

That's how Chico discovered that state and federal authorities really were serious about the irrigation projects that people kept talking about. Most folks dismissed the idea of such huge public works as nothing more than idle talk. They were confirmed in that conclusion when the survey teams packed up and went away. It was a false alarm, they said. But by then Chico had learned that the plans were real and had picked up some clues as to the routes that were the most serious contenders.

When he plunked down a wad of his carefully husbanded cash for 320 acres of land, Chico chose an unprepossessing tract of grazing scrub that he figured would be one of the first to tap into the future irrigation system. Two years later, when the survey teams returned in force and he watched them mark out a canal route on the edge of his property, Chico knew his bet had paid off. He and the boys hitched up the land-plane to their biggest tractor and began to scrape the field down to an even surface, flattening the hummocks and filling in the depressions. Fields need to be level to benefit optimally from irrigation water, and Chico believed in benefitting optimally.

He walked back to his pickup truck. The boys would be finishing the morning shift in the dairy barn and would be ready for breakfast soon. Their mother and sister would be setting out a table for the ravenous sons, the man of the house, and the two hired men. Then it would be back into the dairy barn to arrange the milk cans for the daily pickup by the truck from the local creamery and out into the fields to tend to the crops. Everyone would work nonstop until a break for lunch, following which the afternoon shift would begin. Cows need to be milked twice a day and their rhythms determined the daily routine on a dairy farm. And on a dairy farm, the daily routine applied to all seven days of the week. Cows did not take weekends off.

Chico thought about his family with deeply mixed emotions as he drove home. He knew that his wife Teresa missed the Old Country and had marked the ten-year anniversary of their arrival in the United States with ill-concealed anguish. Hadn't the original plan called for ten years of hard work in the land of milk and honey, followed by a triumphant return to the Azores?

Of course, mused Chico, it hadn't been a *firm* deadline. He and Teresa had always agreed that they would return to their homeland when the time was right. Unfortunately, he had taken that agreement as tacit approval of an extension of the ten years, while Teresa had taken it as an unspoken promise that he would take them home sooner. Now twelve years had elapsed and their future was looking both brighter and more American.

Chico couldn't come right out and say it, but he suspected that the Francisco family was here to stay. Their only daughter was an adult now and had a serious beau. Teresa had confided to him that she suspected Fatima would be engaged soon. No crystal ball was necessary. If they returned to the Azores now, Fatima would insist on staying behind. The worry lines on Teresa's face deepened. Chico began to wonder if it would help or hurt the situation if he announced that the Azores were no longer home.

Home was California now and home they would stay.

Chico shuddered at the very thought of trying to say such a thing to Teresa. No, it would never do. She would cry for days after such a blunt acknowledgment that she was forever separated from her sisters and brother. It was better to let it develop gradually.

Chico parked his pickup in front of his house just as his two boys arrived from the dairy barn. They put their rubber boots by the front door as their father climbed down from the truck and they followed him inside in their stocking feet. Chico's sons were teenagers now, not the small wide-eyed children who had trekked across the world with their parents twelve years earlier. Both were brawny young men, hardened like their father by the constant physical labor that running a dairy farm entailed. Neither one was in school, having opted out after graduating from elementary school. They had no time for high school and book-learning. At least the elder son didn't.

The younger son would have probably gone to school if he hadn't seen it as conflicting with his family responsibilities. Chico sometimes felt conflicted about not having encouraged Paulinho to go to high school anyway. He saw how eagerly the boy would read his older sister's books whenever he could steal a few minutes of free time. Still, it was a big help to have him on the ranch full-time, and Chico had not pressured his son to drop out.

He hadn't pressured the older boy either, but that was a moot point. Candido would have dropped out even sooner if given the opportunity. The only thing he had picked up from school was the nickname of "Candy," which Chico didn't particularly like but didn't make a point of objecting to. Nicknames were popular back in the Old Country, where families often seemed to recycle the same names over and over again. It was only natural that Candido would acquire one, even if it wasn't a Portuguese nickname like his father's "Chico."

Candy might yet turn out to be a problem. He was a hard worker, but required constant direction. He didn't need constant supervision, but detailed instructions were always a must. Unquestioned ancient tradition said that the eldest son was supposed to be his father's trusty right arm and successor, but Chico recognized that Candy was an unimaginative plodder. What would become of the Francisco family dairy farm when its stewardship passed into the hands of such a person? It was Paulinho who was enthralled by his father's plans to expand the dairy and acquire more farm land. Paulinho was his father's helper, the son who had accompanied the father in the visit to chat up the survey teams, and thereafter his father's confidant in the plans to prepare for the arrival of water. When Chico had tentatively broached the subject with Candy, the boy had shrugged and said that someone would tell them if big plans were afoot for the Central Valley. (*I am telling you*, thought Chico, before shrugging his own shoulders and giving up.)

Chico knew he would have to think about it some more later.

JUNE 1983

The "Expert" Witness

Her hair was short, her body was stocky, her shoes were sensible, and her dress was blue. A patterned scarf was looped around her neck and pinned with a gold brooch at one shoulder. The urbane young woman lowered her right hand after taking the oath to tell various kinds of truth and climbed up onto the witness stand. She sat down and folded her hands in her lap, a prim smile on her face as she regarded the people scattered about the court room.

Judge Brevard Knight looked in the direction of the petitioners' attorney and raised his eyebrows.

"Ms. Onan?"

Beatrice Onan was a thin, middle-aged woman with angular features and artificially dark brown hair. She wore a pair of half-glasses, which she now snatched off and placed atop the stack of papers she had been shuffling.

"Yes, thank you, your honor." She tugged quickly at the hem of the half-jacket she was wearing over her dark pantsuit and strode over to the witness stand.

At the respondents' table, Dennis Ramos turned to the row of clients sitting immediately behind him and flashed his trademark grin.

"Brace yourselves," he whispered. "This is going to be good."

The Franciscos looked back with hopeful expressions on their faces. They returned their attention to the witness stand as Onan deferentially addressed the woman sitting there.

"Would you please state your name for the record?"

"My name is Peggy Hunter."

"Thank you very much, Ms. Hunter. Please tell me —"

Onan paused as she noticed a movement by the judge. He voicelessly mouthed two words at her when she looked at him. When her face remained blank, he did it again. Onan gave a start and turned back to her witness.

"Ms. Hunter, could you please give the court your *full name* for the record?"

"Oh, I'm sorry! My name is Lysistrata Margaret Hunter. I do business as L. Margaret Hunter and most people know me as Peggy."

Onan glanced at the judge, who gave a small nod. At the respondents' table, Harold Widener and Dennis Ramos exchanged muted smiles at the rival attorney's clumsy start.

"Thank you very much, Ms. Hunter. Please tell us your occupation."

Hunter sat up straight and smiled. "I am a registered handwriting expert who works as an expert witness in legal proceedings."

"Would you please describe your professional qualifications?"

Hunter's smile got broader. "I have ten years' experience as a handwriting expert and I've been a recognized courtroom expert for five years. I have testified in over thirty trials. In addition to being a partner in West Coast Forensics, Incorporated, I belong to the Golden Gate Handwriting Research Institute, and hold a master's degree from the University of California at Berkeley."

Ryan Bowman had been sitting quietly at the respondents' table, his carefully adjusted hairpiece neatly in place, calmly looking through the folder in front of him and ignoring the whispers of his colleagues, Widener and Ramos. Now that Peggy Hunter had finished her litany of professional qualifications,

Bowman lifted his head just as she looked over at the opposing attorneys to see their reaction to her *bona fides*. Bowman startled her with a big smile.

Hunter looked back at Onan for reassurance. The petitioners' attorney did her best to project confidence, although she had been rattled to discover that the respondents had hired three of her least favorite colleagues to oppose her. At least the lead attorney for the Franciscos, Ryan Bowman, was an older man and a bit of a plodder. And his hairpiece was ludicrous. The younger men, however, made her cringe every time she looked at their faces. They had beaten her in four of their last five encounters and she preferred to pretend they did not exist.

"Thank you very much, Ms. Hunter. As you know, this trial involves the forgery of a will —"

Harold Widener was on his feet as if spring-loaded. "*Objection*, your honor! Counsel is stating an unwarranted conclusion. She is declaring as fact a matter under dispute."

"Sustained. Ms. Onan, you will rephrase."

"Yes, your honor," said Onan tightly. "Ms. Hunter, as you know, this case involves a dispute over a will and an allegation by my clients that the signature on the will is a forgery. Have you testified previously in court as an expert witness in similar cases?"

Hunter relaxed visibly as the attorney led her back onto familiar territory.

"Yes, Ms. Onan. I have been engaged as an expert witness in no fewer than eight previous disputes over challenged signatures on last wills and testaments."

"Thank you very much. I have no further questions at this time. Your honor?"

"Yes. Thank you, Ms. Onan. Mr. Bowman, does counsel for the respondents have any questions for the petitioners' expert witness?"

"We do, your honor."

Bowman unfolded his tall and slender frame from his seat at the respondents' table and ambled casually over to the witness stand. He consulted the top page of the sheaf of papers in his hand. He drew out the seconds until the witness became visibly apprehensive.

"Good morning, Ms. Hunter."

"Uh, good morning."

"You did say that you hold a master's degree from Cal? From UC Berkeley, I mean?"

"Yes, that's right."

"Very good. Very good. Ms. Hunter, did you tell the court the field in which you earned that master's degree?"

"I don't recall. I may have mentioned it."

"I don't think you did. In any case, could you refresh our memories?"

"English literature."

"English literature in general?"

"Victorian era English literature."

"Very good. Thank you. Please, if you would, explain to the court how your degree is pertinent to your claimed expertise as a professional witness in handwriting identification."

Hunter regarded Bowman with irritation.

"I don't suppose it's *directly* pertinent, but I do hold an advanced degree."

"Yes, Ms. Hunter. In a field unrelated to handwriting identification. Thank you."

Bowman pretended to consult his notes again, flipping up the top page as if looking for a nugget of information on the second page. While some attorneys preferred to work without props, as if every bit of information lay within easy reach in their huge brains, Bowman felt more comfortable questioning opposing witnesses with a folder or batch of papers in his hands. He felt the jurors would not mind the appearance of a minor human frailty. Besides, some witnesses became conveniently anxious while wondering how much information their interrogator already held in his hands. Hunter appeared to be of that antsy breed. She began to fidget as Bowman framed his next question.

"Could you please inform the court, Ms. Hunter, whether you have any actual qualifications as a handwriting expert? I do believe you made some reference to being a 'registered' expert. What, exactly, does that mean?"

Hunter clasped her hands as she answered.

"It means that I hold a formal certificate of qualification as a handwriting expert, which is registered by the professional institution granting said certificate."

The formal language came out as if it were a rehearsed spiel. Bowman cocked his head at the witness and asked for clarification.

"'Institution,' Ms. Hunter? Does this 'institution' have a name?"

"The Miami Institute of Graphoanalysis," she replied, affecting a calm air and pronouncing the name as though it belonged to an educational institution of great repute.

"Is that a residential institution, Ms. Hunter?"

As much as it pained her to ask, she did not understand the question and needed clarification.

"I'm sorry, sir. I don't understand the question."

"I apologize for being unclear, Ms. Hunter. I mean, is the Miami Institute of Graphoanalysis an educational organization with actual buildings where people go to take classes, or is it a correspondence school where non-resident students take their classes by mail?"

"Uh, there is a, uh, residential *component*, although course work can also be submitted by mail."

"Did *you* take your courses by mail?"

"Yes."

"Thank you. And what did this 'residential component' consist of in your case?"

"I attended a graduation ceremony in person."

"So, no actual in-person course work?"

"Uh, no. Not as such."

"Not at all. Right?"

"Yes."

"Thank you."

Bowman dug into his sheaf of papers again, affecting a slightly embarrassed air as if searching for a lost scrap of information.

"Excuse me, Ms. Hunter." Pause. "I wonder if —" Pause. "Okay." He folded back a page as if marking a place. "I wonder if you could explain what graphoanalysis purports to be and how the Miami Institute of Graphoanalysis describes the qualifications that derive from completion of their certificate program?"

It was a heavily laden question, but it wasn't Bowman's job to make the opposing witness comfortable. Hunter did not seem particularly perturbed as she gave her answer.

"Well, graphoanalysis is the science of analyzing handwriting and the Miami Institute certifies its graduates as professionals in the field of handwriting analysis."

"Interesting. Thank you, Ms. Hunter. But isn't graphoanalysis specifically devoted to identifying personality traits by examining individuals' hand-writing? Things like cheerfulness, generosity, honesty, and other aspects of temperament? Is that supposed to be a 'science'?"

"Um. If you want to be strictly technical then, yes, there is a lot of emphasis on analyzing personality traits, but it is a methodical and scientific approach. It really is."

"That's an interesting claim, Ms. Hunter, since analyzing a person's personality by analyzing his or her handwriting is not recognized as a discipline at any college or university in North America. That is, of course, unless you include the non-credit extension courses that some colleges offer. Extension courses that include casting horoscopes and trance channeling. Isn't grapho-analysis simply a parlor game whose proper venue is birthday parties and bridal showers rather than court proceedings?"

Hunter looked to Onan to rescue her, but the petitioners' attorney was hunkered down at her table, waiting for her witness's ordeal to end.

"I don't think that's a fair characterization, sir," said Hunter to Bowman.

"One wonders. Did counsel for the petitioners hire you to determine the personality of their grandmother when she signed her will? Will you tell this court whether Teresa Francisco was cheerful or morose when she put pen to paper?"

"I will tell the court whether she was the one who actually signed it," said Hunter sullenly.

"One wonders how," retorted Bowman. He paused, looking down on the witness as if in sympathy.

"Let's leave that for now, Ms. Hunter. Let's address the matter of your claims of expertise in a different way. Have you heard of the National Society of Questioned Document Examiners?"

"Yes, I have."

"Please tell the court what the National Society of Questioned Document Examiners is."

"Yes. It's a professional society for experts in the field of identifying disputed documentary evidence."

"Does that specifically include expertise in identifying handwriting as genuine or forged?"

"Yes, it does."

"Ms. Hunter, you did not mention membership in the National Society of Questioned Document Examiners as one of your qualifications to serve this court as an expert witness. Why did you not do that?"

"I am, uh, not a member."

"Ms. Hunter, why are you not a member of the National Society of Questioned Document Examiners?"

Hunter's eyes bored into Bowman as the answer was torn out of her, word by word.

"I do not meet the membership requirements."

"You mean to say that you're not qualified to be a member of the National Society of Questioned Document Examiners, the professional organization for experts in the field of handwriting identification?"

"That is correct."

"Thank you, Ms. Hunter."

Bowman flipped a page of his notes.

"Ms. Hunter, have you heard of the American Association of Handwriting Analysts?"

"Yes, I have."

"Please tell the court what it is."

"It's just a professional society for handwriting analysts."

"Very good. Ms. Hunter, didn't you describe yourself as an expert handwriting analyst?"

"Yes. I did."

"Thank you. Ms. Hunter, are you a member of the American Association of Handwriting Analysts?"

"No, I am not."

"Interesting. Is there some specific reason why you do not belong to a professional society in your avowed field of expertise?"

Bowman waited patiently until Hunter delivered the answer in a resigned tone of voice.

"I don't meet the membership requirements."

"Do you mean to tell me, Ms. Hunter, that the American Association of Handwriting Analysts does not consider you a handwriting analyst?"

Hunter let several seconds tick by before she forced herself to answer.

"No."

"No, you don't mean to tell me? Or no, they don't consider you a handwriting analyst?"

"They don't consider me a handwriting analyst according to their own narrow definition."

"Please, Ms. Hunter, can you tell the court what aspect of their supposedly narrow definition bars you from joining the organization?"

"They require a college degree in the discipline."

"And your mail-order certificate from the Miami Institute of Graphoanalysis does not constitute a college degree in their estimation?"

"No."

"Ms. Hunter, did any of your courses at the Miami Institute of Graphoanalysis treat matters of handwriting *identification?*"

"No, sir."

Bowman squared the sheaf of papers in his hands and lowered it. He regarded the witness with a level gaze and addressed her without looking down at his notes.

"Ms. Hunter. What is the Golden Gate Handwriting Research Institute?"

"It's a professional society devoted to progress in the field of handwriting analysis."

"Ms. Hunter, what is your role in the Golden Gate Handwriting Research Institute?"

"I am a founding member," she replied proudly, but somewhat defensively, a wary look in her eye.

"Ms. Hunter, does the Golden Gate Handwriting Research Institute publish a peer-reviewed research journal?"

"We publish a newsletter."

"With peer-reviewed research articles?"

"No."

"Ms. Hunter. How many members does the Golden Gate Handwriting Research Institute have?"

Hunter slumped a little in her seat.

"Two," she replied.

"Who is the other member, Ms. Hunter?"

"George Gaffney, my partner in West Coast Forensics."

"Ms. Hunter, how many people are involved in West Coast Forensics?"

"Two people."

"You and Mr. Gaffney?"

"Yes."

"Is your business relationship with Mr. Gaffney a professional partnership of equals?"

"Um. George Gaffney is a member of the American Association of Handwriting Analysts. I am his . . . apprentice."

"Thank you, Ms. Hunter. We will leave it to Ms. Onan to explain to her clients why she hired you and not Mr. Gaffney."

Bowman turned and addressed the judge.

"Your honor, counsel for the respondents has offered the court clear evidence that this witness lacks the professional expertise necessary for her to render an informed judgment on the signature on the will of Teresa Francisco. Respondents therefore respectfully petition the court to dismiss this witness and bar her testimony on the grounds that she is not a competent expert. We move that she be excused."

Peggy Hunter stared in horror at Ryan Bowman as he concluded his remarks. Judge Knight calmly regarded the attorney and the witness in turn. "The nature of the signature is the key matter in this dispute," said the judge. "If we were to accept respondents' motion, it would deprive petitioners of their key witness and leave them without a case. The motion is therefore tantamount to ending these proceedings. The court chooses to let the jury hear the testimony of the petitioners' expert, giving it such weight as the jurors deem reasonable in light of the matters brought forth by counsel's questioning of the witness. The motion is therefore denied."

The judge looked up at the clock.

"Since we have had a very busy morning and I think people are probably ready for a respite, court stands adjourned till two o'clock this afternoon." Judge Knight gave a brisk whack with the gavel.

As people stood up and bustled out of the courtroom, Widener and Ramos leaned against the railing that separated them from their clients.

"What did I tell you?" said Widener. "Exactly what we predicted. You guys were looking nervous when she was prattling about her Berkeley degree and this and that and the other thing, but I told you there was nothing to worry about."

"Yeah," added Ramos. "Bowman spent a week up in the Bay Area doing basic shoe-leather investigation work and getting the scoop on her. She's damaged goods now and no one on the jury will forget that while she's testifying on the evidence."

"Peggy Hunter may want to avoid small-town venues for a while. We weren't the pushovers she expected," said Widener.

Bowman ambled up and joined his colleagues and clients. His face was serene, but his eyes glittered with triumph.

"Ladies and gentlemen," he said to the Franciscos, "I have never before had the privilege of examining such an 'expert' witness as I did this morning. We haven't won the case yet, but we definitely have them on the run."

He fumbled in his pocket for a handkerchief and wiped his moist forehead, slightly dislodging his hairpiece as he did so.

"I swear," he concluded, "it was the pinnacle of my legal career."

AUGUST 1980

Odile Has Good News

"Honey, would you like some tea?"

Candido turned at his wife's voice. Odile was standing in the doorway, her short and wide build filling the lower two-thirds of the space. The tone of her voice was neutral enough, but Candido noticed the characteristically doubtful expression on her face as she regarded the mess of ceramic tile and particle board that was scattered around him.

"No, thank you. The contractor and his guys should be back soon and I want to be here when they arrive. I'm not all that happy with our progress so far and I think we need to talk."

"Okay, Candy. I just thought I'd ask. I brewed a pot for me and Cindy and we thought you might like some."

Candido felt a sudden rush of warmth and hoped his wife did not sense his reaction.

"Oh. Cindy is here?" he said with affected casualness.

"Yes. We just got back from shopping and decided a cup of tea would be nice."

"Well, okay. You talked me into it. It's not like I won't hear the contractor's truck when they drive up."

Candido stepped up from the sunken floor of their home's future spa and followed his wife to the kitchen.

"Candy decided to join us after all. You were right to suggest it, Cindy."

Cynthia Parker put her cup down on the kitchen table and smiled up at Candido as he towered behind Odile.

"Hello, Candy. I'm glad you could join us. How's the progress on your project?"

"Too slow," replied Candido, as he sat down at the kitchen table opposite Cynthia.

In addition to the tea service, a plate of small muffins and assorted tarts sat in the middle of the table. Odile could never be without her sweets. In her mind, their small size made them negligible, assuaging her guilt when she ate several at one sitting.

Odile resumed her seat at the side of the table, picked up the tea pot, and poured her husband a cup. She looked around, not finding what she wanted. She raised her voice and called out, "Ferdie, where's the honey?"

There was some clattering from the adjacent walk-in pantry and Ferdinando's voice replied, "Just a second."

Odile turned to her husband. "Taste the tea, sweetheart. Is it good? I made it for all of us to enjoy."

Candido and Cynthia had been staring at each other across the table, but Odile was impatiently looking toward the door that led to the pantry. As Candido hastily raised his teacup to his lips and sipped, the door opened and Ferdinando walked in, a chunky young man carrying a pot of honey. He laid it on the table and said, "Actually, *I* made the pot of tea. I hope you like it."

Candido scowled to see that his son was wearing an apron again, but didn't say a word. What could he say? Odile wouldn't hear any criticism of their youngest son, whom she had successfully shaped into her personal servant, headwaiter, cook, and butler. By now Ferdie was far more skilled in the domestic tasks that Odile had abandoned than Odile had ever been.

Ferdinando brushed a few crumbs off the table and returned to his restocking of the pantry. He maintained a carefully neutral expression as he made his way out of the kitchen. Ferdie had seen the way his father's foot had been sliding across the floor toward Cynthia's when he first emerged from the pantry and the guilty way his father had suddenly pulled it back when his son appeared. Mom clearly had no clue about the flirtation between her husband and her best friend, and Ferdie couldn't see that it was his job to disabuse her. He already had duties enough.

Besides, maybe it was innocent. His father could never resist being insinuatingly sweet to any attractive female, but Ferdie had seen plenty of cool responses. Dad was nowhere near as attractive to women as he thought he was. Anyway, it was all faintly ridiculous. "Candy and Cindy" was a pairing that just begged for mockery.

Odile noted the unhappy expression on Candido's face as he watched Ferdinando disappear into the pantry. She braced herself for some snide remark, but it never came. Candido emitted a small sigh and took another sip of tea.

Odile drizzled some honey on one of the tarts and dispatched it with two quick bites. She washed it down with some tea and then replaced the tea cup on the table with an audible impact.

"I have good news," she said when Candido's attention shifted from Cynthia to her.

"Oh," he replied. "That's — uh — good. What's the news?"

He glanced back at Cynthia, whose face gave nothing away. Neither could he read his wife's face. Candido and Odile had very different conceptions of "good news," so her announcement left him at a loss.

"Cindy drove me to a doctor's appointment today in addition to going shopping."

The tease didn't help. Odile loved going to doctors. Candido had the bills to show for it. His wife had been treated for an unending series of complaints, most of them trivial or imaginary. He had long since given up on trying to track her supposed illnesses, only to have been shocked back into full attention when she had come home the previous year with a diagnosis of advanced heart disease. Earlier her diseases had been too minor to be worth bothering over. Now it was too serious to be able to do anything.

But Odile was claiming "good news." What could that be?

"Which doctor did you see?"

"It was Dr. Hansen," she replied. Odile paused, groping for the word "cardiologist" and not finding it. "The heart doctor," she concluded.

"And he had good news for a change?"

"Yes. Good news. He said he was wrong last year."

"Wrong how?"

"Wrong diagnosis."

"He said you had heart failure."

"Dr. Hansen said it was congestive heart failure," interjected Cynthia.

"Yes," said Odile, nodding her head. "That's what he called it. When he looked at my file again he said it wasn't as bad as he thought."

"He admitted a mistake?"

"Well, he said my condition is a lot better than he thought."

Candido sat stock still, his mind racing. He was sitting at a table with his wife and his girlfriend. He had assumed for the past year that Odile was a short-timer. The home renovations that so displeased her had never been intended for her. Candido had commissioned them with someone else in mind. Someone else who was sitting across the table from him. Now Odile was telling him he had been laboring under a misapprehension. Nothing was going according to plan.

He suddenly realized that he was supposed to be saying something. Odile was watching him expectantly. He forced a smile onto his lips. "That *is* good news, dear. Wonderful news."

He grabbed his teacup and took a big slurp. Across the cup's brim he saw Cynthia looking back at him. Her face was a blank. He made his the same. The three of them were in a trap, but only Odile did not know it.

JUNE 1982

Henry Confronts Elvino

Henry Francisco had not been enjoying his life in recent months. In years, in fact. Things had definitely been better when he was the privileged son of one of the senior partners. Being the mere nephew of the big boss entailed a shocking demotion in status. It didn't help that Uncle Candy was an excessively lackadaisical dairy farmer. Like his father Paulinho, Uncle Candy's younger brother, Henry wanted to do things. Uncle Candy, however, was content to apply himself diligently to treating each growing season exactly like the previous growing season. Why tamper with success?

It drove Henry crazy.

The days when his grandparents had been alive and his father had been a partner in the family business now seemed part of a ridiculously idealized past — Henry's own version of the paradise-lost story. But Paulinho had decamped after years of chafing under his older brother's feckless stewardship, selling out his interest in the dairy farm, leaving Henry to fend for himself as a hired hand.

Henry had had a decade of being low man on the totem pole. While his grandparents had encouraged his involvement in the family dairy farm, and perhaps occasionally nudged their son Candido to give his nephew more attention and responsibility, they were both gone now.

The loss of his grandmother earlier in the year still reverberated throughout the family. Uncle Candy was now an absentee boss, having left his wife the same day that his mother died. He was shacked up with his girlfriend Cindy. His attempts to manage the family dairy farm were complicated by the refusal of his sons to speak to him. Candido was reduced to leaving messages on answering machines and writing notes in his crabbed handwriting on the notice board in the workshop. The passing months had already demonstrated that his boys followed those instructions only when they felt like it. *De facto* operation of the family dairy farm was devolving upon Candido, Jr.

That had made things even tougher for Henry, since Junior had inherited his father's pedestrian style of leadership without inheriting any measure of the senior Candido's natural sociability. While Uncle Candy had bossed Henry around as a matter-of-fact function of running the farm, Junior bossed his cousin around for the fun of it. Henry had already fallen from limbo into purgatory, and now he felt he was slipping into hell.

Today, however, Henry was thinking about his Salazar cousins, not the Franciscos. His late Aunt Fatima had married Louis Salazar some forty years back and had presented him with seven children, six of them boys. The sons helped their father operate a large dairy farm only a few miles from the Francisco place. The Francisco and Salazar families had always enjoyed amicable relations, but now the death of Teresa Francisco had sown dissension among her descendants.

Henry was raising a huge dust cloud as he barreled down a dirt road in his Jeep. It was only a matter of time before he was sure to encounter one of his Salazar cousins in the field. He knew their patterns of operation and their division of labor. He kept an eye open for a particular pickup truck — a Frankenstein assemblage of salvaged parts and coats of gray primer — belonging to Elvino Salazar.

Soon he spotted it. And there was Elvino, walking along the edge of the alfalfa field, checking whether the new growth was ready to produce another crop. At a distance, it was difficult to tell Henry and Elvino apart. Both young men were tall and slender, dark hair poking out from under baseball caps. At closer range, their matching brown eyes made them look more like brothers than cousins.

Henry braked his Jeep to a sliding stop next to Elvino's pickup and climbed out without waiting for the storm he had raised to blow past.

Elvino watched his cousin's dramatic arrival with amazement, which only grew when Henry emerged from the billowing dust and threw a packet of papers at him. It bounced off his chest and fell to the ground.

"What the hell are you guys doing?" spat Henry.

Elvino bent down, picked up the packet, and scanned the first page.

"What's the big deal, Hank? This is just our petition. That's all it is."

"What do you mean 'that's all'? You fuckers are *suing* us!"

Elvino was taken aback.

"No, no! You don't understand. It's just a petition to examine grandma's will."

"'Examine'? Are you and your brothers idiots? This is a petition to revoke probate of *Avó's* will. It's a *lawsuit*. You're *suing* us. Don't you even know what you're doing?"

Now Elvino was really distraught.

"That's not the way it was explained to me, Hank. That's not the way it was explained at all! I would never have signed if I knew it was a lawsuit."

Henry looked at the expression on his cousin's face and his anger subsided a little. He had seldom seen anyone look so confused and distressed. He bit back a barb about his cousin having just confirmed his idiocy and took a more diplomatic tack.

"Okay, Elvis. So how did they explain it to you? And who is 'they'?"

"My dad. And his girlfriend. She's a lawyer. I guess she told Dad there were questions about grandma's will and that it would be good to have it reviewed. She and Dad told us to sign the papers to let the court see if the will divided things up the right way. She said if we signed it, it would be a way to get better information about grandma's intentions."

Henry felt his temper rising again, but fought it under control.

"Elvis, that was just a total load of bullshit. Your dad made you and your brothers party to a lawsuit against the Francisco family, even if you didn't know it. And is this attorney, the name on the lawsuit, is that your father's girlfriend?"

Elvino nodded his head.

"Yeah. Biddy Onan. She said she would help us with the paperwork."

"I'll bet. And your father is paying the legal bills, right? I guess that's one way she can get into her boyfriend's pockets."

"Uh, yeah. He said he'd cover the expenses. We're not on the hook for lawyer's fees."

"Well, *we* sure as hell are! And in case it didn't occur to you, we had to take out a loan to get the cash to pay out your inheritance. It's not like the Franciscos had a spare $70,000 laying around. We're cash-poor and now we're going to have legal bills piling up."

Elvino hesitated before repeating what he had been told, but he decided not to hold it back from Henry. He and Henry were the same age and had always been best of friends. Elvino was desperate to clear the air and salvage what he could of the friendship.

"Yeah, well, you know, that was sort of the point that Dad made. He told us that it was wrong of grandma not to divide up her estate three ways: One third to each of her children. Instead, all of the land went to the sons and just money went to Mom. I mean, to Mom's heirs. Dad said that we needed to do this to honor Mom's memory."

"For fuck's sake, Elvis, that is the stupidest thing I've ever heard!" Henry paused to catch his breath and calm himself down. "This would never have happened if Aunt Fatima were still alive. Your mom would never have stood for this!"

Elvino offered no response.

"Listen," Henry continued. "*Avó* and *Avô* wrote several wills over their lifetime. I've seen them because Dad and Uncle Candy are executors and they were part of the paperwork from the lawyer's office. One was from 1940, right after your mom married your dad. That will contained an appraisal of the Francisco estate and divided it in three parts, just like you mentioned."

He paused to see if Elvino was following him. His cousin gave him a brief nod.

"Okay. Then there's the will from 1952. By then both Uncle Candy and Dad had gotten married. *Avó* and *Avô* revised the will. They took your mom's share from the 1940 will and adjusted it up to allow for inflation. Then they said the remainder of the estate was to be divided between the two sons, who were living on the dairy farm and working to expand it. It's really pretty simple. *Avó* and *Avô* wanted your mom to inherit a share equivalent to one-third of the business at the time she left to marry your dad. *Avó's* last will was written after *Avô* died. And your mom had died, too. She raised your mom's share of the inheritance to $70,000, even though it was a little more than the actual inflation-adjusted amount from 1940 because she wanted to give each of you $10,000. Seven Salazar grandchildren, $10,000 each. Total, $70,000. So why the hell did your father think it should be more than that?"

Elvino had listened patiently to Henry's lecture, a morose expression on his face.

"Look, Hank. Dad said, 'three kids, three equal shares.' That's him talking. Personally, I was *delighted* when I got my check. And I didn't sign the papers because I wanted to get more. I did it because Dad said I needed to. And he said the Francisco share of the estate was worth way more than $70,000."

"Your father is right about that, but Uncle Louis is forgetting that *Avó* wasn't obligated to leave anything to anyone. She could have given it all to charity. Heck, maybe that would have been simpler."

"Now who's shitting who? You don't believe that!"

"No. You're right. I don't. *Avó's* will actually made me part of the business again, because I'm one of the named heirs. But no cash. Is my share worth more than $10,000? Yeah, it is, sort of. If only I could cash out an undivided interest at market prices. But *Avó* didn't draw any lines on the property. Like I said, my interest is 'undivided' and there's no specific piece with my name on it. I'm stuck as a minority partner in the family business."

"Assuming you win the lawsuit," noted Elvino incautiously.

Henry gave his cousin a sharp glance.

"Don't go asking for trouble, Elvis. I'm forgiving you for now because you admitted you did it out of ignorance. Or maybe stupidity. Maybe you didn't notice that your father got only three signatures on the petition. You and Randy live at home, so he could pressure you, and Otelo probably signed because he doesn't care if he pisses anyone off as long as he might get something out of it. Right?"

"I guess you're right."

"You know I'm right. We're going to have a lot of trouble now. You and I are in the middle of it. I'll try to treat you like a neutral party as much as I can because I know now you got sucked into this. But your father should know we're going to tromp his lawyer girlfriend and win this lawsuit. No question about it. It's going to be a bad time."

"I really am sorry, but there was no way I could have known what we were getting into."

Henry shook his head and laughed.

"Here's some advice for you. Don't sign things in the future without reading them."

"Good advice, but it's not like I would have understood it anyway."

Henry plucked the petition out of Elvino's hand.

"Come on, cousin. You should at least give it a try. Did you even look at page two? I think you could have gotten the drift. Check this out: 'decedent was not of disposing mind.' The 'decedent' is *Avó*. And 'not of disposing mind' is just a polite legal way of saying she was nuts or incompetent. You signed a document saying our grandmother was *loca*."

"Geez! I never knew that."

"Oh, it gets better. Try this one: 'decedent did not execute said document.' I think that one means the will is supposed to be a fake or a forgery. Now you're accusing us of being criminals."

"No way!"

"And 'execution of said instrument was procured by fraud, in that decedent could neither read, write, nor understand the English language.' I guess someone forgot to notice that *Avó* had a Portuguese-speaking attorney draft all her legal documents. And that business about speaking English? Say, Elvis, you ever chat with our grandmother?"

Elvino looked extremely uncomfortable.

"Yeah, sometimes. A little."

"But you don't speak any Portuguese, do you? So how did you talk with her?"

"In English."

"Yeah. Don't forget that when we call you to the witness stand."

Elvino swallowed audibly.

"And I love this one: 'decedent was under undue influence,' followed by a list of all of the Francisco heirs, including me. For the life of me I can't figure out why we were exerting undue influence on *Avó* if we were forging the will anyway. That's going to way too much trouble. Fascinating. I do believe what we have here is technically called a 'shotgun' approach. The old lady was incompetent, the old lady was illiterate, the old lady was under duress, and — oh! — it doesn't matter anyway because the will is a fake. Pretty tight argument, I'd say."

Elvino stood speechless.

Henry walked over to his Jeep and climbed in.

"By the way, Elvis, after the Franciscos beat the Salazars, you'd better hope that we don't enforce the 'no contest' clause of *Avó's* will. That reduces to *one dollar* the inheritance of anyone who challenges the will. Be careful not to spend the ten thousand just yet. You might need to give it back."

Henry fired up the Jeep and disappeared in a cloud of dust.

MAY 1947

Boys Meet Girls

"Breeding stock at twelve o'clock!"

Odile reacted to her sister's nudge.

"Ow!" She rubbed her arm where Odette's sharp elbow had made contact. "What? Where?"

Odette gave an exasperated sigh.

"Good-looking guys. *Straight ahead.*"

The Avila girls were dressed in long pink gowns because they had been attendants to the Queen of the Pentecost *festa.* They had marched in the parade, attended the High Mass, dined on *sopas* at the long trestle tables in the Holy Ghost hall (special area reserved for the Queen and her attendants), and now they were free to wander and check out the other young people in attendance.

There were fresh faces in abundance. Many Portuguese families traveled for miles to attend Pentecost celebrations in various towns. The Holy Ghost was revered in the Azores as the special guardian of its nine islands, and most of the Portuguese immigrants in California were islanders. The characteristically Azorean celebration of the *Festa do Divino Espirito Santo* had become an indispensable part of maintaining the immigrant community's unity and identification with the homeland.

It was also a meat market.

Unattached sons and daughters were herded to the annual *festas* in hopes of finding ethnically and religiously suitable partners. The Francisco brothers were decked out in their Sunday finest, taking a day off from the demands of milking cows in the Central Valley to sample the fleshpots of Southern California. As Portuguese boys flocked to the *festa*, more cows were milked by temp Anglo workers on that day than on any other day of the calendar.

Odette had spotted Candido and Paulinho with an appraising eye. She wasn't scouting for herself. Odette already had her hooks deep into a boyfriend whom she would be prompting to propose within a month or two. Odile, on the other hand, needed all the help she could get. Odette was determined to push her sister out there and get her matched up with an appropriate partner. Time was of the essence. Odile was soon to turn nineteen and at risk of becoming an old maid.

The Avila sisters were a study in unfortunate contrasts. Though both girls bore names from Tchaikovsky's "Swan Lake" — bestowed by their father because he thought they sounded classy — it suited only one of them. Odette was tall, slender, and vivacious, while Odile was short, plump, and lethargic. Odette knew they reminded people of Mutt and Jeff, so her plan was to launch Odile into the midst of a promising knot of young men and then stand aside so as not to overshadow her.

"There you are!"

Carmina Soares had emerged from the swirling crowds of young people and joined the Avila sisters. She was intermediate in height and weight between Odette and Odile. Carmina was conventionally pretty and wore her hair in a more successful version of the mid-length perm that Odile had adopted for the *festa*. She also had a well-scrubbed wholesome look that set her apart from Odette, whose high cheekbones and fashionably bobbed hair gave her a more sophisticated aspect.

Carmina inserted herself between the sisters and took each by the arm.

"Isn't this great! Wasn't the parade wonderful! Look at all these people!"

The three girls were a matched set of pink-gowned attendants, sorted in descending order of height and ascending order of weight. Odile was always happy to see her invariably cheerful school chum. She didn't know why exactly, but it was always more comfortable — less challenging — to stand next to Carmina than next to her sister.

"Hey! Who are those guys?"

Carmina had spotted the Francisco boys, who were somewhat ill at ease, standing together and looking at the strangers surrounding them.

Odette saw an opportunity.

"I don't know, Carmina. They're rather cute, though. Why don't you and Odile go over and talk to them? I'm sure they're from out of town. You should welcome them."

"Well, maybe. What do you think, Odile? Want to do it?"

"I guess that would be okay. I'll go if you go."

Odette tried to fine-tune the approach.

"Odile, you should talk to the one on the right. I think he's your type." Odette carefully avoided describing Paulinho as the "shorter" brother. That would have gotten her sister's back up.

"The taller boy looks kind of sad," said Carmina, dragging out into the open the height issue that Odette had been at pains to avoid.

"You could cheer him up, Carmina. I know you could. You should set your cap for him," suggested Odette.

"But Carmina isn't wearing a cap," observed Odile in confusion.

Odette kept the exasperation out of her expression.

"It's just a figure of speech," she replied. "I read it in *Gone with the Wind*."

Odette disengaged her arm from Carmina's hand and nudged her friend and her sister toward the Francisco boys.

"Now go be nice to them. Make them feel welcome. It's the polite thing to do. Go!"

The girls giggled at each other as they moved tentatively toward the brothers. Paulinho noticed their movement.

"*Candy*. It looks like we have visitors."

Candido glanced in the direction his brother was looking.

"I thought *we* were the visitors," he said. "These girls are local. They were in the parade."

"There were out-of-towners in the parade, too," observed Paulinho, "but I think you're right anyway. These girls were attending the hometown queen."

Carmina knew right away that she preferred the shorter and younger Francisco boy. She figured they were brothers from their resemblance to each other, although the taller and older one had a high forehead that exaggerated his age and a long face that gave him a perpetually mournful aspect. The younger one, by contrast, looked bright-eyed and cheerful. He had a nice smile and his wavy hair was a shade darker than his brother's.

She hesitated, though. Odette had made it very clear that the prettier boy was marked out for her sister, leaving the homelier one for Carmina. Did she want to cut in on Odile and get on Odette's wrong side? Would it be better to let Odile have first crack at the cute one?

The moment she asked herself that question, Carmina had her answer. Let Odile go first. She was sure to mess it up. Carmina felt just a little guilty relying on her schoolmate's clumsiness, but it would be better than actively undermining her.

"Um, hi," said Odile.

"Hello," replied the Franciscos simultaneously.

"Hello," replied Carmina.

A long moment of awkward silence.

"My sister said she thought you were from out of town," said Odile, trying desperately to make conversation. She looked back over her shoulder as if to point out her sister, but Odette had vanished.

"Your sister is right," said Paulinho. "Candy and I came down from Tulare County for the day."

"Candy?" asked Odile.

"Yes, my brother is Candido and I'm Paulinho. What are your names?"

"I'm Odile and this is my friend Carmina."

"Not your sister?"

"No. Carmina and I go to school together."

"Is your sister the tall girl you were talking to just a minute ago?" asked Candido.

"Yes, my sister Odette."

"She's very pretty," observed Candido.

"Yes, she is. She's the pretty one," said Odile miserably.

"All of you looked very nice in the parade," said Paulinho, trying to turn the conversation in a more positive direction.

Odile brightened at the compliment as she and Carmina simultaneously said, "Thank you!"

"Yeah, you really did," added Candido.

A couple of silent seconds stretched out. Carmina decided she had given Odile enough opportunity. She spoke directly to Paulinho.

"So what do you and your brother do in Tulare County?"

"As if you didn't know," laughed Paulinho, as he and his brother exchanged amused glances.

Carmina laughed.

"I'm sorry, but I was just trying to make conversation."

All of them laughed again, except for Odile. Candido noticed the confused expression on her face and felt a pang of sympathy. Paulinho was always laughing at things he didn't get and it looked like Odile suffered the same fate with her friend.

"What's wrong, Odile?"

"I don't understand. Your brother" — she didn't remember Paulinho's name —"said 'as if you didn't know,' but I *don't* know. What did he mean?"

Candido smiled at her, the first happy expression anyone had seen on his face that morning.

"Well, if you think about it a little more . . . We're Portuguese boys at a *festa*. What do you think we do for a living? What does your father do for a living? What does Carmina's father do for a living?"

Odile wrinkled her brow at the challenging string of questions.

"Carmina's father has a dairy farm that he runs with her brothers." She paused. "Do you . . . have a dairy farm?"

"Yes! You're right!" exclaimed Candido. "Doesn't every Portuguese boy in California live on a dairy farm? I think it might be the law!"

Odile looked concerned, but decided that Candido was probably joking about the law.

"I guess you're right," she said, a smile appearing on her face.

"And what about your father? Does he work on a dairy?"

"Well, we don't have cows," said Odile, "but he makes his living hauling cow manure for fertilizer."

"Close enough! See? We're all in the dairy business!"

Carmina had been watching the exchange between Odile and Candido and was slightly startled to discover that Paulinho had moved right next to her.

"There's a vendor over there with a soft-drink concession. I'm getting a little thirsty and was wondering if you would like something to drink, too," he said.

"Oh. Yes. Yes, I am a little thirsty. That would be nice."

"Great. We can leave your friend here with Candy. They seem to be having a good conversation and I don't want to interrupt them."

"Oh. Okay. That's a good idea."

Paulinho and Carmina moved away slowly from Candido and Odile. Paulinho was doing a good job of hiding his nervousness as he wondered if it would be too forward to offer his arm as he led Carmina over to the drinks concession. He decided not to risk it. He was happy enough that she was following him willingly where he wanted to go.

Besides, if she took his arm she might notice the hammer-pounding of his heart, which was making his entire body vibrate.

SEPTEMBER 1958

Monsignor's School

It wasn't exactly a coincidence that the local church was named in honor of St. Bartholomew. Many of the region's residents were Azorean immigrants from the parish of São Bartolomeu de Regatos in the island's capital city of Angra and they were the mainstay of the church's congregation. The pastor of St. Bartholomew's Catholic Church was Monsignor Francis X. Pontac, an ambitious young cleric who had been at the helm for four years and had already pulled off the stunt of a lifetime.

St. Bart's had opened a parochial school.

It was almost a magic trick — or maybe it would be better to describe it as nearly a miracle. Monsignor had conjured up a Catholic grammar school in the midst of a tiny rural parish in the middle of Tulare County. How could such a small base support such an ambitious project?

Not to put too fine a point on it, Monsignor shamed the community into it. From the first moment he had arrived, the pastor had been marching to and fro across the church's plot of land. Monsignor had three acres to work with, thanks to the generous donor from the Joaquim family who had made the original bequest. One was quite adequate for the church, rectory, and parking lot. The other two were sufficient for a pair of classroom buildings, a convent for a teaching order of nuns, and a playground.

People who drove by St. Bart's would often see Monsignor out in shirt-sleeves, hammering stakes in the ground, stretching out string, and outlining his dream. He dug much of the foundation himself, gradually drawing in volunteers who couldn't simply pass by while their pastor was toiling alone in the blazing heat. People who stopped to contribute an hour's labor would suddenly realize that they had been there all day. As long as Monsignor didn't quit, they couldn't either.

St. Bart's School would have been completed in half the time if Monsignor hadn't had to say Mass and hear confessions. Whenever he straightened his back, groaned, and dusted his hands to announce he had to get ready for services, his volunteers would snap out of their glassy-eyed trance and use the opportunity to escape until the morrow.

Paul and Jojo Francisco knew a little about the work that had gone into their new school. The cousins had been part of Monsignor's sweat-equity program. Since they were only six years old during the frenetic erection of the cinder-block school buildings, they got to spend most of their time pushing around wheelbarrows of sand. They'd dump the sand wherever they were told to, then wheel their barrows back to the big pile for another load. On good days, there'd be older boys at the big pile to heap more sand into their wheelbarrows. On the bad days, they'd be on their own. Those were the days that they'd end up with blisters from wielding the shovels themselves.

Jojo seemed to think it was mostly fun. Paul regarded it as misery. The school project was eating up weekends when he could have vanished into the upper reaches of the hay barn, built himself a bench out of a couple of hay bales, and lost a morning or an afternoon in the pages of a book. This, by contrast, was cruel and unusual.

"Well, Jojo, we made our bed, and now we get to lie in it," said Paul to his cousin on the first day of class at St. Bart's. He wasn't *exactly* sure what it meant, but he had heard it in a gangster movie and it seemed to fit.

Jojo was accustomed to ignoring anything that Paul said that wasn't immediately clear, so most of the time he just shrugged or grunted whenever his cousin said anything. It was an elegant solution to a difficult problem.

The Franciscos had decided that Candido's three boys and Paulinho's Paul would all attend the new school. Paul's sister Mary Carmen was enrolling in kindergarten at Pleasant Hill public school and their little brother Henry was still too young for school. Jojo had not been successful in Pleasant Hill's first grade, so he was repeating it at St. Bart's, where he would have the additional humiliation of being in the same class as his younger brother Ferdie. Paul was moving up to second grade and Junior would be in fourth.

The biggest surprise at St. Bartholomew's Catholic School was two-fold. Junior, Paul, Jojo, and Ferdie would all have the same teacher, *and* she was Protestant. The four Francisco boys would have the same teacher because St. Bart's was opening as a two-room school, with first through fourth grades in one classroom and fifth through eighth in another. There were two four-room classroom buildings, but only the first building was finished and the initial enrollment was too low to support more than two teachers. Mrs. Knox was a lay teacher who had yet to complete her conversion to Catholicism. Monsignor was willing to overlook that because she held a valid California teaching credential and was willing to work for the wages he could afford to pay. He would have her up to full Catholic speed in no time. As for Mrs. Cruise, the teacher for fifth through eighth grades, she was willing to work for a pittance because her prosperous husband was a benefactor of the school.

To his surprise, Paul was not too unhappy about the circumstances at St. Bart's. There were books he hadn't seen at Pleasant Hill (the readers had Jan and Mary instead of Dick and Jane) and the responsibilities of the multi-grade teachers kept them too busy to bother him very much. He was content to sit at his desk and read. There were more things to memorize at St. Bart's than at Pleasant Hill, and Paul wondered if that was because it was Catholic school or because it was second grade. But it wasn't a problem.

Jojo, on the other hand, was fit to be tied. Within the first few days of the fall term, he had already been warned more than once that he *could* be tied. If necessary, Monsignor would strap him down to his desk to keep him from getting up and wandering about without permission. Jojo didn't know if it was a real threat, but it seemed prudent to accept it at face value.

The classroom was theoretically divided into four sections for the four grades, with Francisco boys in three of the quadrants. Mrs. Knox would circulate from one grade to the next, giving out assignments and warning them to work quietly while she went to check on another grade. During recess, the Francisco boys would sometimes compare notes.

"All the lessons are boring," complained Jojo.

"They're not just boring," corrected Junior, "they're *stupid*."

"I don't know," said Paul. "It's not like we really have lessons. Mrs. Knox doesn't have enough time to explain things. She just says, do this part or do that part, and then we have to read it ourselves. It's okay if you read it carefully. But it would be nicer, I guess, if she explained more stuff."

"I like the teacher," observed Ferdie. "She seems nice."

"If we have to read it all ourselves, then why do we need a teacher?" said Junior. "I think this is a fake school."

"And it's too *hard* to read, too!" added Jojo.

Paul, Junior, and Ferdie exchanged glances. Jojo didn't know how to read. That was the real problem.

The Franciscos spent less and less time with each other during recess as they were increasingly integrated into their separate grades. Ferdie began to shadow Mrs. Knox, becoming her "little helper" and trying to insinuate himself into the position of teacher's pet. Junior soon found it demeaning to hang out with "the little kids" and Jojo had little in common with Paul anyway. Jojo preferred to tear around the playground like a Roman candle while Paul liked the fact that the sandbox was shaded by the only tree of any size on St. Bart's playground. He began to hang out with a fellow second-grader named Luis.

"Your name is like my *padrinho's*," said Paul one day, "except no one ever says the 's' at the end and you do."

"Yeah, well, it sounds funny when you say *padrino*," replied Luis. The boys didn't know how to spell the words, so they couldn't compare.

"Uh-huh, it sounds different. That's interesting."

"Yeah, maybe you say it wrong because you're a Portagee."

"Not *wrong*," insisted Paul. "Just different. And you're not supposed to say 'Portagee.' It's not nice."

Luis seemed surprised.

"It's not? Why not?"

"I don't know. My family just says that it's not." Paul thought for a moment. "And that's kind of funny, you know, because we say it ourselves."

The boys sat in silence for a while.

"Okay," announced Luis. "I know what you mean. My family has words it doesn't like either."

"Yeah? Like what?"

"Greaser, beaner, and spic," recited Luis promptly. "I don't know what the deal is with 'beaner,' because I like beans just fine. But 'greaser' sounds nasty."

"Yeah, it does," agreed Paul. "Okay, if you don't say 'Portagee' I won't use those words you said."

"Sure. But, you know, like you said, we use them in my family sometimes. I guess no one else is allowed, though."

"How do you use them?"

"Actually, the only one we really use is 'beaner.' We use it on my little brother because he farts a lot and it's funny."

Paul winced because he was prissy about language and avoided using words like "fart." But he laughed at Luis's story.

The boys were sketching random patterns in the sand when Luis asked a question.

"What's the deal with your cousins' names?"

"What do you mean?"

"Well, I hear you call them 'Junior' and 'Jojo,' but the teacher and Monsignor call them 'Candido' and 'John Joseph.'"

"Oh, right. Monsignor always uses our baptism names. 'Candido' is Junior's real name. He's named for his father, my Uncle Candy — I mean, Candido. And Monsignor calls Jojo 'John Joseph' because he can't say 'João José'!"

"What did you say? 'Zhwow Juh Zeh'?"

"Hey, that was pretty good, Luis. Yeah, that's Jojo's real name. It means the same as 'John Joseph.'"

"I got it. In Spanish it would be 'Juan José.'"

"Yeah, I've heard that. It sounds totally different."

"Yeah."

Luis had a twig from the tree and was using it as a stylus, writing the letters of the alphabet in the sand.

"I have an older brother named Francisco," he said.

"Really? That's neat. You know, lots of Portuguese and Spanish names are the same. Or a lot alike." Paul paused for a moment. "Say, does your family use nicknames? My grandfather uses 'Chico' because of our Francisco family name. His real name is Paulo."

"What did you say? 'Sheik'?"

"That's what my grandmother calls my grandfather." He borrowed the twig from Luis and wrote CHICO in the sand.

"Oh, 'Chico'!" exclaimed Luis. "That's what we call my brother Francisco, but I didn't hear the oh at the end when you said it."

"My father says that people from the Azores don't like vowels at the ends of words, although they're there, so we just don't say them. I think he's joking, but it really is that way. Sometimes."

The boys sat in contemplation of the mysteries of the universe.

Paul leaned down and obliterated his grandfather's nickname from the sand.

"Look at this, Luis."

He wrote XICO.

"What's *that* supposed to be?"

"It's my grandfather's name again. That's the way I've seen my grandmother write it."

"You're kidding! That doesn't make any sense at all!"

Paul was beside himself with delight as he explained. Sharing odd bits of information with others gave him the keenest pleasure.

"No, remember? Monsignor explained it to us!"

Luis frowned at his classmate and shook his head.

"When did Monsignor ever explain your grandfather's name to us?"

"But he did, kind of! Remember when he took our class to the church and gave us a lesson on the parts of the Mass? And I asked him a question? Do you remember my question?"

Luis shrugged.

"That's okay. No reason you should," continued Paul. "But I asked Monsignor the meaning of that funny thing on the front of the lectern, the place where he reads the gospel. I asked him about the P with the X on it."

Luis brightened.

"Oh, yeah! I remember that now. He said it stood for Jesus."

"That's right. Or 'Christ,' really. Monsignor said the letters are from the Greek alphabet. He said it was the chi-rho and he wrote it down for me. The X is like a C-H." Paul circled the "x" in xico. "So my grandmother was using a chi when she wrote my grandfather's name. I never knew that before."

If Paul had bothered to afflict Junior or Jojo with such a piece of esoterica, they would surely have rewarded him with a shrug or perhaps even a sneer. He watched expectantly for Luis's reaction, hoping anxiously for a positive response.

"Wow," said Luis with a smile on his face. "That really is pretty amazing. Wait till I tell Chico!"

Paul glowed with satisfaction.

PART II

JUNE 1983

Otelo on the Stand

"Petitioners' next witness is Otelo Salazar."

"The court calls Otelo Salazar to the stand."

Heads swiveled and eyebrows were raised as the witness approached the clerk to be sworn in. Otelo was in his mid-thirties and movie-star handsome. His short hair was a shade lighter than that of most of his relatives and his gray-blue eyes were a legacy from his grandfathers. Both men were thought to carry a dash of Flemish blood from a group of fifteenth-century sailors who had spiked the Azorean gene pool with some recessive-trait variety.

Otelo had had a notorious career as the hell-raising bad boy of the Francisco-Salazar clan. The right hand that he held up was missing half its ring finger, a Fourth-of-July souvenir from an unexpectedly successful youthful experiment in homemade firecrackers. He seldom looked directly at people during conversations, which gave him the reputation of being stand-offish. That was true enough, but Otelo actually kept his head slightly turned to favor his functioning left ear. His right eardrum had never recovered from the silo incident, an even greater disaster than the Independence Day accident and the one that finally put an end to his experimentation with explosives.

Although Otelo was one of the petitioners, he had avoided the trial proceedings until the day he was due to testify. Beatrice Onan had wanted the three petitioners in place every day, sitting erect in their seats in righteous indignation at the injustice they were seeking to correct, but the petitioners were singularly uncooperative. Elvino had threatened to send a note to the court withdrawing his name from the petition if Onan did not stop harassing him. Randy was likely to follow suit in any action taken by his older brother.

Otelo, on the other hand, just didn't want to be bothered. He had $10,000 from his grandmother's estate and the lawsuit was an opportunity to get an even bigger chunk. Since his father was footing the bill, Otelo was perfectly happy to cooperate — as long as it didn't inconvenience him. He was unhappy that he needed to testify, but Onan had promised him he'd be in and out within an hour. He could put up with that.

"Please state your full name for the record."

"My name is Otelo Candido Salazar."

Harold Widener leaned closer to Dennis Ramos. "Geez," he whispered in Ramos's ear. "This family has more Candys than a sweet shop."

"Thank you, Mr. Salazar," said Ms. Onan. "If it please the court, I am presenting the witness with an exhibit which I request be labeled as Exhibit A."

"So ordered."

"Mr. Salazar, is that your grandmother's handwriting on Exhibit A?"

Widener was instantly on his feet.

"*Objection*, your honor! No foundation."

"Sustained. Ms. Onan?"

Onan looked puzzled.

"Yes, your honor. All right. I'll rephrase. Mr. Salazar, is that your grandmother's signature?"

"*Objection*, your honor!"

"Sustained. Ms. Onan, the objection is based on your lack of a foundation. Please continue."

Onan did not look enlightened, but she nodded her head anyway.

"Yes, your honor. Thank you, your honor." She turned back to her witness. "Mr. Salazar, whose handwriting do you see on Exhibit A?"

"*Objection*, your honor!"

"Sustained." Judge Knight's glasses had slipped from the bridge of his nose, allowing him to glare balefully over them at the petitioners' attorney. She looked back at him in complete confusion.

The judge came to a decision. He turned toward the witness.

"Mr. Salazar, are you familiar with your grandmother's handwriting?"

"Yes, sir."

"Mr. Salazar, would you recognize your grandmother's handwriting if you saw it?"

"Yes, sir."

"Mr. Salazar, is that your grandmother's handwriting on Exhibit A in your hand?"

"Yes, sir."

"The court thanks you, Mr. Salazar." Judge Knight turned back toward Beatrice Onan. "Your witness, counselor."

"Uh, thank you, your honor."

Ramos nudged Widener. "Looks like someone flunked Moot Court 101," he whispered.

"Mr. Salazar, what is the nature of Exhibit A?"

"Excuse me. I don't understand the question."

In the gallery, Paul Francisco winked at his brother Henry. "*O tolo,*" he whispered. *The fool.* It was Otelo's unavoidable nickname among his detractors.

"I'll rephrase. Mr. Salazar, what is Exhibit A?"

"Oh! It's a birthday card."

"Could you please be more specific?"

"It's a birthday card to me from my grandmother. Probably for my thirtieth birthday, or something like that. Could be earlier."

Otelo's wife had found it in a stack of papers in a chest of drawers. They actually had no idea how old it was.

"If it please the court, petitioners would have this next item labeled as Exhibit B."

"So ordered."

"Mr. Salazar, what is Exhibit B?"

"It's a graduation card I received from my grandmother."

"Can you be more specific?"

"High school graduation. That would be 1965."

The card had been dredged out of the deepest recesses of a desk in Louis Salazar's home, where it had lain for eighteen years.

"Mr. Salazar, are you familiar with your grandmother's writing?"

The judge interrupted.

"Ms. Onan, unless the late Mrs. Francisco was an author and you're asking Mr. Salazar if he was familiar with his grandmother's work, I think you can take it as read that it's already established that he knows his grandmother's *hand*writing. You don't have to rebuild the foundation for each exhibit item."

Someone in the jury box smothered a chuckle, causing the bailiff to raise a finger to his lips.

"Yes, of course. Thank you, your honor." Onan turned stiffly back to her witness.

"She's moving like the judge shoved a fireplace poker up her ass," whispered Widener to Ramos.

"She should be grateful he keeps saving her from herself," replied Ramos in a low voice.

Onan proceeded to run a series of exhibits past her witness, who confirmed that each one was in his late grandmother's handwriting. She had a dozen exhibits in total, comprising birthday cards, graduation cards, wedding cards, and a guest-book signature from a baby shower.

After Otelo handed back Exhibit L, Onan thanked him and informed the judge that she was done with her witness. Judge Knight looked toward the respondents' table, where the three attorneys representing the Franciscos sat.

"Does counsel for the respondents have any questions for this witness?"

Bowman, who had been sitting without saying a word for the entire session, took his cue. He stood up.

"Thank you, your honor. We have no questions. The witness may be excused, subject, of course, to a later call-back."

"Very well. Thank you, Mr. Salazar. You are excused. However, as Mr. Bowman noted, you are subject to recall by respondents' counsel if they later deem it necessary. Understood?"

"Yes, sir."

"Very well. This court stands adjourned until 9:00 tomorrow morning." He banged the gavel, rose, and swiftly disappeared from the courtroom.

Otelo headed for the exit farthest from his Francisco relatives and was gone.

Several members of the Francisco family gathered along the rail to hear any remarks their attorneys might have about the session.

"That might have been a close call," observed Widener.

"What do you mean?" asked Henry Francisco.

"Onan was completely screwing up the introduction of evidence. She forgot that she couldn't ask her witness for his opinion until she established a basis — a foundation — for the validity of his opinion. What good is it to have a witness identify someone's handwriting if he's never seen it before?"

"It was so simple a mistake," added Ramos, "that the judge just couldn't believe she was making it."

"And she kept making it over and over again. I said it was a 'close call' because I was duty-bound to object every time she made the mistake. But rest assured that juries don't like lawyers who keep objecting. The first couple of objections establish that our opponent is incompetent, but the objections after that start to make me look like an asshole."

"Which we should keep secret from the jury," said Ramos.

"Screw you, Dennis. Anyway, the jurors were getting as tired of hearing me say 'objection!' as I was of saying it."

"But the judge intervened. Wasn't that weird?" asked Paul Francisco.

"Definitely. Very definitely. But if the judge hadn't intervened we could still be here trying to get Exhibit A identified as your grandmother's handwriting. He did us all a favor, although I don't think Biddy Onan is as grateful as she should be."

MARCH 1982

Paulinho Sees the Will

Carmina heard the sound of Paulinho's pickup truck pulling into the driveway. She dashed to the door to open it for her husband, watching anxiously as he climbed out of his vehicle and walked toward the house.

Paulinho gave her an absent-minded peck on the cheek as he entered the house, saying nothing. He sat down at the kitchen table.

"I could really use a beer," he said.

Carmina was accustomed to being her husband's remote control for the refrigerator and it never occurred to her to resent it. She fished out a cold bottle of Lucky Lager and carried it to the table. She sat down as Paulinho popped off the top and took a long pull from the bottle. Carmina was bursting with questions, but she folded her hands, waited patiently, and steeled herself for the worst.

"Okay," said Paulinho at length. "Good news first."

Carmina relaxed ever so slightly. There was at least *some* good news.

"We keep the house."

Carmina sagged with relief.

"Of course, there was never any real question about that," he continued.

So they had kept telling themselves, thought Carmina, but who could be certain about anything?

"And Candy gets his house, too, of course. But that's kind of a joke now." Especially since Candy had moved out, leaving Odile in possession.

"What's the bad news?"

Paulinho took another swig of beer.

"Leave that for a second. There's more good news."

Carmina was breathing much more easily now. Their home was safe. That was the main thing. And even more good news?

"I'm co-executor."

"I don't understand, honey. What does that mean?"

"It means that Candy can't do a single damned thing with the estate unless I agree."

The immediate implication filled Carmina with delight. She had been worried that Candy would be as casual and capricious an executor of his mother's estate as he had been a manager of the family dairy farm. If Paulinho was co-executor, any decision would require the mutual agreement of the brothers. It was another huge weight off her shoulders to think that her husband would have parity with his brother.

And that was when she recognized the secondary implication. Teresa was rebuking her elder son from beyond the grave. She had put herself on record as not trusting him to do a good job by himself. She had bound him to his younger brother and given the younger brother an equal say in the disposition of her estate.

"Did Candy show up? Was he there? How did he take it?"

For the first time since he had returned home from the lawyer's office, Paulinho smiled.

"Not well, sugar. He was pretty steamed. In fact, his face turned all red and I thought he was going to have a stroke for a second." A stroke had crippled their father years before the old man's death. Both Francisco boys feared Chico's fate and regarded it as the Francisco family bogeyman. "But he finally calmed down and started acting all nice and polite. I guess he figured out there was no benefit in antagonizing his co-executor."

Carmina wasn't a big fan of soft drinks, but she wasn't a beer drinker either. Nevertheless, the occasion demanded something. She fetched herself a Coke from the refrigerator and popped it open. From that point on she would associate the beverage's fizzy taste with good news and a feeling of relief.

"Congratulations, Mr. Co-executor," she said. They clinked bottles.

"Okay. Now the rest."

Carmina gave a start. The good news had been so good that she had forgotten there was also bad news.

"Mom bequeathed me 7 percent of the estate."

Carmina shook her head in confusion.

"What's that? Is that the value of the house? Is that all we get?" She felt herself starting to babble. Carmina shifted gears. "It doesn't matter, honey. We don't depend on the dairy farm. You went your own way and you're a success. It doesn't matter if Mom didn't divide her share of the family business equally between you and Candy." Carmina referred to her mother-in-law as "Mom" as easily as she addressed her own mother.

"Oh, but she did. Candy got 7 percent."

"I don't get it. I don't get it at all."

A rueful smile played on Paulinho's lips.

"Maybe I don't get it either, but maybe I do. Mom gave *you* 7 percent also. And 7 percent each to Paul, Mary Carmen, Henry, and Alex. Oh, and 7 percent to Magdalena."

Carmina thought for a moment.

"Mom gave equal shares to you and me and each of our children, plus Hank's wife?"

"That's right, sugar. Seven of us."

"But . . . seven times seven. That's . . . forty-nine. She gave us 49 percent of the estate?"

"Actually, I lied a little. Our shares are each a little more than 7 percent. Our combined share is exactly half the estate."

"How does the other half work?"

"Candy and Odile. Their three boys. The two daughters-in-law."

"Seven, again."

"Right. That's what Mom did. She listed fourteen heirs and parceled out equal shares. Actually, 'parceled out' is a bad choice of words. There are no parcels. Our shares are equal, but undivided."

"Why did she include daughters-in-law but not Gerry? If she included sons-in-law then Mary Carmen's husband would have a share."

"I'm not sure, sugar, but think about it. As far as Mom was concerned, wives marry *into* families. She thinks — she *thought* — of Sofia and Rita as Franciscos. Gerry, on the other hand, is the very nice young man who took Mary Carmen *out* of the Francisco family."

"Like Louis took Fatima out of the Francisco family and made her a Salazar. What about the Salazars?"

"Mom didn't forget Fatima. She stipulated that Fatima's children would get $70,000, divided evenly, so that's $10,000 each. Candy and I are going to have to use the estate as collateral to raise the cash to take care of the bequest to Fatima's kids. I guess that's part of the bad news, too."

Paulinho and Carmina sipped their drinks and were lost in thought for a few moments. Then Carmina spoke.

"Alex."

"What about Alex?"

"Our baby is not even a teenager yet. And he's one of Mom's fourteen heirs."

"Yes, that's the way Mom decided to do it. I guess it's a good thing we decided to have him. Perhaps Pope Paul didn't write *Humanae Vitae* for nothing."

"Honey! Don't be disrespectful!"

"Just practical, sugar. Anyway, what Alex doesn't know won't hurt him. He's a minor and I'm listed in the will as his trustee. We're not going to ask an eleven-year-old what he wants to do with his sliver of a big estate. As co-executor and trustee, I'll be able to protect his interests. Maybe he'll be going to college, especially if we can talk him into going to less expensive schools than Paul did."

"Fourteen people. How will we ever agree on anything?"

"Majority vote, of course. If we disagree on something we can have a vote."

"But it's an even split. We could end up seven to seven."

Paulinho laughed.

"You're forgetting something, sugar. Something *very* important."

Carmina thought for a moment.

"Oh!" she said.

"Right!" agreed her husband. "Candy and Odile will never vote together on anything now. If he said the sky is blue, she'd say it's green. They won't even agree on up and down. Candy will be voting with us if there are any disagreements. What else can he do? At least that way he gets in good with his co-executor."

Paulinho looked at the dregs in his beer bottle. He swirled it around. He lifted his bottle.

"A toast! A toast to Mom!" They clinked their bottles again. "She made certain we'd remember her forever, because that's how long it's going to take to sort this all out."

Paulinho tipped back his bottle and drained the last of it.

JULY 1982

Louis Gets a Letter

"Mail!"

It sounded like Elvino. Louis Salazar levered himself out of his recliner and went to see what his No. 5 son had brought in. Elvino was nowhere in sight, but the mail he had brought in was lying in a heap on the kitchen table. Louis eased himself into a chair, wincing as his weight-aggravated bad back gave a twinge. He had been a widower for more than six years now, and it didn't suit him. Fatima had been an excellent wife and had had a knack for moderating her husband's excesses. In her absence, Louis was reduced to subsisting on snack foods and take-out. The three boys who remained at home didn't know how to cook anything that wasn't carved off a cow or a pig, so there wasn't much variety in meals prepared at home. It was an existence, but it wasn't much of a life.

Bills, of course. You could always count on plenty of bills. One from the irrigation district and a batch from Southern California Edison. Dairy farms sucked up lots of water and lots of electricity. A check from the creamery. Someone without dairy experience would have been impressed by the creamery's payment to the Salazar dairy, but the bills had impressively large numbers on them, too. The balance didn't always work out in the dairyman's favor, although Louis prided himself on being one of the more successful dairy operators in Tulare County.

Louis tossed aside some sales papers for things that didn't interest him and discovered the personal letter. He didn't see many of those. He scanned the return address. It was from Paul Francisco, his godson and nephew. Or, to be a little more honest about it, *Fatima's* godson and nephew. Was the boy dutifully sending his godfather a birthday card? It was too early for that. He tore it open.

Paul was a puzzle and Louis wasn't especially keen on puzzles. What weird mix of Francisco and Soares genes had produced *that* boy? He had no special complaint about his nephew. He just didn't get him.

Now Fatima, that was a different matter. His late wife had been able to tune in effortlessly on the boy's wavelength. It was also clear that Paul had adored his Aunt Fatima. Worshiped her, even. It was always *madrinha* this and *madrinha* that, addressing her as she was entitled by virtue of having held the little guy during his baptism thirty-one years before. Paul also addressed his Uncle Louis as *padrinho*, but Louis didn't sense any special warmth in it. Just the perfunctory politeness of a well-trained Portuguese boy.

Fatima had been the most educated and best-read of the Francisco clan. Paul had been drawn to her like a paper clip to a magnet. He borrowed books from her. He'd give her books as gifts. They'd discuss music and argue over the merits of different composers. Fatima was no particular fan of Wagner, but she had a soft spot for *Lohengrin*. (Louis knew to stay out of the house on Saturday mornings when the Metropolitan Opera's live broadcasts would pour out of the stereo system in the den.) Paul liked Wagner a lot and would try to persuade his godmother to have a greater appreciation of his own favorite. Louis couldn't remember which one that was. He remembered *Lohengrin* because his wife would play it sometimes on the phonograph and he had once wondered aloud why Wagner had composed an opera about the star of the TV show *Bonanza*. Fatima had laughed her beautifully musical laugh while explaining Louis's mistake to him.

Louis was surprised to find several sheets of regular paper in the envelope. He had assumed its weight indicated heavy stock, such as a greeting card. But it was just sheets of ordinary paper. The first page was a personal letter.

Uncle Louis:

That was unusually brusque. No "Dear" or even "Hello." And certainly no "*padrinho*."

If your attorney has not seen fit to bring it to your attention, you may be ignorant of the position into which you and three of your sons have maneuvered yourselves. It's bad enough that you're supporting Otelo in his greedy attempt to seize more of Avó's estate, but it's even worse that you're permitting (or, perhaps, even forcing) Elvino and Randall to place themselves at similar risk.

Louis's heart was pounding and his hands were shaking. What sort of insolent nonsense had Paul gotten himself up to?

I write this letter so that you will understand clearly my own position in this matter. As I have been named among the defendants, I will stand against the petitioners at every stage. That includes testifying against my cousins in any subsequent perjury proceedings, since their petition is a tissue of lies and they will undoubtedly perjure themselves on the witness stand by repeating these lies.

Louis was hyperventilating. He put the letter down and struggled to control himself. He could not believe it had come to this. He paced back and forth until he finally felt calm enough to read the rest of it.

It is unseemly for young people to rebuke their elders, especially elders toward whom they had previously felt nothing but affection and respect. Nevertheless, that is what I am doing. I rebuke you for supporting a legal action that attacks my father and slanders my grandmother. I will stand against you.

Paul Francisco

Louis looked at the other pages. They were photocopies of pages from the California criminal code. Paul had sent him the sections defining perjury and subornation of perjury, along with the one that set the penalty for perjury: "not less than one nor more than fourteen years."

He slammed the pages down on the table so hard that it rattled and he felt a sharp pain in his hand. He heaved himself to his feet and marched down the hall.

"Elvino! Elvino, where are you?"

Elvino popped his head out of the door at the end of the hallway. The sound of his father's voice had startled him — it sounded different — but the expression on his father's face was actually frightening. He had never seen the old man in such a rage.

"What's the problem, Dad? Is everything okay?"

Louis stopped in the hallway outside his son's door. His face was flushed and beads of sweat had popped out on his forehead. His breathing was rapid and ragged.

Elvino watched in apprehension as his father got himself under control. He didn't know what to say, so he waited for his father to speak. Louis sounded more like himself when he finally did.

"Elvino, tell me. You still see Henry around? You still talk to him?"

"Sure, Dad. Every now and again."

"You're getting along okay? You're not fighting?"

Elvino thought for a moment before replying. His father knew about the way Hank had gotten in his face after being served with the petition to revoke probate, but Elvino hadn't mentioned telling Hank that he had been duped into signing the paperwork. He didn't know what answer his father was hoping for, so he simply told the truth.

"No, Dad. We're not fighting. We don't talk about the lawsuit, of course."

"Did you tell him that this isn't aimed at him or any of the kids? That it's all about Candido and Paulinho and the way they've taken advantage of us and your mother's legitimate interests?"

Elvino felt acutely uncomfortable.

"Sort of, Dad. Well, I tried. Really, Hank doesn't want to hear anything about it. When I tried to pass along what you said about, you know, it being about Uncle Candy and Uncle Paulinho, Hank got kind of pushed out of shape. He said, 'So why is *my* name on it?' And he wouldn't listen and I dropped it."

Louis had been telling anyone who would listen that the lawsuit was really a matter for the grownups. It wasn't about the grandchildren. It was about Teresa's sons versus her son-in-law. Louis had been encouraged by the responses. He said, "Three children, three equal shares," and people would nod their heads in agreement. It was simple justice, as far as Louis could see.

But the Franciscos didn't see it. Otherwise why would Teresa's sons dishonor their sister's memory by cutting her share down to a mere $70,000? Louis had persuaded himself that he was in the right and it wounded him to be accused of launching a vendetta.

Or suborning perjury.

"What's going on, Dad?"

"I have a letter from your cousin Paul. I guess Henry hasn't told his older brother that it's nothing personal. It's an extremely hateful letter. My godson sent me a hateful letter. What would your mother say if she saw how your cousin is acting toward his *padrinho?* It's disgraceful! He called us liars!"

Is it a lie when you fool two of your sons into signing a petition to revoke probate? Elvino was smart enough to keep his thought to himself.

JULY 1982

The Legal Eagles

The dark wood of the wall paneling matched the wood of the long rectangular conference table. The big chairs were upholstered in dark leather. It was a thoroughly traditional and unimaginative conference room for a legal firm, the kind that made clients feel like they had come to the right place.

The effect of stodgy solidity was spoiled slightly by the fluorescent lights. While the ceiling panels flooded the room with the kind of light necessary for long productive sessions of poring over reams of fine print, one of the tubes behind the frosted plastic was in need of replacement. At random intervals it would dim for a couple of seconds before flickering back to normal brightness.

It did so at the exact moment that Ryan Bowman ushered his two colleagues into the conference room, reminding him that he had meant to have it fixed that morning. Feeling subtly undermined by the inconvenient coincidence, Bowman made a snap decision to reassert his dignity by sitting at the head of the table. He abandoned his original plan of sitting across from his fellow attorneys. As he took the seat at the end of the table, his colleagues promptly claimed the seats to his immediate right and left. Bowman was uncertain whether he had divided and conquered or been caught in a flanking maneuver.

He poured himself a glass of ice water from the crystal decanter that his assistant had placed on the table earlier. Harold Widener helped himself to the ceramic carafe of coffee and filled one of the mugs that had been provided. He raised his eyebrows at Dennis Ramos while still holding the carafe aloft, but Ramos gave his head a slight shake. Widener put the carafe back down and busied himself with adding a remarkable amount of sugar to his coffee.

Bowman took a couple of sips of ice water and noticed that his assistant had also laid out long yellow legal pads in accordance with his boss's previously intended seating pattern. He gave a mental shrug. So much for the dominance games. His younger colleagues had probably already noticed that he played the first round of maneuvers by ear. It was probably time to stop playing one-upmanship.

"Dennis, would you hand me that pad next to you? Thanks." Bowman smiled at his younger colleagues. "I don't suppose that there's too much question about what we need to do."

Widener and Ramos shook their heads in joint negation.

"No question at all," said Widener. "This whole business has escalated from a simple division of an estate among contending parties to a full-blown lawsuit. So let's get this council of war rolling."

"Okay. This is potentially one of the biggest messes we've ever had to untangle. Most of the Franciscos have signed waivers accepting me as their attorney despite my partnership with John Simoes, who drafted Teresa Francisco's will, the one being challenged by three members of the Salazar family."

There was no question that Simoes would be subpoenaed by the petitioners as a witness, creating an awkward situation when he would be questioned by his law partner. That theoretical concern paled, however, in contrast with the need to have the Francisco family represented by the law firm with the greatest depth of knowledge concerning the complicated details of the families involved and their business connections. That law firm was unquestionably Simoes & Bowman, which had drafted every legal document for the Franciscos since John Simoes was a kid right out of law school, working for a legal practice then known as Simoes & Son. Still answering in those days to "João," John had sat in on his father's consultation with Chico and Teresa Francisco when they drafted their original 1940 will. John had prepared Teresa's final will and testament in 1979, when the old lady revised the document to reflect the deaths of her husband and daughter — and lack of faith in her older son.

"Dennis and I talked about this before we came over. We fully agree that you are the lead attorney in the current proceeding. We'll turn and rend each other to shreds after we've ensured that the Franciscos have something to fight over. For your information, I am now attorney of record for Ferdinando

Francisco as well as his mother. I'll therefore be representing both Odile and Ferdinando in this dispute. Since both of my clients were named by Teresa as heirs in her estate, my role will be to protect my clients' interests in preserving the integrity of Teresa's estate and her bequests, after which I will shift gears and represent Odile in her efforts to strip Candido stark naked in the divorce proceedings."

"My clients are Candido's other sons," said Ramos. "That would be Candido Junior and João José." Ramos shared the Franciscos' Portuguese heritage and had no difficulty pronouncing the names, although as a second-generation Californian his ability to speak Portuguese was limited. "Junior and Jojo are going to sue their father over their joint business interests. My clients and their wives were all named heirs in Teresa's will, so I have four people keenly interested in preserving her estate from their cousins' petition."

"And the rest are mine," said Bowman. "That basically means Paulinho and his family, along with his brother Candido."

"Who has no place else to go!" laughed Widener. Bowman and Ramos smiled.

"Candido makes a really tempting target, you know," said Ramos. "Does he know we'll be sharpening our knives for him all the time we're cooperating during the trial?"

"If he doesn't," replied Widener, "I'll *tell* him. The more anxious he gets, the easier time I'll have getting a good settlement for Odile."

"Gentlemen, gentlemen," admonished Bowman. "As Candido's attorney, I'll thank you *not* to stab him with your sharpened knives until after the trial."

"Don't worry, Ryan. We know how to bide our time," said Ramos. He didn't see any reason to tell Bowman that his clients were discussing whether they could force their father into bankruptcy, which could result in an auction of his farm assets. That could create a pile of cash against which Junior and Jojo could make their claims. They felt no residual loyalty toward the father who had abandoned their mother.

Widener saw no reason to tell Bowman that Odile wanted to oust her estranged husband from management of the Francisco estate during its period in probate limbo. Widener was considering opening discussions with Ramos about whether his clients would like to make common cause with their mother in forcing out Candido and making Junior the *de jure* instead of just the *de facto* manager of the Francisco dairy farm.

"So," said Ramos brightly. "Shall we talk about *her?*"

Spontaneous laughter burst from both of his colleagues.

"Okay," said Bowman, "*who* can explain what's going on here?"

"You should ask Ferdinando, not Odile. He's much more alert and attuned to family gossip than his poor mother," said Widener. "Ferdie says that Biddy Onan is sleeping with their Uncle Louis."

"Gentlemen, gentlemen! Let us not engage in idle gossip," said Bowman. The younger attorneys looked at Bowman with indulgent expressions on their faces. Was Bowman really this prissy behind closed doors?

"We should talk *facts* only," continued Bowman, but then he smiled. "And as a matter of fact, the Simoes & Bowman private investigator has confirmed that Biddy Onan's car is frequently parked overnight at Louis Salazar's place. If she's not sleeping with the old man, then her only choices are Leo, Elvis, or Randy, ranging in age from thirty-four down to twenty-one."

"At least they're all legal," laughed Widener.

"Yeah, but none of the boys will take a second look at Biddy unless they're necrophiliacs!" said Ramos.

When the laughter died down, Ramos poured himself some ice water while Widener topped off his coffee. Bowman sipped his water with a pensive expression on his face and Widener dug back into the sugar.

"You know, gentlemen, although there's an element of opportunism in Beatrice Onan getting hired as legal counsel in a court action underwritten by her boyfriend," said Bowman, "what is she even doing here in the first place?"

"Good point," agreed Widener. "She shook the dust of this two-bit town off her shoes — and didn't mind saying so — when she moved up to San Francisco to seek her fortune. So why is she trying cases down here on her old stomping grounds?"

"She's still based in San Francisco," observed Bowman. "And her stationery boasts a street address in The City, not a P.O. box."

"You know," mused Widener, "I'll bet it's a front. A mailing service address that just makes you look like a big success. I'll bet if you go there you just find a walk-in with rows of numbered boxes. Her 'suite' is probably just a lock-box in a mail drop."

"That's certainly no disgrace for a fledgling attorney," said Bowman. "Might even be a canny investment in one's image. But Biddy is no spring chicken and she wouldn't be down here trolling for cases if she had a full docket up in Frisco. I've heard that she has — or had — some financial difficulties."

Ramos looked thoughtful for a moment and wrote a note to himself on his legal pad. "That might be worth following up," he said.

"Oh?" said Widener, raising his eyebrows.

"Sure," said Ramos. "It wouldn't hurt to find out more about what makes her go."

"Oh, we already know that," said Widener. "It's Louis Salazar."

The three men laughed.

"Speaking of Louis," said Ramos, "why isn't he a party to this case?"

"That's not too big a mystery," replied Bowman. "He'd be vulnerable in terms of establishing his standing as one of his mother-in-law's heirs. Teresa didn't make a bequest to Louis in any of her wills. Only to Fatima. And with Fatima gone, she bypassed her son-in-law and went right to the grandchildren. Of course, Louis could point out that Teresa made bequests to her daughters-in-law, so why not her son-in-law, but there's no inherent point of law there. And it sounds greedy, especially since his dairy farm is even larger than the Francisco operation. Louis probably realized that it made more sense to make it all about his children and got three of them to go along with the plan."

"Why only three?" asked Widener. "Why not all seven of the Salazar children?"

"Rumor has it that the two oldest sons, Tony and Manny, refused outright to have anything to do with the scheme," explained Bowman. "Then there's the problem of Leo and Catarina. I hear that they're a bit 'slow' and have speech impediments. Leo's is especially bad. It might look as if they were manipulating him if they pushed him forward as a party to the lawsuit. It could look bad. Otelo, however, was willing to give it a shot and the two younger sons who live at home, Elvis and Randy, were inveigled into putting their names to the petition. Louis stays in the background while his three sons serve as front men."

"Do you think Biddy told him he had a better chance this way?" asked Ramos.

"Ha!" exclaimed Widener. "If she did, it's the first bit of good legal advice she's given anyone in her entire career!"

"That reminds me," said Bowman. "Of the three of us, Harold, you're the one who has most recently tangled with Beatrice Onan. Right?"

"Oh, yes. I cleaned her clock in a ridiculous reckless endangerment lawsuit. That woman really is an ambulance-chaser."

"Very good. Then I think you should be the one who issues objections on behalf of the respondents. What do you think of that?"

"I think that's a very nice idea. I get on her nerves anyway, so nothing would please me more than to interrupt her as often as I can. We can count on her to make plenty of mistakes, so I won't lack for opportunities."

"Great. And Dennis, why don't you take on the responsibility of being our repairman? You can be the guy who smoothes things over when we need to issue clarifications or do follow-ups in awkward situations."

"You mean the guy who makes excuses for mistakes and tries to mitigate blunders!" interjected Widener.

"Well, if you want to be blunt about it," agreed Bowman. "But we should take advantage of the fact that Dennis is a likeable 'aw, shucks!' kind of guy and juries warm to him. If we have those skills on our team, they're best used to out-point Onan if things get nasty."

"You know, Hare, Ryan is absolutely right. I can't help it if I'm younger and prettier than you and people like me better. We need to play to our strengths. You get to be mean lawyer and I get to be nice lawyer."

Widener answered him with a grin.

"Screw you, Dennis. And enjoy it while you can!"

There was a moment of simultaneous silence from the three men until Dennis Ramos tapped his pencil a couple of times on his notepad and turned to Bowman.

"Tell me. Have you decided what we're going to do about the black sheep of the family?"

Bowman pretended not to understand.

"What black sheep?" he said.

Widener chimed in.

"Come on, Ryan. Full disclosure, please. Dennis and I both know about the loose cannon on the deck. He threatens to upset the apple cart on us."

"Thank you for the cascade of clichés, gentlemen," said Bowman, putting off a direct response.

He had once had the habit of running his fingers through his hair during moments of stress. These days that would serve only to dislodge his hairpiece. Sensing the old feeling coming upon him again, he redirected it by picking up his glass of water and taking a sip.

"Very well, then," continued Bowman. "Apparently we all know that Paul

Francisco sent a letter to Louis Salazar accusing him of suborning perjury. I have a copy of that letter, including the attachments from the state civil code. As his attorney, I have advised Paul to take no more unilateral actions. I believe he has accepted that advice."

"The letter is a threat," said Widener. "Plain and simple. It could be used against our side in the trial. Biddy could portray it as an attempt to extort a withdrawal of the lawsuit."

Bowman sighed.

"No question about it," he replied. "I have cautioned my clients to that effect and I am confident that there will be no more incidents like the letter to Louis Salazar."

"Who is this Paul Francisco anyway?" asked Widener. "My client Ferdinando says his cousin could hardly wait to get away from the dairy farm and is uninvolved with the family business. What's his big beef in the matter?"

"I can answer part of that," said Ramos. "Louis Salazar is Paul's *padrinho* — his godfather — and that's a big deal in our Portuguese-American community. He must feel like his godfather betrayed him. That's personal."

Bowman nodded his head.

"Dennis is correct. Paul Francisco went off to college, got a couple of degrees, and is up in Sacramento. He's working as a civil servant in the State Treasurer's office and as an adjunct faculty member at one of the colleges in the capital region. He's the only one of Teresa Francisco's descendants to have left Tulare County. But he stood up to be counted when the lawsuit was filed, even if he did it a bit too enthusiastically. Family loyalty runs deep among my clients, apparently even with the so-called 'black sheep' who went his own way."

"That's a funny thing to say," remarked Widener. "There are three of us here because the Francisco family is broken into three factions."

"I concede the point," said Bowman. "We'll just have to paper over the rifts till the Salazar lawsuit is settled. I'm sure we can maintain that much family unity for the short term, right?"

His colleagues nodded their heads. Bowman smiled and reached into his portfolio, extracting a thin manila folder.

"Harold asked for full disclosure a moment ago. I confess that I have yet to fully disclose. Just between you and me, I'm inclined to forgive Paul his impetuous outburst toward his godfather because he has somewhat redeemed himself in my eyes."

Bowman opened the folder and extracted a single sheet of paper. He held it up toward his colleagues.

"This is not the letter he sent to Louis Salazar. It is, rather, a letter that was sent to Paul almost three years ago. Gentlemen, I present to you our secret weapon."

FEBRUARY 1954

Catarina Is Born

The two oldest Salazar boys peered through the glass window of the nursery in the hospital's maternity ward.

"She still looks the same," said Tony, the eldest at twelve.

"Give her a break! She's only been here a couple of days!" retorted Manny, ten.

"You know, actually I think she looks a little smaller."

"That's because her face isn't as red and puffy."

"Is she coming home today?"

"I think so. We'll know when Daddy comes back out."

The boys had yet to see their mother after the difficult birth of their sister. No children of any age above zero were permitted anywhere in the maternity ward except the nursery's visiting room.

In one of the maternity ward's rooms, Fatima was talking to her husband.

"You're my second visitor today," she told Louis.

Louis sat at her bedside, holding her hand. There was a small bandage where the needle for the intravenous drip had been. He was extremely happy to see it gone.

"Was the doctor here? What did he say?"

"Oh. My mistake. You're my *third* visitor. But maybe the doctor doesn't count. He was just making his rounds. And he said I'm doing fine. I told him

I want to go home and he said he'll decide this afternoon." Fatima paused, trying to remember what she was going to say. "Who's watching the boys?"

"My sister," said Louis. "Except that Tony and Manny are with me. I left them looking at Catarina."

"Maybe we should have named her 'Catherine' instead. Would that have been better?"

"Don't be silly, Fatima. 'Catarina' is a perfectly good name. I know you chose it because it was my mother's name and my father was very pleased to hear about it. He cried when I told him." Louis squeezed his wife's hand. "You were going to tell me about your visitors."

It wasn't like Fatima to let her mind wander. It was further evidence, as if he needed any, that the delivery of their fifth child had been the worst ordeal of all. The labor had lasted hours longer than for even the fourth child, who had been marked by the experience.

"Yes, you're right. I had a visit from Monsignor."

Louis felt a spasm of fear and a sudden chill. He didn't like to talk about priests while visiting people in the hospital, especially when the person in question was his wife.

"What was Monsignor doing here?" he asked hoarsely.

Fatima caught the concern in his voice and smiled. Louis basked in its warmth and his fears receded into the dark recesses of his mind.

"Monsignor makes regular visits here. I also saw him earlier, when I was still in labor. He gave me a blessing and brought me a new rosary." She looked around. "Where is it? I hope I didn't lose it already."

"It's here." He reached over to the nightstand and picked it up from behind the box of tissues. Louis placed it in Fatima's free hand. She brought the little crucifix up to her lips and kissed it.

"Thank you, sweetheart."

Louis was chewing his lip as he regarded his wife. He resolved to speak his piece.

"Fatima, you know I'll support you in anything you decide, right?"

His wife's eyes narrowed in puzzlement.

"Of course. What are you talking about?"

He took several seconds to screw up his courage. It was amazing how long a second lasted when your wife was gazing at you expectantly.

"Fatima . . . I really think Catarina should be our last child. We have a daughter now, the first granddaughter in the whole family, and can stop if we want to."

More long seconds as his wife's expression became unreadable, completely immobile. He waited for words, but they weren't coming. He kept waiting, but there were still no words. Fatima lay motionless in her hospital bed, her rosary clutched in one hand, the other held by her husband, until Louis noticed that she was trembling ever so slightly. Trembling as if she were struggling not to. Then he saw that her eyes were watering. They overflowed and tears began to course down her cheeks.

"*Louis!* How could you *say* such a thing!"

Now she was sobbing and had lifted her free arm to hide her face in the crook of her elbow.

"Fatima, Fatima, Fatima!"

Louis reached up and took his wife's arm by the wrist. She resisted for a moment, then let him gently pull it away from her face. When he saw her eyes again, they were looking to the side, not at him.

"Fatima, listen to me! Having Catarina nearly killed you! I love my daughter and thank God for her, but we should have learned the lesson with Leo. He'll never be quite right and we can't deny that. I hope Catarina will be fine, but most of all I want *you* to be fine. We have five beautiful children. *Five,* because Leo is beautiful, too, despite everything. That should be enough for anyone. *Enough.*"

Fatima was amazed by her husband's outburst. Louis was a man of very few words. Entire days passed without her getting more than a grunt or two out of him, but now he was pouring out a passionate stream of words. She was drowning in the flood of his argument.

"Enough," she said.

"Yes! Yes! Enough."

"No," she replied. "You don't understand. 'Enough' from *you.*"

"Enough from me?" he repeated, numbly.

"Yes," said Fatima. "How can you even say these things to me? And after Monsignor's visit." She shook her rosary at him, and the cheap glass beads made a tinkling sound as they dangled from her fingers. "Do you know what Monsignor said when he gave this to me? Do you know?"

Louis shook his head, awash in a deepening misery.

"He said I was brave. He said I was a vessel of life. He said I was a gateway for souls clamoring to enter the world. *That's* what he said! He blessed me and said that motherhood was my sacred vocation. Are you denying that?"

Louis plucked some tissues from the box on the nightstand and silently handed them to his wife. Fatima took the crumpled tissues and dabbed at her eyes. She was amazed to see how moist the tissues became and was momentarily distracted by the sight. Louis gave her some more.

His small gesture of silent assistance touched her heart and calmed her.

"Louis. Louis, I'm sorry. I apologize for my outburst. I know you meant well. *Mean* well. But we can't second-guess God. We have to submit to his will."

Since when did Monsignor become God? Louis kept his thought to himself. His defeat was already complete. He might as well go out into the battlefield and put the wounded out of their misery.

"We'll have more children if it's the Lord's intention," Fatima continued. "We have to be faithful. Do you agree?"

"Yes, dear."

Fatima was not entirely satisfied with Louis's terse capitulation, but she had tired herself out and wanted to reserve her strength for the longed-for trip home with her daughter. Then she remembered.

"Louis? I forgot something. Something else that Monsignor told me."

Louis didn't want to hear it, but he squeezed her hand slightly and said, "Please tell me. What else did he say?"

"Carmina is here. Monsignor saw her this morning. She had a little girl! Paulinho and Carmina have a little girl named Mary Carmen! Isn't that — *ow!*"

Louis released her hand.

"I'm sorry, dear. I was surprised."

Inside, however, he was thinking, *God damn those Franciscos! It's always something with them! Fatima nearly dies giving Chico and Teresa their first granddaughter after — what? — eight Salazar and Francisco grandsons and — wouldn't you know it? — they go and pop out a second granddaughter right on our heels! Damn, damn, damn!*

"That's okay, sweetheart," said Fatima. "But isn't this the greatest news? Catarina will grow up with a playmate her own age. I just know that she and Mary Carmen will be the *best* friends. Like sisters! Practically twins! It really is a gift from God. I am *so* happy!"

Damn, damn, damn.

Want to Be a Priest?

Paul was used to Monsignor Pontac's customary brusqueness, so it was very strange to see another side of him. The priest carried him into the rectory's living room and lowered him onto the sofa. Monsignor tucked one of the pillows under Paul's head and sat down beside him. He gently placed his hand on the third-grader's forehead and rested it there for a moment.

"No. I don't think you're running a fever," said Monsignor.

The pastor of St. Bartholomew's unfurled a comforter that had been lying folded at Paul's feet and draped it over the boy.

"Just rest there quietly for a while. I'll call your parents. Do you need anything? A glass of water?"

"Thank you, Monsignor. A glass of water would be nice."

The priest walked briskly but quietly out of the room.

St. Bart's Catholic School did not have an infirmary or a school nurse. When Paul leaned over the side of the sand box after lunch and emptied his stomach onto the ground, Mrs. Knox had turned to the one solution for everything and sent one of the boys running to fetch Monsignor. The priest-principal of St. Bart's had rushed over to take charge. Monsignor had picked Paul up as if he were weightless and conveyed him to the priest's residence, the one place where the boy could lie down until one of his parents arrived to collect him.

The interior of the rectory was almost completely foreign to Paul. He had been in the entryway a few times while running errands to and from the school, but he had never seen the priest's living quarters. The schoolyard was rampant with rumors over what Monsignor had in his house, but Paul had glimpsed no barred dungeon during his quick passage in Monsignor's arms into the living room. Of course, the dungeon for bad children was supposed to be in the basement. He probably wouldn't have seen it anyway.

Paul turned his head to look around the living room. It was unlike any he had ever seen before. There was no television set anywhere, and the walls were lined with book-laden shelves. Hundreds and hundreds of books. Paul was fascinated.

Monsignor was back at his side. He helped Paul to a sitting position. He used one hand to support Paul's back while the other held the glass of water in front of Paul's face. Paul leaned forward and took a sip. It eased the acrid taste in his mouth. Paul used one hand to tilt the glass further and slurped more eagerly, but Monsignor tilted it back.

"Slow down, Paul! A little at a time."

Monsignor let Paul have a few more sips, after which the boy pulled back and nodded his head.

"Thank you, Monsignor. That was good."

"You're welcome. Now you rest easy until your mom gets here. I called her and it shouldn't be long."

"Yes, Monsignor."

The priest lowered Paul onto to the sofa and returned the glass of water to the kitchen. Paul closed his eyes and rested.

He started thinking about his grandmother. *Avó* was always making remarks in Paul's presence about the sterling qualities of priests. Apparently they were the agents of Christ on earth — the pope's deputies. Sometimes Paul thought it sounded a little silly. He couldn't imagine Monsignor with a deputy's badge. At other times, however, his grandmother's comments intrigued him. Priests were a breed set apart, special people who inspired awe and perhaps just a little fear.

Sometimes *Avó* would ask him, "Don't you think it would be nice to be a priest?" Paul was shocked by the very idea. It seemed the height of arrogance to assume he could be one of God's elect. He always replied with a diffident, "*Não sei, Avó.*" I don't know, Grandmother.

Paul had not yet figured out that Teresa Francisco was performing the vocational triage among her grandchildren that Portuguese grandmothers normally practiced. With ten grandsons among the Francisco and Salazar families thus far, Teresa was looking for the one who might be sacrificed as a tithe to the Church. Blessings were known to rain down upon devout Catholic families who sent a son to the seminary or a daughter to a convent. Teresa had only the two granddaughters, so she couldn't spare either one, but a good Catholic woman with ten grandsons should be embarrassed if she couldn't find at least one priest among them.

The choice was clear. It had to be a boy with a bent for learning. At one stroke, most of Teresa's young male descendants were eliminated from the competition. She was left with Tony Salazar, Fatima's eldest, and Paul Francisco, Paulinho's eldest. She couldn't absolutely rule out the two youngest grandsons, who might have some potential, but Henry Francisco would be needed to succeed Paulinho as a dairyman. Paulinho could, however, spare his bookish elder son for ecclesiastical purposes.

Paul was the obvious choice over his cousin. The Salazar boy was personable and outgoing, while Paul was already showing signs of being a standoffish loner. If it came down to a matter of being willing to spend long hours at one's desk studying Latin and theology, Teresa could imagine Paul at that task much more easily than Tony.

So far, however, she had had minimal success in eliciting any positive reactions from Paul about a priestly career. She would say a few more rosaries for the intention of stimulating Paul's sacerdotal vocation. If God willed it, it was certain to happen.

Only vaguely aware of his grandmother's motives, Paul lay on Monsignor's sofa and thought about her gentle but constant reminders about the glories of the priesthood. As his eyelids grew heavy, he wondered why *Avó* had never played the obvious trump card: Monsignor's living room contained a veritable library, more than he had ever seen in a home before. Priests apparently lived surrounded by books. It was like heaven on earth.

Paul dozed, dreaming of never running out of books.

APRIL 1960

A Son Back Home

It was one of those clear mornings when the span of the San Joaquin Valley became visible. The shadowed peaks of the Sierra Nevada serrated the eastern horizon, the foothills rising from the flat plain of the valley floor. In the opposite direction, the more distant mountains of the Coast Range were dimly visible, their eroded eastern slopes catching the day's early light.

Chico Francisco gazed at the washed-out blue vista of the coastal mountains to the west. The San Joaquin was long in the north-south direction and narrow in the east-west. Only about a hundred miles separated the Sierra Nevada behind him from the Coast Range in front of him. Chico smiled at the thought that it was "only" a hundred miles or so. His native island of Terceira was merely eighteen miles long in its greatest dimension. He drove his pickup truck farther than that every time he ran an errand to the city of Tulare.

Everything was bigger in California. Much bigger.

Chico walked toward the dairy barn, which was relatively quiet. The morning milking had begun at 2:30 a.m. and finished up around 6:30. The milkers had gone home for breakfast and a nap. After lunch they would be back for the day's second shift from 2:30 till 6:30 in the afternoon. The routine continued around the clock, seven days a week.

A quick inspection showed that the milkers had done their job well. As usual. The pipes had been flushed out with water and drained, preventing the accumulation of spoiled milk — a haven for bacteria. The concrete floor of the dairy barn had been carefully hosed off. The refrigeration system was humming, keeping the stainless steel milk tank cold. The tank was nearly half full. With the completion of the afternoon milking, it would be brimming. Then the creamery's tanker truck would arrive to drain its contents.

As he passed through the dairy barn, Chico heard some cheerfully tuneless whistling coming from the direction of the calf pens. That puzzled him. Although he prided himself on treating his workers well, they didn't usually express their contentment to everyone within earshot. He emerged from the barn and discovered it was Vidal, merrily feeding the calves that were old enough to dine on hay.

Chico's employee was a short, wiry man whose stature was common among men born and raised in the Azores. Those who grew up in the United States, however, displayed an unexpected talent for growing tall. Chico's two sons both overtopped him by a few inches. Judging from Fatima's two eldest sons, it seemed likely that Chico's grandsons would be even taller.

As Chico watched, Vidal whacked a hay bale with a hatchet, severing the twine that held it together. He then tore slabs of compressed hay from the bale and tossed them into the manger that ran along the side of the calf pens. Eager calves were poking their heads through the stanchions to nibble at their morning fodder. Vidal noticed his employer watching him from the direction of the dairy barn.

"*Bom dia, patrão!*" he called out. *Good morning, boss!*

"*Bom dia, Vidalinho,*" replied Chico, addressing his worker with the familiar diminutive form of the man's name. Depending on the relationship between employer and employee, such familiarity could be seen as either affectionate or patronizing. Vidal flashed a big smile that made it clear how he took his boss's greeting.

The smile was, however, even bigger than usual.

"You seem especially happy today," said Chico in Portuguese. "Has good fortune smiled on you?"

"Yes, *patrão*. She has smiled very generously on me!"

Vidal walked over to Chico while fishing in the bib pocket of his denim overalls. He produced a folded letter and held it toward his boss. Chico cocked his head slightly to one side as he took Vidal's letter and unfolded it. He scanned its lines. A peculiar expression passed over his face. Chico raised his eyes back to Vidal and looked at the pride and delight glowing on his employee's face. He swallowed, folded the letter, and gave it back to Vidal.

"Your wife says that she had a son," said Chico diffidently.

"My wife says that *we* have a son!" declared Vidal in light-hearted correction of his boss. "*I* have a son!"

Chico was accustomed to thinking quickly on his feet. He was seldom at a loss for words, but words were failing him now. Vidal was looking at him expectantly. He had to say something.

"You seem very pleased."

"Of course, *patrão*, I have a son! I am *very* pleased!" said Vidal, some exasperation creeping into his voice at his boss's apparent obtuseness. "My wife says the boy is healthy and strong. Just like his father! This is the happiest day of my life!"

Another long awkward silence stretched out between them until Chico finally asked a question, although it was in the form of a statement.

"Vidalinho, you have been working for me for some time now."

"Yes, of course," said Vidal, with a quizzical look. "Four years. I keep track. Soon I can go back to Terceira to my wife and my son. Maybe in only one more year."

Chico cleared his throat. He decided to speak plainly.

"Vidalinho, you have been here for four years. You have not been with your wife in four years. She has a son . . . but it is not yours. You understand that, don't you?"

Vidal recoiled as if Chico had struck him.

"Do not say that, *patrão*! Do not say such a thing! How can you say such a thing!"

Vidal was angry. He pointed to the calf pens.

"You see those calves, *patrão*? You call them *your* calves. Your cows have calves, they are *your* calves. My wife, she had a son. She is *my* wife. She had *my* son. It is the same thing! I have a son!"

Chico solemnly regarded his worker. At length he nodded his head.

"Very well. I understand and I apologize. I congratulate you on your son. I wish you and your wife and your son much health and happiness."

Mollified, Vidal ventured a small smile.

"*Obrigado, patrão. Muito obrigado,*" he said. *Thank you, boss. Much obliged.*

Chico nodded his head in acknowledgment. Vidal tucked his letter back into the bib pocket of his overalls.

"I need to finish feeding *your* calves, *patrão*," he said.

"Yes, Vidalinho. *My* calves. You do that very well. Keep up the good work."

Vidal fell upon the bale again and tore off some more slabs to feed the calves. He was pleased with his boss's praise, but that faded away as to nothing compared with the good news from home.

NOVEMBER 1971

Gerry Meets the Family

Gerry Chamberlain didn't know what to do with his hands. Mary Carmen had been willing to hold one of them while they were strolling through the small orchard between her parents' home and her grandparents', but she dropped it just before they emerged from behind the big fig tree at the orchard's edge. He considered shoving his hands into his pockets, but decided that would look nonchalantly disrespectful. So they dangled at his sides and he tried not to let them fidget.

"You'll do fine. Trust me! You already know most of the people."

Gerry didn't share Mary Carmen's positive outlook.

"'Most' of them?" he said. "I hardly think so."

"Okay, maybe not 'most,' but *a lot*. My brothers will be there. You know Hank pretty well because he goes to our high school. Paul is up for the weekend, like usual."

"I know Alex."

"Well, I'm not sure the baby really counts but, yeah, you really know him and he likes you. If Mom hands off my baby to me, you can help me keep him entertained. Folks will like that, when they see that Alex accepts you as family." She thought a moment. "And Ferdie went to our high school. You remember my cousin Ferdie. He'll be here."

Mary Carmen pulled her boyfriend up the steps that led to the side door of her grandparents' home. Only traveling salesmen and other people who didn't know any better tried to use the big front door. Gerry still found it peculiar that Mary Carmen simply opened the door and walked in. No family member ever knocked on Chico and Teresa Francisco's door. It was a perpetual open house and you simply walked in.

When Mary Carmen had dragged Gerry inside on their first visit to her grandparents, he had asked her later how the custom had been established. She was puzzled, never having thought of it before, then she figured it out. It was simple. As far as her father and Uncle Candy and Aunt Fatima were concerned, this was just their childhood home. You don't knock to enter your own house. Naturally their numerous children simply followed suit. It made sense, in a way, but Gerry was thinking that he would start locking the doors when his future grown children moved out.

Gerry had never before seen the home of the senior Franciscos jam-packed with family for a major holiday. The modest home lacked a separate dining room, but the kitchen was large and two long tables were already set up, making it difficult to pass through to the living room, especially since the kitchen was already crowded with most of the women of the family.

Mary Carmen greeted her grandmother, bending down to give the old lady a kiss on the forehead.

"*Abença, Avó.*"

Gerry knew she was asking her grandmother's blessing. He knew virtually no Portuguese, but he had heard the ritual phrases often enough to know their significance.

"*Nosso Senhor te abençoe*," said Teresa, giving the response that "The Lord has blessed you," invoking the deity because her own mortal blessing would be too puny. She reached up with her hand, putting it behind her granddaughter's neck, and hauled the girl down lower so that she could plant a firm kiss on her cheek.

"*Chega aqui*," said Teresa to her granddaughter. *Get over here.* She led Mary Carmen over to the kitchen counter and whisked an immaculately white dish towel off a small bowl. There were *filhozes* inside. Mary Carmen's mouth immediately started to water at the sight of the Portuguese confections. She picked up one of them and took a bite. It had cooled off since her *avó* had fried up a huge batch earlier that morning, but it was light and toothsome and dusted with sugar and cinnamon.

The yeasty dough had risen in large bowls stashed in the pantry and covered with damp towels. Dollops were then dropped into a deep fryer until puffy and brown, after which they were shaken in a brown paper bag with sugar and cinnamon. When prepared by someone as skilled as Teresa, the *filhozes* were as light as bubbles and melted in the mouth. Mary Carmen fed one to Gerry, who gave a little moan of pleasure.

"*Avó* saved a few for us," said Mary Carmen, helping herself to another. "The rest were scarfed up by the first to arrive. *Muito obrigada, Avó.* Thank you!"

Having paid her respects to the matriarch, Mary Carmen then repeated the ritual with Aunt Odile, who was her *madrinha* from baptism and whose response was rather more perfunctory than her mother-in-law's. Odile had a strong scent of cinnamon about her.

Finally, it was Aunt Fatima's turn. Fatima was Mary Carmen's *tia* rather than her *madrinha*, but Mary Carmen was very fond of her aunt and Fatima returned her greeting with real warmth.

Her principal obligations met, Mary Carmen retrieved her boyfriend, grabbing him by the arm and pulling him toward the door to the living room. Apparently it was all right if she held on to his arm, as long as she didn't do anything quite as shocking as actually holding his hand in public. Gerry nodded his head toward Teresa and Odile and the other women as he and Mary Carmen squeezed through. He said "hello" a few times in what he hoped was a cheerful and friendly voice, fearing all the while that he might get an incomprehensible Portuguese response from someone.

Mary Carmen and Gerry now stood in the doorway of the living room. It was noisier and even more crowded than the kitchen, with adults all over the chairs and couches and wall-to-wall children on the floor. Gerry literally could not understand a single word anyone was saying. It didn't help that the television was tuned to a Spanish-language station. In the absence of Portuguese-language broadcasting, Spanish was the best anyone could do.

Mary Carmen was still holding Gerry's arm. She plunged into the living room, wending her way through the moving obstacles of the little ones and dragging her boyfriend behind. She was aiming for the overstuffed couch at the far end of the room, where her brothers had gathered. The two older ones were trying to persuade Alex that he should drink the baby formula in his bottle and settle down. It was Mary Carmen's opportunity.

"Hi, Paul. Hi, Hank. Let me have him."

With a look of pure relief, Paul handed his baby brother up to his sister. As she cradled him in one arm, she reached with the other and took the bottle from Henry.

"Okay, make room for us."

Henry shifted to the floor and Paul moved up to the arm of the sofa.

Mary Carmen looked over her shoulder at Gerry as she held the bottle in Alex's face.

"Sit down, honey. There's room next to Paul."

"Ooooooh! 'Honey'!" snorted Henry from where he was sprawled.

"Shut up, Hanky."

As Gerry obediently sat down in his assigned position, Mary Carmen squeezed in next to him. Alex had decided that his sister had the authority to feed him and was nursing rather noisily on the bottle.

Paul looked down on his sister's beau with a sympathetic smile on his face.

"How are you doing, Gerry?"

"Um, okay. At least so far."

"Good for you. Is this your first all-up Francisco family event?"

"Yes. Definitely. This beats anything I've seen before. Even the August birthday party at your mom and dad's."

"Well, birthdays at Mom and Dad's are not command performances. Easter, Thanksgiving, and Christmas. If you're a Francisco or a Salazar and you miss one of the three High Holy Days, *Avó* will excommunicate you."

"Don't listen to him, Gerry! Paul's lying, as usual."

"Thanks for the warning, Hank, but I've already learned that your big brother deals in figurative rather than literal truth."

"*Shit!*" said Henry in a low voice so that it wouldn't carry in the general din. "It just got too intellectual around here. I need to get my rubber boots to wade in it. Call me when there's turkey on the table."

Since Henry was already on the floor, he decided to scuttle off on all fours. The younger children shrieked at the sight of a teenager crawling among them and scrambled out of his way. At the door to the kitchen, Henry stood up and made his escape in upright mode.

Gerry looked at Mary Carmen, but she just shrugged.

"I don't explain my brothers," she said. "I just help take care of them."

She put Alex up on her shoulder and patted him till he emitted a burp. She laid him back on her lap and cuddled him. If Alex would be good enough to fall asleep, Mary Carmen could put him in the crib that *Avó* kept in the spare bedroom.

"Paul, how did you end up with Alex?"

"Mom told me and Hank to watch him while she went back home to get the potato salad. Didn't you see her?"

"No, Gerry and I cut through the orchard. Mom must have walked back along the driveway."

"So, what's school like in Southern California?" asked Gerry.

"It's a love-hate situation. I'm still adjusting to living away from home, and that's embarrassing to admit. And sometimes I wonder why a guy with a dangerously low draft number is enrolled in the toughest science school on the West Coast. Or maybe the entire U.S. Why didn't I hear Fresno State beckoning?"

Mary Carmen grinned indulgently at her older brother.

"Give me a break. You went there *because* it's the toughest. You're a natural-born show-off."

"All right, all right. Guilty as charged. I'm trying to prove something. So it would be really nice if I pass my classes this quarter."

Gerry looked around the room at the chatting groups of family members. He saw Mary Carmen's father sitting on a hassock next to his father's recliner. Chico was an invalid who was unsuccessfully trying to recover from a stroke that had paralyzed one side of his body. He looked shrunken, and Gerry wondered what he had looked like in his healthier days. Paulinho noticed

Gerry gazing in their direction and nodded his head slightly. It was a polite gesture, but distant. Mary Carmen's boyfriend had her father's sufferance, if not his full approval.

"In case you were wondering, Gerry, yeah, they're talking about you."

"For real, Paul?"

"Yeah, for real. Everyone has a comment about you, but no one's said anything really negative. At least, nothing that I've heard."

"So what *have* you heard?"

"The main thing is that they think you're really, really pale."

"Okay. I can't exactly deny that, can I?"

"No, I concur. You are definitely a pasty-face."

"Paul!"

"Sorry, Sis. I didn't mean to be so literal. Would it be better if I said 'exceedingly fair'?"

Mary Carmen and Gerry both said "No!" at the same time.

"Well, you are. And I heard Dad say to *Avô* that you are very polite. That carries a high premium in this family, so that's good."

"Anyone saying anything bad?"

"I already mentioned the 'white as a ghost' part."

"Not in those words."

"Okay. Well, those words were used. I had forgotten that *fantasma* is the Portuguese word for ghost, but that's what you're as *branco* as. Hmm. 'White as a ghost.' I wonder if that's really a Portuguese idiom?"

"What do you mean?"

"We're California Portagees," explained Paul. "An increasing fraction of us were born here. We speak English like natives and we carry American idioms back into the language of the Old Country. If we visited the Azores and said 'white as a ghost,' I'm sure they'd understand the message, but would they regard the expression as peculiar? I mean, do they ever use it themselves?"

"Ask Dad," suggested Mary Carmen.

"I don't think so. He was only three when he came over here. He's a perfect example of California Portagee, although his Portuguese is a lot stronger than yours or mine. But maybe you're right. Maybe I should ask him. A scholar *manqué* like Dad might enjoy tracking it down."

"What did you say?"

"Ignore him, honey. That's just Paul being his weird collegiate self."

"I said 'scholar *manqué*.' It's a French word that implies a lack of something.

Dad didn't get to go to school because the dairy involved so much work, but he would have loved to have gotten a real education. He finally got his GED, so now he's a high school graduate, but Dad would have enjoyed college. He never had the opportunity, so I get to go instead. Of course, he might have preferred I do something sensible with my college education."

"What's wrong with being a math major?" asked Gerry.

Paul shrugged.

"Nothing, of course. But in this room, good luck explaining that a math degree is different from becoming an accountant. It's a completely foreign concept, because numerical stuff is for banks and finance. Or counting cows. That's it. Or take my maternal grandmother, who thinks she learned mathematics in school because she and her girlfriends used to use a number cipher to send each other secret messages. You know, a replacement cipher like 'A equals 1' and so forth and so on. She is *really* confused about what I'm studying."

Gerry laughed.

"Consider getting a job at the National Security Agency. Then it'll all make sense to your Grandma Soares!"

Paul and Gerry chuckled, while Mary Carmen stood up with the sleeping Alex and carried him off to *Avó*'s crib. Paul watched Gerry tracking his sister with his eyes as she left the room.

"The test of fire?"

"Huh?"

"Did Mary Carmen say you had to prove yourself by meeting the entire family?"

"Not in exactly those words but, yeah, that's pretty much the situation. And I haven't really met many people yet. I'm just sitting here talking with you while people look at me out of the corners of their eyes. And talk about me in a language I don't know."

"Don't worry. You'll meet a lot more over Thanksgiving dinner. The day is young. And no one has said anything specifically about you in several minutes. But, boy, you must be crazy in love to put up with this."

"I don't really mind. No one has been rude to me."

"They certainly haven't been talking about you behind your back. They all do it right in your face, right in front of you. That might be a *little* bit rude."

Gerry sighed.

"I am a stranger in a strange land."

"Whoa! Don't quote Bible verses if you value your life!"

"What's the problem with that?"

"Think about it, Ger. That'll just remind folks that you're not a Catholic. You're Mary Carmen's non-Catholic, non-Portuguese boyfriend. Today we're dealing with the non-Portuguese part. Leave the rest till later."

Gerry leaned closer to Paul and lowered his voice.

"I told Mary Carmen that I'd convert if she wanted me to."

"And she said no."

"How did you know?"

"My sister is definitely more religious than I am and she would disapprove of any conversion for convenience. She's big on sincerity, which I'm not prepared to say is a bad thing. *But don't tell anyone else.* They'll give her holy hell if they find out she passed up an opportunity to 'make' you convert. Zip it up and don't mention it again."

"Okay. If you say so."

"I *do* say so. And Mary Carmen will say so, too, if she hasn't already."

"Well, yeah, she did. She told me not to spread it around."

"And shame on you for spreading it around! Fortunately, you confided in the family heathen. Now don't go spreading *that* around."

"But, Paul, that's what everyone already says about you."

"Heck. That figures. Why am I not surprised?"

JULY 1975

Candido Sells Culls

The culls bawled in fear as the handlers secured the rope halters to their heads and led them away. Candido Francisco unhooked the heavy planks forming the ramp down which the culls had been pulled from the cattle trailer. He tossed them into the back of the trailer. The planks were lying in the urine and manure that the culls had voided during their trip to the auction yard, but Candido would hose it all out when he got it back to the dairy farm.

His culls had brought a pretty good price, considering that none of the dairymen had purchased them. Candido had brought their statistics from his herd records, but their milk production numbers had not been quite high enough to persuade anyone that they would be a worthwhile addition to their dairies. Of course, that's why Candido had culled them from the herd in the first place. And today there had been no second- or third-tier dairymen for whom the culls from the Francisco dairy would have been an improvement over their own cows.

Nevertheless, there had been other people present who were willing to bid on the mediocre milk producers. Candido wasn't certain exactly what would happen to the culls, but he figured that dog food was their likeliest fate. The auction yard did not deal in USDA-certified beef products for human consumption, although it was entirely possible that someone would occasionally purchase a cull for private use and deliver it to a meat locker for butchering. Candido's freezer at home still held some steaks from a particularly plump cull that he had retired from the herd earlier in the year.

Having closed up the cattle trailer, Candido made his way to the cashier's office and got in line. When it was his turn, Candido gave the clerk the vendor number he had been assigned upon his arrival that morning.

"Hello, Candy. I see all four of your cows sold."

"Yes. A good day. I don't have to haul any of them back home."

"Lucky you. Okay, let me add up the amounts and cut you a check for the total."

The cashier started punching buttons on a mechanical adding machine, pulling its lever after each amount was entered. He punched the "total" button and pulled the lever one more time.

"Okay, then," said the clerk. The auction yard's check register was a large vinyl notebook with multiple checks on each page. Carbon paper ensured that each check was duplicated by the pressure of the clerk's pen before he tore off the original and handed it to the vendor. The clerk was just picking up his pen when Candido asked him a question.

"Say, Bob, could you make that out to 'Francisco & Sons'?"

The clerk paused, his pen suspended over the first blank check in the check register, and looked up at Candido.

"You mean, instead of 'Paulo C. Francisco & Sons'?"

"Yeah. 'Francisco & Sons' is our new business name, because my dad is no longer involved. Having 'Paulo' in the name doesn't make sense any more now that he's a cripple. And it gets confused with my brother's name, although Paulinho isn't part of the business anymore."

"I guess. Well, you're calling the shots now anyway. Does this mean that old Chico isn't getting any better?"

Candido's natural features made it easy for him to look forlorn, so he amped it up just a bit by letting his face sag.

"It's been over five years, Bob. The physical therapy hasn't worked and Dad's still paralyzed all down his left side. It's very sad."

It *was* very sad. And Candido realized that his words were sincere, even as he was exploiting them to advance his personal scheme.

The clerk nodded his head sympathetically and carefully inked in the check for "Francisco & Sons." He tore it from the register book and handed it to Candido.

"Here you go. I'll keep the new business name in mind for next time. You coming to the next auction day?"

Candido folded the check and stuck it in his pocket.

"Don't know yet. Maybe. I've got a couple of three-year-olds just sitting on the bubble, but I'll give them a little more time before deciding they're culls. But I'll be back soon. Take it easy!"

"Yeah. Take it easy. Tell your dad 'hi' and that the guys at the auction yard miss him."

"I will. Thanks. He'll appreciate the thought."

Candido made room for the man who had been impatiently waiting behind him and strolled casually away from the cashier's office. He climbed into his pickup truck and drove slowly out of the auction yard, keeping a close eye on the cattle trailer he was towing. Should he go back to the dairy farm first and unhitch the trailer, or was there space to park the pickup-trailer combination next to the local Bank of America office? He decided to chance it. After all, he was eager to deposit the auction check in the new "Francisco & Sons" business account he had created.

Candido was a partner in Paulo C. Francisco & Sons, along with his parents and two of his sons. That meant he had a share in the ownership of the cattle owned by the Paulo C. Francisco & Sons dairy business, but Candido was not satisfied. Now that he was running the dairy farm, he felt entitled to more. He would manage his father's business accordingly. Chico's business would continue to sell cattle, but Candido's business was going to collect the proceeds. The trips to the auction yard would definitely increase in frequency.

And then Candido's new business could afford to start *buying* cattle and merging them into the herd. By degrees, Chico's dairy farm would become Candido's dairy farm. Although he was certain that his father's will would designate him as principal heir to the family business, Candido's clever plan would mitigate any downside risk that Chico and Teresa might choose to do something else. He was just helping things along. That's all.

As he brought his pickup-trailer rig to a stop against a conveniently long stretch of empty curb near the bank, Candido wondered if perhaps he was the smartest member of the family after all.

PART III

The "Expert" Testifies

"Ms. Hunter, you may proceed."

"Thank you, your honor."

Peggy Hunter climbed down from the witness stand, where she had just finished enumerating the requirements for establishing a "standard" signature against which a challenged signature could be compared. She moved toward an easel on which a large poster had been propped. Biddy Onan helped her lift the cover sheet and drape it over the back of the easel so that the contents of the poster stood revealed.

"As the court can see," said Hunter, oscillating uncertainly between the judge on the bench and the jurors in the box, "I have made blow-ups of five unchallenged signatures by Teresa M. Francisco. You will observe that Mrs. Francisco had a very strong sense of line, as exemplified by the horizontal linearity of her writing."

Hunter underscored her point by running her index finger across the bottom of each signature.

"One moment, Ms. Hunter."

"Yes, your honor?"

"Would you or Ms. Onan be so kind as to identify the five signatures?"

Hunter looked toward the petitioners' counsel, who had flipped open one of her legal folders and was searching for the requested information. Hunter folded her hands and bit her lip as Onan's search got more frantic. The judge waited for a while before deciding to expedite matters.

"The clerk will please produce Exhibits A through L."

The courtroom clerk dived into the evidence folder and brought out the diverse mix of greeting cards that had been introduced into evidence the day before.

"Please show them one by one to Ms. Hunter."

The clerk dealt the exhibits singly to the witness, who scanned each card and then looked at the poster. The first two exhibits were returned to the clerk. Then Hunter got a hit.

"Sample 1 on the poster is from Exhibit C."

Again.

"Sample 5 is from Exhibit D. Oh! And Sample 2 is from Exhibit E. And Sample 3 is from Exhibit F. Yes, okay. Sample 4 is from Exhibit G."

Hunter put her hand out for the next exhibit before realizing she had already identified all five sample signatures. The clerk returned to his station. The judge gave the clerk a small smile and a brief nod before saying, "Thank you, Ms. Hunter. Please continue."

"Yes, your honor. Thank you. As I was saying, Mrs. Francisco had very linear handwriting. You can also see a characteristically sharp descender in the middle of her M, her middle initial. The uppercase M does not normally descend below the baseline, but you will observe that Mrs. Francisco's Ms have a central descending spike that breaks the baseline."

Hunter waved her hands over the signatures as she spoke, pointing to the specific features as she identified them.

"Mrs. Francisco routinely lifted her pen while signing her last name. Each instance of 'Francisco' has a discernible pen-lift after the first syllable, between the 'Fran' and the 'cisco.' She sometimes lifted her pen between the last two syllables, 'cis' and 'co,' but that is not as reliable an indicator because the pen-lift is not always present. An inconsistency like that is unusual in a personal signature, but not unknown."

In the gallery, the Franciscos shifted uncomfortably as Peggy Hunter gave a persuasive impersonation of a handwriting expert. Her initial jitters had subsided and she ticked off her points with great confidence and authority.

"Please note the initial letter of Mrs. Francisco's first name. She inscribes an uppercase T in a spiky fashion rather than according to the smooth Palmer method cursive. Writers tend to have a special identification with the letters that represent their initials, and you can see that this holds true with Mrs. Francisco, who writes the Ts and Fs of her initials with an almost dramatic flair that is lacking in the other letters — except for the descender already noted in her Ms. What's more, Mrs. Francisco's Ts and Fs are closely matched, the two letters being identical save for the slash that distinguishes the latter from the former."

Hunter turned toward the bench.

"Your honor, may I have the second display?"

"You may, Ms. Hunter."

Judge Knight nodded at the clerk, who then carried a second easel from the side of the courtroom and placed it next to the first easel. Onan arose from her seat at the petitioners' table to assist Hunter with the unveiling of the second poster, but the witness did not wait for her. She flipped the cover sheet over the back of the easel to reveal a single large signature on the new poster. Onan backed up to her table and quietly sat down.

"This is a blow-up of the disputed signature on the will," explained Hunter.

The judge said, "The court notes that the will of Teresa Francisco has already been introduced as evidence."

Onan stood up.

"Objection, your honor! Petitioners object to having the document in question identified as Teresa Francisco's will!"

The judge gave her a long, level look.

"Counsel may wish to consider that she does not get to object to statements from the bench. She may, if it pleases her, make note of them as points of disagreement should there later be an occasion for filing an appeal. I remind counsel that she herself introduced the exhibit in question. Do you care to make any additional objection?"

"No, your honor. Counsel withdraws her objection."

"Thank you, counselor. Ms. Hunter, please forgive the interruption and continue."

"Yes, your honor."

Hunter pointed at the middle initial M in the signature on the will.

"Here we observe that the spike is present in the middle of the M, but that it does not break or even touch the signature line. It's only one element of discrepancy, but a telling one. In the authentic signatures, the M *always* spikes down to break the baseline. Note also that the T in 'Teresa' and the F in 'Francisco' look alike, but have additional differences apart from the F's slash. In particular, the T lacks the angularity found in Mrs. Francisco's authenticated signatures."

Hunter traced her finger along the signature line that had been reproduced from the will.

"Please look at the signature line. See how this signature floats uncertainly above it, lacking the strong linearity that we saw in the authenticated signatures."

Hunter took a step back toward the first poster and stabbed a finger at one of the sample signatures.

"Remember the pen-lifts between the 'Fran' and 'cisco'? Mrs. Francisco always left a characteristic small gap from lifting her pen after writing the 'Fran.' There *is* a pen-lift at that point in the signature on the will, *but* whoever wrote it was at pains to resume the writing so that no gap appeared. This is a common giveaway in forgeries, where the forger slowly and carefully writes each letter, introducing extraneous pen-lifts — to attempt to conceal the piecemeal nature of the writing, the forger ever-so-carefully tries to put the pen down exactly where its previous stroke ended. The writer's overzealous care in this instance resulting in eliminating a gap that always appears in a true signature."

The witness clasped her hands, stood very straight, and faced the jury.

"It is my considered opinion as a professional handwriting analyst that the signature on the will is not that of Teresa M. Francisco."

After a moment's weighty silence, Judge Knight spoke to counsel for the petitioners.

"Ms. Onan, your witness has completed her presentation. Do you wish to ask her any further questions?"

Onan stood up.

"No, your honor. The petitioners do not have any further questions for their expert witness."

"Very well. Mr. Bowman, does counsel for the respondents have any questions for the witness."

Bowman stood up.

"Yes, your honor, I believe there are a few questions we would like to ask her."

"You may proceed. Ms. Hunter, you may take a seat in the witness stand unless Mr. Bowman asks you a question that requires you to approach the posters. Would the clerk please reposition the easels so that their contents are visible from the witness stand?"

The clerk bustled over to push the two easels back between the witness stand and the jury box so that the witness could view the posters by turning slightly to her left.

As Bowman assumed a relaxed stance in front of her, Peggy Hunter felt that something was oddly different this time. Then she realized that Bowman was empty-handed. He had not even a scrap of paper in his hands. As much as she had hated his page shuffling during the previous day's session, she discovered that this change in behavior was unsettling. Bowman smiled at her.

"Ms. Hunter, I believe you stressed the *horizontal linearity* of Mrs. Francisco's handwriting."

"Her authentic writing, yes."

"There is a signature line on the will. Is that not so?"

"Yes, there is. In fact, I specifically pointed that out as showing the lack of linearity in the signature on the will."

Bowman walked over to the poster with the five samples of Teresa's signature.

"Ms. Hunter, do you see signature lines on the five samples?"

"No, sir."

"There aren't any, are there?"

"No, there aren't."

"In your *professional* opinion, Ms. Hunter, do people write their names differently, depending on whether the page is blank or there is a signature line?"

"They might in some cases."

"Was this the case with Mrs. Francisco?"

"I do not know."

"Ms. Hunter, *why* don't you know?"

Peggy Hunter squared her shoulders and replied, "As a professional, I do not draw conclusions in the absence of evidence. Since the authenticated samples of Mrs. Francisco's handwriting did not include signature lines, I did not make any inference about the possible influence of their presence on her writing."

"If it please the court, may I have Exhibit D?"

"The clerk will provide."

Bowman took the proffered exhibit and held it up in front of the witness.

"Ms. Hunter, is this not the source of your Sample 5?"

Hunter peered at the exhibit and then looked at the first poster.

"Yes, it is. I so identified it earlier, and it is the source."

"Ms. Hunter, would you please tell the court what this exhibit is?"

"It is a page from the guest book for Linda Salazar's baby shower. The page with Mrs. Francisco's signature, among others."

"Ms. Hunter, are there *lines* on this page?"

"Yes, but faint gray ones. It's possible that Mrs. Francisco couldn't even see them."

"Do you have information about Mrs. Francisco's eyesight, Ms. Hunter?"

The witness hesitated for a long moment.

"No, I do not."

"Then perhaps it would be wise not to speculate in the absence of evidence. Right, Ms. Hunter?"

"Yes, sir."

"Very good. I see on your poster of samples that the signature line does not appear with Sample 5. Would you agree, Ms. Hunter, that it was unfortunately cropped out in creating the blow-up from the guest book?"

"Yes, unfortunate. I would agree."

"Thank you, Ms. Hunter. *Very* unfortunate. I'm noticing — and perhaps you do, too — that the guest book signature floated rather high above the signature line, which is why it was so easy to unfortunately crop out the line."

"Yes, I'm sure that's why. Mrs. Francisco did not sign on the signature line."

"And the person who signed the will also did not sign on the signature line, did she?"

"*Objection*, your honor! Counsel is assuming that the will was signed by a woman."

"Overruled, Ms. Onan."

"But, your honor, he is implying that the will was signed by Teresa Francisco!"

"Ms. Onan, if you've been paying attention, counsel for the respondents has been *insisting* that the will was signed by Mrs. Francisco. I will allow him to use the gendered pronouns of his choice. You are overruled. You may proceed, Mr. Bowman."

"Thank you, your honor. As I was saying, Ms. Hunter, before I was so peculiarly interrupted, Mrs. Francisco's signature in the guest book is *very* similar to the signature on the will in terms of linearity. Is it not?"

"Well, in terms of *linearity*, yes, in those terms, anyway."

"Which you indicated is a key characteristic trait in Mrs. Francisco's authenticated signatures — or did I not hear you correctly?"

"Yes, it is."

"And which also appears in the signature on the will?"

"I already said that."

"Very good. I just wanted to make certain. Now let's talk about the Ms and their 'central descending spike.' You pointed out that the spike did not break the signature line on the will, right?"

"Yes, I did. And it doesn't."

"And that doesn't happen on the page from the guest book either, does it?"

"No, it doesn't."

"So that's another point of similarity between Sample 5 and the will's signature. Yes?"

"Yes, but those similarities are just with that one sample."

"An excellent point, Ms. Hunter. I am delighted to have discerned so many similarities while using only *one* of your samples. Let's see if we can find even more by looking at the others. Since linearity has been such a productive vein of inquiry, let's consider it a bit further, shall we?"

"I think that question was rhetorical, Mr. Bowman."

"Oh, was it really? Let it go, then. What I want to ask you concerns the *horizontal* aspect you cited. We dabbled with it while discussing Mrs. Francisco's apparent disdain for signature lines, but now I want to know how you determine linearity when there's no signature line for comparison purposes. How do you do that?"

"If you look at the characters without descenders, you can try to draw a line that touches the bottom of each one. If you succeed, you have a distinct baseline for the writing. That's an indication of strong linearity."

"Since you said Teresa Francisco's handwriting is very linear, I presume you were successful in drawing those imaginary lines — those 'baselines' — on your samples."

"Yes, I was."

"And you failed in your attempt to do the same with the signature on the will?"

"Partially. I was less concerned about drawing the line because of the existence of the signature line, which already indicated the absence of proper linearity."

"I'm sorry, Ms. Hunter, but I believe you just introduced a new term by mentioning 'proper' linearity. Was the signature on the will 'improper' because you could draw a baseline but it wasn't parallel to the signature line?"

"Yes. That's right. The lack of parallelism in the will's signature indicated it did not have the strong horizontal linearity I found in Mrs. Francisco's undisputedly genuine signatures."

"I hate to have to disagree with you again, Ms. Hunter, but we may have a problem with the 'horizontal' aspect. Did you rotate any of the sample signatures in placing them on your evidence poster?"

"No, sir. Not really. I mean. Not by design. They may have been adjusted slightly while pasting the blow-ups in place, but not intentionally."

"I think we should find out how much they were rotated, Ms. Hunter, whether it was done intentionally or not. I'm afraid I don't have a protractor on me, but perhaps some rough estimates will suffice. Are you ready, Ms. Hunter?"

"For what? I don't know what you're planning."

"It will be simple. May I please have Exhibit G? . . . Thank you. Ms. Hunter, what is Exhibit G?"

"It's a greeting card that was received by Catarina Salazar on the occasion of her wedding in 1981. It provided Sample 4."

"Thank you, Ms. Hunter. Would you say it's a linear signature?"

"I already said that. Yes."

"Would you describe it as a *horizontal* signature?"

"Not *exactly*."

"About how inexactly, would you say? How much is the baseline skewed? Is it tilted twenty degrees? Thirty?"

"Um. Well, it's really . . . sort of on a diagonal."

"*Forty-five* degrees?"

"No! Not *that* much!"

"But close to that, I guess. Interesting. But it sure looks horizontal if you turn it enough, like the blow-up copy on your evidence poster."

"I didn't turn it deliberately. I already said that."

"Thank you, Ms. Hunter. If I were to summarize, it seems that the description 'horizontal' is an entirely artificial artifact of your linearity argument. After you drew your invisible baselines, you treated them thereafter as horizontal reference lines, even in egregiously tilted examples such as Exhibit G."

Bowman hadn't asked a question and Hunter had no intention of volunteering anything as she glowered at the attorney.

"I believe we have also identified a second source of confusion. Ms. Hunter, did you not point out that the M in the signature on the will does not break the *signature line?*"

"Yes, I did. And it does not."

"But does not the M in the signature on the will break the so-called *baseline*? If we look at your poster of that signature, does not the spike in the middle of the M break the *baseline* in the same way as the M's in the authenticated signatures break their baselines?"

"I can't be certain without actually drawing the baseline on a copy of the signature, as I did during my investigation, but it's close."

"Would you agree, then, that it is inconsistent to use the signature line as the standard of reference when discussing the M in the signature on the will while using imaginary 'baselines' instead while talking about the M's in the samples?"

"It would be better to use the same standard of reference in each case."

"I will take that as a lengthy way to say 'yes,' Ms. Hunter."

Bowman gestured at the exhibit still in the witness's hand.

"By the way, can you tell me how Mrs. Francisco signed the card that she gave to her granddaughter on the occasion of the granddaughter's wedding?"

"I can't read all the words."

"That's quite all right, Ms. Hunter. The words 'querida neta' mean 'dear granddaughter,' but I'm talking about the signature itself."

"Okay. I see 'Francisco,' of course, but I don't know how to pronounce the first name, which I guess is a nickname or something."

"That's the point, Ms. Hunter. This is one of two samples that you chose because of supposed 'linearity,' but which lacked Teresa's first name." Bowman walked over to the easel of samples. "I draw the court's attention to Samples 3 and 4, both of which Teresa Francisco signed as 'Ava Francisco,' where 'Ava' is a phonetic rendering of the Portuguese word for 'grandmother.'" Bowman positioned himself back in front of the witness stand.

"Ms. Hunter, did you discover that it was Mrs. Francisco's habit to sign her legal documents 'Grandma Francisco'?"

Jurors and observers burst into laughter. Judge Knight gave a sharp rap with his gavel.

"The court cautions its guests to remain quiet or it will require them to leave. The court similarly admonishes the jury to restrain itself. Mr. Bowman, do you have any more questions, as opposed to punch lines?"

"Yes, your honor. Thank you. Ms. Hunter, please disregard the previous question. Permit me to ask you instead why you limited yourself to family greeting cards in creating your set of authenticated samples? The will is an important legal document. Why did you not seek comparison signatures from other legal documents? Signatures written on signature lines? Signatures with Mrs. Francisco's full name? You have only three samples with her full name and yet you testified that five authentic samples are a minimum. How can you support your strong conclusion about her Ts and Fs although you were two samples short?"

"Mr. Bowman, I said earlier that I draw my conclusions from the data available. I reviewed all of the samples provided by the Salazar family and most of them were greeting cards. She only occasionally signed her full name to those, so my options were limited. I carefully chose those signatures that could be considered exemplars for the key characteristics that I had identified. I am a responsible expert witness."

"Thank you for your detailed answer, Ms. Hunter. However, a responsible expert witness should have examined the writing on Mrs. Francisco's checking account signature card. Why did you not do that?"

"That's a confidential financial document. My clients did not have a copy of anything like that."

"Ms. Hunter, that is what subpoenas are for. You can ask Ms. Onan about that when the court recesses. She might remember."

Bowman paused, a thoughtful expression on his face. He moved closer to the witness stand and leaned toward Hunter slightly. Confidingly, he said, "Ms. Hunter, did you know that Mrs. Francisco was an alien?"

Peggy Hunter's eyes went suddenly wide. For one surreal moment, she thought Bowman had said something completely insane. Bowman carefully did not smile at her reaction, which he had hoped for, but had not expected to be quite so dramatic. He savored her confusion for a few seconds.

"That's right, Ms. Hunter. Mrs. Francisco never became a citizen. She had permanent resident alien status. Every year she was required to file a form with the Immigration and Naturalization Service. The INS files must have over fifty authentic Teresa Francisco signatures on file."

"I did not know about that, Mr. Bowman."

"Make a note of it, Ms. Hunter. Professional document examiners know these sources of reliable official signatures."

The witness was not completely successful in keeping a sour expression from her face.

"One final question, Ms. Hunter. Would you agree that you violated the minimum standards you said were mandatory for evaluating disputed signatures, and that you violated these standards because you were unaware of good sources of authentic signatures?"

Hunter stared at Bowman, struggling to control her anger. Bowman kept his level gaze on her without saying another word.

"Ms. Hunter?" said Judge Knight. "The counsel for the respondents asked you a question. You need to answer it."

Hunter took a deep breath.

"Yes," she said, in a low voice.

"Thank you very much, Ms. Hunter. I have no further questions, your honor."

JUNE 1981

Catarina's Wedding

So it's true, thought Linda Salazar. *All brides really* are *beautiful on their wedding day.*

She reached up and gently adjusted her sister-in-law's hat, tilting it just a little more and giving it a bit of a rakish air. The hat had been a stroke of genius, the brim mitigating Catarina's high forehead as well as providing maximum control and concealment for the bride's difficult hair. The tendrils that had been allowed to escape were delicately curled and had an elegant look.

Linda stepped back and gave her sister-in-law the once-over. The fidgety hands were occupied by holding the bridal bouquet. The gangling height was downplayed by sensibly flat shoes that were invisible under the white satin skirt. Linda had applied Catarina's makeup herself, and had wisely chosen discretion. The coral pink lipstick enlivened the bride's lips in a contrast quite sufficient to their normally colorless state. A hint of eyeliner gave an accented visibility to Catarina's eyes as they peeked out from under the hat's brim. Her eyes had always been one of her stronger assets, but now they were even a bit alluring and mysterious. Catarina's features were generally nondescript, but regular, so they had not resisted Linda's attempts to bring out some feminine comeliness.

And Catarina had a highly uncharacteristic smile on her face, manifesting an extremely rare genuine happiness that was certainly the most important reason she had been transformed into a radiant bride.

"You look great, Cat. You really do."

"Yeah, really?"

Linda was used to Catarina's voice, so she did not wince at its guttural hoarseness. Years of speech therapy had been more successful with Catarina than they had been with her older brother Leo, but it was still not a euphonious sound. At least the stutter was gone.

"Yes, *really*. If only your mother could have been here to see it. She would have been so *proud*."

Catarina smiled, but did not say anything. She seldom spoke a word unless she really had to.

"Now you wait here and I'll come back to get you when it's time for the procession. Remember, you can't sit down! We don't want any wrinkles. Just stand there. It won't be very long. I have to see if Manny is ready and check my own makeup. Then I'll make sure Father Garrity is in place and I'll be right back. Just a few minutes. Okay?"

Catarina nodded.

Linda was a lot shorter than her sister-in-law. She stretched up on tiptoe and gave Catarina a quick peck on the cheek. She bustled out to make her rounds.

Manny Salazar was not difficult to find. Linda encountered her husband waiting just outside the vestibule.

"Is she finally ready?" he asked impatiently.

Linda grinned at him.

"Stop fretting. She's actually going to be on time for her wedding, even if she's never been on time for anything else. Have you seen Father?"

"Yeah. He's in the sacristy and he's already in his vestments. The altar boys are ready, too. Paul has the wedding program and the cues. No problems."

"The guests?"

"*Avó* has already been seated in front. Were we worried about anyone else?"

"Not really. Is Dad ready to escort the bride?"

Linda was referring to her father-in-law, Louis, to whom she had become a second daughter in her twenty years of marriage to Manny. She had also become Louis's indispensable right arm in all matters domestic. When Catarina withdrew further into her shell after her mother's death, Linda had stepped forward to ensure that domestic help was engaged to keep the Salazar home from descending into squalor. Linda was also responsible for the fact that there were still a few home-cooked meals placed before her father-in-law and the offspring that still lived at home, but that was a battle she wasn't winning.

"Yeah," said Manny, smiling. "Dad's all tricked out in his tux and looking prosperous. It's not every man who can afford to buy his little girl a husband."

"*Manny!* Don't you dare repeat that!"

Linda was mortified.

"I promise, honey. But that won't stop everyone else from saying it."

"I don't care about that. I *do* care that Cat's brothers are saying it. That's just mean!"

Linda didn't like to remember last year's outburst from her father-in-law. Louis had been in a snit over the imminent arrival of Paulinho and Carmina Francisco's second grandchild, their daughter Mary Carmen being pregnant again. They had been standing in Louis's den when he broached the subject with his daughter-in-law.

"Mary Carmen has been married for — what? — five, six years? And my Catarina is still single. And now Mary Carmen has a second baby on the way and my Catarina is turning into a spinster. This is not acceptable!"

"Seven years, Dad," said Linda, family data always at her fingertips. "Mary Carmen married Gerry seven years ago. And Catarina is only twenty-six. That's hardly a spinster or old maid."

"Ha! Her mother was twenty when I married her and people said I had waited too long. Too long, they said!"

"Gee, Dad. That was forty years ago. It's not such a big deal to wait till late in your twenties anymore."

"Twenty-six is already 'late in your twenties.' What are we going to do about it?"

"Do about it? I don't know, Dad. Catarina doesn't go to all the *festas* and then doesn't mix with other people when she does. We introduce her to boys around her age but she doesn't want to talk. I really don't know what to do."

"It was better in the Old Country," groused Louis. "The old women would talk among themselves and decide these things. When the *velhinhas* made their decisions, people listened, because the old ladies knew what they were talking about."

"I'm afraid the *velhinhas* don't have as much clout in this country as they do back in the islands. We can't just go up to an old lady and tell her we need her to assign Cat a husband."

"Then I'll do something about it myself."

Linda gave her father-in-law a quizzical expression.

"Dad, I can't imagine what you have in mind. What do you have in mind? What are you talking about?"

Louis Salazar wrinkled his brow and started pacing to and fro. He was silent for a couple of minutes as he walked and pondered and his daughter-in-law waited patiently. Finally, Louis stopped and faced her again.

"I know what to do, but I'm not sure how to do it."

"I'm listening, Dad. What do you mean?"

"Her dowry. I'm talking about Catarina's dowry. We need to let people know about it. The rest will take care of itself."

"Cat's dowry? I've never heard anything about her dowry before. What is Cat's dowry? I thought people didn't do that anymore."

"If my daughter needs a dowry, she'll have a dowry. We just need to decide what it should be. You can help me."

Thinking back on that exchange with her father-in-law, Linda knew that Manny was right. Kevin Lineman was less in love with Catarina than he was with the financial security that she represented. As much as it distressed her to admit it, Louis Salazar had purchased a husband for his little girl. It had been extremely easy to spread the news that Catarina had a generous dowry. Louis kept baiting the hook with bigger and bigger worms until someone bit. Today they were reeling him in.

"Say, have you seen Kevin?" asked Linda. She didn't know where the groom was. "Is he in place yet?"

"No, I haven't," replied Manny. "Let's go see if he's in the front lobby."

Manny and Linda walked arm-in-arm down the side hallway that led to the church lobby. Their entrance into the lobby attracted the attention of the wedding guests, who paused on their way into the church to look at people who were obviously members of the wedding party, Linda in her matron-of-honor gown and Manny in his best-man's tuxedo. Most of the bridesmaids and groomsmen were already clustered in the lobby, trying to stay out of the way of the arriving guests as they awaited the processional. The flower girl and ring-bearer were there, looking vaguely uncomfortable and impatiently hoping for something more interesting than standing around and waiting.

"Hi, Manny! Hi, Linda! You guys look sharp!"

"Thanks, Ferdie," said Linda to her husband's cousin. "Have you seen Kevin? We're supposed to start in a couple of minutes and we need the groom."

Ferdinando Francisco extracted himself from the line of guests awaiting the attentions of the ushers and came over to stand closer to Manny and Linda.

"He's at the house," said Ferdie in a low voice. "Elvis and Randy have gone to collect him."

Linda immediately understood that "house" meant the three-bedroom home two blocks away from the church that Louis had purchased for the use of the newlyweds. They had been using it as the staging area for most of the final preparations for the wedding. She wondered why Ferdie had lowered his voice, but found herself following suit as she whispered back.

"Is something going on? Why did Elvis and Randy have to go after him?"

Ferdie smirked.

"Well, I'm not saying this myself, you understand. I'm just telling you what I heard, okay? But from what Elvis and Randy were talking about, I guess that Kevin had beer for breakfast. A *lot* of beer for breakfast."

Manny smothered a chuckle, but not before his wife gave him a sharp look. Linda had had five years of serving as the Salazar family matriarch, and she was equal to the task.

"Manny, you should take Leo with you and with Elvis and Randy there'll be four of you to escort Kevin to the church. It's only a couple of blocks, so he should be able to make it even if he's staggering a little. I'll go find Father and warn him we might be a few minutes late. He'll be okay with that. Then I'll tell Dad — Anyone know where he is?"

"I just said hello to him out front," said Ferdie. "He's grabbing one last cigarette before it's too late."

"Okay, thanks. Manny, you tell Dad what's going on — if he doesn't already know — as you head out and I'll go back in to stay with Cat. Got it?"

Linda sped off without waiting for confirmation.

"Well, I have my orders," said Manny to Ferdie. "Want to come with?"

"No, I don't think so. I'll go catch a seat and stay out of the line of fire. Good luck!"

Leonel "Leo" Salazar was wearing his tuxedo and standing awkwardly in a corner of the lobby, on the periphery of the wedding party. He was broad-shouldered and extremely strong, perhaps the hardest worker in the Salazar family, but almost as reserved as his sister. His speech impediment was worse than Catarina's, but he was more friendly and seemed fairly cheerful and easy-going most of the time. After reading *Of Mice and Men* in high school, Elvino had asked, "So why didn't we name him Lenny?" — provoking Linda's wrath and a promise from Elvino not to repeat his witticism.

"Leo. Come with me. We're going to Cat's house."

Leo immediately fell in at Manny's side and marched out of the church with his brother. As they passed their father at the foot of the stairs, Manny said, "We're going to get Kevin. Be right back!"

Louis threw down his cigarette and ground it out under his foot. He watched his tall sons striding down the sidewalk, slender Manny and broad Leo. Earlier he had seen Elvino and Randall breeze by, heading in the same direction.

"Hi, Louis. How are things going?"

Louis turned toward the familiar voice. Paulinho and Carmina were approaching him, walking with their hands clasped. He felt a widower's spasm of jealousy at seeing a happily married couple.

"Hello, Paul. Carmina. Things are going okay, I guess. We may be running a bit late, but this time it's the groom and not the bride."

"If you remember, we had something similar at Mary Carmen's wedding," said Paulinho. "But it was the groom's tuxedo that hadn't arrived. Gerry was on the verge of having to swap clothes with one of the ushers when the rental service finally delivered his outfit."

Louis nodded.

"If it's not one thing, you know, it will be something else. Go on in and get settled. I'm sure it won't be too long."

Louis looked back in the direction that his sons had disappeared. To his relief, he saw a squad of Salazar boys pacing toward him, Elvino and Randall in the lead and Manuel and Leonel right behind them, with Kevin bracketed between the latter two. Kevin was definitely unsteady, but Leonel had an iron grip on one arm and Manuel was holding the other. Louis observed the spectacle for a while, then walked serenely into the church and took his assigned post in the lobby.

His boys soon appeared in the lobby themselves. Elvino and Randall peeled off and entered through the double doors to find themselves seats in the nave of the church, among all the wedding guests. Manuel and Leonel steered Kevin to the side door that admitted them into the hallway. Kevin's face was an ashen color, but he was managing to walk at the pace set by his future brothers-in-law. Louis gave a sniff as the three disappeared into the hallway. He was proud of his boys, but he was less than delighted with the young man who had volunteered to be his son-in-law. He winced at the recollection of Kevin's clumsy delivery of the proposal of marriage, sitting next to Catarina on the couch in the Salazar living room, mouthing the lines that Linda had suggested to him.

Linda's prepping of her sister-in-law had prevented Catarina from being astonished when the boy who had been coming over and hanging around for a few weeks finally said, "Will you marry me?" — but none of the eavesdroppers had exactly cheered when the only response she could think of was, "Oh, okay."

Louis was thinking his daughter's lack of enthusiasm had been entirely appropriate as he awaited the bride's appearance.

And here she was, being guided into position at his side by his wonderful daughter-in-law. Louis's mouth fell open. He had never seen Catarina looking so lovely. He looked at Linda, who had noticed his reaction and was savoring it. Louis knew it would be a bad idea to congratulate his daughter-in-law on her miracle-making in front of the miracle herself, so he left that for later.

"Catarina, *querida*, you look *so* beautiful! You remind me of your mother. I know she is looking down on you from heaven right now."

His eyes were watering as his daughter smiled at him. She took his arm and they faced the double doors, awaiting their cue. Linda was chivvying members of the bridal party into their prescribed order. The groomsmen had been dispatched down the side hallway to make their entrance at the front of the church, where they would stand erect, clasp their hands in a dignified manner, and await the procession of the bridesmaids and bride.

The groom and groomsmen were all gathered in the sacristy, where Father Garrity and his two altar boys looked at the party with poorly veiled skepticism.

"Kevin, are you ready for this?"

The groom focused his eyes on the portly priest.

"Oh, yes, Father. Uh-huh."

Garrity recognized the cadences of alcohol-influenced speech. He was a man who liked his wine, and was occasionally at pains to speak carefully so that people would not know how much he had recently imbibed. Kevin Lineman's speech wasn't particularly slurred, but it was right on the margin. He addressed the older Salazar boy.

"Manny, is he ready?"

"Yes, Father. Just barely," said Manny.

"If you say so," said Father Garrity dubiously. "All right. It's showtime, gentlemen. Get on out there and take your positions." He paused. "But stay close to Kevin, okay?"

Manny decided that he would take the liberty of tweaking his wife's plans. The groomsmen marched out from the sacristy two at a time instead of single file. That gave Manny, as best man, an excuse to walk next to Kevin, just in case the groom started to weave.

The guests watched attentively as the men appeared at the front of the church. Manny heard whispered murmurings as they noticed the condition of the groom. He stood at the penultimate location next to Kevin, whose post was farthest from the altar. The junior groomsman was the closest to the altar. They all formed a line facing the guests and stood with their hands clasped, as Linda had coached them, except for Manny, who deemed it more prudent to leave his hands free, just in case.

A movement at the other side of the altar drew the attention of the wedding guests. Paul Francisco had appeared, wearing a plain dark suit instead of a tuxedo. He was serving as the lector for the service. He had performed the same function at his *madrinha*'s funeral five years before. Paul placed his missal on the lectern and said, "Please rise!" That was the cue for the audience to stand up as Father Garrity entered the altar area, preceded by the two altar boys.

The bride's side of the church, Portuguese Catholics to almost the last person, stood up in one smooth synchronous motion. The groom's side, a collection of family members and school friends, most of them Protestant, struggled to their feet in clumps.

Father Garrity took his place in front of the altar and behind the two-person kneeler that awaited the bride and groom. The altar boys flanked him. After Father took a moment to stand straight and compose himself, Paul Francisco said, "Please be seated!"

This time the groom's side was almost as efficient as the bride's side, all the guests dropping into their pews in unison. Organ music started and the double doors at the end of the aisle opened. The first bridesmaid started slowly toward the altar, looking straight ahead without any expression on her face. Linda had wanted dignity throughout the wedding service and had coached everyone to avoid looking at the guests and getting distracted.

When the first bridesmaid reached a point one-third of the way toward the altar, the second bridesmaid entered, her mien matching that of the first.

The junior groomsman stood forward and moved to meet the first brides-maid as she drew near. They walked the last few steps arm-in-arm toward Father Garrity, nodded their heads briefly, separated, and moved to the sides of the church, where they circled around and took their reserved seats in the front pews.

Each groomsman similarly greeted a bridesmaid until four couples had paid their respects to the priest and been seated. Manny placed his hand behind Kevin's back to steady him as they watched the progress of the ring-bearer and flower girl down the aisle, followed by Linda, the matron of honor. Linda had decided it was better to keep the youngsters together as a team in the lobby instead of splitting them up with the groomsmen and bridesmaids. She had also positioned them in the procession so that she could keep an eye on them. Everything was swimmingly under control.

Or so she hoped. She eyed the groom nervously and noticed how closely Manny was standing next to him. Linda marched with a measured pace, keep-ing her face immobile and maintaining her prescribed one-third of an aisle distance behind the ring-bearer and flower girl. To her delight, the youngsters paused right in front of Father Garrity and gave him a charming bow from the waist. And almost simultaneously. Linda had considered having the little girl curtsy, but that was just asking for trouble.

The children were following instructions and waiting for Linda and Manny to catch up to them. Linda and Manny bowed to the celebrant, each collected one of the youngsters, and then proceeded to the pews, where they deposited them. The best man and matron of honor then solemnly marched back to the altar, taking positions on either side of the bridal couple's kneeler and facing the guests.

Kevin was now standing by himself, and most eyes in the church were on him. He was still under control, but he was clearly the likeliest source of some real entertainment during the service.

The central aisle stood empty and the double doors had been closed after Linda's entrance. The organ struck up a bridal march. Paul Francisco intoned, "Please rise!" and everyone came to their feet. The doors opened again and there stood the radiant bride on her father's arm.

Louis swelled with pride as they proceeded slowly down the aisle. He saw the expressions on people's faces as they observed his transfigured daughter. He was supremely happy. And yet he was fighting a bizarre impulse to shake his fist at the surprised people and mock their incredulity. *See! See! I knew all along. None of you knew! But I knew! Screw you all!*

The bride's side of the church was packed with relatives. Louis saw his sister and her family. And cousins. And in-laws. Paulinho and Carmina were smiling at him. Mary Carmen and her Anglo husband, with their toddler standing wide-eyed between them and their infant napping in his mother's arms. And the loathsome Candido and his pathetic Odile. Louis felt as if he towered above them, and he savored the moment.

They were nearing the front. Louis looked at his daughter's fiancé. *Damn, that boy looks sick!* He glanced at his daughter. She was still smiling as if in a beautiful dream. *Well, I guess it is. I hope it's not followed by a nightmare.*

Kevin wobbled over and took his bride's arm. Louis gave his daughter a kiss on the cheek and reached out to shake the groom's hand. He couldn't help himself. He squeezed hard and watched Kevin's eyes bulge. He gave Kevin a warning look, let go, and paid his respects to Father Garrity with a curt nod. As the bridal couple approached the celebrant, Louis walked to the front pew and took his seat next to his mother-in-law. Teresa Francisco was clutching a handkerchief and occasionally dabbing at her eyes. She also had a rosary in her hand, and Louis was startled to see that it matched the rosary that Monsignor had given Fatima when Catarina was born. Perhaps it was even the same one. He didn't know, having lost track of things like his wife's rosaries, medals, and scapulars. Linda might have given it to her as a remembrance.

Paul Francisco had the best seat in the house — except that he had to stand — from which to view the bridal couple. The lectern was directly adjacent to the altar and stood at the same height. From his vantage point he was looking down at the bride and groom, who were now kneeling in front of Father Garrity. *Kevin does not look good*, he thought. *Not good at all. I guess your face really can turn green. I always thought that was a figure of speech.*

The priest launched into the wedding ritual, pointing out for the benefit of his mixed audience that the Roman Catholic Church regarded marriage as a sacrament, a rite replete with special graces that would shower down upon the newly married couple. He quoted some of the statements of St. Paul, the bachelor saint who wanted women to shut up in church but said that it was better to marry them than to burn. Garrity did not, however, choose those particular passages. Instead he quoted Ephesians to the effect that wives should submit to their husbands and that husbands should love their wives. He was rattling off all the standard boilerplate.

Paul Francisco listened to Father invoking his namesake saint and marveled at the spectacle of a celibate celebrant using the words of an unmarried saint to explain the joys and responsibilities of marriage to a bridal couple. He suspected they'd get better advice from their parents, who had the benefit of actual experience.

The bride and groom stood up to exchange vows and give each other rings. Father proclaimed them a sacramentally wedded couple, at which point they sank back down to their knees for the priest's blessing. Kevin went down hard, his knees striking the padded kneeler with a *thud* that could be heard throughout the church. His legs had gone limp as he had started to kneel and he had dropped in free fall.

Catarina looked at her new husband in concern as Father Garrity bent down urgently.

"Kevin! Are you all right? Shall I stop? Do you need a break?"

Kevin was breathing noisily as he clung to the kneeler's armrest. He opened his mouth, but nothing came out.

That was a good thing.

"Manny!" Linda hissed her husband's name in a loud whisper.

Manny jammed his left hand under Kevin's right armpit and grabbed the right elbow with his right hand. He pulled Kevin up to his feet and dragged him toward the door to the sacristy. Moving at a speed belied by his size, the reliable Leo appeared on Kevin's left side and the Salazar brothers proceeded at flank speed out of the altar area with their brand-new brother-in-law.

They had barely vanished from the sight of the wedding guests before the sounds of Kevin's Vesuvian-scale retching filled the church. Except for the noise from the sacristy, complete and utter silence reigned.

Father Garrity gave Paul a meaningful look before bustling off after the indisposed groom. Paul dropped his eyes to his prompt sheet and raised his voice in an announcement for the benefit of the guests, and to cue the bride.

"The soloist will now sing Schubert's *Ave Maria* while the bride places her bouquet before the statue of the Blessed Virgin Mother."

Recognizing that the show must go on, Catarina gathered herself up and walked solemnly over to the side chapel dedicated to the Virgin Mary. People turned their heads to watch her as she knelt in front of the life-sized statue of the Blessed Mother, arrayed in the white garments that characterized her apparition as the Immaculate Conception before the devout Portuguese peasant children of Fatima. Catarina placed her flowers before the statue, bent her head, and began to pray. The calming strains of the *Ave Maria* soothed the nerves of those in attendance.

In the sacristy, Father Garrity looked down at the disgorged contents of Kevin's stomach. It appeared that Kevin had chosen Cheetos to accompany his morning beer drinking. Kevin himself was slumped miserably in Father's vesting chair, which was normally used during preparation for Mass. Manny and Leo had already pulled a roll of paper towels from the cupboard and were trying to sop up the mess. As Leo tore sheets off the roll and dropped them to the floor, Manny strode over to the closet and pulled out the mop and bucket. As a former altar boy, he remembered where everything was.

Father walked over to the sink, filled a glass of water, and took it to Kevin.

"Take a sip, boy. Get some of the nastiness out of your mouth."

Kevin took the glass carefully, as if he did not trust himself to hold it.

"Is it holy water?"

Father laughed.

"No, no, no, no! Just tap water. Drink a little. Drinking a little can help after drinking a lot."

Kevin took a sip and swished it around in his mouth. Father looked at what Manny and Leo were doing.

"That's enough, gentlemen. It's under control, right? Leave the details till later. We'll deal with the mess after we've dealt with the Mass, okay?"

The soloist had finished singing the *Ave Maria* as Catarina returned to the kneeler in front of the altar. Her husband was not there to greet her, so she stood there patiently, her back to the wedding guests. Her eyes flicked over to Paul, who nodded slightly. He considered giving her an encouraging smile but was afraid it would look like amusement at her expense and so refrained.

Paul was as aware of the dowry scheme as anyone else in the family, and therefore regarded the wedding as a business proposition, not a romantic occasion. And, upon reflection, somewhat to his surprise, he did not object to the idea. But, nor did he feel obligated to play along when Linda would tell people that Kevin and Catarina were really "in love." At the same time, he was willing to give the arrangement his blessing as a practical solution to an awkward situation. Catarina liked the idea of being married and Kevin liked the idea of being financially secure. And Louis Salazar was in a position to make that happen.

Happily ever after.

Unless puking your guts out at your wedding was grounds for an annulment.

Kevin was back, walking under his own power and steadier than before. He was followed by the Salazar brothers and Father Garrity. Kevin took Catarina's hand. "Sorry!" he whispered, as they knelt down again. She gave his hand a small squeeze. Manny resumed his position and Father was back in front of the newlyweds. Father raised his hands.

"Let us pray."

He gave the bridal couple a blessing and then started the nuptial Mass, which would occupy another forty minutes in high-church Catholic fashion. Eventually, however, Father spoke the concluding lines of the ceremony, giving Paul his final cue.

"Please rise!" said Paul Francisco.

Father Garrity came forward and stood behind the newlyweds. He had them turn toward the wedding guests.

"Ladies and gentlemen, it is my privilege to introduce to you our newly married couple. Please give your love and support to Mr. and Mrs. Kevin Lineman!"

Applause filled the church as Catarina and her husband progressed down the aisle. Her smile was genuine, even if the marriage was an artificial construct. Kevin struggled to maintain a steady pace even though his knees hurt. He avoided the curious eyes of the wedding guests. *I can make this work*, he thought. *I can make this work!*

From the lectern, Paul watched the receding couple, the wedding party trailing behind them.

La commedia è finita! he thought.

Paul Reads Fourth Grade

The first-grade class at Pleasant Hill Elementary was occupied with a drawing exercise when the door opened and a stout middle-aged woman slipped inside. Mrs. Miller looked up to see who had entered her classroom and smiled upon recognizing her colleague from the fourth grade. She walked over to where Mrs. White was waiting for her.

"Hello, Agnes," she said quietly. "To what do I owe the honor?"

"I'm looking to teach some students a lesson, naturally," said Mrs. White to her younger colleague, but her mildly humorous remark had an undertone of exasperation. "I think, Dolores, that you have just what I need."

Paul Francisco looked up from his drawing to where his teacher was conferring in whispers with her visitor. He was startled to see that they were looking at him. He decided the best thing to do was bend his head down over his work and make a show of coloring busily. Maybe they would notice his cousin Jojo instead, who sat right behind him and was always getting in trouble.

It didn't work. Mrs. Miller had come over and was standing over his desk. He accepted his fate and looked up at her.

"Paul, I'd like you to do a favor for Mrs. White."

Paul glanced at the door, where the chubby old lady was waiting. He knew she was the fourth grade teacher, but he didn't know what she was doing in his classroom.

"A favor, Mrs. Miller? What kind of favor can I do for Mrs. White?"

"Just go with her for a few minutes and then come back to class. Could you do that for us?"

"Go where?"

"To her classroom. Like I said, it will be only a few minutes. Okay?"

"Okay, Mrs. Miller. If you want me to go with her I will."

Paul put his crayon back into the box, making sure to place it in the order of the spectrum he had learned, which started with red, orange, and yellow and made its progression to the odd-ball colors brown and black. Those last two weren't colors in the rainbow, but they had to go somewhere. He put the lid back on the box and stood up. He followed Mrs. Miller over to the door, where Mrs. White greeted him.

"Hello, Paul. Mrs. Miller says she thinks you'll be able to help me. I would be very glad of your assistance."

Paul liked the way Mrs. White talked. It sounded very formal and sophisticated.

"I would be very glad to give you assistance," he said, as politely as he could.

The women exchanged grins over his head.

"Oh, he's a live one, isn't he?" said Mrs. White to Mrs. Miller. Then to Paul: "Thank you very much, young man. Let us repair to my classroom now and I'll show you what is needed."

Paul didn't recognize the usage of the word "repair," but perhaps she needed him to fix something in her room. Dad had a really big dictionary at home, so maybe later he could check what Mrs. White meant. In any case, he knew it was his cue.

"Yes, ma'am," he said.

He wasn't a kindergartner anymore, so he didn't offer his hand to be led. He simply followed Mrs. White out of the door and down the hall to her fourth-grade classroom. Paul could hear noise from behind the door as Mrs. White reached for the knob, but the hubbub died down instantly as she twisted it and pulled the door open. She held it open and indicated that Paul should precede her. Paul stepped inside uncertainly and waited for instructions. Every eye in the classroom was fixed on him. The big kids did not look friendly as they stared at the boy who was below average height for his first-grade cohort.

"Class, I want you to meet Paul Francisco. He is from Mrs. Miller's first-grade class. Say hello to him."

The big kids favored him with a ragged chorus of greetings.

"Please follow me, Paul."

The students' heads swiveled to follow Paul as he accompanied Mrs. White to the front of the room and to the side of her desk. She picked up a book from her desk. The stout matron put on her glasses, which had been hanging from a chain around her neck, and adjusted them slightly. She held up the book.

"Class, would you please tell our guest what this book is?"

There was some incoherent mumbling until one student near the front of the room raised her hand.

"Yes, Coral?"

"It is our class reader, Mrs. White," said Coral primly.

"Very good, Coral. Thank you."

Mrs. White flipped it open and found the page she was looking for.

"Class, do you remember what is on page 102?"

There was a flurry of activity as students flipped open their own books to the indicated page. Some of them had put their books away during Mrs. White's trip to visit Mrs. Miller and they slammed down their desktops after retrieving the readers. The ruckus ebbed and three-dozen young faces were poring over page 102.

Several hands went up.

"Yes, Gene?"

"It's a poem about the moon," said the curly-headed boy.

"Thank you, Gene. If I remember correctly, some of you said the poem was too hard to read, right?" Heads were nodding, some vigorously. "Let's have a show of hands, shall we? How many of you feel that the poem is too difficult for fourth graders to read?"

A forest of hands shot up. Paul could not tell if it was unanimous, but it looked like it. The boy named Gene had both hands up and was waving his arms like a semaphore.

"Thank you, class. Please put your hands down."

She handed her open book to Paul. The poem "The Moon" occupied half of page 102.

"Mrs. Miller has kindly consented to allow young Master Francisco here to visit our class for a few minutes. I will now ask him to read the poem for you."

Paul was initially delighted when Mrs. White called him "Master," because it reminded him of what he had heard about his great-great-grandfather. According to his *avô*, his *avô*'s own grandfather had had the nickname "*Mestre*" back in the Old Country, because the old man had been so clever. It was like being called "master" or "professor." Paul was similarly pleased when he heard someone called "*maestro*" when he watched music programs on television with his father, because they seemed like something special related to his family heritage.

But his delight changed instantly to horror when he realized that Mrs.

White had set him the task of reading from the fourth-grade reader in front of an entire fourth-grade class. His face felt hot and flushed.

Although he had grown up speaking Portuguese at home, Paul had taken quickly to reading and speaking English. Kindergarten had been a full-immersion language-learning program for him. It had been quite successful, although the pervasive sibilants in Portuguese had translated into a noticeable lisp in Paul's English speaking. Several weekly sessions with the school's speech therapist had yet to bring it entirely under control.

Paul looked down at the page and drew a deep breath.

"Oh, just one minute, Paul. Let me get you a chair to stand on."

As Mrs. White walked to the other side of the classroom to collect a kid-sized chair from a work table in the corner, Paul scanned the poem. He quickly calmed down. The words made sense. *Most* of the words made sense. What is "quays"? He had never seen that one. Is it pronounced "kways," with a long-A sound? He really didn't know.

Mrs. White placed the chair next to Paul and he dutifully climbed up on it.

Wait a minute, he thought. *This is a poem. Poems rhyme. What word goes with "quays" in this poem?*

He looked back down at the page: It appeared that "quays" rhymed with "trees." That seemed stupid, but Paul knew how poems were supposed to work. The die was cast. He cleared his throat.

"The Moon," he recited. He paused.

"The moon has a face like the clock in the hall;
She shines on thieves on the garden wall,
On streets and fields and harbour quays,
And birdies asleep in the forks of the trees."

Paul peeked at Mrs. White out of the corner of his eye. She was smiling. Apparently it was all right to read "quays" as "keys." *Weird*, he thought.

"The squalling cat and the squeaking mouse,
The howling dog by the door of the house,
The bat that lies in bed at noon,
All love to be out by the light of the moon."

One more verse, he told himself. *Only one more.*

"But all of the things that belong to the day
Cuddle to sleep to be out of her way;
And flowers and children close their eyes
Till up in the morning the sun shall arise."

The poet's name appeared at the bottom of the poem, so he read it: "Robert Louis Stevenson." He pronounced the middle name as "Louie" because that's how everyone said the name of his *padrinho*.

Paul took in a deep breath and looked up. The fourth-graders were staring at him, but not in a particularly friendly way.

"Thank you, Paul. That was very nice. Class, you should congratulate Paul for his fine reading."

There was a smattering of coerced applause as he climbed off the chair.

"It's time now, Class, for me to return Paul to his own classroom. I will be back very soon. When I return, we will read 'A Sudden Shower' by James Whitcomb Riley and *no one will complain that it's too difficult.* Am I understood?"

A chorus of "Yes, ma'am" replied.

When he was back in his classroom, Paul discovered that the drawing period was over. Fortunately, Mrs. Miller was about to do a lesson on counting, which was one of his favorites. As he settled into his desk and put away his drawing and crayons, his teacher paused by his desk and leaned down.

"Paul, I'm sorry to ask you two favors in one day," she said quietly, "but would you mind helping me sort the bookshelves during the recess period?"

"Of course, Mrs. Miller."

Paul was puzzled why Mrs. Miller wanted him to help her sort books during the recess period that the first-graders shared with the grades up through fourth, but he didn't particularly want to be out on the playground with the fourth-graders anyway. He decided it would be perfectly all right with him to stay in the classroom today.

Linda and Candido

Linda Salazar parked the red-and-white El Camino in the back driveway of Candido and Odile's home. She grabbed her purse, a simple woven bag with a hand-strap, and walked up to the house's back door. It was the family entrance and all of the Franciscos and Salazars used it to the exclusion of the front door. She didn't bother pressing the doorbell. Something had gone wrong with it years before and neither Candido nor the boys had ever gotten around to fixing it. Linda gave the doorframe a sharp rap.

"Come in!"

It was Candido's voice, not Odile's. Linda cracked the door open and stuck in her head.

"Hi, Unk. Is Aunt Odile at home?"

The door opened into the house's service porch. It contained the washer and dryer. One door led to the walk-in pantry, which connected to the kitchen, a second door connected to the garage, and the third was a shower-equipped bathroom. The bathroom also served as the family's mudroom, where rubber boots and work shoes were left, lest they track dirt and manure into the house.

"No, she went shopping. Again."

Candido was standing in the doorway of the bathroom. He was in his jeans and stocking feet, with a terrycloth towel hanging from his neck. He rubbed at his face with one end of the towel.

"No problem. She asked me for my recipe for bread pudding." Linda started poking around in her purse for it. "I can just leave it for her."

"For Ferdie, you mean."

Linda smiled awkwardly.

"You're probably right, Unk."

She didn't know what else to say.

Candido approached her, grasping the two ends of his towel in his large hands, wearing it like a halter. He had a prominent farmer's tan, his face and neck tanned down to the vee demarcated by the open-necked work shirts he usually wore. His torso was a pasty white.

"He's a good kid, though Odile's turned him into the daughter she never had."

"He *is* a good kid. And he works hard for you and his mom. It's not fair to run him down just because he has a *jeito* for cooking." Linda used the Portuguese word for "knack."

Candido laughed and slapped his protuberant stomach with a loud meaty sound.

"You're right, Linda. The boy does keep me happily fed. But Odile really, really wanted a girl and you have to admit Ferdie's a near miss."

Linda wondered if Candido was clever enough to have intended the word play. She doubted it.

"I don't mean to put him down," said Candido. "He'll even leave the raisins out of the bread pudding, if I ask him. I love all my boys. You have to love your children."

"Of course. No question about it."

"You know," said Candido, his voice becoming slightly insinuating. "It sure is too bad that you and Manny don't have any children. Not even after ten years."

Linda caught the disquieting glint in Candido's eye.

"Eleven. Yeah, well, sometimes things work out that way. Or don't work out."

"I'm sure it's not for lack of trying, what with Manny having such a fine-looking wife and all."

Candido's smile was uncomfortably close to a leer. He had moved a little nearer.

"That's a little too personal, Unk," she said, a warning note in her voice.

"I'm just being sympathetic. You know, it's probably Manny's fault. I'm not saying that the Salazars have, like, *bad* blood, but maybe it's not just Leo and Catarina that have problems."

"I don't want to talk about this, Uncle Candy. Stop it right now."

"Don't get me wrong," he said. "When I say 'Manny's fault,' I'm not really blaming him. It's not like he can do anything about it. He's just not all that healthy. He's got that bad hay fever, for one thing."

"It's asthma. I thought you knew that. It's not hay fever. And it has nothing to do with fertility, okay? This conversation is over."

He loomed over her. She took a pace back, but he slowly moved forward to close the gap.

"Okay. I didn't mean to upset you. We can stop talking. I'm sorry I brought up that stuff. But I really do care. And you — you should be doing whatever you can to give your family a child. There are ways, you know. Lots of ways. But you don't want to talk. I don't want to talk either. I can think of something better than talking."

Candido moved forward a half-step, which for him was as much as a full step for Linda. He looked down at her and gently touched her hair with one hand. Linda stood stock-still in shock, dismay, and disbelief.

"Uncle Candido. You have one last chance to stop right now."

Linda's voice had a tremor in it. Candido misinterpreted it as sexual tension. She dropped her handbag. Candido thought it was a sign of physical numbness. Linda thought of it as a convenient way to get both hands free.

Candido's nipples were large and fleshy. They gave Linda's hands good purchase when she reached out to grab them and twist. Twist *hard*.

Her husband's uncle shrieked in a soprano register that he hadn't been able to reach since puberty. A peculiarly detached and analytic part of Linda's mind noted that she had twisted in opposite directions. She hadn't planned that detail. It just seemed the right way to do it.

Candido tore himself free and staggered back several steps from her. Linda stooped down quickly and grabbed her purse.

"For future reference, *Unk*. I may be half your size, but I'm also twice as mean. If you *ever* get within arm's reach of me again, you will be sorrier than you can imagine. *Believe me.*"

She reached into her bag and dropped a piece of paper, which fluttered to the floor.

"Make sure Odile gets that. Let her know I came by. I'm sure you don't want *me* to tell her. I'm sure you don't want *me* to tell her *anything*, right?"

Linda slammed the door behind her so that it rattled on its hinges. Seconds later, Candido heard the El Camino peel out in a spray of dirt and gravel.

Chico Is a Citizen

"Raise your right hands and repeat after me."

Chico Francisco raised his right hand.

"I hereby declare, on oath . . . ," said the man from the naturalization office.

"I hereby declare, on oath . . . ," said Chico and the other two dozen people standing in the room with their right hands raised.

"That I absolutely and entirely renounce and abjure . . ." said the man from the naturalization office.

"That I absolutely and entirely renounce and abjure . . . " said Chico and the others.

"All allegiance and fidelity to any foreign prince," said the man.

"All allegiance and fidelity to any foreign prince," said Chico and company.

"Potentate, state, or sovereignty . . . ," said the man.

"Potentate, state, or sovereignty . . . ," said Chico and the other citizenship candidates.

"Of whom or which I have heretofore been a subject or citizen," said the man.

"Of whom or which I have heretofore been a subject or citizen," said Chico, thinking, *Adeus, Portugal!* Goodbye, Portugal!

The oath of naturalization continued for a few more lines in antiphonal style. When they reached the end, the representative from the naturalization office said, "Congratulations, you are now official citizens of the United States of America."

Chico walked over to where his family was waiting for him.

"Congratulations, *Pai*," said the boys. They shook his hand.

"*Bem feito*," said Teresa, *well done*, as she gave his cheek a kiss. "Now I'm married to an American, I guess."

"Yes, you are," said Chico, smiling at his wife. "This will be all for the good, just as we discussed."

Chico was looking forward to checking the box identifying him as a citizen on loan applications and other documents. Being an American would simply make life easier. He had asked Teresa if she wanted to join him in becoming naturalized, but his wife had balked. It would have been convenient to naturalize the entire family at one time, but for Teresa it was too much. Chico realized that her acquiescence in his naturalization was a tacit acknowledgment on her part that the Azores were gone forever.

Of course, that had been clear enough when Fatima had married Louis Salazar. She had already presented her parents with two grandsons, on whom Teresa doted. Instead of her sisters back on the islands, she now had Tony and Manny to fuss over. She was mollified, if not entirely reconciled.

"*Mãe*," said Paulinho, addressing his mother. "Now that *Pai* is an American citizen, can he have you deported if you give him trouble?"

Teresa smiled at her younger son, always the cheekier of the two.

"If only," she said. "But don't forget. He can put *you* on the boat, too!"

Chico gently took the arm of his foreign wife and led his family out.

JUNE 1963

The Wrong Grandmother

"I have the wrong grandmother."

"Huh? What is *that* supposed to mean?"

Ferdinando thought for a moment before venturing an answer.

"It just means that my grandfather didn't mean to marry my grandmother."

Now it was Paul's turn to wrinkle his brow. He and his cousin were sitting on the haystack, fearlessly dangling their legs over the side. A flatbed trailer below them showed the fruit of their labors. The boys had pushed thirty-two bales off the top of the haystack and restacked them on the trailer — two deep in two rows of eight. Each bale weighed over a hundred pounds, making it a little heavier than Paul and a little lighter than Ferdinando. Each boy had wielded a pair of wickedly pointed hay hooks to wrangle the bales into place.

Later the trailer-load of bales would be used to distribute hay to the cows for the afternoon feeding.

"That doesn't make a lot of sense, Ferdie. Are you saying that your *Avô* Avila married your *Avó* Avila by accident? By mistake?"

"No, not that. I mean that he was engaged to someone else."

"Okay. I get it. The engagement was broken and he ended up marrying someone else."

"Yeah," agreed Ferdie, "but it was weirder than that. My Aunt Odette told me the story because she thought it was funny, but it made my mom mad when I asked her about it."

"Maybe your mom got upset because it means she was almost never born."

"Uh-huh. Could be. And then I guess I wouldn't be here either."

"That sounds right to me. So what happened?"

"*Tia* Odette told me that my *avô* came to this country when he was still single. He was engaged to a girl back home."

"In the Old Country. The Azores."

"Yeah, back home," said Ferdinando.

Paul thought it was interesting how they had picked up the expression "back home" to refer to a place that neither of them had ever seen. They had learned the phrase from their grandparents and it was a natural part of their language.

"Anyway," continued Ferdinando, "*Avô* worked for a few years until he thought he had enough money to get married. So then he wrote back to his girlfriend to come to America so they could get married."

"I've heard stories like this before," said Paul, thinking about tales told by *Avó* Francisco. "Our *avó* said lots of men came to the U.S. by themselves, some married and some not. They meant to go home after they earned enough money to have a good life back in the Azores. *Avô* says that's what his grandfather did — except he went to Brazil instead of the United States. Sometimes, though, the men didn't come back, even if they had wives and children back in the Old Country. I think that's why *Avó* came here with *Avô* and brought our dads and *Tia* Fatima with them."

"Yeah, probably," agreed Ferdie. "But when my *avô* wrote back to get his girlfriend, he didn't get an answer from her. He got a letter from her father instead."

"Oh, oh," said Paul.

"Right. The father said that my *avô's* girlfriend got tired of waiting for him and married someone else."

"Ow!"

"Yeah. But then in the letter the father said, 'She has a sister. You want to marry her sister instead?' My *avô* thought about it and said yes. So my *avó* isn't the *avó* I was supposed to have."

"Good story, Ferdie! But you're forgetting what we were talking about earlier. If your *Avô* Alberto had married someone other than your *Avó* Odolina, you wouldn't even exist. I'd be talking to someone else!"

Ferdinando screwed up his face in a combination of deep thought and existential distress.

"That is *creepy!*"

"You want to hear something even creepier? Your mom wanted to marry my dad and my mom was supposed to marry your dad. Mom told me that was your Aunt Odette's idea. Neither one of us would exist. Or maybe we'd swap places!"

"You're welcome to my brothers," said Ferdinando.

"No, thank you!" replied Paul. "I'll stick with my own brother and sister."

"I don't want to think about this anymore," said Ferdinando.

"Then think about this," suggested Paul. "*Avó* told me what the bachelors did when they wanted to get married and didn't have fiancées waiting for them back home."

Ferdinando's curiosity was piqued.

"What did they do?" he asked.

"*Avó* said that the men would go shopping for a bridal gown. They'd mail the dress back to their parents in the Azores and ask their folks to fill the dress and send it back."

Ferdinando burst into gleeful laughter.

We Have Lift-off

Thirteen years of age is like full adulthood for a farm boy. Henry Francisco was driving his father's Jeep, a vehicle he fully expected to have in his own name by the time he reached sixteen and was technically eligible for a driver's license. He was already putting as many miles on it as his father, since Paulinho preferred to drive a recently acquired pickup truck.

Henry turned off the county road and onto the dirt lane that ran between two parcels of land. One belonged to Henry's grandfather and the other to his Uncle Louis. There were two large mounds of earth at the edge of Louis Salazar's field. Henry downshifted the Jeep as he drove up the side of the taller mound and parked his vehicle at its highest point.

Most of the mounds on Tulare County farmland were manure piles, the accretion of scrapings from the cow corrals. Each spring the piles were reduced as the dried cattle waste was scooped into manure spreaders and scattered as fertilizer on the fields. Uncle Louis's two piles, however, were different. Henry was on a mountain of topsoil, expensively hauled in on dump trucks. Next to the heap of topsoil was a smaller mound of sand. Leo Salazar was operating a skip-loader — a tractor with a hydraulic scoop on the front — to load up a dump truck with sand from the smaller pile.

Henry climbed out of the Jeep and looked out over the field. A huge Caterpillar earth mover was traveling toward him, raising dust as its large underbelly scoop scraped along the ground. The scoop was not digging into the surface. It was already full of sandy soil gouged out of a groove that wandered across the middle of the field.

The groove followed the track of a sandy streak that was the remnant of an ancient creek that had existed some hundreds of years earlier. Such sand streaks reduced crop yields and diminished the value of farmland. Most farmers simply put up with these riparian relics, but more aggressive men like Louis Salazar sometimes tried to reduce or even eliminate them.

It was a chancy proposition, but Louis was gambling that the time and trouble and expense of replacing sand with topsoil would pay off in the long run. He was also defraying part of the cost of his project by selling the sand to a local concrete firm. If things penciled out as he had estimated, the Salazar operation would have recouped its investment within a decade or so.

The bright yellow Caterpillar earthmover pulled up next to the sand pile on the opposite side from where Leo was working and its hydraulics lifted and opened its scoop, dumping the load of sand. The Cat's driver turned the big machine back into the field and parked it. The door of its cab opened and Elvino Salazar climbed out. He waved at Henry and started toward the dirt pile.

Henry was intensely jealous of his younger cousin because no similar project was going on at the Francisco dairy farm. He had driven lesser Cats in smaller-scale work, but he longed to operate an earth-moving giant like the dusty monster before him. Perhaps Elvino would let him take a turn.

"Hi, Elvis," said Henry as his cousin trudged up the side of the topsoil mound.

"Hey. What's going on?"

"Nothing. Just passing through. Nearly done?"

"Maybe. With the scraping part, anyway. Got most of the sand, I think." Elvino kicked at the dirt underfoot.

"Dad'll come out and decide if it's enough," he continued. "Then I get to break up this little mountain here and fill in the creek bed."

"Neat."

The honk of a horn caught their attention. Leo had parked the skip-loader and was poised at the door of the dump truck. He waved at Elvino and Henry, slammed the door shut, started the truck, and drove it down the dirt lane.

"Another load of sand for Tulare Redi-Mix," said Elvino.

"Where's everybody else?" asked Henry.

"Like I even know. Leo and I are doing most of the work here this afternoon, but Tony and Manny took in some loads of sand this morning. We ought to have one of the other dump trucks here right now, getting loaded up, but I don't know. Haven't seen Otelo all day. He's probably back at the ranch."

The boys looked toward the south, the direction of the Salazar dairy. Two clusters of buildings were visible less than a mile away. One was dominated by the old wooden barn of Darrin MacDonald, whose spread lay between two Salazar tracts, and the other encircled three tall metal silos. The silver cylinder in the middle was emblazoned on the side with "SALAZAR DAIRY" in big red letters.

Henry opened his mouth to make some inconsequential remark, but later he would not be able to remember what it was. He and Elvino were fortuitously looking right at the silos when all hell broke loose.

Vertical bright lines of actinic yellow instantaneously seared the eyes and scored the side of the center silo, like parallel claw marks tracing the cylinder's riveted seams. Henry's unspoken words strangled in his throat as he watched his cousin's family name breaking up into "SA LA ZA R." The air shuddered with the noise and impact of the explosion, the sound lagging a split-second behind the burning visual image.

The cousins reflexively and belatedly reached their hands up to cover and protect their ears from the boom. As they did, the silo's conical top separated from the cylindrical body with a burst of sheeting flame and arced into the sky. The upper ends of the cylinder were curling back like a cartoon exploding cigar.

Henry was accustomed to watching televised live coverage of rocket launches, but he had never expected to witness one in Tulare County. While not up to NASA standards, the Salazar silo rocket was spectacular in terms of proximity and astonishment. The blunt conical missile moved along a flat parabolic trajectory toward the MacDonald place, gaining little height. It wobbled with a slight spin, making less than a full rotation before crashing down right next to MacDonald's barn. The noise of its impact made little impression on Henry and Elvino's ringing ears.

Henry realized that Elvino was yelling at him, trying to be heard.

"Otelo! It's got to be Otelo!"

He had grabbed Henry's arm and was pulling him toward the Jeep. Henry climbed in behind the wheel as Elvino scrambled into the passenger seat. Henry revved up the vehicle and they tore down the side of the mound and bounced onto the dirt lane, speeding toward the Salazar dairy.

Silos can accumulate volatile gases from fermenting corn or contain explosively flammable grain dust suspended in air. If Elvino was correct, Otelo had picked the wrong place to practice his hobby of homemade explosives.

PART IV

Jackpot Day

"It's jackpot day, Paul."

"Is it? All right. Happy jackpot day, Harold."

Odile's attorney was rummaging in his pockets.

"You have any change, Paul?"

"Yeah, in a jar on my dresser and in the ashtray of my car."

"Never mind. Here." Harold Widener handed him a pair of dimes. "Now go to the basement and make a phone call."

"Okay. To whom and why?"

"It absolutely doesn't matter. It only matters what phone you use. Or, to be more precise, *try* to use. It's a perfect set-up."

"I need just a little more direction, Harold."

"Biddy just went down to the pay phones, okay? Who are the people in the courthouse that she hates the most? There's *me*, a badge I wear with pride, and there's *you*, the ungrateful nephew who wrote a nastygram to her boyfriend. Start to go into her booth and then back out. Make it look accidental. Can do?"

"Sure, Harold. Sounds like fun."

Paul loped down the stairs to the basement level and looked for the bank of pay phones. He saw why Harold had said they were perfect for a little harassment of the enemy. Their doors had tinted glass for privacy, which also made it difficult to tell if the booths were occupied, and the doors didn't close very well either. Paul made a beeline to the first booth whose door was mostly closed. When he got close enough to see that it was actually empty, he changed course and moved toward the next prospect.

It was jackpot day.

As he pulled the door open, Biddy Onan looked up and snarled.

"It's *occupied*! I am *using* this phone!"

Paul was holding the dimes up in one hand and feigned momentary confusion.

"Oh. Sorry. Please excuse me."

He looked left and right before backing up a step.

"I'll try a different phone."

"Yes, I think you'd better," she said frostily. As she pulled the door as shut as it would go, Paul heard her mutter, "Today *everyone* needs to use the phone."

Paul returned to the lobby, but Harold was not in sight. He went to the courtroom assigned to the family feud. As usual, the room was swarming with Franciscos, but there were no Salazars anywhere. None had ever appeared, except when Otelo had given his testimony. Paulo wondered if the jurors had noticed that the Franciscos were united (however temporarily) while the Salazars were invisible. If they had, would it tend to benefit the respondents?

Harold Widener was at the respondents' table, conferring with Bowman and Ramos. Paul waited until Harold noticed his presence, and then approached.

"I did as you asked," he reported.

"And — ?"

"She was very unhappy to see me hovering over her. And she said something about 'everybody' suddenly needing to use the phones today."

Harold grinned.

"Take care of those dimes, Paul. Consider them your generous fee. They are experienced dimes. I hope Biddy didn't recognize them."

"*You* did this earlier?"

"Oh, yeah! Biddy's been running back and forth from the phones all morning. There have been lots of opportunities to get on her nerves today."

"Is that good or bad? Could she be up to something?"

"Biddy Onan is *always* up to something. Dennis! Come over here. Paul has a question."

Ramos got up from the table and joined them.

"Paul wants to know if Biddy is up to something. This is your bailiwick, right?"

Dennis gave what was for him a very subdued smile.

"Biddy is trying to put out fires," he said. "She is the victim of a *very* unfortunate coincidence."

"Dennis *set* the fire," said Harold.

"I most certainly did not," said Dennis primly. "It's all a matter of simple justice and asking questions in the right places."

Paul felt a touch on his shoulder and moved aside to let his sister Mary Carmen join the scrum next to the respondents' table.

"This sounds like a war on multiple fronts," she said. "We're fighting both inside and outside the courtroom. Are we trying to beat them or destroy them?"

"You have to understand, Mrs. Chamberlain," said Harold. "This is as close to war as makes no difference. Your Uncle Louis declared it. He set this in motion and Biddy Onan is his willing moll and mouthpiece. If we win, your grandmother's wishes prevail. If we lose, her wishes are ignored and your parents are potentially homeless. The situation does not call for half-measures."

"He's right, Mary Carmen," added Paul. "It's not a time for playing nice. We've been scoring points off the opposition and we need to press our advantage."

"I told you it's jackpot day," said Harold. "You ain't seen nothin' yet."

"I think you're right, Hare," agreed Dennis. He swept an arm toward an evidence easel by the side of the courtroom. It held a covered poster like the ones Hunter had used for her testimony. "That's your letter over there, Paul. Ryan calls it our 'secret weapon.' Our expert witness was delighted with it and today we're going to hear all about it."

"Last time we kicked the feet out from under their pseudo-expert and knocked them all over," said Harold. "Today we jump on them while they're down. With both feet. In boots."

Mary Carmen stood with her arms crossed and a frown on her face. Paul gave his sister a small nudge, but all she did was heave a resigned sigh.

JUNE 1982

The Salazars Get Mail

"Mail!"

Elvino dropped the bundle from the mailbox on the kitchen table. It fanned out upon impact. He had already noticed that there was more mail than usual today, but now he noticed the identical letters. That was peculiar. Normally it happened only when the electricity bill came. The Edison company insisted on sending separate bills for each meter on the entire dairy farm. But these weren't electricity bills.

"Hey, Dad! Look at this!"

Elvino pawed at the letters. Four of them. Each had the same return address from a law office in Tulare and each was addressed to a different family member. One had his name on it.

Elvino wasn't accustomed to getting much mail, especially not fancy-looking mail like this. He ripped it open as his father stepped into the kitchen, his girlfriend just behind him.

"*Holy shit!*"

Elvino stared in amazement at the contents. When he became aware of his father's presence, he gave a sickly grin.

"Sorry, Dad. I was just surprised. *Really* surprised. This is a check for *ten thousand dollars!* For *me!*"

Louis Salazar regarded his son as the boy clutched the check. He gripped it as if he were afraid it would vanish. Louis became aware that Biddy couldn't see very well and stepped aside so that she could come through. They exchanged solemn glances.

Elvino was shuffling through the mail again. "There are letters here for Leo and Randy, too," he said. "And Catarina. Why did they mail Catarina here?"

"I don't know," said his father. "Perhaps it's the address that *Avó* Francisco gave her attorney when she filed her will. That part might not be up to date."

"This is from *Avó?*"

Louis had known about the provisions of the will since soon after his mother-in-law's death, when he had been briefed by Paulinho, but he had kept the information from his children. Now the cat — and the money — was out of the bag.

"Your grandmother's will gives each of you ten thousand dollars," he said. Elvino yelled down the hallway.

"Leo! Randy! Are you home? Come here! Quick!"

He turned back to his father.

"This is amazing, Dad. I had no idea."

"We're going to need to talk about this, Elvino."

The tone of his father's voice caused Elvino's joy to ebb swiftly away.

"Is something wrong, Dad?"

"I want you to think about something, son. Seven checks of ten thousand each. That's only seventy thousand dollars."

Elvino's eyebrows went up when he heard his father say "only," but he kept his peace.

"Don't you think your mother was worth more than seventy thousand dollars?"

Now Elvino was befuddled as well as worried.

"Mom? What about Mom? Of course she's worth more than seventy thousand, but what does this have to do with Mom?"

Biddy inserted herself into the family conversation.

"It's an *insult*, is what it is. Your father doesn't want to say it, but it's true. It's an insult to your mother's memory. The Francisco dairy farm is worth over a million dollars easy, but instead of getting a third of that, your mother gets only seventy thousand dollars."

Elvino found himself growing angry. He tolerated Biddy because his father was fond of her, but he resented her interference. She rattled about clumsily in the mom-shaped hole in their lives.

"My mom is not here. *Avó* couldn't leave anything to her if she tried. *Avó* would never do anything to insult Mom's memory. She wouldn't do that!"

Elvino feared he was going to start to cry. He wasn't a teenager anymore and he had to maintain his dignity. This was a conversation among adults, and he was an adult.

"I'm not saying that *Avó* did that, Elvino." His father's voice was soothing compared to Biddy's. "We would never say anything bad about your grandmother. No one ever loved her more than your mother and your grandmother loved her back. What Candido and Paulinho did, though; that's another matter."

"What they did? What did they do?"

Biddy hadn't noticed that her intrusion was not welcomed by her boyfriend's son, so she interjected again.

"Your father doesn't know exactly what they did, but it's clear that your mother's share of your grandmother's estate should be worth at least four hundred thousand dollars, maybe more. You should have gotten fifty or sixty thousand, not just ten."

He still didn't like Biddy, but now she had captured his attention.

"Are you *sure*?"

"No one is sure about anything, son, but it would be only fair to your mother's memory to find out. And it would be fair to you, too, and your brothers and sisters."

"I guess, Dad. But I don't know what to do."

Elvino could not believe how rapidly he had crashed from the pinnacle of his happiness. Everything had gone horribly wrong in an instant.

"Biddy has been working on some papers. She's a lawyer and she knows what to do. We can ask the court to check whether the will really reflects your *avó*'s intentions and if your mother's share was determined fairly."

"Papers?"

"Yes, I've already drafted them," said Biddy. "We just need you to sign your name and that will let me go to the court and ask them to find out more information. Certainly no one could object to that."

"Yeah, that sounds reasonable, I guess. Probably."

A door slammed behind him. Someone was coming in from the outside. Randy burst into the kitchen and skidded to a stop upon seeing the static tableau in front of him.

"You have mail," said Louis, nodding toward the kitchen table.

Randy pounced on his letter and tore it open. He glanced at the fancy stationery and then noticed what was attached to it.

"*Shit!*"

"Calm down," said Elvino. "Now we get to talk about it."

DECEMBER 1949

Paulinho's House

The house was nearly ready. The front yard was nothing but dirt, but it was already cleared of most of the construction debris. Paulinho had planted a small evergreen tree that he intended to use as a local landmark when it grew larger. "The house with the fig tree" was his father's. His would be "the house with the evergreen."

At this hour of the morning the little tree was rimed with frost. The dirt of the front yard crunched as Paulinho walked across it. He still lived next door at his parents' house, but soon he and Carmina would be married and this would be their home.

The sound of a pickup truck approached. It was coming from the direction of Candido's home, which Paulinho could see from where he stood because the crops in the intervening field were not too high at this time of year. It was indeed Candido's pickup, which swung into Paulinho's driveway. To his dismay, his brother was carrying a small bundle when he climbed out of his vehicle.

"It's looking good," said Candido, nodding toward the house.

"Thanks," Paulinho said to his brother.

Candido was awkwardly adjusting his small bundle, which started to make protesting noises.

"Candy, what are you doing carrying Junior around again?"

Candido paused before answering.

"Odile has one of her sick headaches this morning. The boy can't stay with her."

"Maybe you should take him to Mom's," suggested Paulinho. "He's just — what? Has it been three months yet? You can't tote an infant all over the farm."

"Yeah, three. I might do that. But Junior likes tractors. They put him to sleep. I can hold him on my lap while I run the harrow over the cotton field and he'll take a nap. Then I'll stop by Mom's."

The cotton fields were bereft of cotton, having been harvested and plowed under. But Candido was going to drag the harrow behind a tractor to break up the clods and rake the surface.

"I hope Odile feels better soon."

"Me, too. You don't know how it is when she gets those headaches."

Actually, Paulinho did know. Twice he had pulled up outside his brother's home in the months since Junior's birth and heard the screaming and the smashing. Odile was having less a post-partum depression than a post-partum mania. Both times Paulinho had waited long enough for things to settle down before knocking on the door and pretending he hadn't heard anything.

Candido decided to change the subject.

"You know, I'm glad you're building next to the dairy yard. When something goes wrong at night, the milkers will be knocking on your door instead of mine!"

Since his brother seemed to think he had said something clever, Paulinho indulged him with a chuckle.

"That's right. You're safe and secure a mile away in your home on the far edge of the property. Clever of you. And that makes it cozy for you and Odile."

The barb sunk home. It reminded Candido that home was anything but cozy when he had to keep his son away from his wife.

"Of course," continued Paulinho, "Carmina and I will probably have it easier when we want Mom to babysit the children, depending on how many we have."

Candido played along by giving his brother a manly smile.

"That's a good idea, too. You know, before I do the harrowing I should go see Mom and Dad. Junior is fussy and maybe he needs his bottle. I don't know how much Odile fed him this morning."

Candido decided he was saying too much and fell silent.

"Yes," agreed Paulinho. "Mom will be able to tell."

NOVEMBER 1975

Junior Needs a Raise

The arc welder in the dairy farm's workshop was one of Candido's favorite toys. He vaguely remembered something his sister Fatima had once told him about the Greek god of the forge, although the name Hephaistos had long since slipped his mind. The details, however, didn't matter. It was enough to imagine himself as a godlike figure with the power to burn and bind metal.

Candido finished welding the seam on the broken hitch of the hay rake, flipped up the nearly opaque visor on his welding helmet, and peered out through its rectangular opening to examine the results. He saw that it was good.

He also saw that Junior had entered the workshop. His eldest son had an anxious expression on his face. Candido figured they might as well get it over with.

"Hi, Junior. What's up?"

Junior walked up to his father's work area.

"I need to talk to you about something," he said.

"About what, exactly?"

Junior dragged over a wooden crate and sat on it, facing his father. He leaned forward with his hands clasped earnestly. It was uncomfortably close to a begging posture.

"Sofia is pregnant again. I talked it over with her and there's no way we can make the budget work. It's all we can do to take care of the one that we already have. I need a raise, Dad. I need more to take care of my wife and your grandchildren."

Candido was glad that Junior's characteristically bad timing had caused him to approach his father while Candido's face was hidden behind a welding mask. He didn't want his son to see the calculating look on his face.

"You know, son, this is not a good time."

"I'm just telling you what I need, Dad."

"We don't have the cash. It cost us a lot of money to buy out your uncle. We still owe Paulinho three more years of payments. Things are tight, boy."

"Can't you do *anything?*" pleaded Junior.

"You *do* know, don't you, that you and your brother draw the exact same salary as me? The exact same. You and Jojo are getting the same salary as *me*, the head of the family. Do you think it's reasonable to expect *more?*"

"No, Dad. No, I don't. But Sofia and I are still in a bind. The kid and all, you know."

"Listen: I'll talk to your mother. If we can't raise your salary, maybe we can do something else. Maybe help you with household expenses. Maybe we can do that."

"That would ... *help*," said Junior.

"Okay, it's a deal." Candido flipped down the welding visor and concealed his eyes from his son. "Your mother or I will talk to you real soon and let you know what we can maybe do about your housing allowance."

"Thanks, Dad. And thank Mom, too."

"Don't mention it. You're welcome. I just wish we could do more."

"Yeah, me too."

Candido fired up the welder and did a little unnecessary touch-up on his repair job until he was certain his son had left the shop.

At noon, he stopped at home for lunch. Miracle of miracles, Odile was there. As he helped himself to some leftovers that Ferdie had stashed in the refrigerator, Candido summarized his conversation with their son.

"What do you want me to do about it, Candy?"

Candido sat down at the table, popped a beer and started to eat.

"Not a lot," he said, around a mouthful of ham and cheese. "You need to give him more groceries, I think. Something on a pretty regular basis. Something to keep him and Sofia happy."

"If we give Junior more then you know that Jojo will ask for more, too."

"Yeah, if he hears about it, I'm sure. Anyway, I told Junior that he gets the same salary as me. That cooled him down a bit."

"But that's true, right? I think it is the same."

Candido took a long pull at his beer and smacked his lips.

"Of course it's true. Exactly the same. But I didn't tell him it's also exactly the same amount that *you* get."

"What?"

Candido rolled his eyes, but fortunately Odile was not looking right at him at the moment.

"*Your* salary, honey. When we deposit those two checks each month, one is made out to *you* and the other is made out to *me*. You earn as much as me."

"Oh, I see, I think. Yes. But the amount on the check is exactly the same as Junior's."

"Yes, and we have *two* of those."

"Oh. Okay. I remember now, but I never worry too much about it. That's your job, right?"

Yeah, thought Candido darkly, *you never worry about how much money there is. You just spend it.*

"Right," he said aloud. "So you and I and Junior and Jojo all get the exact same amount. And Ferdie gets half-pay because he still lives at home with us."

"Ferdie gets only half?"

Candido was sorry he had mentioned it.

"Right, because he gets room and board with us."

"Maybe Ferdie should get *more*, don't you think?"

"No, I don't think. Anyway, we were talking about Junior. Let's get him some groceries on the business's supermarket account. Charging expenses to the business is a perk for the boss, but we can toss a little of that in Junior's direction. It'll keep him happy and it won't cost that much. At least, not as long as we do it instead of letting him charge things directly. Like I said, that's a boss perk."

"Whatever you think is best, Candy."

Paulinho Takes Electronics

"Mr. Francisco, got a sec?"

"Sure thing, Mr. Harper."

"I want to talk to you a bit."

"Okay."

George Harper waved at the chair next to his desk. It was break time at the night school and it would be ten minutes before the students returned to the classroom. Paulinho settled down in the chair and looked expectantly at his teacher.

"This stuff isn't entirely new to you, is it, Mr. Francisco?"

"No, not entirely."

"So where did you pick it up?"

"Heath Kit," replied Paulinho. "I built a pair of CB radios that my wife and I use to stay in touch when I'm in the field. I really enjoyed putting it together and went on to other projects, too. The electronic organ in our living room is from a Heath Kit."

"Well, you have a knack for it, but there's more to it than that. The kits are great, and I've built a couple myself, but they're paint-by-numbers. Anyone who can follow directions can do it, as long as they're careful and don't skip steps. Good practical experience in wiring and soldering, but it doesn't explain *why* you're doing things."

"That's why I'm in this class."

"And I'm glad you are. Mr. Francisco, you have the potential to go well beyond an introductory electronics course in night school."

"Thanks, Mr. Harper, but I don't know about that. I really started taking classes to prepare for the GED. But this class is just for fun. You don't need a circuits class to pass your high-school equivalency."

"You're not going to have any trouble passing the GED. But I don't want you to think you're just goofing off or merely taking this class for fun. If you take intermediate electronics in the spring semester, I think it'll open up some real possibilities for you."

"I'm a dairyman. This class really is for fun. It doesn't fit into any long-range plans for me."

"Okay, then. You know your mind better than anyone else. But if you sign up for my next class, maybe it'll be more than just fun."

"I might do that. And you never know. We might be getting more electronic in the dairy business and it could be good that I'm learning this stuff. I'll have to think about that."

"Okay. Well, that's what I wanted to talk about. Don't forget what I said. You have real potential, Mr. Francisco."

"Thanks, Mr. Harper. Thanks very much. I really appreciate hearing that."

MAY 1960

Junior Tells on Jojo

Junior had deigned to join the shade-lovers who were sitting in St. Bart's sand box. The heat wave had sapped even Jojo's endurance, bringing him in from the sun to play with Paul and Luis. Junior hunkered down next to the tree and sat with his back against the trunk.

"Piss be to you," he said.

"That's not funny anymore," said Paul.

Monsignor had launched a campaign to encourage overt religiosity at St. Bart's Catholic School. He particularly liked it when students addressed each other with such pious ejaculations as "Peace be to you." Junior had promptly created his own version. Paul had looked up "ejaculation" in his father's big dictionary and promptly added it to the list of words he knew but wouldn't say.

Jojo had been alternately building and demolishing sand mountains. He scowled at his brother's crude greeting and returned fire.

"Hey, Junior, did you know today is named after you?"

"What?"

"Yeah! It's *Turd's Day!*"

The laughter was muted, because no one wanted to provoke Junior. He was large for a fifth grader and perfectly willing to use his fists if he didn't see Monsignor or the teachers nearby.

Junior shrugged contemptuously, as though Jojo's joke had been beneath notice. It was too hot to go over and slug his brother because that would be sure to turn into a lengthy brawl. Jojo was physically strong and could hold his own with his older brother. Junior didn't relish the prospect of an equally matched fight that would leave both of them sweaty, bloody, and probably on Monsignor's discipline list. He opted for psychological warfare instead.

"Hey, you guys know that Manny is graduating from high school soon?"

None of the Salazar boys were attending St. Bart's. The older boys were beyond elementary school and Fatima was willing to do almost anything for Monsignor except consign her younger boys to an understaffed school.

"Yeah, so what?" rejoined Paul. "Tony graduated last year already."

"I'll tell you what," said Junior. "I've been talking to Tony and Manny about high school. I was there when they were warning Otelo about it."

Despite himself, Jojo was intrigued.

"Warning him about high school? What's so scary about high school? How is it different from St. Bart's?"

Junior smiled. His brother had taken the bait.

"High school is *very* different," declared Junior. "When they have recess time like this" — he gestured with one arm at the playground — "they have to wear special outfits, including shorts."

Some of the boys nodded their heads. They had noticed this when driving past the high school during P.E. periods. The Francisco boys never wore shorts except for things like trips to the beach. You'd get your legs all scratched up if you wore them around haystacks or working on the dairy farm. It was bad enough that Monsignor made all the boys at St. Bart's wear white shirts and salt-and-pepper corduroys as the school uniform (especially on a day like today!), but being told what to wear during a recess period seemed like the worst sort of tyranny.

"And afterwards," continued Junior, "they all have to get naked."

"*Naked?*"

"Yeah, naked. The teachers make them all strip in this big room and then they pour water over them."

"That's just the shower room in the school gym," objected Luis. "My brother Chico told me about it. That's just to get cleaned up after exercising. It's no big deal!"

Not everyone shared Luis's nonchalance. Paul was shocked at the very idea of being naked in front of strangers. Jojo seemed to think it was amusing.

Junior was basking in the rapt attention of the younger students. He relished the sense of authority, just as he enjoyed being the eldest in his family.

"That's right," he said, though he didn't call Luis by name because he couldn't remember it. "It's a shower room, but it's still true that you have to get naked and everyone sees you naked. Tony and Manny says it happens every day. Of course, some of us have an advantage."

His listeners' sense of horror was now piqued with curiosity.

"What kind of advantage do you mean?" asked a third-grader named Lloyd.

Junior smiled.

"I mean, the boys with chewed-off dicks can't make fun of the boys who *don't* have chewed-off dicks!"

Jojo's face turned bright crimson, but he escaped notice for the moment because all eyes were on his brother.

"What on earth are you talking about?" demanded Paul.

"I mean — and Tony and Manny will back me up on this — I mean that some of the boys are missing the end of their dicks."

In a group of Portuguese and Mexican boys, the concept was bizarre in the extreme.

"You are shitting us," declared Lloyd.

"No. I swear. You need to pay more attention in religion class."

Paul frowned at his cousin's smug expression. It was unconscionable that his cousin should claim superiority on a point of academics.

"That doesn't make *any* sense!" he said.

Junior was supremely happy as he regarded his classmates with an air of magisterial disdain.

"I'm surprised at you, Paul. Don't you remember your Holy Days of Obligation?"

"Sure I do! What about them?"

Junior suddenly realized he was on uncertain ground. He knew which holy day he meant, but he was afraid he would mispronounce it and he couldn't remember exactly when it was. Fortunately, he could take advantage of Paul's eagerness to play Mr. Know-It-All.

"Can you name them?"

"Of course! There's Christmas and the Assumption and Ascension Thursday and All Saints' Day and Immaculate Conception and Circumcision!"

"Bingo!" said Junior. "And when is Circumcision?"

"On January 1. That's why we're obligated to go to Mass on New Year's Day."

"And why do we have that holy day?"

"To start the New Year?" suggested Luis.

Paul's mind was working frantically. He felt that Junior was showing him up and he didn't like it. His cousin's remarks about holy days had reminded him of what he had discovered when he looked up "circumcision" in the big dictionary, but all it had said was something unmemorable about a "Jewish rite" for baby boys.

"No," said Paul. "It's about taking Jesus to the temple when he was a baby boy."

"That's right," agreed Junior. "And that's when the Jews chewed off the end of his dick."

Bedlam erupted as students bombarded Junior with questions and exclamations. He waved his hands for silence.

"That's what 'circumcision' is, guys. They chew the end of your dick off. They *bite* it off."

Loud groans from the audience.

"Your brother is shitting us," said Lloyd to Jojo, noticing for the first time that Junior's kid brother was hunched up and looking miserable.

"Paul, do you know the official name of the holy day?"

Paul hated to be dancing to his cousin's tune, but he had to give the answer.

"It's called the 'Feast of the Circumcision,'" he said.

"Yeah! See? 'Feast.' They took Jesus to the temple and the Jews ate the end of his dick. Jesus didn't like having his dick shortened, which is why he replaced the Jewish religion with Christianity and made his friend Peter the first pope. That's all in history, guys!"

Junior waited for the general babble to die down before continuing.

"So when you go to high school, just remember that Jesus doesn't like chewed-off dicks and that gives you an advantage when you have to go naked."

"Wait a minute," said Luis. "Something doesn't make sense. Do we know any Jews around here? Why do boys have shortened dicks in high school if they're not Jews?"

"That's the sneaky part," said Junior. "My dad told me it's probably because of when the Jews took over the government with Roosevelt."

"Roosevelt wasn't a Jew!" exclaimed Paul. He knew that FDR had been an Episcopalian because he had looked up the presidents' religions when someone said that Senator Kennedy couldn't be president because he was a Catholic.

"He didn't have to be," continued Junior, channeling his father's prejudices and conspiracy theories with some additional garbling of his own. "The people around him were, because of the bankers and stuff. And lots of doctors are Jews, so they think boys should have their dicks chewed off."

"That's just crazy!" cried Paul. "Jewish doctors aren't waiting around for a chance to bite the dicks off baby boys!"

"I didn't say they were using their teeth," replied Junior serenely. "They use knives now." He smiled at his brother. "*Isn't that right, Jojo?*"

"*It wasn't my fault!*" screamed Jojo. "*It was an accident!*"

"I'm pretty sure they used a knife, though. Right?"

"I don't know! I don't know!"

Jojo had drawn himself up with his knees to his chin and his arms clasped tightly around his legs. He was rocking back and forth in misery, tears streaming down his face and his nose running.

Paul knew exactly what Junior was talking about. He was both appalled by Junior's cruelty and frightened by his unexpectedly clever ploy.

"It's not fair, Junior! It *was* an accident!"

Heads swiveled toward Paul.

"Jojo ran his bike into a barbed-wire fence. It was an *accident*. He didn't mean to hurt himself."

"That may be true," said Junior, "but that's when Jojo became Jewish!"

"*That's a lie!*" screamed Jojo at the top of his lungs. "*Liar! Liar! Liar!*"

Junior sat back against the tree trunk in sublime satisfaction. At that moment they heard Mrs. Knox ringing the end-of-recess bell, but it was far too late for anyone to be saved by it.

Paul Gets a Calculus Book

Paul Francisco unlocked the car and climbed in on the passenger side, carrying his bag of bookstore purchases. His first week of college was fast approaching. He had ventured onto the junior college campus to get his books in advance. The bookstore bag contained four impressive texts, which Paul spread out on the car's front seat: Pauling's chemistry, Halliday & Resnick's physics, Bailey's U.S. history, and Thomas's calculus. And a pair of Hostess cupcakes, impulse-purchased right at the bookstore's checkout counter.

The calculus book was the focus of Paul's attention. He had paid the princely sum of $12.50 for it, so he knew it was a particularly valuable text. Paul opened it up and began to browse. It was a garden of delights.

It might also be his ticket out of Tulare County. Paul was happy enough to attend the community college in his hometown for now, but he was steeling himself to be the first member of the Francisco family to leave the dairy farm behind. If things worked out, he was two years from "going away" to a full-fledged college or university.

Paul carefully unwrapped a cupcake and began munching on it as he looked at his calculus book. He paged through until he found the introduction to the derivative. There it was! The limit definition of derivatives, exactly as he had learned it from the Aleksandrov books. The Russian mathematician and his coauthors had written a three-volume tome titled *Mathematics: Its Content, Methods, and Meaning*. An English translation had been offered as a membership premium by the Library of Science book club, which had prompted Paul to join.

Paul strongly suspected that he had been the only student at the high school with his own set of the Aleksandrov books.

He had pored over the contents of volume one and found relief from a fear that had haunted him since intermediate algebra in his junior year of high school. When asked what calculus was all about, the algebra teacher had helpfully explained that calculus was the branch of mathematics that used pretense to solve problems. Short segments of curves were treated as if they were segments of straight lines. Thin strips of curved areas were treated as if they were simple slices of a rectangle. Paul listened in horror as it seemed that the future of mathematics lay awash with approximations. Farewell to exactitude!

Aleksandrov was tough going, but it was clear that the Russian authors weren't trifling about with approximations. Calculus was an *exact* mathematical tool. Now Paul had an American text specifically designed to teach calculus to college freshmen.

What could be more wonderful?

DECEMBER 1977

Chico's Final Vision

Until the stroke reduced him to an invalid, Chico had run the dairy as its benevolent despot. But he contented himself with making all the *big* decisions. His boys were welcome to use their own judgment in implementing their father's directives. Chico was training his sons to succeed him, but he didn't ruminate about it — he wasn't even that conscious about it — till he reached middle age. That was when he realized something was going wrong.

Whenever Chico issued orders that he had issued before, Candido would spring into action and replicate all the steps he had performed on the previous occasion. If, however, the orders were new, Candido would hem and haw until Chico gave him precise instructions. As a man who was always thinking how to turn circumstances to his advantage, Chico was increasingly unhappy with his elder son. Candido was a robot. Chico wanted a son, but he had an automaton.

Paulinho and Candido had been born in the wrong order, but there was no way to repair God's mistake. Chico's younger boy was someone he understood because he was an improved version of his father. Paulinho was always thinking, always strategizing, always dreaming of better things. Yet Paulinho had to trail along in his brother's wake, walk in his brother's shadow, wait for his brother to make the first move.

Chico had seen Paulinho chafing under the burden of his older brother's plodding ways, but Chico could never figure out a way to resolve things — nothing short of breaking the business in two and giving each boy his own theater of operations. It had been the solution adopted by many despots throughout history. Too many sons? Then why not give each a slice of your kingdom?

But Chico couldn't bring himself to do it. He was still pondering the dilemma of his two sons when he woke up one morning and could not get himself out of bed. That had been the beginning of his living death, trapped in a body whose left half was completely inert. Chico's existence devolved into a completely predictable series of laps around a very circumscribed track. Only he couldn't run the track himself.

One of his sons or grandsons would come by each morning to carry him from the bedroom to the living room. One of them would come by each evening to carry him back to bed. Teresa would fuss over him all day, shifting him and fluffing his pillows and preventing him from developing bed sores. She would point out activities going on outside the window by his chair, but he wasn't interested in activities in which he couldn't participate. One might as well be watching TV. So he did. He watched TV, he ate his meals, he dozed in his chair, and then he had a restless night in bed.

The visits of the physical therapist tapered off to nothing, and that was a relief. The earnest young man had been a nuisance. Chico watched TV and occasionally put up with the well-intentioned visit of a grandchild or great-grandchild. His memory began to dissolve backward, as he stopped recognizing the most recent additions to the family. The days added up and collected into years.

Today was a peculiar day. Chico was agitated. Things felt odd.

He was too restive to doze and the television could not hold his attention.

He mashed the button on the remote control with his good hand and turned it off.

"*Terezinha!*"

His wife was trying to clean house. She heard her name and appeared in the doorway.

"What do you want, Chico?"

He pondered for a few seconds.

"*Nada.*"

She regarded him solemnly for a long moment, and then went back to work.

Chico didn't know what he wanted. His need was indefinable, a vague tic that was distracting him today.

"*Terezinha!*"

His wife reappeared.

"Did you remember what you wanted, Chico? What do you need?"

He sat silent for several beats, then found his voice again.

"*Nada.*"

Teresa tried to resume her household chores. Not even five minutes passed before Chico paged her again.

"*Terezinha!*"

His long-suffering wife was in the doorway, trying not to wring the hands that she had clasped together.

"*Estou aqui,*" she said. *I'm here.* "What is it this time?"

"*Nada.*"

"*Credo!*" muttered Teresa under her breath. *Can you believe it?*

She gave up on the housework and crossed the living room to her over-stuffed chair. She would sit in her chair where Chico could see her and she would write a letter to her niece in Brazil. Perhaps her presence would be enough to calm her husband. Sometimes it was.

Chico sat slumped in his chair. If he sagged a bit further, his wife would come over and tug him into a more upright position. Sometimes he would deliberately lean as far as he could over the arm of the recliner. That was always good for a full minute or two of tugging and prodding as Teresa wrestled him back into position, muttering quietly under her breath. Little moments like that broke up the long, long hours of the day.

But Chico was not trying to play games today. He wanted something, but didn't know what. It was like an itch in his imperfectly functioning brain, but he had no way to scratch it.

He wondered why Fatima never visited anymore. She had always been a responsible and loving daughter who never neglected her parents and had presented them with a large brood of Salazar grandchildren. Chico had become accustomed to her regular Sunday afternoon visits, but yesterday had been Sunday and she had not appeared. Or had Sunday been the day *before* yesterday? He wasn't sure about what day it was, but he was certain that Fatima had not visited.

Perhaps she was sick again. Fatima had often been sick in recent years. One day he had asked Teresa why their daughter no longer came over, but she had not given him a straight answer. Chico had been persistent that day and finally asked if Fatima was feeling bad.

Teresa had surprised him with a quick answer.

"No, no, Fatima is not feeling bad."

But she turned her head away quickly as she spoke the words, and Chico knew something was wrong.

Of course you know something's wrong! But they don't know that you know things!

That was the little voice in his head. It came and went. Sometimes he knew who the voice belonged to, putting things together in his damaged head while drifting back and forth across the boundary between sleeping and waking.

The voice was his. It was the voice of his old self — which was to say a much younger and healthier self. It was peculiar to drift through a fog while his old self whispered or shouted in his mind's ear.

They're not telling you things, but you can tell they're not telling!

Sometimes he managed to think how nice it would be if his old self started speaking aloud through his mouth, investing himself once again with the conversational coherence and vigor of his middle years, but the voice did not cooperate. It spoke in brief spurts and devoted itself to mildly paranoid statements. If it couldn't do any better than that, he wasn't going to encourage it to speak aloud.

Besides, Teresa wouldn't like it. He was pretty certain of that.

If only Fatima would come and visit him again. Her presence was always such a comfort and eased the burden on her mother. Chico was always on his best behavior when Fatima visited. She would sit in that couch over there, smile comfortably at him and speak intelligently in her sweet voice about things that he didn't understand. That hardly mattered, as long as he heard those things in her sweet voice, a voice so like her mother's.

Chico trembled with an almost subliminal spasm and blinked his eyes. His daughter Fatima was sitting in her usual place on the couch, clear as day. A lop-sided grin stretched his face as he gazed at her.

She's here! How good to see her!

A small, inarticulate moan escaped his lips. Teresa looked up sharply and watched her husband for a while. She was relieved to see he didn't appear to be in distress. He was looking at the couch and smiling. Teresa bent her head down toward the letter to her niece and resumed writing.

Chico noticed that it was getting difficult to focus on Fatima's face, which had been so clear at first. She was smiling at him. He could tell that, but his vision was blurred and dark around the periphery. His daughter's face was a spot of pale light amidst darkness. Chico blinked several times to clear his vision. The blurriness was still there.

It didn't matter. Fatima was so lovely. He felt another tiny shudder.

Oh, she looks so much like her mother!

Chico stared as hard as he could.

Wait! It is her mother! That's Teresa!

Without his realizing it, Chico's head had lolled a bit to one side, moving the focus of his vision from the couch where he had imagined his daughter to the chair where his wife sat in reality. He was staring at the timeworn and careworn but still beautiful visage of his dear wife. His vision continued to contract. Teresa's face was the only tiny spot of light in the rising tide of an ocean of dark. The point of light seemed to be shrinking or fading, but a sense of profound peace was creeping over Chico. The agitation he had been feeling all day was evaporating.

By slow degrees, Chico Francisco grew calmer.

And then, cooler.

PART V

Expert Testimony

Harold Widener has his hands on the railing separating the respondents' table from the gallery. He leaned forward as he addressed the Francisco family members who had assembled for that morning's court session.

"As I was saying earlier today, this is jackpot day," he gave a nod toward Paul. "And the day is just beginning. Ryan has our expert witness ready to go, Dennis has been up to a little bit of investigative work himself, and I — well, I get on Biddy's nerves. We are the perfect team. Lean back and relax, but fasten your safety belts just in case. There will be bumps in the ride!"

The door to the jury room opened and the bailiff herded in the people who would decide the outcome of the case. They had been schooled to avoid any sign of favoritism toward either party in the lawsuit, and so far they had been carefully neutral in their facial expressions.

The attorneys took their places, the temporary alliance of three lawyers back at the respondents' table and the single lawyer seated at the petitioners'. The bailiff called for everyone to rise as Judge Brevard Knight entered the courtroom and told them to be seated once the judge himself had sat down.

Judge Knight got off to a brisk start.

"Mr. Bowman, am I to understand that you have an expert witness ready to testify on behalf of the respondents?"

"We do, your honor."

"Very well, you may proceed."

"Thank you, your honor. The respondents call James Franklin Foster."

James Foster was sworn in and took his seat in the witness stand.

"Mr. Foster, would you please state your full name and your occupation."

"My name is James Franklin Foster and I am a retired postal inspector. I still work, however, as an expert witness in handwriting forensics."

"Thank you, Mr. Foster. Would you outline your professional activities for us, please?"

"Of course. I belong to all of the usual professional organizations for a handwriting forensics expert, such as the National Society of Questioned Document Examiners and the American Association of Handwriting Analysts. I am the chair of the Standards and Practices Board of the National Society and I am past regional vice president of the American Association's western states division. I am also an adjunct professor of criminology for various campuses of the California State University."

"Thank you," said Bowman. He repositioned himself before continuing, partly to be facing the jury, but mainly to put Biddy Onan in his field of vision. The expression on her face was satisfyingly sour.

"Mr. Foster, would you please tell the jury of the impression you formed of the qualifications of Ms. L. Margaret Hunter to be an expert in handwriting forensics?"

"Her qualifications do not exist, Mr. Bowman. She meets none of the criteria that would characterize a competent handwriting examiner. The evidence of her supposed expertise, as provided to this court, demonstrates neither academic nor professional training in the field. She is not an expert."

"What about her position with West Coast Forensics?"

"West Coast Forensics is the operation of a Mr. George Gaffney, who is carried on the rolls of the American Association of Handwriting Analysts as a member in good standing. Ms. Hunter has described herself in court papers as being his apprentice. If she aspires to be what Mr. Gaffney is, I believe that several years of diligent practice and study might bring her to the point of qualification. As of today, she is not qualified."

"Thank you, Mr. Foster."

Bowman had had enough of watching Onan droop at her table. He turned back toward his expert witness.

"Mr. Foster, did you have an opportunity to examine the will of Teresa Francisco in detail?"

"Yes, I did."

Widener and Ramos look at each other in surprise. Onan hadn't jumped to her feet to insist on it being the "alleged" will of Teresa Francisco. Was she holding her fire till later, or had they broken her?

"Did you arrive at a conclusion, Mr. Foster?"

"Yes, I did."

"And what was that conclusion, Mr. Foster?"

Now Widener and Ramos were truly astonished. Wasn't Onan going to object to the lack of a foundation? It had been deliberately provocative of Bowman to ask for Foster's conclusion before introducing the basis for that conclusion. But Onan didn't budge from her seat.

"I concluded that the signature on the will was that of Teresa Francisco and that there is no reasonable doubt about it."

Widener and Ramos had their heads close together.

"You know, I'm *almost* disappointed," whispered Widener.

"A win is a win, Hare," whispered Ramos back. "But we do miss out on some of the fun. *I* almost feel bad about what's coming down today."

"Oh, *I* don't, Dennis. I can hardly wait."

Since Onan hadn't demanded that he establish the basis for his witness's conclusion, Bowman now proceeded to back-fill. He felt the eyes of the judge on him and figured that Knight knew what he was going to do.

"Mr. Foster, let us please review the process that brought you to your expert conclusion. Would you please tell the court how you became acquainted with the characteristics of Teresa Francisco's signature?"

"Certainly, Mr. Bowman. If the clerk would please turn on the slide projector on the evidence table, I will be glad to explain."

"The clerk will do so," said Judge Knight.

The projector's light flashed against the wall of the courtroom opposite the jury, giving the jurors a direct view. The wall was painted a matte white, dispensing with the need for a projection screen. The first slide appeared.

"This is the exhibit labeled P," said Foster. "It is Mrs. Francisco's most recent signature card from Bank of America. As you can see from the date, it was executed shortly after her husband's death in 1977. The exhibit is an excellent example of one of Mrs. Francisco's signatures on official documents and is therefore a good comparison for the challenged signature on the will. Next slide, please."

The clerk clicked the projector to the next slide, which filled the wall with a Warholesque display of repeated signatures.

"Exhibit Q — or, more accurately, Q1 through Q6 — contains the signatures excerpted from the last six resident alien registration forms signed by Mrs. Francisco. Aliens granted permanent resident status in the United States are required by law to file such a form every year. Again, these are signatures on official documents and are excellent comparison samples for a contested will. Furthermore, there is no doubt about their authenticity, given their internal consistency and consistency with her bank signature, which was signed in person. Next slide, please."

Knowing what was coming, and considering that the court clerk had his hands full, Bowman motioned to the bailiff and indicated the easel in a corner of the courtroom. The bailiff quickly fetched the easel and set it up between the witness stand and the jury box.

A single signature appeared emblazoned on the wall.

"This signature is excerpted from Exhibit R. It is a little different from the other samples, but I nevertheless deem it a good sample. It is taken from a personal letter that Teresa Francisco wrote to her grandson Paul Francisco in January 1980. In addition to the date on the letter itself, we have the canceled envelope, whose timestamp confirms the date. In addition, the letter is addressed to Paul Francisco at an address he occupied for only two years, between 1979 and 1981. This sample is as well established in time as any of the samples on legal documents. Furthermore — next slide, please — the signature comes in the context of a full-page letter."

The courtroom wall now displayed a blow-up of a handwritten letter, the previously displayed signature appearing at its bottom edge. Bowman pulled the cover sheet off the poster on the easel, revealing a duplicate of the letter. Several of the jurors focused on the nearby copy instead of looking at the projection on the wall.

"This is Exhibit R. To give you a sense of its proportions, the letter was written on personal letter paper that was six inches wide and nine inches long. The paper has lines, although Mrs. Francisco did not always pay too much attention to them. She signed the letter with her full name, which may seem strange in a letter written to a grandson, but the letter has a formal tone and the signature is in keeping with the overall content. I cannot over-stress the importance and significance of having a well-established sample with so much content and so firmly established in time. I point out that the letter is dated approximately one week after the signing of the will. This is an ideal sample."

Henry Francisco gave his brother Paul a hearty thump on the shoulder, congratulating him for having preserved their grandmother's letter. Mary Carmen winked. Other members of the family were smiling at Paul or giving him a discreet thumbs-up.

Paul noticed that Ms. Onan was staring in his direction. *Since I'm still alive,* thought Paul, *that means that she doesn't have laser beams in her eyeballs.*

He looked toward Harold Widener, who was twisted in his seat and looking back at him. Harold was silently mouthing a single word.

Jackpot!

DECEMBER 1971

Henry Sees the Future

Henry Francisco listened to the receding sound of his father's pickup truck as it departed toward town. Paulinho had received a phone call right after the family returned from Christmas morning Mass and had immediately bolted out the door. Still wearing the Sunday finery he had worn to church, Paulinho promised Carmina he would be back in plenty of time for the midday feast next door and departed.

Carmina looked slightly irritated as she headed toward the master bedroom to change into her everyday clothes. She would have preferred that her husband remain at home, but she knew that he was as good as his word and would not linger on his errand. Paulinho would be in his place at the adults' table in his mother's kitchen when it came time to gather at the home of Chico and Teresa. She needn't worry.

Henry, however, was worried. He rolled in his hands the Magic 8-Ball that had been one of his Christmas presents, a gag gift from his older brother.

"Outlook not so good," it said.

"Damned thing is probably right," muttered Henry to himself.

At sixteen years of age, Henry was wondering if his future was unraveling. Things he thought he could count on were turning out to be unreliable. His father, for example, was clearly pulling away from the family dairy farm. Paulinho had gone out on a Christmas Day service call, responding to a plea from a client for help setting up his new television. Such calls were occurring with increasing frequency as Paulinho helped out as a part-time technician at Challenge Electronics in town. Word was getting out that Paulinho Francisco was available when others were not. Even on Christmas.

What would happen to Henry's dreams and expectations of helping to run a family dairy farm if his father abandoned the business to his older brother Candido? Would Henry end up working as his Uncle Candy's hired hand? It wasn't an appealing prospect.

Everything had seemed so clear in the past. Henry thought his future was all around him on the dairy farm where he lived. His older brother would pose no obstacle or offer any competition. Henry and Paul were clearly on different trajectories. Although Paul looked a little anxious after returning from his first battery of final exams at Tech, Henry had no doubt that his brother would overcome any academic difficulties on his path away from Tulare County. By the same token, his older brother was giving him a clear path to the family farm, uninterested in eclipsing Henry with his seniority.

Henry couldn't help thinking of the parallel situation with his father and uncle, where it was similarly true that the younger brother had the greater devotion to farm life. By contrast, however, Uncle Candido had no viable alternatives to living and working on the family dairy farm. Candy was also completely willing to use his position as elder son to relegate Paulinho to a lesser role. Chafing at his situation, Henry's father had found another outlet for his talents.

Mary Carmen interrupted her younger brother's reverie by walking into the room with sixteen-month-old Alex on her hip. The toddler was giddy with the excitement of his first real Christmas. Mary Carmen lowered her baby brother to the floor.

"Go on, Alex. Go show Hanky what you have," she said.

Alex walked with a toddler's waddling gait over to his brother, something clutched in his fist. He leaned against the sofa where Henry was sitting, patted his brother's leg with his open hand, and waved his fist at him.

"*Tack*-ter, Hanky! *Tack*-ter!"

Henry put out his hand and Alex dropped a small toy tractor into it.

"*Tack*-ter!" the toddler repeated.

"Yeah, Alex, that's a nice one. Very nice."

Henry's favorite toys as a child had been scale models of farm equipment. He wondered whether Alex would emulate him in retaining that interest as he grew up. Alex may have belatedly and unexpectedly supplanted Henry as the baby of the family, but he was hardly likely to take his brother's place as the most avid agriculturalist in their generation of the Francisco clan. Henry also wondered if the family dairy farm would still exist by the time Alex grew up. He no longer felt confident of that and the uncertainty gnawed at him.

Alex snatched the toy tractor back from his brother's hand and ran to their sister. She led him into the kitchen, where their mother was preparing some dishes to take to the feast at *Avó* and *Avô's* house next door.

Henry watched them go, then picked up the Magic 8-Ball again.

"Will I get to keep working on our dairy farm?" he asked it.

"Without a doubt," it said in the ball's circular window.

Henry felt unduly pleased. And a little silly, too.

"Will I get to run our dairy farm in the future?" he asked, rolling the ball in his hands and keeping his voice low so that no one in the kitchen would hear him. He held the ball still and watched for the answer to appear.

"Don't count on it," said the Magic 8-Ball.

"*Damn!*" muttered Henry under his breath.

He paused, thinking. Then he smiled and rolled the ball again.

"Will I get to run our dairy farm in the future?" he repeated.

"Reply hazy, try again," said the ball.

"Hmph!" said Henry.

"Will I get to run our dairy farm in the future?" he said, turning the ball a couple of times.

"Signs point to yes," said the ball.

Henry grinned.

"Okay. That's more like it," he said.

Sometimes it helped to make your own luck. He would try to remember that.

A Parting of the Ways

Paulinho was hanging up tools on the peg-board in the workshop when Candido came in.

"Where were you this morning?"

"Why do you want to know, Candy?"

"I could have used some help dehorning the heifers."

"What were your boys doing?"

"They were doing the irrigation."

"I seriously doubt that, Candy, because *I* was repairing the irrigation valves. Two of them were leaking in the west forty and I never saw any of your boys passing through there. The valves are fixed now, by the way."

"You could have told me, at least. How can I plan things if I don't know where you are?"

"The problem is that you *don't* plan things. If you had told me that you were going to dehorn heifers this morning, I would have been there to dehorn heifers. But you didn't tell me because you didn't know you were going to dehorn heifers until you got up this morning."

"That's not true! I decided yesterday that it was time to do it."

"So why didn't you tell me *yesterday*, huh?"

Candido was trying hard to work up a case of righteous anger, but Paulinho was making it difficult. He decided to settle for ordinary anger. It was simpler.

"All I know is that I don't like the way things are going!" he said.

"That makes two of us," retorted Paulinho.

That triggered Candido's temper very nicely.

"You know, I don't have to put up with this! I should quit! I *do* quit! I am walking away from this whole fucking mess!" he roared.

Paulinho declined to make it easy on his brother. Instead of yelling back, he asked a simple question in an even voice.

"And just where are you walking away to? Where do you think you'll go?"

Candido realized that the only image in his head involved his riding off in a cloud of dust in his pickup truck. Alone. It was a momentary fantasy image that didn't have a sequel. He could not imagine what the next step after that would be. His contingency plan didn't go beyond Step 1: *Leave.*

Paulinho watched his brother trying to come up with an answer. He was familiar with that blank facial expression. Paulinho decided to take the big, big step that he had been contemplating for months.

"Or *I* could go."

Candido snapped out of his reverie.

It was the solution to all their problems. Paulinho would go away and Candido would suffer no more of his disrespect and interference. It was ideal. Still, Candido wanted to even the score, if only just a little.

"Oh, yeah? But where would *you* go?"

Paulinho appeared to be unruffled by the question.

"I'll go to work in town. I could get a job at Challenge Electronics. I think Bob Challenger would be happy to have me. I've got the qualifications to be a service technician. Or maybe I could get a local franchise. The only place in town that does authorized repair service for RCA equipment is the K-Mart. Bob says that RCA would be happy to license an independent operator in the area. That would let me do sales, too."

Candido listened to Paulinho's musings with his mouth hanging open. Even he recognized that his brother was not engaging in idle chatter. Paulinho had clearly been thinking about these things for a while. He had already collected opinions from people about what was feasible. He was already halfway out the door.

Paulinho noticed the surprise on Candido's face.

"What? You didn't think I had an answer? I have an answer all right, Candy. My answer is all ready to go. And *I* am all ready to go!"

Candido felt as if he were on the verge of a panic attack. Paulinho really *could* go. They weren't just blowing off steam like on previous occasions. Now that it seemed on the brink of turning into reality, Candido realized he wasn't ready. But Paulinho was. And Paulinho wasn't finished.

"You can buy out my interest in the partnership if you do it with your boys," said Paulinho. "It's just a matter of your buying out my share of Paulo C. Francisco & Sons. The land and buildings are Dad's personal property, but the company holds the dairy's cows and its creamery contract. It won't be such a big-ticket item with the land out of the equation. Junior, Jojo, and

Ferdie could join the company by helping you finance it, supposing they've saved up some of their earnings from working on the dairy farm. Depending on what you can scratch up for financing, you could have me paid off in ten years. Maybe less. You'll become senior partner and your boys would be official junior partners, holding two-thirds among you and Dad having his original third."

It made sense. Candido could see it working. He wanted the land, of course, but there was no way he could afford it. Besides, he was presently working it as though it belonged to him anyway and he was enriched by its harvests. And it would eventually actually be in his name when it passed down to him as inheritance from his father. That thought nudged Candido in the stomach, which clenched in anxiety at a sudden fear.

"Okay. That could maybe work. We could get an appraiser out here and see the bank about financing. And I can ask the boys if they want in."

"Sure," agreed Paulinho. "Simoes & Bowman can draw up the agreement."

Candido nodded, then spoke in studied casualness: "We'll need some kind of clause in there about you giving up any claim on the estate, of course."

"Like hell."

"What do you mean, 'like hell'? It's only fair! If you walk away from the dairy farm then you can't just come walking back in when Mom and Dad die!"

"What our folks do with *their* property is *their* business. You live on the dairy farm and so do I. Mom and Dad own our homes. It's understood that we'll eventually inherit them. I'm not signing anything that takes away my home."

"Okay, okay. We could make an exception for that."

"Are you or are you not listening? I said that Mom and Dad get to decide what to do with their property. If they leave all the land to you, I'll be unhappy because I built up a lot of its value and it would seem unfair. But if they at least give me the house I worked for, I'll deal with it. And you will, too! I am selling you my interest in a business, not applying to be disinherited."

Candido was pondering how to make Paulinho's scenario about getting only his house come true. He'd have to think about it some more. Obviously, Paulinho would be going over the sales agreement with a microscope, so his best bet would be to influence their parents' will. That didn't really sound any easier, but at least it was a problem for later. Not *too* much later, now that their father was an invalid, but perhaps a decent interval after they got Paulinho bought out.

"Okay," said Candido. "I guess you're right. Maybe you're *always* right, huh?"

Paulinho heard the resentment in his brother's voice but decided to be gracious. He was still assimilating the thought that he was going to be free of any further business entanglements with Candido. His immediate happiness tempered his anxiety about trying to launch a new career in a completely unrelated field.

"I'm not *always* right, Candy, but this is certainly the right thing for us to do. It will be good for you and me and your boys. There's going to be a new Francisco & Sons in town, and it's going to be you and your boys."

Candido brightened at the thought of it. *He* would be *the* Francisco. *He* was the winner.

AUGUST 1973

Ferdie Buys a Round

"Hey, David. Saving this seat for anyone special?"

"Hi, Ferd. No, make yourself at home. I'm desperate enough for company that I'll let even you sit there."

"Flatterer!"

Ferdinando Francisco settled onto the bar stool and signaled the bartender to get him a long-necked bottle of beer like the one David was sipping.

"You seem in a particularly good mood. Any special reason?"

"Why, is a reason necessary? I'm young, beautiful, and rich. Why shouldn't I be cheerful?"

"And a chronic liar, too. Especially about the rich part."

"Thanks for not saying it's about the beautiful part."

Ferdinando's beer arrived.

"Here's looking at you, kid!" he said, and took a long pull. "Wow! That is *good* after a long, hot, dusty day's work."

David had been taking a swig from his own bottle when Ferdinando made his remark and he began to choke and cough. Ferdinando gave him a couple of hard thumps on the back.

"Hell and damnation, Ferd! You should warn me when you're going to say shit like that! A 'long day's work'? What's that? Something you read about in a book?"

"That is not fair at all. I work plenty hard! And I don't read books; I *keep* them. And *that*, my dear friend, is how I earn my fabulous wealth."

"Let me get this straight — if you'll excuse the expression. Your work as your father's errand boy is pulling in major *dinero*? Is that right? If so, then I need to find out if Daddy wants to hire another messenger boy."

"You go get your own Daddy and leave my father out of it. Besides, I am way more than a mere messenger boy. I am the dairy farm's financial manager."

David came to a stop with his beer bottle almost touching his lips.

"I absolutely swear that you are trying to kill me! If I had been drinking when you said that, I would be dead of asphyxiation right now. By what stretch of the imagination are you a financial manager?"

"Well, I can't really say 'accountant,' can I?"

"I should say not. You flunked accounting, kiddo!"

Ferdinando looked subdued for a moment. He took a sip from his beer.

"You remember wrong. I never got to accounting. I had to pass business math first. And I didn't."

David was turning his head and looking in all directions and peering into the darker corners of the bar. Ferdinando got an exasperated look on his face.

"David, what *are* you doing?"

"I'm looking for the hidden camera. Any second now Allen Funt is going to come over and tell me I'm on *Candid Camera*. Then I will tell him to start using more realistic situations if they want to fool anyone."

Ferdinando was piqued.

"Okay, listen. It's not that complicated. Dad got tired of paying a lot of money to accountants to tell us stuff we already knew. I mean, we have bank account statements to tell us how much money we have and checkbook registers to tell us how much we spent. It's not rocket science, even if accountants do a lot of extra stuff just for show."

"I'm sure it takes only half as long if you do 'entry' bookkeeping instead of 'double-entry' bookkeeping."

"Thanks. I'll laugh later. But I was telling you what Dad decided. I just keep all the bills and receipts in one place — that way we can find them at tax time — and I make deposits at the bank and write checks to pay the bills. I said it's simple and we're keeping it simple. And Dad says it keeps other people's noses out of our business."

"I'm not exactly following that part."

"Dad says our old accountant does the books for my grandparents and my Uncle Paulinho and my Aunt Fatima's family. If one accountant knows the business of everyone in the family, he could be the source of leaks."

"Yeah. And then you'd have to call in the plumbers. I don't think Nixon needs his anymore. Maybe you could hire them!"

"Geez, David. Give me a break. I'm trying to explain! Dad was going to go to another accountant and then he thought, 'Hey, let's save some money!' And that's when he decided we should do the job ourselves. Junior and Jojo spend all day bouncing their butts on tractor seats, so I was the obvious person for the job. I was already doing a lot of the bills and deposits anyway."

"I sure hope that you and your father are right about that. You could end up in trouble. What about a tax audit by the IRS? How about that?"

Ferdinando had on his face the smug smile of someone who had anticipated the question.

"That's an easy one! If the IRS audits you, *then* you hire a tax attorney or a CPA or something, but why waste money on them unless and until you have to? I keep telling you it's simple and you keep not believing me."

"No, no, Ferd. I believe you. I believe that your father gave you the job. I just hope that you stay steady in your recordkeeping in the long run. That sort of thing has never been your strong suit."

"You're forgetting my motivation. As long as I do this job well enough, I get to keep it and I get to keep being a high-earner."

"Really? You're getting a good salary for doing simple ledger work and not knowing any accounting?"

Ferdinando pursed his lips and rocked his head from side to side just a little while deciding how much to say.

"Look, we've been friends since high school."

"Yeah, ages and ages and ages. Whoops! Sorry! Only four years. Plus two years of JC. But I guess that's something. I knew you back when you were still chubby."

Ferdinando had become rather obsessive at fighting off his mother's genetic legacy of obesity. His dieting had been successful enough to quiet *Avô* Alberto Avila's boasts about Ferdinando taking after the maternal side of the family.

"Okay, but here's the point: if I don't explain things carefully enough, it'll sound bad. I'll have to trust you to understand it."

"I have no idea what you're talking about right now, so it sounds fascinating."

"It's all about being part of a *family* business. That's the thing. Our salaries are small. Not a living wage at all. But you get perks in a family business. The Francisco business owns houses, and family members don't pay rent to live in them. Why, even my Uncle Paulinho lives in a house like that, right on the dairy farm, and he's not in the family business anymore. Dad thinks he should pay rent, but my *avô* and *avó* won't hear of it."

"Your grandparents?"

"Yeah, my grandparents. They live in a house on the dairy farm, too. It's one of the perks. And then there are things like accounts at businesses — accounts that you can charge things to, if you get authorized to do that. I'm authorized at about all of them by now. Because I'm doing what Dad wants and doing a good job of it. Even Junior and Jojo don't have the access I do, and they used to be paid a lot more than me."

"And now they're not?"

"Well," began Ferdinando slowly, "*officially* they're still a lot more and it's on the books that way. But now I have a job as important as anything *they* do, so I should earn the same amount. I could ask Dad to raise my salary, but if I have the responsibility for the money and records, then I can sort of do it myself without bothering him about it. I mean, it's *my* job. I just charge things to reduce my expenses and bring me up to about the same level as my brothers. It's only fair, you see, so that's why I do it."

"Ferd, Ferd, Ferdie! Say, do you know the meaning of the word 'rationalization'?"

"Why are you asking me that? You know math isn't my thing."

"Never mind. But I have to warn you that people wouldn't like the sound of it. Especially not your brothers. They'd go apeshit."

"Yeah, probably. You're probably right. I mean, nothing I do affects their salaries at all, but they'd probably bitch. I'm just helping myself out to rise to their level. It's just *fair* is what it is. And they *owe* me!"

"How you figure?"

Ferdinando remained silent for a while as he pensively swirled the remaining beer in his bottle.

"It goes back a long way," he finally said. "*All* the way back. Did you know I'm a C-section birth?"

"I don't think you ever brought it up before. Is that significant?"

"Well, you know that I'm the baby of the family. There's a reason for that. When Mom got the Caesarian, she also got a complete hysterectomy."

"Okay, that explains why you're the baby of the family, but I'm still confused why you even brought it up."

"It's complicated, but the doctors talked Mom into the hysterectomy because she used to go nuts after every delivery. *Really* nuts. And Dad would have to keep us kids away from her until she settled down. Some women get post-partum depression, but Mom would get post-partum hysteria. I think it was something Dad told the doctors about and then the doctors told Mom she'd be much better off without her ovaries and without any more kids. After I was delivered, they gave her a radical hysterectomy."

"So, did it work?"

"Kind of. But she had a long period of bed rest and drugs after all that surgery. She was too weak to scream at Dad and throw things at him and yell at us kids that we had ruined her life. Maybe she just needed more tranquilizers and stuff in the first place."

"Maybe. I suppose."

"Mom was still in her twenties when I was born. She said the operation put her into menopause and she's been complaining about it and blaming me for it ever since. Twenty-one years of that shit and still counting."

"Damn! But I really don't think it works that way."

"Try telling *her* that. And how would *you* know? Anyway, the operation meant that Mom would never have a daughter, which pissed her off, but in a less spectacular way than before. She decided Dad had enough boys for working the farm and kept me at home as her trainee. I grew up as her maid."

"Ferd, if this is another 'my mother made me gay' story, I beg you to spare me."

That got a laugh out of Ferdinando, even if it was a rather weak one.

"Look, I don't know about all that. Okay? I just know that I grew up waiting on my mother hand and foot and doing cooking and cleaning and laundry and stuff from the time I was able to walk."

"I know you're a good cook, Ferd, but you never told me you'd been practicing your whole life."

"Yeah, they owe me back part of my life. Mom bossed me around and my father and brothers made fun of me. Especially my brothers."

He sipped some beer.

"Screw them anyway," he added mildly. "I'm doing okay now and Dad depends on me for important stuff. I'm worth every bit as much as they are to the business."

"'The laborer is worthy of his hire,'" said David.

"Don't quote stuff at me. I'd hang out with my cousin Paul if I wanted that kind of thing."

"It's just a Bible verse."

"Then even worse. I don't hang out with priests either."

He drained the rest of his beer.

"Anyway," said Ferdinando, "now you know what's going on and why it's my way of getting a little justice. Getting a little of my own back. Hell, they owe me a ton of back-wages for domestic services! I'm just collecting for some past-due bills."

"Okay, okay, Ferd. I get it. I see it, but — damn! — you really need to be careful. I just see trouble."

"You need to relax. Be calm like me. Let's get you another drink. In fact, I think I'd like to buy a round for the house. I've never done that before and I think it would be fun to treat everyone in the Buckaroo tonight to a drink on me."

"You're the moneybags."

"Cool. And after the drinks, I'll take you outside and show you my new car!"

Candido and the Accountant

"Mr. Francisco, I'm not a lawyer, but I really should caution you about making threats that open you up to charges of extortion."

"Why would it be extortion to put an embezzler behind bars?"

"That's not what I'm talking about, Mr. Francisco. You said to me that you threatened to put your son in jail. If you said that to your wife in hopes of getting more leverage in the divorce settlement, you are definitely opening yourself up to counter-charges. That's all I'm saying. Talk to your attorney before you talk to your wife again. Or to your son!"

"I will. Okay, I will. But you still haven't told me if I can charge my son with fraud or embezzlement or something."

"Very well, Mr. Francisco. My professional opinion as an accountant is very simple: *Who the hell knows?* The books and records you have brought me are exemplars of incomprehensibility. I defy anyone to say what was going on."

Candido sat in the chair next to the CPA's desk. He was kneading his large hands together in anxious movements. The accountant was looking at him over the top of the half-glasses that he had perched on his nose. The accountant's eyes were a watery blue, but their gaze was steady.

"But that's why I brought you this. I need an accountant to figure out what went where and who got what. My son was stealing the business blind and I need to do something about it. Tell me what you can do to find these things out for me."

The accountant sat back in his chair and steepled his fingers.

"Mr. Francisco, this firm has not provided accounting services for you or your family business since 1973. That's when you decided, for whatever reason, to do your own accounting and bookkeeping. Am I right?"

Candido nodded.

"And that's when you turned the books over to your youngest son. Is that correct?"

Candido nodded again.

"And this is the son who flunked business math at the community college."

It was a flat statement, but Candido took it as a question and nodded his head again.

"Incredible. Mr. Francisco, were we to attempt to reconstruct the family business accounts for the past ten or eleven years, we would need receipts, canceled check stubs, bank statements, bills of sale — literally every scrap of paper that recorded or implemented your financial transactions during the last decade. What you brought me falls rather short of that, doesn't it?"

Candido nodded. He anticipated a lot more nodding before this consultation was over.

"Most people believe that accountants hate shoeboxes. You know, when people bring in their records in a shoebox and say 'Here, do my taxes.' Well, I have news for you. We love shoeboxes. If people with shoeboxes really put all of their receipts and pay stubs and checkbook registers in them, we *love* shoeboxes. The key is completeness. We'll fish out the pieces of paper one by one, record the information, put it in order, and figure out what it means. And we'll charge you for the time it takes, of course, but it's *not* difficult. Give me a comprehensive shoebox and — if you'll excuse the expression — I am as happy as a pig in shit."

The accountant was looking down his nose at Candido and his glasses were slipping. He pushed them back up and continued.

"What you brought me today, however, that's just shit. You need a team of forensic accountants to comb Tulare County, looking under every rock and every cow pie for missing information. You'll want attorneys to subpoena bank records for accounts whose numbers are mysteriously stamped on the backs of canceled checks made out to companies you never heard of. And many checks were made out to 'Cash.' Good luck with *those*. And so many are simply missing. Your ledgers contain unreadable entries and random time gaps ranging from two months to four. What happened in those intervals? Who knows?"

Candido's long, sad face got longer and sadder as he listened to the accountant's litany.

"I don't think you could afford the bill, Mr. Francisco, for so many people working the amount of time it would take to untangle the mystery. And I don't see much hope that you could recover any amounts sufficient to put you in the plus column. Did you say there was also a bankruptcy?"

Candido finally spoke again.

"Yeah. At the end of '82."

"Perhaps you're better off considering that bankruptcy as a clean slate and just worry about what has happened *since* then. That is often the way people view a bankruptcy. May I ask what that was about?"

"When my mother died early in '82, we started getting hit with all kinds of bills we didn't have to pay before. We had to start paying rent to the estate for the land we were farming. And our inheritance was locked up in court, so we had new costs but no new income. Then my two older boys sued for their share. That was in '82 also. I had to file for bankruptcy to protect the assets I still had." Candido sighed. "You know divorce papers were filed then, too. By the time the estate was settled, which finally happened a couple of months ago, it was way too late to salvage much from my business."

"What was your business name, Mr. Francisco?"

"It was 'Francisco & Sons.'"

"I'm confused, sir. Wasn't that your father's business name? This firm provided him with accounting services for decades under that name."

"No, his business was 'Paulo C. Francisco & Sons.' Mine was 'Francisco & Sons.'"

The accountant shook his head in dismay.

"A terrible, terrible choice, Mr. Francisco. Whatever were you thinking? It's an open invitation for confusion. I can see people failing to make the distinction and cutting checks for one company when they mean to pay the other, acknowledging payments from one but crediting them to the other." He glanced down at the haphazard array of Francisco financial records on his desk. "I daresay we would find many examples of such confusion if we combed through this carefully enough. It invites fraud!"

Candido avoided looking the accountant in the eye as he concurred.

"Yeah, I should have thought of that," he said, as innocently as he could.

"Look, Mr. Francisco. You want some advice? I'll give you advice. Forget anything from before your 1982 bankruptcy. That's over and done with. It's hopeless anyway. You need a detailed financial profile of your assets and liabilities so that you know what's up for grabs in your divorce contest with your wife. Is the lawsuit with your sons still pending, or was it settled?"

"Settled. After the fight over the will, my boys took their shares and ran with it. They tried to sue for some of my share but had to give up. We agreed that the lawyers were going to get it all if we stayed in court. They couldn't wait to cash out and go get their own dairy farms."

"That's one small mercy, then. Mr. Francisco, I tell you truly that I have never in my career seen anything like this before."

Candido was heartily sick of hearing those words from attorneys and relatives and farmers and dairymen and reporters and judges and — now — accountants.

"But we can help you take stock of your current situation and perhaps start building a foundation for some future security."

"It's worth a try," said Candido.

"And let's have no more talk about trying to put family members in jail, all right?"

"I was just talking about the one family member, but I guess you're right. I guess there's no point in trying to put my youngest boy in prison. Anyway, Ferdie's such a big sissy he'd probably enjoy it."

"Excuse me, Mr. Francisco. I want to be clear on one thing. We're here to offer you accounting services. We are not here to give tacit approval to your prejudices by remaining silent while you speak them."

Candido looked at the accountant, who was staring disapprovingly at him through his half-glasses. *Damn*, he thought, *the queers really* are *taking over everywhere.*

AUGUST 1982

Odile Gets a Bill

Odile Avila Francisco gripped her cane tightly as she lowered herself into the chair that Harold Widener was holding for her. She breathed a deep sigh of relief as she settled into it. The bone spurs in her heels made it especially painful to move her bulk around.

Odile had turned into a scale model of her late father Alberto, the man who had given his pampered daughters French names to mark them out as special — better than other Portuguese girls. Odette had shrugged it off and grown up poised and self-reliant, but Odile was weaker and had grown up spoiled. Odile's self-control had never been good, but the remnants of it had flown out the window when her husband had flown out the door. She blamed her most recent fifty pounds on him.

Widener was surprised that Odile had come to his law office alone. Normally she would have been accompanied by her son Ferdie, but the young man was not in evidence today. Since Widener was providing legal representation for both mother and son, he was accustomed to seeing them as a pair.

"Where is Ferdinando today, Mrs. Francisco?"

"Ferdie went out this afternoon to be with friends," she said, panting because of her chronic shortness of breath. "I couldn't wait for him to come home. I had to come see you right away."

That much had been apparent. Widener's legal secretary had not been able to make any sense of Odile's frantically incoherent phone call. It was about money and a letter and Odile's dark suspicions that her estranged husband was behind a scheme to destroy her. When the secretary put Odile on hold and tried to summarize the conversation for her employer, Widener had decided there was no help for it but to tell Mrs. Francisco to come in.

Odile was rummaging through her large handbag. She extracted a legal-sized envelope from it and handed it to Widener.

"This came in the mail right after lunch. They're trying to get money out of me and I don't know why. I need you to fix this!"

Widener was startled to see the return address on the envelope.

"Mrs. Francisco, this is from the court-appointed receiver. Didn't you recognize the name? I told you about it."

Odile shook her head.

"I don't know anything about that."

Widener wearily rested his arms on his desktop.

"We've been over this before, Mrs. Francisco."

"Well, I don't remember anything about it. Is Candy behind this? I know Candy is involved somehow. Maybe Cindy put him up to it!"

Widener shook his head.

"Candido is involved only to the degree that he fought and lost the argument over appointing a receiver. And *we* won. Do you remember now?"

"We won something?" Odile seemed impressed and momentarily heartened. "What did we win?"

Widener exhaled in exasperation. He wished Ferdie were here.

"Let me remind you about a few things, Mrs. Francisco. After you and your husband, uh, *separated*, you and your son were concerned that Mr. Francisco would do things that would diminish the value of your bequests from your mother-in-law's estate. Remember how we talked about that?"

"Yes, that's what I think Candy is doing right now!" she said.

"Just a moment, Mrs. Francisco. We're still talking about what happened a few months ago. You and Ferdinando asked me what you could do to protect your interests, right?"

That sounded right. Odile nodded her head.

"I told you that a court-appointed receiver would have the power to prevent even the co-executors of the estate — your husband and brother-in-law — from doing anything that would alienate the estate's assets or reduce the value of the legacies assigned to your mother-in-law's chosen heirs."

Odile's eyes were fixed on him, but Widener didn't see any particular comprehension behind them. She was waiting for a punch line of some sort. He decided to indulge her.

"So we petitioned the court to put your mother-in-law's estate under the control of a receiver and the co-executors opposed us, *but we won!* The court-appointed receiver has been in charge for a couple of months now and the co-executors have to clear their plans with him before they do anything. That's what we wanted."

Widener hadn't asked her a question, so Odile didn't say anything.

"The receiver's job is to make sure that the estate of Teresa Francisco is managed in such a way as to preserve its value. That means crops are to be planted and harvested, the buildings are to be maintained, etcetera. Everything that is required to keep things going until the estate is probated and the heirs take possession. Candido and Paulinho are still co-executors, but we have the receiver to keep an eye on anything they do. This is what we wanted, right?'

It sounded good, so Odile nodded.

"But if the receiver is supposed to be watching what Candy does, why is he asking me for money? That's not the job we gave him!"

Reminded of the letter Odile had brought, Widener picked it up from his desk and pulled out its contents. He scanned it quickly and his eyes widened.

"Mrs. Francisco, do you know what this is?"

"I think so. He's telling me to send him money. Right? But I don't have to give him money and I want you to stop him!"

"Mrs. Francisco, this is a rent bill for your house."

Odile looked at him with a deeply puzzled expression.

"Rent? But we never pay rent for the house. It's *our* house. Who would we pay rent *to?*"

Widener had an overwhelming impulse to just smash his forehead down on his desktop. He controlled the impulse with difficulty.

"Mrs. Francisco, do you mean to tell me that your house is part of your mother-in-law's estate?"

"No, I don't mean to tell you that. Why?"

Widener took a deep, deep breath.

"I know the court-appointed receiver. He was selected from a list of acceptable candidates that we provided to the probate court. This is a man who knows what he's doing. This rent bill indicates that Teresa Francisco was the owner of your home and the parcel it sits on. The cover letter explains that the billing was computed according to prevailing rent levels for comparable homes in your region of the county. The receiver explains that he is managing your mother-in-law's estate so as to preserve its value and ensure that its assets are properly managed. Just like I told you a minute ago. That means no free lunch; that means no free rent."

"So he can charge me rent now? But I never pay rent! And I don't have any money to pay it! Ferdie says we don't have any money coming in! Why doesn't he give me money if he wants me to pay bills?"

Widener was doing a lot of sighing. He did it again.

"Mrs. Francisco, you can't expect the receiver to provide either stipends or free housing to people who just happen to live on the estate. Your income is cut off because Candido is no longer at home."

"You mean this man can bill me for living in my own house *and* he can cut off my money?" Odile was aghast and her chin was trembling. She fumbled in her purse and pulled out a wad of tissue. She blew her nose and crumpled the tissue in one white-knuckled fist. "What am I going to *do!*"

"Let me do two things, Mrs. Francisco. First, I'll talk to the receiver. Perhaps we can charge the rent against your anticipated share of the estate. Perhaps we can arrange to get you some spending money in a similar way. You have pending assets, so I'll try to get you some consideration on that basis. Second, I'll talk to Ferdinando and give him some pointers on working under this receivership." *And maybe Ferdinando has a clue about what's going on around him and can share that with me*, thought Widener.

Widener got up from his desk to indicate that the meeting was over. He helped Odile lever herself out of the chair and walked her to the door. She wobbled out the door, shaking her head in wonderment and dismay. She wanted to talk to Ferdie, too. She still suspected that Candy was behind it all. He was always behind everything.

Widener watched her depart. Amazing. He was deeply chagrined that he had never suspected that Odile lived on her mother-in-law's property. Of course, he had read the legal definition of the property in the will, but county township designations don't carry street address labels. Besides, it was so bizarre for a client to agree to put herself under a receiver in this way that he had never made the connection. He turned toward his legal secretary.

"Take a note, Marcie. In the future, 'due diligence' includes verifying the client's sanity. Okay?"

Teresa Gives Free Advice

Teresa Francisco was at her command post. The overstuffed chair was stuck right next to the window in a corner of the living room. She could see Paulinho and Carmina's house through the thin stand of fruit trees in the old orchard that Chico had planted forty years ago. The calf pens were behind their house. Next to that was the dairy barn. Nothing could enter or leave the dairy yard without being subject to Teresa's inspection.

It was only right and proper. She was the *patroa*, the patroness, and the senior partner in Paulo C. Francisco & Sons. Teresa regarded the empty recliner across the room, sitting next to the other window.

She looked at it every day and thought about Chico. What would he think if he were still alive? Teresa could not be certain.

She wasn't even certain what *she* thought. She put her swollen feet up on the hassock and leaned back into her chair. She gave thanks every day in her prayers for her comfortable life and stable health. The aches and pains were manageable. The gnawing hurt in her heart was more of a problem.

Teresa fished the rosary out of the pocket of her housecoat. It was a rosary that had once belonged to her late daughter. She took the little crucifix of Fatima's rosary and kissed it, then made the sign of the cross with it. She started to pray. Soon she was on autopilot, clicking through the beads automatically, repeating the *Hail Mary* effortlessly.

Teresa was distracted by a movement outside. It was the little white pickup again. She hadn't seen it for a few days, but now it was back, driving past her window and into the dairy yard. The pickup's door sported one of those magnetic signs, but she could not read what it said. She wondered why it was back.

The white pickup parked next to the dairy barn and a man in a baseball cap climbed out. Teresa thought it was the same man she had seen the week before, except today he was not carrying a clipboard. Last week he had had the clipboard with him every day for three consecutive days as he wandered to and fro across the dairy yard. Today, however, he was carrying a manila envelope. He headed off in the direction of the workshop.

The workshop was next to the barn, but just out of Teresa's field of view. She figured, however, that the man was looking for Candido, who might be in the workshop's small office. He often went there to work on the herd records before visiting his mother for a morning cup of coffee.

Teresa brewed a pot every morning in anticipation of her son's visits. Candido could be relied upon to drop in, but he would stay exactly as long as it took him to drink one cup. Teresa had bought larger mugs, but Candido just drank faster. He felt obliged to visit his mother regularly, but he did not feel obliged to linger.

The pickup driver was back at his vehicle in only a few minutes. He climbed in and drove off. Today, for some reason, he didn't feel compelled to walk all over the place.

No sooner had the man left than Teresa saw her grandson Jojo driving a tractor with the automatic feeder wagon in tow. It was apparently Jojo's turn to do the morning feeding, which was a task he usually alternated with Junior.

The wagon would be loaded with corn silage from the huge mountain of silage stacked up behind the corrals. Teresa knew she would smell the heady aroma of the fermenting corn if she stepped outside, but she was comfortable where she was and had smelled it quite often enough in her lifetime. Besides, corn silage had become the cattle feed of choice on the Francisco dairy farm this season and its scent often hung in the air.

Jojo would drive the tractor-wagon combination along the corrals with the feeder wagon spewing out corn silage into the mangers. Teresa had noticed that one wagon load no longer sufficed to feed all the cattle. These days Jojo always doubled back and came out with a fresh load to finish the job. The herd must have grown, though Candido hadn't mentioned it to her. He didn't seem to think it was any of her business, despite the fact that Paulo C. Francisco & Sons *was* her business. It would be rude, however, to remind him of that.

It might also raise issues that were better not discussed openly, for the sake of peace in the family.

Teresa heard the porch door open, followed by the heavy tread that characterized her older son. Candido appeared in the living room doorway and nodded politely to his mother.

"*Bom dia, Mãe,*" he said.

"*Bom dia, filho,*" she replied.

Teresa pulled her feet down from the hassock and shoved them into her slippers. She tucked Fatima's rosary back into her pocket and walked toward her son. He stepped back so that she could pass into the kitchen. He bowed down so that she could kiss his cheek.

"How are you today?" she asked.

"Fine," he said. "How are you?"

"I'm fine, too."

"It's going to be hot today," said Candido.

Conversations with her older son were always excruciatingly dull, but that was inevitable if the only acceptable topics were health and weather. Teresa poured her son a mug of coffee and placed it on the table next to the sugar. She opened the refrigerator and brought out a cruet of cream. The cream was, of course, from the Franciscos' own cows.

Of course, thought Teresa to herself, *the real question is whose cows they actually are.*

As she put the cream on the table, she saw that Candido was checking the mail she had left on the table's corner. All the business mail was supposed to go directly to Candido's home these days, but mail delivery was often an approximate service in rural Tulare County. Teresa, Paulinho, and Candido had consecutive box numbers on "Rural Route 1," so it was inevitable that the sorters would sometimes mix up the Francisco mail. When Teresa found mail for her sons in her mail box, she would place it for them on the kitchen table.

Teresa sat down at the table opposite her son as he dumped cream into his coffee and started to mix it. Soon he would start gulping it down and then run out the door.

"Anything interesting in the mail?"

Candido shook his head.

"Only sales notices and an auction flier."

Candido carefully sipped to check whether his coffee was too hot to drink.

Teresa was thinking about the time Candido had found the mail *extremely* interesting. To tell the truth, so had she. The envelope had been addressed to Francisco & Sons and appeared to be a bank statement. That was a couple of years ago, before Candido had told his mother that she didn't need to open the business mail anymore. She had been accustomed to opening it all and leaving it neatly organized on Chico's desk for his review, but Candido did not require that service.

Teresa had been miffed at the omission of her husband's name, but she assumed it was meant for Paulo C. Francisco & Sons and sliced it open. Inside she found the expected bank statement. However, she did not recognize the account number. The statement contained a familiar pattern of deposits that suggested receipts from the auction yard, except that the amounts were larger and more frequent. The intervals were generally a week apart and the auction yard held its auctions weekly. The deposits suggested that Francisco & Sons were selling two to four cows or heifers each week. That meant that somewhere between one hundred to two hundred head of cattle during the course of a year were passing through the auction yard, assuming that the other months were similar. The money was going into the Francisco & Sons account, but where were the cattle coming from?

It seemed likely that they had been in the cattle trailers she had seen from her window as they passed out of the dairy yard.

She had put the statement back in the envelope and asked Candido about it the next day. His face had flushed red when he saw it, but he explained that she didn't need to worry about it, he would take care of it, and he was sorry that someone had forgotten to use the business's full name. Teresa decided not to mention that the account number did not match that of Paulo C. Francisco & Sons.

When several days went by without her bringing it up again, Candido began to seem more at ease. Occasionally, though, he acted spooked.

He was a little antsy today, as if sensing his mother's unasked questions. Candido preferred that questions remain unasked. He slurped his coffee as his mother sat across from him with her hands folded.

"Who was that young man with the white pickup truck?"

Damn! She does *have questions,* thought Candido. *But at least it's an unimportant one.*

"Oh, that was just the man from the consulting firm."

Teresa pondered that for a moment.

"What was he consulting about? I saw him several days last week, but then no more until today."

Candido wondered if it would be worthwhile to create a new driveway into the dairy site that wouldn't pass next to his mother's house. Probably not. She had a good vantage point from her living room chair and he couldn't very well move the dairy barn.

"He's helping us raise milk production. He was here looking over the operation. Today he came back to give me his report."

Teresa nodded her head. Then she said:

"I hope he told you that the boys are feeding the cows too much corn silage. Cows need dry hay, too. I know it's easier to feed them silage, but the hay is important."

Candido shocked his mother by getting up from the table, going over to the counter, and pouring himself a second cup of coffee. He would have preferred to bolt from the room, but this was the smoothest way he could turn his back for a few seconds. Candido took a deep breath, composed himself, and sat back down at the table. He smiled at his mother as he laced his coffee with cream and sugar.

"Um, right, *Mãe.* I'll mention that to the boys."

The report was stuffed in Candido's pocket. He had already looked at the executive summary on its first page and knew what it said. The consultant wanted the Franciscos to feed more dry hay to their milk cows. Their diet was too heavy in corn silage.

Candido slurped his coffee. He couldn't help wondering. If he asked his mother how much her advice was worth, would it match the consultant's bill of $5,000?

Candido Visits an Address

Candido's eyebrows quirked upward when he saw the familiar logo of a fireman's helmet on the envelope. Today's mail had brought a letter from the insurance company. He hoped it contained a check.

He ripped open the envelope and shook out the contents. A few folded sheets of paper fluttered out. There it was. He picked up the check and looked at it. He nodded to himself. Figuring the deductible and the amount of repair work required, it seemed reasonable. He picked up the accompanying statement to read the details.

Yes, there was the windshield replacement. Most of that was charged to the deductible. The body work to fix the dented door panels. The paint job. Everything appeared to be in order.

Candido looked to see if there were any notations related to the insurance premiums. He was afraid they might go up. But he could find no indication of that. They had made claims on the insurance before, but that was for Ferdie's fender-bender. This was the first time they had had to cover repairs for vandalism.

Candido noticed that he had clenched his fingers and wrinkled the statement. He was slightly surprised that he had reacted so strongly to his recollection of the vandalism. While he was angry at the unknown vandal(s), he was also embarrassed by the failure to protect the family's personal property. He didn't want to blame Ferdie for something that was some barbarian's fault, but he couldn't resist the notion that he, Candido, would have done a better job. It was a weird notion, as if he thought that he would have sensed his vehicle's danger and been there in the nick of time to confront the vandal and beat the snot out of him. Candido relished his vague revenge fantasy for a while.

Of course, in reality there would probably have been no difference. What did it matter whether Candido or Ferdie had parked the car and later come back to find its windshield smashed and its doors dented and scratched? It probably didn't matter at all.

A thought struck him. Had Ferdie been careless in choosing a place to park his car? Now that Candido came to think of it, Ferdie had said only that it had happened in the city of Tulare. He had never, that Candido could recall, reported just where it occurred.

Candido looked again at what the insurance company had mailed them. One sheet of paper was a photocopy of the incident report. It contained an address on Bardsley Avenue where the vandalism had occurred, but Candido didn't recognize it. He knew Tulare well but couldn't place the address. He tried to visualize the stretch of Bardsley Avenue indicated by the address, but he had only a vague impression of nondescript shops or businesses he had never had occasion to patronize.

Now that he was thinking of businesses in the city of Tulare, Candido recalled he had been meaning to visit the hardware store on K Street. Since he had a reason to drive to Tulare on business, he could swing down Bardsley Avenue and check out the address on the incident report. It was a good idea and would satisfy his curiosity.

Less than half an hour later, he was driving his pickup truck down K Street. He turned onto Bardsley and looked for the numbers on the buildings. He didn't have far to go. In fact, it was that free-standing building surrounded by an ill-kempt parking lot. Candido did not care for its appearance.

He pulled into the parking lot and slowly circumnavigated the building. Where was the business sign? It was an undistinguished rectangular building constructed out of cinder blocks and painted gray with purple trim. The windows were small and tinted.

Where the hell is the sign? thought Candido.

As if in answer to his question, a small sign appeared as he steered around a corner of the building. It was not very well placed if it was intended to draw in passers-by. In fact, the sign was mounted on a side of the building that was perpendicular to Bardsley, not on the side facing it. Given its size and location, you practically had to be in the parking lot before you could see it.

The sign read "Buckaroo." Now that Candido had stopped, he noticed the shapes of neon lights in the tinted windows. Turned off, they were hard to see through the glass, but he could tell they were beer ads. As far as Candido was concerned, the Buckaroo was awfully low-key for a Western bar in a Western city. And since when was Ferdie hanging out in Western bars?

That was when Candido noticed the building's patchy paint job. Roughly rectangular patches of the wall slightly mismatched the building's overall color. It looked like someone had sprayed graffiti on the walls and the bar owner had tried painting over the words. One such rectangle was right in front of Candido, but the gray paint did not do a good job of covering the black letters. The bar owner should have used a second coat to make "FAG" invisible.

Candido decided it wasn't a Western bar.

It was perhaps the least surprising discovery Candido had ever made.

Junior at the State Line

Candido Francisco, Jr., was happier than he had been in a long time. His convoy of cattle transport vehicles was approaching the Oregon border. Although he had precious little in common with his cousin Paul, at least Paul had managed to escape from Tulare County. Now Junior would be the second member of the Francisco clan to shake that dust off his heels, but he would go his cousin one better. He would leave the state. Soon California would be behind him for good.

"For good." He hoped that was literally true.

It was too easy for Junior to lapse into an unhappy reverie of disappointed dreams if he did not watch himself. He was still furious over the final results of the Francisco-Salazar feud and resented that he was starting over in Oregon with less of a grubstake than he had hoped for. Thank goodness that *Avó* had seen fit to include Sofia as one of her heirs. Together, Junior and his wife could scrape enough together to seek a fresh start in a new state.

The bulk of that fresh start resided in the three cattle transports. Each tractor-trailer rig could hold nearly forty head of dairy cattle. Junior was hauling 112 cattle with him, his share of the Francisco & Sons herd after swapping Junior and Sofia's bequeathed interest in Teresa Francisco's estate with other members of his family.

To Junior's surprise, Jojo had decided to go his own way instead of throwing in as his brother's junior partner. The convoy was therefore smaller because Jojo and his share of the cows were staying in Tulare County. Junior was certain it was at Rita's instigation that Jojo had found a small dairy to rent not far from the Francisco estate. Only Jojo's wife had enough influence to keep him from following his older brother's lead. Junior resented his sister-in-law's intervention, but he was determined not to dwell on it. After surviving lawsuits and bankruptcy to get to this point, Junior felt he had overcome the worst obstacles that fate could throw in his path.

His path at this moment was Interstate 5.

"Look, honey. There's the 'Welcome to Oregon' sign!"

Sofia straightened up in her seat and looked ahead. She had not complained during the long trip, but she was pregnant again and not feeling well. The timing of their relocation was not good for her, but Junior had been eager to shake the dust of Tulare County off his feet. She had not been willing to argue against his haste. He had his own cows now and he had to put them somewhere right away. In a couple of days they would be settled in Oregon, and a couple of days after that they could send for their children. Junior had joked that there was enough excess capacity in the cattle trailers to accommodate them, but that was just the latest example of Junior's strange sense of humor. Sofia's sister would take care of them for a week or so until their parents could send for them.

"When do we get to the ag station?" asked Sofia.

"It's right on the state line," said Junior. "It's a big space, too. I checked it out when I traveled up 5 to scout for an Oregon dairy for us. We'll be able to offload the cows long enough to feed and water and milk them."

The milk would perforce be spilled on the ground. Junior had no means for storing it under refrigeration. He wouldn't be selling his milk to a creamery and earning money for it until they were ensconced in the dairy farm he had rented. He had told Sofia that his plan was to avoid crying over spilled milk. Sofia had not found it as amusing or clever as he did. Junior had long been aware that no one really appreciated his sense of humor as much as he did himself. He was his own biggest fan.

Junior followed the signs that directed livestock transports to the Oregon State Agricultural Inspection Station and parked his tractor-trailer rig in the designated area. His hired drivers pulled their rigs up alongside his. The drivers were also skilled milkers, so soon they would start draining the cows' udders by hand. They wouldn't be getting a lot of rest while they were at the ag station — not with more than a hundred cows to milk.

They were approached by an official of the Oregon Department of Agriculture. His garb reminded Junior of the California Highway Patrol uniform.

"Welcome to Oregon, gentlemen. How are you doing?" he asked Junior and his two drivers.

"We're fine," answered Junior. "We're a little tired, but we're about to do a lot of old-fashioned cow milking."

The ag official nodded his head.

"We see more beef cattle than milk cattle. I'm sure you appreciate the difference."

Junior was in the right mood to appreciate the official's remark.

"Yeah, I learned when I was little it didn't do any good to milk steers!" he said with a grin on his face.

The ag official smiled back, not letting on what he was thinking. The Californians puzzled him. They were hauling milk cattle from one state to another. It wasn't unheard of, but it was definitely rare. Even a short trip could spook milk cattle into "going dry" and stop giving milk. If these guys were traveling up to the dairy country in the north state, they were hauling the cattle hundreds of miles even without taking the California leg of the journey into account.

The usual way to move a dairy was to convert the cows to cash: You sell your cattle in one location, take the money to your new location, and buy yourself a local herd. Folks who moved actual cows ended up with a dairy full of dry milkers that would produce no more of their valuable product until they went through another pregnancy and began to lactate anew. As with humans, that took nine months. In the meantime, no milk and no cash flow.

But that was not the ag official's concern. The Californians could do as they liked so long as they crossed their t's and dotted their i's.

"I know you need to get to work, so I'll get out of your way now. Let me have your livestock transportation forms and I'll process your entry into the state of Oregon."

Junior's sense of well-being suddenly evaporated.

"'Transportation forms'?" he said.

The official gave him a funny look.

"Right. I presume that you have your Brand Inspection Certificates? If you give them to me I can push your paperwork through."

Junior remained silent. His drivers exchanged glances and raised their eyebrows at each other. They certainly did not have any certificates, but that was their employer's responsibility. Surely he had taken care of the requirements for admission of California cattle into Oregon state.

"I don't think we have any certificates," said Junior.

The ag official gritted his teeth and put his hands on his hips.

"I'm sorry to hear that. I'm afraid that means you are stuck in this location until we can get you your certificates. I'll get the process started for you, but I have to warn you it'll take a couple of days. This is the sort of thing that's supposed to be done in advance. I'm sorry for the inconvenience, but you are not going anywhere today unless it's to go back into California."

"No," said Junior. "We definitely don't want to do that."

The ag official looked sympathetically at the crestfallen Californian.

"Like I said, I'll start the paperwork. I'll try to expedite it, but there are officials who will need to come down to the station to perform the inspection. I hope we have one already in the field instead of waiting for someone to come down from Salem. It's a tough situation, folks. Sorry!"

The official turned on his heel and started back to the station office to place some calls.

Damned idiots, he thought. After two days in the ag station, penned up most of the time in their trailers, the dairy cattle would be extraordinarily discontented cows. *Their owner won't be able to get a drop out of them by the time he gets to where he's going.*

MARCH 1968

Jojo Drives Two Tractors

João José "Jojo" Francisco was riding a tractor and he was a happy teenager. It was a redundant statement because the one followed from the other. As long as he was bouncing along on a tractor, Jojo was in a good mood, the degree of his mood being directly proportional to the speed at which he was traveling. His happiness was maximized when he was going flat out.

His joy was therefore not perfect today because he was towing a hay wagon that reduced his speed. Nevertheless, powerful mitigating factors were in play. Jojo was on his way to chop alfalfa, and it was a task involving his operation of three pieces of heavy equipment at the same time. It was almost too much fun for one person.

Jojo pulled up alongside the chopper rig and parked. He was pulling the hay wagon with a Massey-Ferguson 50, a sporty little utility tractor used to move things around and handy with smaller attachments like seed spreaders and cotton-stalk choppers. Its bright red paint job was obscured by dust and sun damage, but the spunky vehicle was one of Jojo's favorites. The Fifty suffered by comparison, however, with the massive Massey-Ferguson 85. That was a tractor muscular enough to pull both the chopper rig and the hay wagon at the same time.

The Eighty-Five was already hooked up to the chopper rig, the chopper attached to its hitch and mated to its power take-off shaft. When the operator of the Eighty-Five engaged the power take-off clutch, the PTO shaft would spin, transmitting power to the chopper to drive the scythes that would cut the alfalfa stalks near ground level and the bladed fan that would chop the hay while blowing it into the following hay wagon. To Jojo's eyes, it was as elegant an array as the tripartite Apollo moon vehicle, which NASA had put together with Command, Service, and Lunar Modules.

Besides, so far as Jojo knew, none of the components of the Apollo moon rocket sported dual sets of whirling blades.

He unhitched the hay wagon from the Fifty and moved the smaller tractor out of the way. He climbed up on the Eighty-Five to start it up and carefully back up the tractor-chopper combination until he could hitch the wagon to the back of the chopper. It was at least as elegant a docking maneuver as the astronauts ever performed in orbit. Jojo pressed the starter.

The Eighty-Five's engine turned once, choked, and stopped. Jojo jammed the starter again. The Eighty-Five gave a weak gasp.

"*Shit!*"

The battery must be dead. If he had had jumper cables, he would have considered using the Fifty to give the Eighty-Five a jump, even despite the mismatch in their batteries, but his jumper cables were in his Jeep back at the dairy yard. Jojo sat on the tractor seat and fumed.

He would have to go back to the dairy and fetch someone to give him a jump or a tow. A jump would ideally use well-matched batteries, but the dairy farm's other Eighty-Five was on duty elsewhere and not readily available to drive to the alfalfa field. The alternative was a tow. If someone towed the Eighty-Five while it was in gear, with Jojo holding down the clutch till it gained speed, then Jojo could pop the clutch and the Eighty-Five would sputter into life as its turning wheels cranked the engine through the drive train.

So far all of the obvious solutions involved Jojo fetching help from someone else. That left him less than satisfied. Jojo was a young man of meager scholastic attainments whose stock-in-trade was being a hard and tireless worker on his grandfather's dairy farm. He was usually content with his lot, but that depended on his ability to succeed at his tasks. Going back to the dairy yard for help would put him at risk of suffering his older brother's contempt. Junior treated the simplest act of assistance as an aching burden of *noblesse oblige* and would be at pains to make Jojo feel like an incompetent peasant.

Ferdie knew how to drive tractors and could do the job, but it would be a nuisance prying him away from his domestic chores; Mom might actually forbid it and tell Jojo to go find someone else.

His cousin Paul would be difficult to find, of course, holed up in the haystack, up in the tree house, or hiding in his parents' basement — no doubt with a book. He wouldn't give Jojo any crap about giving the tractor a tow, but tracking him down would be a time-waster.

Hank would be the perfect assistant, but he was the guy operating the other Eighty-Five several miles away on the west forty. Jojo and his cousin operated on the same farm-loving wavelength, but Hank was simply out of range right now.

Was there anything that Jojo could do *by himself?*

Just to be certain, he tried to crank the Eighty-Five's engine one more time and failed. That settled it. Extreme measures were called for.

The chopper had a tall, curving chute through which the chopped hay was blown into the trailing wagon. The tractor operator could control the position of the chute by reaching back and turning a crank that yawed the chute back and forth. The operator could also pull on or loosen a long rope that was attached to a baffle at the chute's exit spout. If the baffle were all the way up, the ejected hay would shoot all the way to the back of the hay wagon. If the baffle were pulled down a little, the hay would fill in the front part of the wagon. Jojo enjoyed using the crank and the rope to fill the wagon to the very edge of maximum capacity, thereby demonstrating his expertise.

The rope could come in handy.

Jojo climbed up on the chopper rig and detached the rope from the exit baffle. He returned to the Eighty-Five, put the inert vehicle into gear, pushed down the clutch as far as it would go, and tied it in place with one end of the rope. He used a slip knot, which he tested by pulling on the rope. The slip knot came undone and the clutch popped back up.

Jojo grinned and tied the clutch down again. He fetched the Fifty and backed it up in front of the Eighty-Five. The Fifty had a length of chain in its equipment slot. Jojo judged that it was adequate to the task. He attached one end to the front of the Eighty-Five and the other to the Fifty's hitch. He drove the little tractor forward until the chain was taut, then he put the Fifty back into neutral, climbed down, and fetched the loose end of the rope from the Eighty-Five. He paid it out as he returned to the little tractor and settled down in its seat.

Jojo paused to take stock. The Fifty was chained to the Eighty-Five. The Eighty-Five was attached to the chopper. Jojo considered whether he should unhitch the chopper, but decided not to. It would be a nuisance to go to all that work only to have to put it all right back together again. Besides, the chopper's bulk would keep Jojo's mated vehicles from accelerating too quickly. He hadn't been able to hitch up the hay wagon, but that was just as well. It was superfluous to his present scheme and would only have complicated matters. He'd have to think of some excuse in the future to move four pieces of heavy equipment at the same time. For now, three was his limit.

He coiled up most of the slack in the rope and tucked it underneath himself. By sitting on the rope's end, he would keep it from getting away. He'd be able to grab the rope when he needed to. Everything was now ready.

His heart thumping, Jojo put the Fifty in gear and slowly released its clutch. The little tractor strained against the chain holding it back with the weight of the tractor-chopper rig. Jojo was afraid for a moment that the tires would slip on the alfalfa stubble underneath, but they gained traction on the ground and Jojo's bizarre caravan began to creep forward.

Now timing was everything. He had to be going fast enough so that the Eighty-Five's engine would start, but not so fast that Jojo couldn't switch from one tractor to the other. Jojo had one hand on the Fifty's steering wheel and the other was holding on to the rope near the edge of his seat. He waited a few long excruciating seconds as the velocity mounted, chose his moment, and yanked the rope.

The Eighty-Five's clutch popped, its gears grabbed, the world jerked, and the engine roared into life. Jojo yelled in triumph.

The Fifty was no longer towing the Eighty-Five. The chain had gone slack and the Eighty-Five was now bearing down on the little tractor.

Jojo jumped off the Fifty and stumbled over an extra step to allow for the Eighty-Five's greater width. As the big tractor started to brush past him, he jumped toward it.

The caravan was still speeding up, both tractors now alive, in gear, and unmanned. At the end of the field was the irrigation canal that bordered Chico Francisco's property. The banks were too low to prevent the tractors and the chopper from ending up in the canal if Jojo did not bring them to a stop.

The acceleration made it difficult to judge, but Jojo jumped right after the Eighty-Five's front wheel passed him and before the giant rear wheel arrived. As his left hand grabbed the steering wheel and his right hand struggled for purchase on the seat, Jojo felt the impact of the big tire on his trailing right foot. *Ow!*

But it didn't grab him. He was hauling himself up onto the tractor seat and turning to sit down and take control. Jojo pushed down the Eighty-Five's clutch with his left foot to take it out of gear. Then he slowly depressed the brake pedal with his tingling right foot and the tractor began to slow down. The chain went taut again and the Fifty's engine was lugging as it strained against its renewed burden. The effort was too great for the Fifty as the Eighty-Five's brakes took hold. Its engine was overloaded and gave up, sputtering into silence.

They were stopped at last, halfway across the field from their starting point. The Fifty was now off, but the Eighty-Five was idling with its characteristic stutter. The only thing still racing was Jojo's heart.

He savored his victory for a few minutes before climbing down from the Eighty-Five and unhooking the towing chain. He'd leave the Fifty where it was until he was done chopping the alfalfa and filling the hay wagon. Then he'd walk over and drive it back to hitch up the hay wagon and return to the dairy yard as if nothing unusual had happened.

His right foot didn't hurt too much as he climbed up on the chopper to reattach the rope. It was probably just bruised a little.

It was a good day. Jojo was riding tractors and that always made him happy.

PART VI

Beatrice vs. Javier

The messenger came down the central aisle of the courtroom and quietly delivered a note to Dennis Ramos at the respondents' table. Beatrice Onan was momentarily distracted from her questioning of James Franklin Foster.

"Ms. Onan?"

"Oh. Sorry, your honor. As I was saying, Mr. Foster, you have to admit that there is at least a possibility that you are incorrect in your opinion that the signature on Teresa Francisco's will is genuine. Is that not so?"

"Of course that's so," agreed Foster smoothly. "It is also *possible* that a bolt of lightning will strike you down the moment you step out of the courthouse today. Or me. Or anyone else in this courtroom. I'm not going to worry about that, of course, and hope that you won't either. I said that there is no *reasonable* doubt about the authenticity of Teresa Francisco's signature on her will. I have presented my evidence to the best of my ability and the evidence is strikingly clear."

"The witness is filibustering," whispered Widener to Bowman. "Good for him!"

Bowman nodded his head. He avoided whispering during court sessions. It seemed more professional to refrain. Widener turned to Ramos for more satisfying feedback and saw that his colleague was folding up his message and grinning broadly. Widener raised his eyebrows questioningly. Ramos leaned toward him and spoke in hushed tones.

"It looks like Biddy *should* be worried about lightning striking."

"Oh?"

"Javier Joaquim is in the building."

"Hot damn! Jackpot day continues!"

Onan was retiring from the field of battle.

"Your honor, I have no further questions of this witness."

"Thank you, Ms. Onan. Gentlemen, is it time to excuse your witness?"

Bowman stood up in his usual slow-motion manner.

"Yes, your honor. We have no further questions for Mr. Foster and he may be excused with our thanks."

"Mr. Foster, the court thanks you for your testimony today and excuses you. You may step down."

Judge Knight looked at the clock on the wall.

"Court stands adjourned until two o'clock this afternoon."

He banged his gavel and left the courtroom. The jurors filed out through the jury room door. The Franciscos gathered in conversational knots, chatting happily about their witness's performance. James Foster paused to shake several proffered hands before he left the courtroom and nodded in acknowledgment of Harold Widener, who had clasped his hands over his head and was shaking them in a sign of victory. As he walked down the central aisle toward the courtroom's main doors, Foster stepped aside to make way for a large man who had seized the opportunity of the court recess to charge inside.

"I see the lightning," said Dennis Ramos.

Javier Joaquim appeared to be about forty. The beard on his jowly face was brindled with gray and he had a substantial paunch, but he carried himself ramrod straight. He had dressed up with a tie, but not a jacket. The eyes behind the horn-rimmed glasses were dark and blazing with anger.

Onan had been watching Foster's departure with ill-concealed loathing. Her expression had changed to one of fear and anxiety when she saw the familiar figure of Javier Joaquim push past the handwriting expert and charge toward her.

"Aunt Biddy, I need to talk to you."

Joaquim's voice was higher than one might have expected in so large a man, but it was a resonant heldentenor voice. Siegfried had come to slay a dragon.

"I can't talk to you right now, Javier. I'm in court!"

"No, you're not. You're in recess right now. We *can* talk and we *must* talk!"

Joaquim was wearing dress slacks with deep side pockets. He pulled a folded sheaf of papers from his left pocket and brandished them at his aunt.

"We have to talk about *this!*"

The fingers of Onan's right hand were clutching at her throat, as if she were protecting her neck.

"Not *here*, Javier, and not *now*. We should get away from here first."

"Why should we? Why not get this cleared up right this minute? Why wait till later? I want answers *now*."

"Settle down. I don't want us to talk like this in public."

"Why the hell not, Aunt Biddy? Because you're a *thief?* Are you afraid people will find out?"

"*Javier!*"

Joaquim was swollen with rage and seemed fit to burst. The Franciscos watched in stunned fascination, mouths agape. Widener was sitting on the respondents' table, dangling his legs and looking like he wanted some popcorn to munch on. Bowman had struck a pose of calm watchfulness, seated at the table, while Dennis Ramos was standing quietly next to the more animated Widener.

Joaquim was holding his papers in his left hand while stabbing at them with his right index finger.

"This is a summons from the U.S. Attorney's office. They want me and my brother to come in for questioning. Aren't you interested in what they want to talk to us about? Doesn't it *interest* you? We're going to be *very* cooperative, Aunt Biddy. *Very* cooperative. We're going to tell them *everything* we know because *we are not going to take the fall for you!*"

Onan surrendered to the inevitable and finally did what she should have done the moment Javier Joaquim had appeared. She grabbed her legal portfolio with one hand, Joaquim's arm with the other, and began walking him briskly toward the door. Having vented his wrath, Joaquim now seemed somewhat deflated and did not scream further accusations at his aunt as she hustled him out the door and toward private quarters.

"I wish the jurors had seen that," said Ferdie Francisco.

"Oh, God, *no,*" replied Widener, who was his attorney as well as his mother's. "That would have been a disaster. Judge Knight might have ruled a mistrial and made us start over again after the jurors saw something that extraneous and that prejudicial. We'll just have to be content with the thought that Biddy is a destroyed woman."

"But what was it all about?" asked Paul Francisco.

Widener didn't speak, but just nodded his head toward Ramos. Ramos shrugged.

"What can I say?" he said. "Someone commented that it was odd how Biddy was spending all of her time in Tulare County when her practice was supposed to be based in San Francisco. It looked like she couldn't have been drumming up much business in the Bay Area, so I did a little bit of poking around. Not only was she not doing well up in Frisco, it turned out that she had filed for bankruptcy two years ago. That sort of thing is public record and wasn't hard to find once I started looking. I kept looking and then I found her name on the deeds of sale of two farm parcels here in the county. What is a bankrupt attorney doing selling farm land?"

"That sounds like a good question, Dennis!" said Widener, chuckling.

"The parcels were her inheritance from her father's estate, which she received *before* filing for bankruptcy, but she 'forgot' to declare them as assets. Then she came down here and quietly sold the parcels to her nephews. There was no way she could keep her name out of the paperwork at the recorder's office, *but* she volunteered to do the title search for her nephews. That would save them money, of course, but it would also allow her to overlook little things like her bankruptcy, which a legitimate title company would have uncovered."

"How did the U.S. Attorney's office get involved?" asked Ferdie.

"Simple!" cried Widener. "Dennis told them!" He laughed.

Dennis Ramos shrugged his shoulders again.

"That's right. I tipped off the U.S. Attorney's office of a possible case of bankruptcy fraud. The summons to the Joaquim brothers informs them that they are under suspicion of collaborating in their aunt's effort to conceal assets. After all, *why* didn't they insist on an independent title search? She knew she could play them for dupes because they were greedy enough to want to avoid the fees, but the boys never imagined what they were getting into."

"Damn!" said Jojo Francisco, in apparent partial admiration of the scheme. "What's going to happen to her?"

"Disbarment, for certain. Revocation of bankruptcy and reinstatement of debts, *very* likely. I imagine her clandestine property will be seized by the court and auctioned to raise money to pay off the creditors she bilked. If the Joaquim boys are lucky, they might be able to afford to buy the parcels in a fair bid. The money they paid her earlier will probably go into her pot of assets to pay off her creditors — which her nephews will then become, since they'll demand a refund, no doubt — but they'll get pennies on the dollar. How many pennies is the big question. The land is going to cost them more than they ever imagined."

"How will the disbarment affect us?" asked Paul Francisco.

"Not at all," replied Widener. "This little case will long be over by the time the mills of justice have ground poor Biddy Onan to dust. Its inevitability may, however, put her off her game during the final rounds."

"Ha! *What* game?" demanded Ramos.

"Ouch! Good point. *I* should have been the one to say that," said Widener.

"I want to know one more thing," said Paul. "Is jackpot day over now?"

"Oh, I hope so. I hope so! I've had as much fun as a mortal man can stand for one day. Tell you what, though," said Widener. "Let's go outside to see if she got struck by lightning. That would be the perfect end to a perfect day!"

JUNE 1983

Beatrice Faces Life

The corner booth in the back of a family restaurant had at least one advantage over a law office: her coffee cup was automatically topped off at regular intervals. Beatrice Onan lifted the mug to her lips and took a swallow. As advantages went, it wasn't much.

Onan put the mug back down on the faux-wood tabletop and considered the list she had scrawled on a yellow legal pad. The first item was "Joaquim." Just the sight of the name rankled her, especially since it should have been hers.

The Joaquim family was one of the most prominent Portuguese-American families in central California. Members liked to suggest that the San Joaquin Valley was their namesake — and too bad about the common misspelling. Beatrice had dated Vasco, the eldest of the Joaquim sons, until the day he suddenly broke up with her and became engaged to her sister. When Javier Joaquim had been born as an eight-pound "premature" baby six months after the hasty marriage, Beatrice finally understood.

Now that same Javier Joaquim had humiliated her in front of her opponents in the Francisco case. Worse, he had made it clear that the Joaquim family would sacrifice her to save themselves.

Again.

This time, of course, she had a measure of responsibility for the situation. Her unsuccessful legal practice had forced her into bankruptcy. In an act of desperation, she had concealed some assets from the bankruptcy court. She had been loath to see the farmland she inherited from her father going to her creditors. Beatrice had persuaded herself that she had a right to protect the paternal legacy and the skills to conceal it from the mechanisms of the legal system.

She had obviously been mistaken. It didn't occur to her that the bankruptcy of her legal practice was a hint that her skills were not equal to the task.

In her mind, humanity was divided into two groups: the users and the used. She had dedicated her life to making the transition from the latter group to the former. It was a bitter disappointment that becoming a lawyer had not done the trick.

The second item on her list was "BA." The bar association.

Beatrice Onan would be suspended and deemed ineligible to practice law in the state once the U.S. Attorney's office indicted her for bankruptcy fraud. She might be able to have the suspension stayed, enabling her to continue to work as a lawyer. Conviction, however, would cause permanent suspension and disbarment. She could write a letter of resignation to the bar association. That would have the effect of immediately halting any disciplinary proceedings against her, but it would have no impact on the bankruptcy fraud case.

There was no point in going that route. She scratched off the item.

"Louis Salazar."

Her liaison with Louis was unraveling at the same time as her case against Teresa Francisco's will. Louis had attended none of the court proceedings, but he had heard in detail the humiliation of Onan's star witness. He felt that his girlfriend had misled him about their prospects for a successful lawsuit.

And she felt the same about him. Louis's argument had been so persuasive. Clearly the Salazar family was being cheated by the machinations of the Franciscos. Any jury would recognize the injustice of Teresa's alleged will and find it easy to believe that it was forged by her sons. Louis had blinded her to the simple language of the will, which made the brothers co-executors. Candido Francisco could not possibly have agreed to such a thing. His fingerprints were nowhere on the will, yet he was the focus of Louis's wrath. It amused Onan that some people gave her credit for inspiring the Salazar lawsuit. That train was going to leave the station no matter what. She had merely climbed aboard for the ride — a ride to nowhere.

She slowly and sadly drew a line through Louis's name.

It was depressing to consider the men in her life — a string of poor choices.

Louis Salazar pushed her around with the force of his determination and the energy of his vendetta. Vasco Joaquim had been even worse, shattering her life with the same act of betrayal that broke her heart. In between, there had been the ill-advised and short-lived marriage with Benedict Onan, the law school classmate who had apparently been looking more for a study buddy than a life partner. She put her ex-husband out of her mind. The less said about him, the better.

Perhaps Beatrice should have become a nun, as she had briefly considered after the business with Vasco. But that was never a serious option.

"Dennis Ramos."

She had underlined his name several times. It was the buzz among the attorneys of Tulare County that Ramos had instigated the investigation against her. Since the rumors had percolated throughout the legal profession, perhaps Onan could find evidence that he had slandered her. It might not go anywhere, but a complaint of unprofessional conduct could subject Ramos to a bar association investigation of his own. That might be worthwhile in itself. She drew a check mark against his name. She would draft a formal complaint letter.

Beatrice would have liked to launch a similar reprisal on Harold Widener, but she couldn't discern an angle of attack. He had confined himself to an elusive campaign of psychological warfare against her, so she couldn't cite anything specific. She had a greater animus toward him than toward anyone else in the clannish boys' club — and it was overwhelmingly a *boys'* club — of local attorneys, but she had less to work with. She hadn't even bothered to put his name on her list. She considered the final name on her legal pad.

"Paul Francisco."

The letter-writer and letter-keeper. The creepy young man had roundly abused his godfather in a nasty missive that Louis had shared with her. And he had saved that conveniently full-page letter from his grandmother. Damnably convenient. She circled his name. Perhaps — just perhaps — she had one more roll of the dice.

Received by the Receiver

Dinis Costa slowed his car, drove off the county road, and parked on the shoulder. He climbed out and walked into the field, the short stalks of mown alfalfa crunching under his feet. It was an experience that he hadn't had in several years, but it was familiar and comfortable.

It was hot under the early August sun. His fair and prematurely thinning hair gave his scalp little protection. Costa had been smart enough to leave his jacket in the car, but now he loosened his tie and rolled up the sleeves of his dress shirt. He had grown up on a farm but left it for college and law school. Now he had a legal practice that combined his life experience with his education, specializing in agricultural law. Costa made his living representing farmers in disputes over things like water rights, property lines, tenancies, and crop allocations. It was more than enough to keep him busy.

Now he was again playing the role of a court-appointed receiver.

Costa was on an inspection tour, looking over the land in Teresa Francisco's estate before visiting the Francisco dairy itself. No doubt nervous family members were already awaiting his arrival, but they could wait a little longer. He pulled a small notebook out of his shirt pocket and began jotting down a few observations that he would later expand into a memo that would go into the Francisco file.

He was walking across an alfalfa field that, judging from the season, would have been harvested at least a couple of times by now. The alfalfa would have been mowed and raked into swaths, after which a baler would come along, suck up the hay swaths into its maw, and squeeze out tightly bound hay bales from its other end. The bales would then get hauled out of the field and stacked in the hay barn, after which the field would revive with yet another stand of alfalfa and the cycle would repeat. An efficient farm would reap several harvests before colder weather brought it to a halt.

A green carpet of young alfalfa sprouts was pushing up through the brittle stubble of the most recent crop. Costa noticed that the green was frequently interrupted by yellowish rectangles, each about the size of a hay bale. Someone had clearly dawdled in clearing the field of bales. The etiolated sprouts in the rectangles were off to a bad start, having been denied the sun longer than they should have been. Their contribution to the next harvest would be meager.

The entire field was divided into irrigation segments that ran the field's length from east to west. The segments were called "checks," and each check would have at least one irrigation valve at its end. The checks were bounded by parallel berms that controlled where the water would go when the valves were opened. A field that was properly leveled for irrigation would have a nearly imperceptible slope that coaxed the water to flow from the valves at the high end all the way down to the low end. With a practiced eye and a modicum of attention, a competent farmer would turn off the valves at just the right moment so that the waters would flow precisely to the far edge of the field, irrigating the land evenly.

Costa was seeing signs of haphazard irrigation practices. The checks looked different from each other, whereas careful farming would tend to make them all look very similar. Sometimes, if a farmer opted to alternate the irrigation between the even-numbered checks and the odd-numbered checks, there might be a subtle alternating pattern reflecting the impact of slightly differ-ent watering times. But Costa didn't think that was the case. What he was seeing looked random, where some checks had gotten too much water and others too little. Apparently the land was being watered by the three bears from *Goldilocks*, and "just right" was not getting its fair share.

It would be Costa's job as court-appointed receiver to ensure that Teresa Francisco's estate did not lose value while it was going through probate. The probate court had been petitioned by Odile Francisco's attorney for a receiver, indicating that the heirs were divided into factions. What's more, a second petition had been filed by some members of the Salazar family, asking for revocation of probate and challenging the will itself. Costa could easily en-visage a contest over the will that went beyond the normal probate process, in which case the decisions he made today could determine the condition of Teresa Francisco's dairy farm for months to come.

There were three dairy farms visible from where he stood. The closest one was less than a mile away, and he knew it belonged to the Francisco family. A tall evergreen tree rose up at one end, where two residences were located. Mrs. Francisco had lived in one and her son Paulinho in the other. Costa knew there was a third residence on the property. It was the home formerly occupied by Candido Francisco and sat on a parcel at the far edge of the estate. Candido's estranged wife had been the one who petitioned for a receiver, leading to Dinis Costa's appointment.

As he walked back to his car, he wondered if the Franciscos would expect to speak to him in Portuguese. He knew hardly any. His branch of the Costa family had been in California a long time and was in an advanced state of assimilation. As a third-generation Californian, Costa was right on schedule for loss of the ancestral tongue. The first generation tended to be bilingual, the second generation usually picked up a smattering, and the third generation . . . *nada*. Sometimes he regretted it, but being monolingual wasn't a big disadvantage as long as the language was English.

Costa had been given a warning about dealing with the Franciscos. Candido and his sons were estranged since he had walked out on his wife Odile. They had agreed to meet with Costa in the living room of Teresa Francisco's empty house, everyone accepting the matriarch's abode as neutral ground. Candido was supposed to be waiting inside. The boys would not come in until they saw the receiver's car parked in their late grandmother's driveway. Paulinho had spoken to the receiver by phone and had decided not to attend. His son Henry, however, would be present.

There was a pickup truck already parked next to Mrs. Francisco's home. Costa assumed it was Candido's. He parked his car behind the pickup, shrugged on his jacket, and approached the house. As he climbed the stairs to the side door, the one he had been told to enter, he noticed that three young men had emerged from the workshop next to the barn and were coming in his direction.

The door opened before Costa could knock. He looked at the man standing in the doorway and jumped to a correct conclusion.

"Hello. Are you Candido Francisco? I'm Dinis Costa."

The man leaned forward and offered his hand, which completely engulfed Costa's as they shook.

"Yes, come on in. The living room is this way."

They walked past Teresa's kitchen table, which lay under a film of dust that she would never have allowed in life. They entered the living room, where a young man was waiting, a fellow not even thirty years old.

"This is my nephew Hank."

Costa shook hands with Henry Francisco.

"Pleased to meet you, Hank."

"Would you do me a favor, Hank?" asked Candido. "Would you let your cousins in?"

As he walked through the kitchen, Henry heard the door knob rattle. Candido had not unlocked the door. He opened it and let his cousins in.

Junior pushed past him without a word, but Jojo said hello and Ferdie nodded at him. Henry followed his cousins back to the living room.

Candido had been bold enough to co-opt his father's old recliner. All three of his sons chose to move to the couch farthest away from their father. Not wanting to appear to choose sides, Henry dithered a moment before reluctantly deciding that his grandmother's overstuffed chair was the closest thing to a neutral corner.

Having shaken hands with the boys as they filed by, Dinis Costa was now in the awkward situation of standing in the middle of a room that had people on three sides of him. It was theater in the round. He cleared his throat.

"All right, gentlemen. As I said during the introductions, my name is Dinis Costa and I am an attorney-at-law. My specialty is ag-related litigation. The probate court has appointed me the receiver for the estate of Teresa Francisco. My brief is easy to state, but rather more challenging to discharge. It is now my responsibility to ensure that the late Mrs. Francisco's estate is operated in such a way that it retains or even increases its value. I have the authority to appoint people to accomplish the necessary tasks, which include the operation of the dairy and the cultivation of the farm. I'm sure you know what the obvious solution is."

"Yeah," said Junior. "Get out of our way and leave us alone. We're doing fine!"

"That is not *quite* the obvious solution I had in mind, but it is perhaps closer than you might have feared."

The man made Jojo nervous. People who talked the way the lawyer did always made him anxious about whether they were deliberately trying to confuse him or trick him into something. Dinis Costa reminded Jojo a little of his cousin Paul.

"My version of the obvious solution is *this*," continued Costa. "I intend to appoint a Francisco to manage the Francisco estate. Who better to run a family dairy farm than a member of the family?"

"Yeah," rejoined Junior, "that's what I —"

He stopped in midsentence when Costa's hand snapped up with its open palm facing him.

"Excuse me, Candido Junior, but you should let me finish my remarks before you react to them. You need to remember that you operate under my sufferance."

Jojo didn't know why the lawyer was talking about making Junior suffer, but things appeared to be taking a turn for the worse. On the other hand, this guy could make Junior shut up. That had to be a good thing.

"I was going to tell you how I intend to do this. It's very simple. I regard all five of you as candidates for the position of estate manager. Under my court-appointed authority and under my supervision, you will ensure that Teresa Francisco's assets are operated as a going concern. All of you have a personal knowledge of this family dairy farm and can presumably offer me cogent reasons why you should be the one I select."

Junior insisted on being combative.

"If you pick *him*," he said, pointing at his father, "I will not work for him. He belongs up in Fresno with his bitch."

"*Junior!*" Candido was half out of Chico Francisco's chair, but Costa thrust his hand out again.

"Gentlemen! Please remember we are in Teresa Francisco's home and I think you owe her memory some respect."

Candido sat down heavily while Junior had a smug expression on his face, pleased at having provoked his father. Costa faced the couch on which Candido's three sons were sitting and addressed Junior.

"*If* I choose your father, Mr. Francisco, it's entirely *my* concern. If you decline to work under his supervision in that instance, then I will have you discharged. You draw a salary from Paulo C. Francisco & Sons, but that salary is contingent on your actually working here."

He looked at Jojo and Ferdie.

"Please note that I am not talking about cutting anyone off who wants to work on the estate and contribute to its maintenance. All decisions of that sort will be made on a strictly business basis. You should also keep in mind that nothing I do affects your status as your grandmother's heirs. I will simply be working to ensure that your inheritance is as great as it can be. I hope that reassures you."

It didn't seem to assuage Junior, but Jojo and Ferdie brightened significantly.

Costa turned toward Henry and then back to Candido, sweeping across his entire audience.

"Now let's talk about the grace period."

"What's a 'grace period?'" asked Henry.

Costa faced him to reply.

"This is more specific to your uncle and cousins than to you, Hank. They have a vested interest in harvesting crops that they've already planted on your grandmother's land. They retain that interest and the estate will respect that."

Costa directed his remarks to Candido.

"Sir, you currently have approximately 450 acres of prime agricultural land under cultivation, land which is in your mother's name, inherited from your father. If your separate business of Francisco & Sons — *not* to be confused with Paulo C. Francisco & Sons, as I'm sure you appreciate — has been responsible for planting and tilling the crops on those lands, its interest will not be alienated. There are, of course, many details to be settled. We will need to audit the value of the contributions of Francisco & Sons to the operation of lands belonging to Teresa Francisco and credit you for that. We must determine the fair market rental value of the lands for the period of time necessary to complete the harvest, and charge Francisco & Sons accordingly."

Candido didn't like what he was hearing.

"What exactly does that mean, Mr. Costa?"

"It means, Mr. Francisco, that your mother may have allowed you free use of the lands in her name, but I cannot. It is my responsibility, answerable to the probate court, to ensure that the estate receives fair value for all of its components, including a fair rent for the use of Mrs. Francisco's land."

Junior exploded.

"You are going to charge us *fucking rent* to farm our own land? Are you fucking *nuts?*"

Costa regarded Junior patiently.

"Mr. Francisco, the lands in question are your *grandmother's*. While you may very well end up with a portion of them in keeping with your status as one of her heirs, it currently is manifestly *not* your land and a fair-market rental value will be determined from comparable lands in this region."

Ferdie had been feeling detached from the discussion, but now he was dismayed.

"But you don't *understand*. You want to charge us rent for family land? We're not into paying rent!"

Dinis Costa was at a loss how to respond to such remarks, so he decided not to.

"Gentlemen," he announced, "I'm going to walk about the dairy yard and inspect the operation."

He reached into his jacket pocket and extracted a stack of business cards. He handed one to each of the Franciscos as he concluded his remarks.

"I would welcome the opportunity to chat one-on-one with each of you. You can call me at my business office and we can arrange meetings. Or you could take turns escorting me around the dairy and we can converse on foot."

He looked at Candido.

"Mr. Francisco, would you care to take the first turn, or would you rather wait till later?"

"I'll go now," said Candido.

They were all on their feet. Ferdie was looking at Costa's business card and fingering it nervously. He finally got up the courage to speak again.

"Mr. Costa, I don't really need this. I'm not the one you want. We don't need to talk about it. I'm just not the one."

"Thank you for telling me," said Costa. "I don't mind if you think that's the case. I presume you know your own mind."

Costa looked at Jojo, whose anxiety had risen to a high level during the final minutes of the lawyer's presentation, but Jojo kept his peace. Costa shifted his eyes to Junior.

"This is *shit!*" proclaimed Junior. "But you need to know a few things. *He* can't do this because no one wants him around here. You need to talk to *me*. Talk to *me* because I know what's what and I'm the eldest. With *him* out of the picture, I have the seniority. So *you* call *me* when you see it's the only way this can work!"

Junior stalked out, but Costa noted that he had retained the business card.

Ferdie hesitated, but he had already taken himself out of the running, so he followed his brother. Jojo took the opportunity to nod his head awkwardly at Costa and take off after Junior and Ferdie.

Costa looked back and forth at Henry and Candido.

"What do you think, gentlemen? Is Junior right?"

Henry waited for his uncle to say something first, but Candido kept quiet. So he spoke.

"Mr. Costa, choosing Junior would be a big mistake. You won't get good work out of him unless you supervise him constantly. If he wants the job at all, it's because he likes to boss people. And because he can't think of anything else to do."

Henry paused. Candido still didn't speak, so Henry continued.

"Junior is right about one thing, though. Uncle Candy burned his bridges when he took off to Fresno. His authority here is gone and it's not coming back. You should pick *me*, Mr. Costa. I know I can do this and I'm ready. I promise I won't let you down."

Still nothing from Candido. Costa prompted him.

"What do you think, Mr. Francisco? Do *you* think your nephew is ready?"

A few seconds ticked by before Candido finally answered.

"Hank is just a kid. He's a good boy and a hard worker, but he's a kid."

"Well," said Costa, "I think I have my contestants."

He shook hands with Henry.

"Your uncle and I are going for a walk, Mr. Francisco. Where can I find you in about an hour? We need to have a chat."

APRIL 1972

Paul and Gio Have a Chat

"So, do you speak Italian?"

"A little. I want to study it someday so that I can become fluent in it."

"I wish I knew more languages. I wish I knew them *well*."

"You're being greedy. Two isn't bad."

Paul Francisco and Giovanni Machiavelli were in the latter's room in Fleming House on the Tech campus. They were going over problems from their advanced calculus class. As a transfer student, Paul had lacked priority to get a room in student housing and had ended up living off campus. Sometimes he hung out in his classmate's room. It was a kind of refuge, where the like-minded young men could unwind from the intensely competitive Tech environment.

Besides, they were both Catholic and grandsons of immigrants, a demographic combination that seemed to be poorly represented in the Tech student body.

"I'm thinking of giving up the battle, Paul."

"What battle?"

"My name. Everyone writes it as J-O-E. Maybe I should just go along."

"That *is* the way you pronounce it, Gio."

"Sure, but I get tired of explaining it to people and then having them forget all about it anyway."

"The Anglos are trying to grind you down, Gio. You must resist the *bastardi*."

"*Si*," replied Gio.

"'*Non carborundum*' and all that," added Paul in mock Latin.

They weren't getting any work done, but it was pleasant to bandy words, even if some of them weren't real. There were imaginary numbers, so why not words?

Paul found Gio's easy-going manner particularly congenial. He felt lucky to have a friend who put him at ease and distracted him from anxious thoughts about success and failure in the challenging curriculum. He could let his guard down with Gio and engage in self-mocking word games.

"I don't think there are many Portuguese-speaking students at Tech," observed Gio.

"What? Are there *any*?"

"Besides you? Yeah, I think we should count the guy from Brazil."

"Oh, right. Yeah, he counts."

"Who speaks Portuguese in your family?"

"Well, my folks, obviously. It was their primary language when I was growing up, which is why I learned it first and still retain a significant amount. And I still use it on the weekend when I go home and visit my grandparents. Except for my baby brother, who is growing up in what's become an English-speaking household, my siblings speak it, too. Somewhat, anyway."

"In my family, the Italian died out with my father. I'd hear him use it with his parents sometimes, but he never used it at home."

"How many people at Tech speak Italian, do you think?" asked Paul.

"Probably a whole lot more than speak Portuguese!"

"Obviously. You know, I think I may be an oppressed minority!"

"Really? Good thing for you that you can pass for Anglo."

"Yeah, right. It's like a superpower. I can speak their language just the way they do and pass for one of them."

Gio had an amused expression on his face.

"That's not exactly true," he said.

"What's not true?"

"That you talk English 'just the way' others do. Have you ever listened to yourself?"

"I do not deign to honor such meretricious calumnies with a response."

Gio laughed indulgently.

"Yeah, like *that*. You're playing right now, but you do that more than you probably realize. Perhaps you can't help it."

Paul winced at Gio's well-placed barb.

"Yes, you're probably right, but I don't know if I'm happy or sad about it. My words spill out in funny ways sometimes." Paul paused a moment, pensive. "Did you know that Gauss considered becoming a philologist instead of a mathematician?"

"Ha! Close call! People remember you when you're the greatest mathematician of the late 18th and early 19th centuries, but who ever made his mark as the greatest philologist in the world? Gauss definitely made the right choice." Gio did a quick mental playback of Paul's last remark. "Excuse me, *amico*, but did you actually draw a comparison between yourself and *Carl Friedrich Gauss?*"

Paul flushed in embarrassment.

"What? No! No, no, no, no, no, *no*! We have clearly established that I am not a super-genius, just a perfectly ordinary *average* genius. Average for Tech, anyway. I am a humble scholar without pretension."

"Ha! And a liar, too, it seems. Maybe it's genetic. A lot of that going around in your family?"

"The genius? Or the lying? I don't think I can characterize my entire family with a few unqualified descriptors. It's much more complicated than that. Big family, too."

"Are your younger sibs going to follow in your footsteps to Tech?"

"Nope. And a blessing to Dad, too, who is digging deep to pay my tuition here. He doesn't need more semi-geniuses to send to big-ticket academies. My sibs will go in their own direction. They're not following me as I try to escape from the family farm."

"Cousins?"

"Even less likely. One of them stopped at high school with a diploma he has difficulty reading and the other two will make do with junior college. I think all of them see the family farm as their one and only option. It's the way of the world, after all: You do what your dad did."

"Hardly. Like me, you're part of an immigrant family. Clearly your grandfather wasn't content to do what his father did. Part of your family tradition is to *change* the family tradition."

"*Touché!* 'It is a very palpable hit.'"

"*Hamlet*, Act Five."

"Ouch! Another point. I think I should meekly surrender now."

Gio had been idly flipping the pages of their advanced calculus text. It was a set of notes in typescript, custom-bound by the college's print shop. Paul had been deeply impressed upon first seeing a custom-printed textbook with the Tech name and logo on the cover. He was fascinated at the thought of being able to make one's own books.

Gio was looking at an item on the homework sheet for their class, nudging his friend back toward some actual schoolwork.

"Do you remember Morera's theorem? What is it?"

"Closed loops and path integrals, I think," said Paul. "Just a minute." He pulled out some folded pages from the middle of his textbook and consulted them. "It's on page 232."

Gio flipped his book open to the indicated page and there was Morera's theorem.

"Okay. How did you do that? Did you memorize the book?"

"No, Gio, I just checked the index."

"Our book doesn't *have* an index. It's a bound typescript."

"But you saw me do it. I have an index on some pages I keep tucked in the book."

"And where, exactly, did you get an index?"

Paul was smiling, pleased to have surprised his classmate.

"I made it."

"You *made* an index? You indexed our entire textbook?"

"Yeah, it didn't have one and I thought it would be useful. So I made one."

"Okay, I got that bit about your being 'average at Tech,' but I want to assure you. That kind of behavior will never be 'average.' It's not in any way normal."

"I thank you for your words of high praise."

"Don't mention it. Now when can I get a photocopy?"

AUGUST 1982

Henry and Dinis Have a Chat

Dinis Costa found Henry Francisco right where Henry had said he would be, sitting on the bench under the big evergreen tree in his parents' front yard.

"Thanks for hanging around, Henry," said the court-appointed receiver, extending his hand for another handshake.

"No problem," said Henry, standing up and shaking hands. "Would you care to go inside to talk? I'm sure Mom and Dad won't mind. Or we could stay here."

"Or we could take a stroll. I'd rather walk and talk. Your uncle and I tramped back and forth on the north side of the dairy. How about if you and I do the south side?"

"You're the boss," said Henry.

Costa smiled.

"Why is it that you've already managed to grasp a concept that continues to elude your relatives?"

"It could be that maybe I'm smarter or maybe more practical."

"Let's hope it's both."

The irrigation canal was not far from Paulinho and Carmina's house. Henry followed Costa as the attorney trudged up the side of the canal's bank and began to amble west. Each bank was topped off with a dirt road. Since the canal ran parallel to the dairy's south-side corrals, the two men had a good view of them while walking along the embankment.

"I'm going to cut to the chase, Henry. I intend to designate you as the manager of your grandmother's estate."

Costa heard the young man suck in a surprised breath.

"That's good news, Mr. Costa, but — uh — I mean, I thought we needed to talk first."

"Call me 'Dinis.' We've already talked as much as we need to. My mind was just about made up before I even came out here. The meeting with the five of you was to make sure I wasn't making a mistake."

"Well, uh, okay, . . . Dinis. But I don't understand how you picked me, sight unseen."

"I did my real research in advance. I wanted to be sure I used due diligence in handling your grandmother's estate, so I asked a lot of dairy farmers what I should do. I asked the people who know the business first-hand."

"What did you ask them?"

"The obvious things. First, I asked who they would hire if they could have one person from the Francisco dairy farm. You and Jojo were usually the ones mentioned. Junior and Ferdinando — not so much. Your Uncle Candido was specifically ruled out by several people who said they didn't think he would take orders."

"Uncle Candy likes to be boss."

"I heard that many times. So then I went to my second question. I asked people who they would choose to *run* a dairy farm, not just work on it. That's when Jojo dropped off the radar screen. No one saw him as management material. Folks could imagine Candido in the job, probably because he was already doing it, but many added the comment that nothing would improve if he kept managing the dairy farm. Ferdinando got a few plugs from dairymen who saw him in town frequently on family business. They figured he had learned the ropes from his father and would have a fighting chance. Ferdinando even did better than Junior, because people said Junior was making a botch of things in his father's absence. The guys who suggested your name were sometimes concerned that you have no experience running anything, but a few of those people said they thought you had potential. No really negative comments."

"I'm grateful for that. Really grateful."

"The overall pattern is unmistakable. The local consensus is that your uncle is an unimaginative plodder."

"My uncle is at his best when he plods unimaginatively. It's never good news when he decides to be creative. If he gives you any trouble about not getting the estate management job, just ask him about green cotton."

"What about green cotton?"

"I'm surprised no one mentioned it to you. Probably from an abundance of other examples. Remind me and I'll tell you all about it later. Or ask Dad."

"Deal."

"So what was the run-down on the rest of the contenders?"

"Junior is apparently a sociopath. Jojo is a follower, not a leader, but definitely a hard worker. You might ask Jojo to stay on as an employee of the Francisco estate."

"I might, but he'd refuse. It would be disloyal in his mind if he stayed. You can bet that Junior will drag him off into a new dairy farm operation as soon as they have their inheritance money."

"You'd know them best. I'll leave that decision to you. And your other cousin, Ferdinando, is a mama's boy who can't cut the apron strings because he's wearing it."

Henry wasn't especially close to his cousin Ferdinando, but he winced.

"That's a mean thing for people to say, even if it's true."

"And also irrelevant. He's taken himself out of consideration. As did your father, for some reason."

"Dad is happy doing what he's doing. His TV business is doing well and he now has two shops in town. He still loves the dairy farm, but he hopes I get it. He says his time as a dairyman is past and it would be a mistake to come back after moving on like he did."

"I respect that. I presume, however, that he wouldn't be averse to giving you fatherly advice in the event you were to look to him for assistance."

"Oh, no. Not averse at all."

The men were walking past the hay barn. Costa noted that some of the bales had darkened along one side. That probably indicated water damage. Henry followed Costa's gaze and saw what he was seeing.

"We left those out in the field too long, Dinis."

"And how did that happen?"

"Uncle Candy thought my cousins were going to do it and my cousins thought their father had hired professional hay haulers. Or they pretended to think that because they didn't want to do it. We've gone back and forth because sometimes my uncle thinks we'll save money by doing it ourselves, but it's backbreaking work that you can't do unless you're really toughened up. Overall, it's faster and cheaper to let the pros do it. They have the gear and the muscles. When Uncle Candy would have us do it — Junior, Jojo, and me — we'd have to rent the gear, which is expensive, and end up all broken down with sore muscles, backs, *everything*. And we'd take two or three times as long as the pros to get it done. The hay hauling situation is a typical Uncle Candy problem: no one knows quite what to do and no one knows what the orders will be until it's almost too late. Or just too late."

"Tell me about irrigation on the Francisco farm."

Henry shook his head in dismay.

"It's like the Three Stooges or something. Uncle Candy will tell Junior to irrigate a field. Junior will tell Jojo to do it. Then Jojo may tell me or Ferdie to do it. But Ferdie might drive off without doing it. I'll do it, of course, but it'll be a few — or several — days late. And they don't like it if I do it on my own initiative because I'm supposed to wait for instructions. I'm a hired hand, you see, and need to be bossed."

"I saw evidence of flooding in the alfalfa field north of the dairy."

"Yeah, and dry spots, too, no doubt. You don't have leeway on when to turn off the water like you do when it comes to turning it on. You have to be there to shut the valves before you let too much into the checks. You need to watch it instead of forgetting it all day and ending up with standing water at the far end. I've suggested the simplest fix, which is a drainage ditch across the low end of the field to take away the extra water. It's wasteful of your water allocation, but so is flooding a check and drowning the crop in it."

"So why didn't your uncle go for it?"

"He said it takes acreage out of cultivation and reduces the crop, but I say we lost more to the check-flooding. I also think he didn't do it because some people think it's an admission that you don't think you'll shut the water off on time — an admission of incompetence."

"One might think that dead crops might constitute an even less ambiguous admission of incompetence."

"Damn betcha! I also suggested alternating the checks. If you leave half of them dry while irrigating the other half, all it takes is a shovel and a few quick channels sliced through the berms to bleed excess water from the flooded checks into the dry ones. It's not an automatic remedy like a drainage ditch, but it doesn't take any space and you can easily put things to rights by block-ing off the channels again."

"Why didn't that one go?"

"It supposedly takes longer. But that's nonsense. You normally do only a few checks at a time anyway, to maintain pressure at the wellhead. Open all the valves and the water pumped from the canal seeps out slowly. Open just a few, and it gushes out. I guess the only problem with alternating checks is that you have more to keep track of, but that's not much of a reason."

"Soon, Henry, you'll be able to handle irrigation on the Francisco place however you deem appropriate."

"You're going to think this is silly, but that makes me amazingly happy. Just amazingly happy."

"I don't think it's silly at all. If you didn't feel that way, you might not be the right person to manage Teresa Francisco's legacy."

"I'll do right by *Avó*'s memory. Just watch me."

"Every step of the way. That is, at least until the estate is settled and you're running it in your own right."

"I hope that's a prediction, Dinis."

AUGUST 1973

Jojo Finds a Keeper

Gerry Chamberlain was learning to enjoy the holiday and birthday gatherings of the Francisco and Salazar families. Now that he and Mary Carmen were married, his status had been elevated in the eyes of the people who had become his in-laws. Also, as his wife, Mary Carmen could now freely engage in such shocking behavior in public as sitting on his lap when all of the chairs and couches were full — or when Mary Carmen pretended they were.

Also, Gerry was the beneficiary of a slow but distinct trend toward the English language in the Francisco-Salazar clan. While the majority of the adults spoke Portuguese to each other, more and more of the younger people preferentially defaulted to English, especially among themselves.

One of the notable exceptions to this rule was sitting on a couch on the opposite side of Paulinho and Carmina Francisco's living room. The young woman was sitting primly at one end of the sofa while Jojo Francisco was cross-legged on the floor, sitting right at her feet. He had left her side only to fetch her cake and ice cream or to freshen her iced tea.

The August birthday party was celebrating the natal anniversaries of Chico and several of his descendants, including his daughter Fatima and his grandsons Henry and Alexander, plus his daughter-in-law Carmina and his grandson's wife Linda. The birthday cake listed all their names, with the exception, of course, of Chico himself. He was identified by his title of "Avô" rather than by his name, as was only proper. Since Alex was just a toddler turning three, he would be having a separate party on his actual birthday, a special celebration that was devoted just to him.

Today, however, was the official joint party for all of the August arrivals. It would therefore be the biggest and most crowded family event of the month. The regular attendees were always quick to single out and gossip about any new guests. There was no reason to expect this party to be any different.

"Who is that?" whispered Gerry into his wife's ear.

Mary Carmen tightened the arm she had around her husband's neck as she pulled herself closer to whisper back.

"Jojo's new girlfriend, obviously. He snagged one right off the boat."

Paul Francisco was sitting right next to his sister and brother-in-law, but the room was noisy enough so that he couldn't hear what they were saying.

"What did you say, Mary Carmen?"

Gerry, Mary Carmen, and Paul put their heads unself-consciously close together in a *tête à tête à tête*. There were several other similar conversational knots amidst the hubbub of the crowded room.

"Her name is Rita Branco," reported Mary Carmen. "She's a cousin to in-laws of cousins on the Francisco side of the family, so she's not actually related to us."

"From Terceira?" asked Paul.

"Yes," replied his sister.

Paul looked at his brother-in-law and rolled his eyes.

"'Not actually related to us,' my foot! Get a load of it, Gerry. *All* of us are descended from the same little island in the Atlantic. I swear that we California Portagees are *all* cousins. What an incestuous lot we are! This is hardly a case of bringing new blood into the family."

Gerry wisely kept his own counsel. He liked to describe his own ethnic heritage as "Heinz." When people reacted in puzzlement, Gerry would say, "It's easier than trying to list all fifty-seven varieties." He was still fascinated by the density of Portuguese heritage in the Francisco family and understood why he had been viewed suspiciously as the possible vanguard of a barbarian invasion.

"She doesn't speak a word of English," said Mary Carmen.

"That's interesting," observed Paul, "since Jojo's Portuguese is pretty bad."

"What's the problem?" asked Gerry. "From where I'm sitting, it looks like the only words he needs are '*Sim, querida.*'" Through practice, Gerry's pronunciation of "Yes, dear" in Portuguese was approaching the gold standard. Mary Carmen gave him a quick pinch, because he always used it with a mocking servility.

"You have a point, Gerry. You know, Mary Carmen, 'Branco' is a good family name for her. She is as pale as milk."

"And 'Rita' is a good name to help restore Jojo to his ethnic tradition," said Mary Carmen.

She grinned at her husband and brother as they pondered her set-up. Since her gag was obviously going to be language-based, Gerry let Paul feed her the straight line.

"And why is that?"

"It's simple. If they get married, Jojo will be able to answer every question with '*Chama Rita*'!"

Paul tried to give his sister a long-suffering stare, but started chuckling involuntarily. Mary Carmen was laughing a lot more loudly at her own witticism. Gerry waited patiently for the explanation that he knew would be forthcoming. As usual, it was his brother-in-law who was prepared to deliver a mini-lecture.

"The *Chama-rita* is a very popular dance form in the Azores. But as separate words it can be translated as 'Call Rita.' We can all see Jojo as the obedient spouse who responds to all questions with 'Ask my wife' or something like that. Mary Carmen scored a good one."

"I'm not in the best position to appreciate bilingual puns," said Gerry, "but I've been getting used to them occurring around me."

"Paul can't criticize my efforts. *Chama-rita* is way better than his lame effort at Junior's wedding."

"I remember that one," said Gerry. "He said it was about time that Junior got some 'Sofistication' when he married Sofia. I thought it was pretty funny."

"A strained effort," proclaimed Mary Carmen.

"Let me try again, then," said Paul.

"Okay. Just give Gerry and I a chance to brace ourselves."

"'Gerry and *me*,'" said Paul, correcting automatically.

Mary Carmen and her husband exchanged indulgent grins. Mary Carmen shook her head.

"Just shut up and tell us your joke," she admonished her brother.

"I will do the best I can despite your paradoxically impossible command," Paul replied. "I was merely going to point out that perhaps Rita Branco is a 'keeper' in both senses of the word."

Mary Carmen cocked her head while thinking. Gerry wrinkled his brow instead. Gerry spoke up first.

"If you're talking fishing, a 'keeper' is a fish that you don't have to throw back."

"Good one, honey," said Mary Carmen. "That would be nice, you know, if Rita is the one that Jojo should hang on to."

"And the other meaning?" prompted Paul.

"I've got that one," said his sister. "It could be someone who takes care of things. Like a keeper at the zoo or at the kennel. Or a groundskeeper."

Gerry was smiling.

"Paul, are you suggesting that Jojo needs a keeper?"

Mary Carmen answered her husband's question.

"Can you doubt it, honey? I can't think of a better candidate for a keeper than my cousin Jojo. Of course, I think it's probably true that *most* men need keepers."

A related conversation was going on in another quarter of the room. Paulinho was sipping a soft drink as his sister-in-law Odile sat nearby, demolishing a piece of birthday cake.

"Who is Jojo's girlfriend?" he asked her.

Odile's fork paused with the next bite near her mouth.

"Rita is a very nice girl who just got here from the Azores. She's not related to us," she said quickly, before popping the frosted morsel in her mouth.

Paulinho smiled. Odile's last sentence was almost obligatory in conversations about courtship. Sometimes it seemed that the gene pool was more of a tiny puddle. He looked over at his nephew, who was staring up adoringly at Rita from his place on the floor. Rita was clearly adhering to the strict rules of the Old Country. Jojo wasn't being allowed to hold her hand in public lest it scandalize everyone.

Funny how tight a grip she has on him despite not touching, he thought.

"Jojo and Rita are certainly on their best behavior," he commented to Odile. "I like seeing that."

Odile smiled as she wiped some icing from her lip and sucked it off her finger.

"I like it, too, but they have company right now. I caught them mooching with each other when they thought they were alone the other day."

Her plate empty, Odile struggled to her feet and headed to the kitchen for another helping. If she ate it in there, no one in the living room would see her. She firmly believed that multiple helpings were more fattening if they were eaten in the same place in front of witnesses.

"'Mooching'?"

Paulinho turned at the sound of Henry's voice. His son had evidently overheard his father's conversation with his aunt. Sharp ears.

"That's what she said, Hank. But that's Aunt Odile for you. My sister-in-law is the only person I know who's illiterate in two languages."

As Odile passed their couch, Mary Carmen got up to accompany her aunt into the kitchen and left her husband and brother to fend for themselves for a while.

"Are you looking forward to life among the mortals?"

Paul did not need to ask what Gerry meant.

"I have at most minor regrets," he said. "Going to Fresno State gives me a chance to catch my breath after two years of Tech."

"Do you have any definite plans?"

"Pretty definite. I transferred to Tech after two years at JC and earned my bachelor's in only two more years. Since I haven't been letting any grass grow under my feet, I see no reason to let it happen at Fresno State. I'll shoot for a master's in one year."

"Sounds a bit ambitious."

"Sure, but why not? It's at least partly compensatory. If I'm going to a public university after earning a degree at the most elite school on the West Coast, I don't want people to get the idea that I've lost it and I'm going to rest on my laurels. If I do the master's in one year flat, that'll put people on notice that I am not slacking off."

"Have you talked to an advisor?"

"Yeah. The math department chair assigned himself as my advisor. He told me that they don't 'normally' recommend trying to finish grad school in only two semesters, but he also said I was welcome to try it."

"A one-year program would be a money-saver, too."

"That's actually sort of part of the deal. Tech was *expensive* and I had minimal financial aid. I didn't qualify for the super-genius merit grants and the family isn't poor enough for me to qualify for the financial-need grants. Mom and Dad dug deep for my two years and I did my best to make sure there wasn't a third. The Cal State University is a hell of a lot cheaper and now the need for speed is related more to my personal priorities than to financial ones."

Paul paused to consider.

"Still, I have to admit. My folks support my being a full-time student. That's a sweet deal and I have to prove they're backing a winner. It's personal and family pride."

"It's a dirty job, but *someone's* got to do it," said Gerry, smiling.

"Ah, you're making fun of me, Gerry. I shouldn't make it so easy for people to do that. I'm bitching about things when I should be quietly grateful."

"I don't see the 'quietly' part ever working out," said Gerry. "And you already seem to have the 'grateful' part in place. You do, however, sometimes forget who you're talking to."

"*Touché!* You'll be doing your business bachelor's at Fresno while I'm doing my math master's, but I'm Mr. Free Ride and you're doing it on your own dime. I can be an insensitive lout."

"But I can't really complain. Mary Carmen and I both have jobs lined up. She'll be working full time while I'll be going to school and working part-time. I'm going to college on the spousal-support plan. If you decide to continue past your master's degree, you should consider getting a wife to support you during doctoral studies."

"I dare you to say that again in front of your wife."

NOVEMBER 1973

A Strange Duet

"Memorial switchboard. How may I direct your call?"

"Room 464, please."

"Just one moment."

The switchboard operator put the call through and there was the sound of the phone ringing in Room 464. Once, twice, three times. There were many reasons, of course, why a patient in the oncology ward of Fresno's Valley Memorial Hospital might not be responding immediately to her bedside phone. However, the fourth ring was interrupted by a click and the sound of the phone being picked up.

"Hello?"

The voice sounded tired and a bit raspy, but stronger than one might have feared for a patient undergoing yet another round of chemotherapy and radiation treatment.

"*Abença, madrinha.*" Bless me, godmother. "I just wanted to say hello this afternoon."

"Hello, honey," said Fatima Salazar, her voice brightening a little. "*Nosso Senhor te abençoe.*" The Lord has blessed you. "How are you?"

"I'm fine, *madrinha,*" said Paul Francisco, thinking that he really should have asked *her* how *she* was, but he feared the answer. "Is this a good time for a call? I hope I'm not bothering you."

"No, honey, this is a good time. You're not bothering me at all. I just woke up from a brief nap after lunch. My accomplishment for today is that lunch stayed down. I'm taking that as a good sign."

Paul was perfectly willing to grasp at straws with his godmother.

"That *is* good news. Congratulations!" He paused, wondering what to say next. "Have you had any visitors today?"

"Yes. Yes, I have. Linda brought Catarina to see me and they were here during lunch. Perhaps having company made it easier to eat the dreadful hospital food."

Fatima gave a small chuckle, which Paul echoed.

"You're probably right, *madrinha.* Perhaps I should visit you during mealtime."

"Don't worry about that, honey. I'm doing all right. You should be concentrating on your studies. You're in grad school now," she said, with a hint of wistful envy in her voice. "You're the first one in the family to go that far. It must be keeping you busy."

"It does, *madrinha,* but as long as I'm right here in Fresno with you it's no big deal to cross town to get to Valley Memorial."

"You know that you're welcome at any time, but I want you to focus on your education. You know I have my eye on you. I have expectations."

"Thanks, *madrinha,* I know you do. I won't disappoint you." He hesitated before asking his godmother a question. "Have the doctors told you when you get to go home again?"

Fatima sighed, the weariness back in her voice.

"I want to be home for Thanksgiving. I'm counting on it. That's very important to me."

"That's important to me, too, *madrinha*. We're all counting on your being there."

Paul went off on a tangent, hoping he had something that would entertain his godmother and briefly provide some diversion from her travails.

"*Madrinha*, I made an interesting discovery at the university library. I thought you would be interested in it, too."

"What's that, honey?"

"The library has an enormous music collection on its second floor. I spend most of my time between classes in one of their listening rooms. I've been listening to rare recordings of Wagner and Mahler and Strauss almost every day. I know you'd love it if you could see it."

"I'd love it more if I could hear it. But it sounds great. I'm glad you found it, as long as it doesn't distract you too much."

"Oh, no, it doesn't. I put the headphones on and do my homework. Real analysis is more fun with a sound track provided by Mahler's seventh symphony."

"Uh-huh."

"And this week I made a discovery that I think you'll find amusing. It's by Rossini."

Rossini was one of Fatima's favorite composers. She adored *Il Barbiere di Siviglia*. Her godson had her attention.

"It's a comic duet," he said.

Fatima could hear some fumbling on her godson's end of the conversation. She wondered what he was doing.

"From one of his operas?" she asked.

"No, *madrinha*. I think it's a standalone piece. I recorded it from the music library and I have it here. Dad made me an adapter cord that plugs my cassette recorder into a headphone jack. It's called *Duetto buffo di due gatti*."

"A comic duet for two cats?"

"That's right, *madrinha*. It's just a couple of minutes long. Listen."

Fatima heard a click and the hissy sound of a cassette player coming through the phone. A mezzo-soprano and a bass-baritone began to sing to the accompaniment of Rossini's music. The only word they ever sang was "meow," with variations of intonation and the occasional hint of purring or hissing. She recognized the music as having been derived from Rossini's opera *Otello*, although she was quite certain the feline lyric must have been added later for comic effect. She laughed quietly as she listened.

Paul heard his godmother's gentle laughter as he hunched awkwardly over the phone, the mouthpiece of the handset held close to the tape recorder's speaker while the earpiece remained pressed to his ear so that he could hear his *madrinha*'s reaction.

Under normal circumstances, a conversation between Paul and his godmother would have been free-wheeling and wide-ranging. Now, however, he was conflicted between his need to talk to her and his fear of overtaxing her illness-impaired resources. He anxiously wanted to ease her mind and distract her from her troubles — but without making himself a nuisance. His tension ebbed slightly as he heard the evidence of his *madrinha*'s enjoyment of the recording.

The Rossini pastiche came to an end. Paul clicked off the cassette player and straightened up.

"How did you like it, *madrinha*? Wasn't that bizarre?"

"Very much, honey. Thank you for sharing that with me. Thank you for thinking of me when you discovered that."

"I think of you all the time, *madrinha*. And I'll be thinking how great it will be to have you home for Thanksgiving."

"I'll be there. But right now I think I should rest some more."

"Oh! Of course. I hope I didn't tire you out."

"No, honey. I'm just tired all the time. But I hope to be feeling stronger soon."

"I hope so, too, *madrinha*. Take care."

"You, too, honey. Good-bye."

"Good-bye."

There was a click on the other end of the line as Fatima hung up her phone. Paul wiped the tears from the handset and returned it to the phone's cradle.

Third Time Is Not the Charm

It felt a little peculiar to be walking across the Francisco dairy yard. Paul had walked this path from his parents' home to his grandparents' innumerable times, but now it was beginning to feel foreign.

His two years in Pasadena had been punctuated by weekends back in Tulare County. You can't get too homesick if you don't really leave home. The year in Fresno had been even closer to home base — close enough, in fact, to allow a quick round trip in an afternoon or evening, if circumstances warranted. It had taken Paul's first two years at the University of California, living more than two hundred miles north of the Francisco dairy farm, for him to begin to transform his sense of where "home" was. He was back in Tulare County for the summer, but the geographical fulcrum of his life now lay well to the north.

And it didn't help, of course, that his baby brother Alex had taken over his old room, relegating him to the back bedroom.

This might well be his last summer spent in the place where he grew up. He could visit his elderly grandparents on a daily basis and there'd be opportunities to see his *madrinha* Fatima, who was battling a recurrence of breast cancer. Paul was fretful over the condition of his favorite aunt, but Fatima Salazar had survived the initial onslaught of her disease as well as the arduous delivery of seven children. His *madrinha* was tough, and he was hopeful she would achieve remission again. No one else in the family was as *simpático* to him as his *madrinha*.

As Paul neared his grandparents' home, he was startled to hear Junior's voice calling his name. His cousin seldom deigned to call people by name. His preferred technique was to yell "Hey!" at the top of his lungs, drawing everyone's attention, and then pointing at the person he actually wanted.

Junior was standing in one of the open doors of the workshop next to the barn, a big corrugated metal building full of the tools and equipment that a dairy farmer would use in doing his own maintenance. His cousins, however, had also used it for other things. One of the shop's work bays — the one with the block and tackle — had practically been converted into a dune buggy factory. Paul noticed that a stripped-down chassis was in place, but didn't show much sign of recent work. Now that Uncle Candy's two oldest boys were married, family responsibilities were keeping them from escaping as frequently to Pismo Beach to test out their big-wheeled creations.

Junior was actually waving at him and smiling, acting almost human. Everyone had been surprised when he managed to court and marry Sofia Silveira, but even more surprising was the doting and solicitous father he had become when their daughter Filipa had arrived. People were beginning to think there might be hope for him after all, and began ending their routine criticisms of his bumptious behavior with, "but he sure is a good dad to his little girl." Sofia was great with child again and near her time. Paul had a sudden intuition that he knew what news Junior wanted to share.

"Hello, *primo*," he said, addressing Junior with the Portuguese word for "cousin." "How are you doing?"

"I'm fine, thank you." It was as if Junior had learned a foreign language he had never spoken before. "And Sofia is doing fine. And Filly is doing fine at her grandmother's. And my son is doing fine." His smile broadened into a grin.

"Your son? My congratulations!"

Paul shook hands with Junior, thinking to himself that they hadn't touched hands in any kind of amicable way for at least a decade. More likely two.

"Thank you," said Junior again, the miracle transformation persisting.

"Have you chosen a name yet?"

"I wanted to talk to you about that." Junior paused. "Sofia picked Filly's name and she said I could choose the boy's. I'm not sure that 'Candido' is the right name to give him."

"I'm not sure what to tell you, Junior, but I do rather think that each child deserves his or her own name. That's not exactly our style in this family, but you don't have to make him 'Candido Francisco the Third.' That's going to be rather unwieldy, especially when you include the middle name."

Junior was pensive.

"I don't know," he said.

"Speaking of your middle name, why not use that? In fact, switch your names and let him be 'Gabriel Candido Francisco.' He'll be the only Gabriel in the family and he won't have to deal with Roman numerals or the dread prospect of being called 'Little Candy.'"

Junior was nodding his head slightly.

"I guess that's not a bad idea."

"It isn't as though you like your own name that much. You'd be giving your boy a break."

A vehicle had turned in from the road and was audibly crunching the gravel on the driveway next to their grandparents' house. It was Ferdinando's car.

"Let's try out your idea on Ferdie," said Junior.

Paul noticed that Junior had refrained from such comments as he had heard before, such as "Oh, look, here comes the fagmobile!" or "Hey! My baby sister is here!" He had to consider that a major improvement.

Ferdinando climbed out of his car and walked toward them.

"It's worth a trip to see the boy, Paul! He's as cute as his mother!"

Junior was taking Ferdie's implied dig in stride. *Only a cameo appearance by Rod Serling would make sense of this day*, thought Paul.

"Paul has an idea about naming the boy," said Junior. "What do you think of 'Gabriel Candido'?"

To Paul's surprise, Ferdie looked aghast.

"No, no, *no*! You have to name him after yourself. Everyone is expecting it!"

"I wasn't," demurred Paul. "And I don't think that Junior considered it obligatory."

Ferdie was adamant.

"This is Junior's chance to put another link in the chain. We've never had 'the Third' of anything. It would be really classy and sophisticated!"

Junior's face had darkened, and Paul saw signs of his cousin's more customary demeanor. Ferdie's plummy pronunciation of "Third" had triggered a thought.

"I don't want my boy being called 'Candido the Turd.' I won't have it!" Junior said.

For a moment it looked like Paul's proposal might return to favor, but Ferdie was resourceful on this occasion.

"That's not a problem, Junior. You don't have to call someone 'the Third' because there's a Roman numeral three after his name. The nickname for boys like that is 'Trey.' That's how they do it. Like I said: It's classy!"

Junior actually seemed to be listening to the younger brother he usually disdained. Paul wondered if Junior was thinking in dynastic terms. It seemed like he might be.

His poor son!

Jojo Has a Wreck

Carmina Francisco was pleased that alfalfa had been planted on the east forty. The field lay across the street and directly in front of her house. She often looked out across that field through the kitchen window over the sink. It was a nice view while washing dishes or peeling potatoes.

It made her unhappy, however, when crop rotation turned the field into a stand of corn. It gave her a feeling of claustrophobia. What was the point of living in the open country if you couldn't see farther than a wall of green across the street?

But even the most lush alfalfa crop preserved her sight lines and her equanimity. It would grow two to three feet high before the men or boys would take to the field in swathers and cut it down. The process would repeat several times during the growing season.

Carmina was up to her elbows in suds when a swather near the far end of the field finished cutting hay for the day and turned toward the dairy. She knew that her nephew Jojo was the operator because she had seen how rapidly the machine had moved back and forth through the field on its harvesting runs. Of all the members of the family, Jojo was the speedster, always pushing the envelope. Paulinho sometimes complained to his wife that it did no good to save money by using family members as workers if those family members ran up spectacular repair bills. It was almost always Jojo at the center of such stories.

A swather is an ungainly piece of farm equipment that sports a huge reel in front that looks like the paddlewheel of a riverboat. The reel turns as the swather moves through the field, sweeping the standing alfalfa toward the machine's scythe (or sickle bar), a horizontal array of reciprocating blades that cuts off the alfalfa near ground level. Depending on the manufacturer of the swather, there would be either conveyor belts or large augers to move the harvested hay toward the midline of the swather, where it would pass through the machine (sometimes through rollers) and be left heaped on the ground in a long trail behind the swather. Once the swaths of hay had dried sufficiently (but not too much), it would be time to bring out the hay balers and pack up the hay into large twine- or wire-bound blocks for storage in the hay barn.

The reel and scythe assembly — or harvesting head — in the front of the machine is large and heavy, so the swather has a triangular chassis with the trailing point loaded down with ballast to offset the weight of the harvesting head. The driver of a swather sits behind a low screen or railing separating him from the reel and normally uses a pair of steering levers instead of a steering wheel.

Now that Jojo no longer had to worry about cutting alfalfa, he had opened up the throttle and was driving the swather as fast as he could down the dirt road adjacent to the irrigation canal. He had raised the reel from its normal harvesting position near the ground and it was now locked for transport in its upright position at the end of two hydraulic arms.

The dirt road was not very level. Whenever the swather hit a bump in the road, the hydraulic arms holding the reel and scythe would bounce up into the air a bit and drop back down onto the supports that kept them from falling any further, such as back down into harvesting position. Since Jojo was pushing the swather to its top speed, the harvesting head was often floating up into the air before dropping back down onto its supports.

Carmina could clearly see what her nephew was doing during his race down the dirt road. In addition to using the steering levers for their intended purpose of pointing the swather in the right direction, Jojo was also clinging to them to keep his seat during the jouncing journey. He was a small figure in the distance, but it seemed to Carmina that Jojo was having a great time, hitting a bump at top speed and becoming slightly airborne over the driver's seat as the floating reel assembly simultaneously rose up on its hydraulic arms. Jojo's butt would crash back onto the seat at the same time that the reel assembly crashed back down onto the support rests.

Carmina was neglecting her dishes as she watched her nephew in rapt attention. She had seen him do foolish things before, but today he was in full daredevil mode. Bump! Float! Crash! Bump! Float! Crash!

The reel assembly shuddered every time its arms banged again the support rests. Bang! . . . Bang! . . . Bang! . . .

Then came the moment that seemed unnaturally prolonged. The swather launched its ungainly self into the air after a particularly bad bump, the reel and scythe rose to their fullest upward extension, and the entire assembly smashed down onto the support rests with a force that the rests could not withstand. They snapped and the hydraulic arms came free from their mountings. The entire harvesting head — reel, scythe, and augers — fell onto the ground in front of the rest of the swather — the triangular chassis with its driver — and was instantly hit in a bizarre one-vehicle collision of the swather with itself.

Before the noise of the impact and subsequent grinding stop reached Carmina's ears, she saw the eruption of dust and debris as her nephew did an involuntary handstand on the steering levers, to which he was clinging for dear life. Then he flipped over and vanished between the severed and colliding components of his vehicle.

Carmina didn't scream. She couldn't even move. She was paralyzed in shock.

A few seconds later, her eyes widened in disbelief as she saw Jojo emerge from the wreckage and climb back up to the driver's station, where the seat leaned drunkenly to one side and the steering levers were twisted beyond their design limits. The two stub ends of the reel's hydraulic arms had jammed into the swather's chassis and created a thin rectangular slot into which a scrawny teenager could fit.

Jojo had had the instantaneous sensation of being crushed before the two parts of the swather wreckage suddenly recoiled and freed him. He dragged himself out of the narrow slot and found himself atop a crazily canted chassis section. He noticed that the driver's seat had been hit from behind by one of the concrete ballast blocks and partially torn from its mountings. The ballast blocks from the trailing point of the swather had been launched into the air and Jojo now observed the scatter pattern, which left heavy blocks to the left and right of the remains of the swather as well as a couple in the middle.

Jojo realized he had survived a bombardment as well as a wreck. Later he would undoubtedly find bruises, but at the moment he couldn't even find any scratches. Something came unplugged inside of him and he started to laugh.

He was still clutching the broken seat in hysterical laughter when his Aunt Carmina reached him.

~~~~

The Soareses Visit the Franciscos

~~~~

Although it was only two o'clock in the afternoon, it was already a hot day. Six people sat in the sheltering shade of the front porch. Lunch had been pleasant and companionable. Paulinho Francisco and Carmina Soares were relieved that their parents appeared to be getting along. Their fathers seemed particularly pleased to be making each other's acquaintance, while the mothers were significantly more subdued.

Paulinho was ready to declare the visit a success and escort his future in-laws to their getaway car. He wasn't eager for Carmina to leave, but he was still anxious that something might go wrong. Carmina, on the other hand, was as cool as could be. Paulinho was impressed by his fiancée's equanimity and wished he had the same kind of *sang-froid*.

The Franciscos' rectangular front porch was furnished with a wooden bench that ran along three sides. Paulinho and Carmina ended up sitting together on the center section, not by accident, where they could conveniently and discreetly hold hands. Chico and Teresa settled down on the bench adjacent to Paulinho while Carmina's parents sat down on the one next to her.

Teresa had placed a pitcher of lemonade and some glasses on a low table in front of the benches. She poured the icy beverage into the tumblers and began to distribute them, starting with Paul and Beatriz Soares.

"*Muito obrigado*," said Paul Soares. *Much obliged.*

Beatriz nodded politely.

Paul Soares and Chico Francisco both had the name "Paulo" written on their baptismal certificates back in Terceira, but Soares had been in the United States long enough to Anglicize his name by dropping the final vowel. For his own part, Chico could not remember a time when anyone had addressed him as "Paulo." Both men nevertheless found the coincidence of their first names amusing.

"There is a shortage of first names in the islands," laughed Chico.

In many ways, what Chico said in jest was true in fact. Strong traditions caused most families to name sons after their fathers or grandfathers. Many Portuguese men were therefore known by an *apelido* — a nickname — which made it possible to distinguish among people bearing the same name. In addition to Paulo Francisco having become "Chico," he and his wife had tagged their younger son — also named "Paulo" — with the diminutive "Paulinho," which had persisted into his adulthood.

Soares and Francisco had more than a birth name in common. Both men were also dairymen, but Chico had hundreds of acres under cultivation with diverse crops, while Paul had devoted the entirety of his comparatively meager eighty acres to alfalfa and hay crops for his cows. That was often the lot of dairymen in Southern California, where urban encroachment was making open land too scarce and expensive to afford in farm-sized spreads. Paul had been jealous of the expanses of cotton, corn, wheat, oats, alfalfa, and barley he had seen on either side of the road as they drove to the Francisco dairy.

Everyone was speaking Portuguese, except that Paul Soares would casually patch in chunks of English in a way that was foreign to Chico and Teresa. Soares and his wife were immersed in English-speaking culture in Southern California to a degree that the Franciscos were not in Tulare County. Paul dropped in an English term as he told a mildly amusing anecdote at his daughter's expense.

"Chico, your boy is going to have a lot to teach my girl after they get married. When we passed the cotton processing facility on the way here this morning, Carmina asked me what it was. When I told her it was a 'cotton gin,' she said, 'Oh, I thought that was a drink'!"

Chico held back his laughter for just a moment, until he saw that Carmina was taking the story in good humor. His future daughter-in-law had colored slightly, but she was smiling. The parents laughed, Paul the loudest and Beatriz the most subdued, while Paulinho smiled at Carmina and squeezed her hand.

"That's not fair, *padrinho*," he said to Paul Soares, using the Portuguese word for "godfather" as a sign of respect. "How can Carmina know about cotton gins when you don't grow cotton?"

Everyone except Beatriz seemed to be having a good time, but even she participated in the conversation about plans for the wedding, which was a year and a half in the future. She rather disapproved of such a short engagement period, but young people today were extraordinarily impatient.

The Soareses and the Franciscos sipped lemonade as the hour progressed. Soon it would be time to leave. Beatriz was wilting in the Central Valley's dry heat and was fanning herself. She leaned toward Teresa and said, "Is it always this hot here?"

"Oh, no," Teresa replied. "It's often much hotter."

An expression of dismay flickered across Beatriz's face. She sat back and looked toward her daughter, who was at her right hand. Carmina noticed her mother's attention and raised her eyebrows slightly. As the fathers were launching into a renewed discussion of the virtues of Holstein cattle as milk cows, Beatriz beckoned to her daughter and leaned toward her.

Carmina cocked her head in her mother's direction as Beatriz whispered in her ear.

"You see what it's like here, Carmina Maria? I tried to warn you. It's not too late, you know!"

Beatriz was not good at whispering. The fathers were engrossed in their conversation, but Teresa heard every word clearly, as did Paulinho. Carmina turned her face toward her mother and hissed, "*Mãe! Stop it!*" Beatriz sat back in her seat, spine straight, with both hands clasped around her nearly empty lemonade glass and an innocent expression on her face. Teresa's face was serenely neutral and Paulinho followed his mother's lead and affected not to have heard anything.

"Beatriz, would you like more lemonade?" asked Teresa politely.

"Oh, *sim. Muito obrigada.*"

When it came time to leave, the fathers gave each other hearty backslaps and handshakes. Both were clearly delighted with the match their children had made. The mothers were less demonstrative, exchanging a brief handclasp and tiny smiles on their faces. Carmina daringly gave her fiancé a kiss on the cheek before climbing into the car with her parents.

As he put his car in gear and began to roll toward the road, Paul Soares shouted, "*Até logo!*" *Till later!* Carmina was waving at them in the back window as the car traveled away from them.

Chico threw his arm over his son's shoulders as they walked back toward the house.

"Good job, boy. Good job. *Nice* girl."

"She appears to get it from her father's side," sniffed Teresa.

PART VII

JUNE 1983

Paul Gets Summoned

Paul Francisco had barely made it through the front doors of the county courthouse before Harold Widener grabbed him by the arm and dragged him into a corner of the lobby.

"Hi, Harold. I'm awfully glad to see *you*, too," said Paul.

"Listen up, Paul. I don't like surprises and we just got a surprise."

The announcement of a surprise was, of course, itself a surprise to Paul, who blinked a couple of times before asking a question.

"What kind of surprise, Harold? And why are you making a point of telling *me* about it?"

Widener was pumped up like a bantamweight fighter in the final minutes before a title bout. He was eager to swing. The target, however, was uncertain.

"Biddy is putting you on the stand."

"Excuse me?"

"Biddy has decided to use you as a rebuttal witness — hostile, of course. I don't know what she's up to, but I don't see many possibilities."

Widener stuck up his index finger.

"*One.* The bitch is just batty and wants to take a poke at you before going down in flames. Putting you on the stand gives her the opportunity to vent."

"But why me?"

"After Foster presented the letter you received from your grandmother, Biddy knew her case was crap. It was crap *before*, but after that she finally knew it. You provided the final straw to break the back of her case — and it was more like a big, fat hay bale."

A smile flashed across Widener's face at the recollection. He got serious again as he raised a second finger.

"*Two.* Not only does Biddy not like you, she thinks the jury won't like you. She thinks putting you on the stand will give the jury a chance to look at you, decide they don't like Franciscos very much, and turn against the respondents."

Paul frowned at his aunt's attorney. He seemed genuinely puzzled.

"I'm a perfectly nice guy, Harold. Why wouldn't the jurors like me?"

"Frankly, if Biddy plays you right, she could make you out to be a bit of a pedant. Folks don't always like people who are pedantic."

"Pedantic: inclined toward unnecessary displays of knowledge or esoterica," said Paul.

"*Yes!*" exclaimed Widener. "*Exactly* like that! Do that on the stand and the jurors will wonder if you're going to 'beam up' at the end of your testimony. And don't forget the letter you wrote to your godfather accusing him of suborning perjury on the part of your cousins. Biddy could bring that up and try to make you look like a thug. It's a potential problem."

"Sorry, Harold."

Widener stuck up a third finger.

"*Three.* It's a 'Hail Mary' pass where Biddy has no idea what's going to happen but she's hoping that she can get you to spill something that will miraculously turn the case around. Right now she's lost, so she might as well try for a miracle."

"Which do you think it is?"

"The last one. From what I know of Biddy Onan — and I know quite a bit — she's not imaginative enough to project herself into the jury's point of view and visualize how to alter their perspective. You'd think an attorney should know how to do that, but she's demonstrated time and again that she doesn't. Anyway, there's no point in my speculating endlessly and spinning lots of theories. Biddy is a bad lawyer in a bad place and her only hope is to do something. Anything. That's as good and simple an explanation as any."

"Yeah. Occam's razor: don't multiply hypotheses unnecessarily."

Widener look at him sadly for a long moment.

"I swear. It's like you get it and you *don't* get it at the same time. Just hear me on this. No cute games on the stand. No word play. No double entendres. (And if you say that double entendres *are* word play, so help me I will punch you.) Play it straight, cool, and polite."

"I can do that, Harold. Honest. I'm here to defend my family and I can do this for them."

Widener still looked unhappy.

"I certainly hope so. You'd better! Just to keep your mind focused, be aware that I will personally gnaw your bones for my breakfast if you screw it up!"

"Consider me duly warned. I promise to behave myself. Besides, you can still have Uncle Candy for breakfast at the divorce trial. There's a lot more flesh there to chew on, aged to perfection and marinated in quite a lot of wine."

Now Widener grinned and shook his head.

"You know, Paul, sometimes I think this is the case of a lifetime. Yeah. But I wish I knew what I did in a previous life to deserve it."

OCTOBER 1959

The Anointing of the Sick

Seven-year-old Ferdie was serving as doorman. The chubby little boy was the one who opened the door when Paulinho pressed the buzzer.

"Good morning, *Padrinho* Paulinho. Good morning, *Madrinha* Carmina."

"*Muito obrigada*, Ferdinando. Thank you."

Ferdie stood aside so that his uncle and aunt could enter. He greeted his cousins less formally, nodding at Paul, Mary Carmen, and Henry as they trailed behind their parents. Since Henry was only three, his five-year-old sister had firmly taken charge of him and they walked in hand in hand.

Ferdie closed the door behind his guests and ran ahead to the living room.

"*Mãe! Padrinho* and *madrinha* are here!"

They followed Ferdie into the living room, where Odile was relaxing in a recliner. She had mellowed in the nearly eleven years of her marriage to Candido, but she had also grown fatter. It did not unduly handicap her. Odile was still young enough and strong enough to move briskly when the occasion suited her. But it seldom did.

She rose to meet her guests as Ferdie took up his post by his mother's side.

"We brought Jojo a get-well card," announced Carmina to her old school chum. She handed the card to Odile. "We don't need to bother him if he's resting or asleep."

"No, that's okay. I think he's awake anyway. We can go see and give him his card. Jojo is on the divan in the den."

The visitors followed Ferdie and Odile into the den, where a television was playing cartoons with the sound turned low. Eight-year-old Jojo was lying on a couch with his head propped up on a pillow and a knit blanket over him. His eyes were half-closed, but he wasn't quite asleep.

"You have visitors, João José!" said his mother as she lowered herself into a chair next to Jojo's couch.

Jojo blinked up at his uncle and aunt.

"*Bom dia, Tio. Bom dia, Tia,*" he said.

"Good morning to you, too, sweetheart," said his Aunt Carmina as she leaned over him and brushed his hair back from his forehead.

The adults then proceeded to talk about Jojo as if he were not there, while Paulinho and Carmina's three children stood in a close cluster, looking with concern at their cousin, but not knowing what to do.

"What did the doctors say about him?" asked Paulinho.

"He will be very sensitive for two or three more days," replied Odile. "But it'll be over a week before he's completely comfortable."

"Were they able to . . . *fix* things?" asked Carmina.

"Yes, I think so. The doctors said he should be okay," said Odile. She was uncomfortable trying to say more because she had not understood much of what their family doctor had told her and Candido. Words like "prepuce" and "glans" had flown right by her. The one thing that was clear in her mind was that her middle son was now missing his foreskin. The doctors had decided to trim away its remains after Jojo had torn it on the barbed wire fence that separated their yard from the field.

Odile looked at the clock on the wall.

"Oh, look at the time! I'm supposed to freshen his ointment every four to six hours."

Ferdie hustled over to the end table next to the couch and picked up a tube that was lying on it. He handed it to his mother. She uncapped the tube and then matter-of-factly turned down Jojo's blanket. Her son wasn't wearing anything from the waist down. His mutilated penis was on display for the entertainment of his visitors. Jojo's face flushed red and he closed his eyes tightly.

"The doctor says it can't be bandaged because it needs the air," said Odile, as she daubed the ointment along the angry red lines that showed where Jojo's foreskin had been. Paulinho and Carmina seemed as unperturbed as Odile, but Paul felt queasy and fought an impulse to bolt from the room.

Mary Carmen was a model of clinical detachment, having been her mother's little helper during Henry's innumerable diaper changes. She proceeded to enlighten her baby brother.

"Oh, look, Hanky! Jojo has a bad owie on his winkie!"

Paul made a sudden odd noise. He was stifling an impulse to chuckle.

"Winkie"? he thought to himself. *Jojo won't be doing any winking with* that *again!*

He was embarrassed to be finding amusement in his cousin's plight. His scrotum, however, felt shriveled in sympathetic horror, so he knew he was not entirely callous.

Junior had heard the noises attendant on the arrival of visitors and burst into the den to see what was going on. He paused in the doorway for a moment.

"Oh," he said, seeing who was present and not evincing any particular enthusiasm for their guests. Then he looked toward his reclining brother and grinned.

"Hey! Looking good, Jojo!"

Then he was gone.

Odile was shaking her head as she capped the ointment tube and pulled the light blanket back over her son.

"I don't know what gets into Junior sometimes. He's a puzzle."

DECEMBER 1982

The Lasagna of Death

Paul's mother was already on the front porch when he pulled into the driveway. She must have been watching the road for his approach. He got out of his car and walked up to her. He had never seen her looking so drawn and tired.

"Where is he, Mom?"

She reached out and took his hands.

"In his usual place. In the family room. He's watching TV."

"How is he doing?"

"All right, I guess. He seems calm. Calmer than *I* am," she said, the last words coming out in a strangled voice.

"I'm sorry, Mom. Are you okay?"

"No. Of course not. But I'm managing. Your father seems very fatalistic. I don't know how he can be so calm."

His mother was repeating herself. Paul started to steer her back toward the house.

"Let's go inside. Let's sit down with Dad."

Paul took his mother's arm and walked up the steps with her. He finally noticed that Alex was standing in the doorway.

"Daddy's going to get better, you know. We're going to beat it!"

His little brother was cloyingly upbeat. As far as Paul was concerned, the preteen simply didn't understand the situation. People did not "beat" inoperable lung cancer.

"You never know, Alex. Nothing's certain."

Alex stepped out of the way to let them into the house, but he had a pugnacious expression.

"But I *am* certain! I *know!*"

"Right, Alex."

Paul didn't know how to handle his baby brother. The twelve-year-old was Daddy's pet. Of course he was in denial over his father's illness.

"Go in and see your father," said Carmina Francisco. "I'll get some dinner ready."

The family room was in half-light. Paulinho was sitting in his favorite chair, facing the large-screen TV and holding the world's most complicated remote control in one hand. The volume was unusually low. Paul normally avoided the family room when his father was watching TV because his dad liked to crank it up. But nothing was normal today.

Paulinho stood up without any sign of impairment. He wasn't dead yet. That wasn't scheduled for another six months or so. Paul approached his father awkwardly for a clumsy hand-clasp and half-shake. Things never go smoothly when two undemonstrative people have to deal with a quintessentially demonstrative situation.

"You didn't have to come down, son."

"Sure I did, Dad. And they can do without me in Sacramento for a couple of days."

"I appreciate it, but there was no hurry. They say I still have months to go, which is all any of us have anyway. It just depends on how many. Two- and three-digit numbers are nicer than one-digit, of course." Paulinho paused. "But look who I'm telling!"

Paul gave his father a pained smile at the man's game effort.

"That's a good point."

"Sit! Make yourself at home. You *are* at home, after all."

Paul sat down without comment. His father's remark was probably inadvertent, but it reminded him of the time that he had referred to returning to Northern California as "going home." Dad had bristled and corrected him: "You *are* at home."

But not really. Not anymore.

"I guess I'm going to see your grandparents and your *madrinha* a little sooner than I expected," said Paulinho.

"Be sure to give them my best," said Paul, trying to play along with his father's casual mood. "I hope you won't mind too much if it's postponed a little. I think Alex needs your company more than they do."

"Yeah, but I don't know that I have much say in the matter."

The conversation had petered out. Paulinho filled the awkward silence by pointing his remote control at the TV and bumping up the volume. They sat and pretended to watch the show on the screen without any of it registering. They successfully wasted several of Paulinho's precious and increasingly scarce minutes.

Carmina appeared in the doorway from the kitchen.

"Honey, are you hungry? I have the nice lasagna that Ferdie brought over."

Both men turned toward her, but Paul waited a beat to let his father answer first.

"Not now, sugar. Maybe I'll have a bite of something later."

Paul stood up, wondering at the peculiar expression on his mother's face. She was . . . irked. How could she be irked at her dying husband?

"I could eat," he said. It was also an opportunity to take a break from the awkward effort of keeping his father company.

Several minutes later, he offered his compliments to the chef.

"Ferdie made this? It's really good. Dad doesn't know what he's missing."

The expression was back on his mother's face.

"He won't eat it," she said.

Paul was puzzled. There was a weird sideshow going on in the midst of a family tragedy.

"Why not? Dad likes Italian food just fine."

"You know why."

Paul had a forkful halfway to his mouth, which he left hanging open at his mother's remark.

"He's not eating it *because* Ferdie made it?"

"That's exactly why," said Carmina, her lips pursed in disapproval.

Paul had difficulty grasping the surreal moment.

"Good Lord, Mom! My crazy father won't eat something prepared by Ferdinando because his nephew is a gay boy? Jesus Christ. Ferdie is his godson!"

Carmina winced because "gay" was a strictly forbidden word, but she also nodded.

"That's right."

"So what the *hell* is that crazy old man afraid of? He's under sentence of death and he still won't eat his nephew's lasagna. Does he think Ferdie's lasagna might give him a case of twenty-four-hour AIDS? How stupid is *that?*"

"I'll make him a sandwich later, sweetheart. There's no point in talking about it."

"Geez. My father is both sick in the body *and* sick in the head!"

"Lower your voice, sweetheart."

"In case you didn't notice, Mom, the TV is still blasting away. We could sing Brünnhilde's immolation scene without disturbing him."

His mother gave him a wan smile.

In the back of his mind, Paul was trying to figure out whether he was being insensitive. He was remonstrating with his mother over her spouse's irrationality when that same spouse was running out of sand in his hourglass. He decided the silly side issue was a welcome distraction. Mom was probably better for having a minor grievance to nurse. It would make dealing with Paulinho more grounded in reality. They could canonize him later, when he was gone. Right now it was a matter of Carmina finding a way to get through from day to day.

"Don't worry. I won't say anything to him. No one's going to teach him any new tricks at this stage. If he hasn't learned by now that gay bachelor nephews are often the best cooks, that lesson is simply beyond his reach."

"Thank you, sweetheart. I'll be sure to tell Ferdie that we really liked his lasagna. No need to tell him about your father."

Having praised her nephew's cooking, Carmina now pushed it away. Her appetite had been nonexistent since yesterday's shocking news. She went into the family room to sit with her husband while she still could.

Paul helped himself to seconds. Poor old Ferdie. Nature and nurture had appeared to gang up to turn him into the family's stereotyped bogey man and internal exile. Paul wondered again why his cousin had never packed his bags and left for the bright lights of the big city. Perhaps he simply loved his family more than they loved him back — and was resilient enough to deal with it. That might be it. Ferdinando Alberto Francisco was tougher than anyone gave him credit for.

Damned good cook, too.

JUNE 1971

Henry Is a Pall Bearer

"It was his hat what killed him."

"What do you mean, Hank?"

"It happened when he lost his hat. The wind took it. He grabbed for it. Or something."

Or anything, thought Paul. *No one really knows how Terry rolled that tractor.*

He and his brother Henry were in the back seat of the family Buick, while their parents were in front. They were returning from the funeral of Teofilo "Terry" Torres. Henry was in a new navy-blue suit that he had worn as one of the pallbearers. It exaggerated the ashen pallor of his skin. He couldn't stop trying to figure out how the accident had happened.

"Maybe he got distracted and lost control. Or maybe he tried to turn too fast. You know, to go back and get his hat."

Most tractors had a top speed near twenty miles an hour. That might not seem like much, but it was more than enough velocity to kill an unprotected human being.

"Terry was driving down the paved county road near his family's dairy farm," continued Henry. "His brother found his hat about a hundred yards from where they found him. The tractor was laying on its side, still running. Terry was laying on the road. His skull was cracked from hitting the asphalt. His brother told me there wasn't any blood. He looked like he was asleep in the casket. You couldn't see anything."

The tractor had been a three-wheel model, the kind that many farmers favored for cultivating row crops. Two large wheels in back provided the motive power while a single small wheel in front provided the steering. It was easy to drive a three-wheel tractor through a field of young cotton plants. The front wheel traveled between two rows of delicate shoots without crushing any of them, while the spacing of the rows ensured that the two rear wheels did the same.

What was good for row crops was less good for stability on the road.

Henry Francisco and Teofilo Torres had been the same age. Only fifteen. Henry and five other teenage farm boys had carried their friend to his final resting place and stood at attention during the burial ceremony.

"It was like I kept thinking Terry could open his eyes and get up again. I knew it wasn't true, but it felt like it. It felt like it until I saw the hole they dug for him."

Henry's eyes were dry, but his voice was strangled in his throat and the natural color had yet to return to his face.

The Buick pulled into the Francisco driveway next to the tall evergreen tree and the brothers emerged into the warmth of the late morning. Henry peeled off his coat and handed it to his brother.

"Take this in for me. I have to go for a walk. I'll be back in a while."

Henry trudged off toward the canal road and turned to walk parallel to the irrigation ditch, hands deep in his pockets. His brother and his parents watched him go.

"It's always been a dangerous job," observed Paulinho quietly. "Once it was horses. Now it's tractors."

He was rubbing a wrist, remembering how it had been broken when the horse he was riding had stumbled and thrown him. There were no longer any horses on the Francisco dairy farm.

"Yeah," said Paul, agreeing with his father. "This family has been lucky so far."

"That's for sure," said Paulinho. "Come on. We may as well go inside."

"I'll tell you one thing," said Carmina, as they were climbing the stairs. "It's a miracle that Jojo is still alive."

Paulinho laughed humorlessly as he held the door open for his wife.

"And we probably don't know the half of what he's gotten up to!"

MARCH 1990

Trey Makes a Mistake

"Damn! What a piece of shit!"

Candido Gabriel Francisco III had pulled on the control rope to adjust the direction of the hay chopper's spout, but it had no give to it. No doubt one of its guide pulleys had jammed again. He was fairly certain he knew which one. He put the tractor in neutral and clambered down to the ground.

The fourteen-year-old's name was in keeping with a long-lived family tradition of recycling. He and his father, however, adhered to a tradition of more recent vintage in declining to answer to either "Candido" or "Candy," the names by which the boy's estranged grandfather was known. His father was universally addressed as "Junior" and he went by "Trey."

Trey walked back to the hay chopper and looked over the big goose-necked contraption he had been towing. It was still making a huge racket because Trey had not disengaged the power take-off clutch before dismounting from the tractor. The PTO shaft connecting the tractor and the chopper was spinning like a dervish at over five hundred revolutions per minute.

Junior Francisco had purchased the chopper second-hand at a farm auction. His struggling dairy farm could not afford anything newer. It worked pretty well for the most part, although Junior and his sons had a constant struggle to keep the aging machine's quirks under control. The chopper had lost the protective metal mesh that normally screened the PTO shaft, so Trey was careful to stand clear of the spinning menace. The mesh safety screen was now sitting on the ground next to the barn, awaiting the day when Junior would have enough time to weld it back into place.

Trey could have returned to the tractor and disengaged the PTO, but he was impatient to free the control rope and knew to be careful. He climbed up onto the chassis of the chopper and reached up to the rope, tugging a bit. Now he could tell that the suspect pulley was guilty as charged. He took another step up onto the machine and used both hands to work the rope loose from where it was wedged in the pulley, making sure it ran free again through the pulley's grooved wheel.

Satisfied with his quick fix, and hoping it would last, Trey began to climb down, cautiously moving only one hand or foot at a time.

It was on the verge of spring, but the weather was still cool in northern Oregon. Trey had decided that morning that it was cool enough to wear a windbreaker, but not cool enough to zip it up. As he lowered himself from the chopper, a loose corner of his windbreaker touched the spinning PTO shaft. At five hundred revolutions per minute, the shaft reeled it in.

Trey was jerked into the shaft like the crack of a whip. He was barely able to register that his arm was lying on the ground before the lights went out and he fell down beside it.

OCTOBER 1969

Carmina Wants One More

"I've been thinking."

"That's allowed."

"I've been thinking about kids."

"There are lots of kids to think about around here, if that's what you want to do. Personally, I prefer thinking about our three instead of Candido and Odile's three, or Fatima and Louis's seven."

"Fatima says that her seven are a gift from God."

Paulinho gave his wife a sharp look. Carmina was a devout Catholic, just as he was, but it was extremely unusual for her to initiate overtly religious conversations. Their Catholicism was an immutable background to their lives, but normally no one felt a great need to actually talk about it. Carmina's choice of particular topic also made him extremely uncomfortable, since it pushed him near the edge of irreverence.

"I'm sure they are. I've heard my sister say that, too. But it's a gift that nearly killed her a couple of times," he said.

"I know. But it didn't, did it?"

"No, it didn't. You're right."

"And there were no problems with our three."

"No."

"Well, what I was thinking about was . . . what if there were four?"

Paulinho sat stunned, taken utterly by surprise. It took him a while to find his voice again.

"But, sugar, our children are all teenagers now."

Carmina smiled at him, as if he had made a joke.

"It's not *their* age that matters, honey."

He felt boxed in. Paulinho knew it would be a bad idea to tell Carmina she was too old for more children. That would be impolitic. Besides, it was manifestly untrue.

"I know, sugar. You're right. But one more? This late?" He paused. "Why?"

Paulinho couldn't be certain, but he thought Carmina looked slightly disappointed in him, as if he should have figured something out, but hadn't. She was very good, however, at concealing her feelings, so it was mostly a suspicion on his part. It was a suspicion that was quickly confirmed.

"It's been over a year since the pope condemned birth control," she reminded him.

He didn't smite his forehead, but suddenly he understood. Many Catholics had taken the Church's stand against contraception as a medieval tenet that had somehow survived into the modern era. They were therefore surprised when Paul VI had renewed the condemnation so forcefully in the *Humanae Vitae* encyclical. Many Catholic theologians had protested the pope's decree and the laity, especially in the United States, gathered the impression that the matter was not quite settled. The pontiff, however, had not backed down. By degrees, it became apparent that the Vatican's chief executive had not cast off the trappings of his absolute teaching authority. He meant what he said.

Paulinho had been lulled by the initial furor into thinking the matter was on hold, but now it was obvious that Carmina had taken it much more seriously. It was entirely possible for them to have more children. They were both in good health and Carmina was still in her thirties. With just a little luck, they could be blessed anew before her fortieth birthday.

"Maybe we should be obeying the pope," said Carmina.

Paulinho was thinking less about the joys of obeying the pope than the benefits of being a middle-aged man with the bouncing baby proof of his continued virility. If Carmina was willing to put herself through the experience, she could do it for the greater glory of God, but Paulinho would have lots of secondary motivations. He would then have one more child than his older brother. It was a sweet thought. But —

"Oh, God!" he said. "What will we tell the kids?"

Carmina smiled, and Paulinho noticed her dimples were more pronounced than he had seen them in a while.

"We'll just tell them to expect a little brother or sister. That's not too difficult."

"I guess not," he agreed.

But privately, Paulinho expected bedlam to erupt.

APRIL 1967

Paulinho Fixes a TV

Challenge Electronics was a nondescript standalone building with a prime location on Olive Avenue, the main thoroughfare into town. Paulinho Francisco had driven past it hundreds or thousands of times on his business errands. More recently, however, he had taken to pulling into one of the parking spaces next to the building to spend a little time talking electronics with Bob Challenger, the proprietor.

"Hey, Paulie! How're you doing?"

Challenger had the usual cigarette dangling from his mouth as he greeted his visitor.

"Come over here and check this out!" he said to Paulinho, waving him over to where he was squatting down behind the open chassis of a television set.

"What's this, Bob?" asked Paulinho, hunkering down next to his friend.

Bob grinned at him.

"It's a *television*, Paulie!"

Both men laughed.

"Yeah," said Paulinho, "but apart from the *obvious*, what do you have here?"

"A junker. Maybe. Got it as a trade-in. Perhaps worthless. Perhaps not."

"Well, that sounds pretty definite," said Paulinho.

"Yeah, definitely definite."

Bob held up a tube.

"What about it, Bob? That's a 6J6 triode oscillator. A bad one, too, judging from the black smudge on the inside of the glass. What's the deal?"

"Yeah, it's a bad 6J6, right out of the tuner. I replaced it, of course, but the TV still doesn't work."

"Okay. That just means it's not just a tuner problem. Or maybe the tuner has more than just a bad tube in it."

"True that. But I don't want to bother with it. The tuner was an obvious problem, and now it has one less problem. But I don't want to waste time tracking down whatever other problems it has."

"So it's a junker — like you said."

"Could be, Paulie. But I just said I didn't want to waste *my* time working on it. I'm completely willing to waste *your* time." Challenger grinned. "You come in here often enough to talk shop and waste me and my technician's time, so maybe I can keep you out of the way by giving you a project."

The smile indicated that Challenger was engaged in some good-humored kidding, but there was just enough truth in his words to give Paulinho a small pang of conscience. It was true that he enjoyed talking about electronics with Bob Challenger and other techs he had met through Mr. Harper and the evening school electronics classes. It was probably also true that he disrupted the workflow at Challenge Electronics by looking over their shoulders during some of the more interesting repairs, as much as he tried to stay out of their way.

"Here's the deal, Paulie," continued Challenger. "This television is worthless right now. It has multiple problems. It's not worth my time to track down all the fritzes in a junker trade-in. But if you manage to get it working, then it's worth a few bucks as a cheap used TV that I can sell to a customer looking for a second set for his den or game room. I'll cut you in for fifteen percent commission on whatever it sells for, if it sells."

"That could be fun, Bob."

"I sure hope so, because it sure as hell is a terrible deal in terms of finances. You might end up making fifteen bucks for twenty hours' work. Who knows? Or maybe zip!"

"Still sounds like fun. It'll give me something to do when Candy wants me out of his way at the dairy."

"Exactly, Paulie. If your big brother doesn't have room for you in the sand-box, we can take advantage of it."

"You know, you keep describing everything in terms of its benefits to *you*."

"Of course. Why would you expect anything different? In case you didn't notice, I am a *successful* businessman!"

The men laughed. Challenger stood up and clapped his hands together as if dusting them off, although they were both perfectly clean.

"Let's haul this junker over into the corner of the shop where it'll be out of the way and you can work on it at your convenience. What do you think? Is this going to work? I'm guessing maybe a couple of weeks before it's fixed or you decide it really is just a junker."

"Inside *one* week, Bob. Wait and see."

Candido Sees a Sign

Teresa Francisco had made the difficult decision not to wear mourning at home. If she were all in black, it would be impossible to deal with Chico. Her invalid husband had little to do. He would certainly seize upon his wife's black clothing and insist on an explanation. Since she couldn't face the task of telling him that their daughter was dead, she continued to wear her usual garments at home. There was nothing particularly bright or cheerful about them anyway, so it wasn't as if her outfits were disrespectful of Fatima's memory.

She was working at her sewing while sitting in the overstuffed chair that she favored. Her grandson Paul was sitting on one of the couches. It was the couch where he had spent many Sunday afternoons enjoying the company of his *madrinha* Fatima. Whenever Paul was at home at his parents' house next door, he had kept a sharp eye open for Fatima's car in his grandparents' driveway.

There hadn't been many visits during this summer. As Fatima weakened, she began to stay at home. Eventually she went into the hospital. It was there in August that the cancer finished its job of killing her. The Salazar family was left rudderless, with several of the children still at home, and Teresa was bereft of the apple of her eye.

Her eyes had done a lot of crying in the five weeks since Fatima's death. Teresa tried to confine it to the kitchen where Chico could not see her. He had grown concerned at the apparent aggravation of her allergies, which she often cited as the reason for her reddened eyes and frequently running nose.

Teresa was working on restoring her equanimity as well as on her sewing. She was practicing the habit of tranquility, which small domestic chores seemed to promote. Fatima's daughter-in-law had given Teresa a rosary that Monsignor had once presented to Fatima. While her eyes moistened every time she prayed with her late daughter's rosary, she took comfort in fingering the beads that Fatima had once used to count off the Hail Marys. The rosary made a lump in the pocket of her housecoat. It lay under her left hand, which held the sock she was darning. The beads would occasionally shift slightly as Teresa did her sewing, and she felt that she was drawing strength from its tactile presence.

Soon her grandson would be returning to the University Farm to resume his graduate work in mathematics. Paul had spent the summer at his parents', reading up on arcane topics and making daily visits to his *avó* and *avô*. Today he had chatted with his grandfather until the old man nodded off. Teresa was always able to get a lot more work done when Chico had company. She would be sorry when Paul's presence was reduced to holidays and his weekend phone calls.

The window next to Teresa's chair commanded a broad view of the dairy yard. She saw Candido approaching from the direction of the workshop. Soon he let himself in through the side door of the house and she heard her son's heavy tread in the kitchen. He stepped into the living room and paused when he saw that his father was napping, the old man's head slumped to one side against the back of the recliner. Candido tried to walk softly to the middle of the living room, where he greeted his mother. He often declined to sit down, which helped to ensure the brevity of his visits to his mother and father.

"*Boa tarde, Mãe.* How is *Pai* doing?"

Teresa gave a little shrug.

"He is as you see. He hasn't been complaining lately and Paul has been keeping him company this afternoon."

Candido dropped onto the couch opposite his nephew. A question popped into his head.

"Paul, do you know any of the people at the UC Ag Extension office up there?"

"Not really, *Tio.* I'm in the math department. The math and ag units don't have a lot of business with each other."

Candido looked a little disappointed, but not especially surprised.

"Yeah, I guess I see that. But if you have a chance to talk to any of them, I'd like to know if they have any — uh, I don't know — suggestions or ideas for dairy farms."

"I thought they did that all the time. Don't you still get the Extension Service newsletter?"

"Oh, sure, but the advice in there is sort of general and kind of technical. If you had friends in the ag unit it might be nice if they had some special tips for an operation the size of mine, you know."

He says "mine" right in front of his mother, thought Paul in irritation. *Has he forgotten that most of this operation is in Avó and Avô's name? And he wants me to grub for free advice from the University Farm because he can't follow their newsletter.*

"I can let you know if I hear anything," said Paul. *Which is never going to happen.*

"Okay. Thanks. Those ag people at the university are good folks. I like what they do. Most people like that, you know, like professors — they're just in it for the easy money. That's what teaching is. Easy money."

"I really hadn't thought of it that way, *Tio,*" said Paul mildly. *I wonder if he knows I'm teaching. Probably not.*

"Yeah, that's how it is."

Candido lapsed into silence. Teresa plied her needle, Chico snored quietly, and Paul sat with his hands folded. Candido stirred with another thought.

Two thoughts in one day. This must be a red-letter day for him, thought Paul.

"Say, do you know what Proposition Fourteen is?" asked Candido.

"Why do you ask, *Tio?*"

"Well, I don't know much about it, but I know we all have to vote against it."

Proposition 14 was a voter-circulated initiative to strengthen the Agricultural Labor Relations Act that had been signed into law the previous year by Governor Jerry Brown. Paul could understand that a crusty reactionary like his uncle would be opposed to a measure designed to enhance the bargaining rights of farm laborers, but Candido was opposing the measure without knowing its contents.

"Why do we need to vote against Fourteen?"

"This morning I saw a sign on a telephone pole that said '*Sí con catorce.*' That's enough for me. If the Mexicans are for it, we have to vote against it."

"*Gracias por el aviso, Tio,*" said Paul.

Candido gave him a sharp look.

~⚬~

Candido and Odile's Anniversary

~⚬~

Candido and Odile's home was filled with well-wishers. Paulinho popped open the champagne bottle and quickly filled two goblets with the fizzy liquid. He handed them to his brother and sister-in-law.

The guests began to chant.

"Drink! Drink! Drink!"

Candido bent down awkwardly so that he and Odile could intertwine their arms and sip their champagne in linked unison. Their guests laughed and applauded as the couple took quick drinks and unhooked themselves from each other. Candido straightened up in relief.

Paulinho had filled several more goblets, which were being passed among the adults. The children were being supplied with cups of equally fizzy Shasta lemon-lime soda. A second bottle was popped open and the process continued until everyone had a drink in his or her hand.

Paulinho raised his goblet.

"To Candido and Odile! Congratulations on thirty years of wedded bliss!" he said aloud. Inside, he said to himself, *A little exaggeration is allowed on special occasions.* "May you have thirty more!"

There were scattered cheers and a couple of cries of "Hear! Hear!"

People were circulating through the adjoining living room and dining room, sampling items from the hors d'oeuvre trays that Ferdinando had spent the morning preparing for his parents' anniversary. They came up to Candido and Odile in twos or threes to offer congratulations and to spend a minute or two in small talk before returning to the food and drink.

Cynthia Parker came gushing up to Odile and hugged her rotund friend.

"Oh, Odile, this is just wonderful! Congratulations! You are *so* lucky to be married to a wonderful man like Candy!"

Cynthia gave Odile a peck on the cheek and turned to Odile's husband.

"And congratulations to you, too, Candy! My best friend is the luckiest woman in the world to be married to you!"

Cynthia had had to bend down to embrace Odile. Now she rose up on tiptoe to give Candido a quick buss on the lips. Candido tingled at her touch.

"I just can't say how happy I am for you!" exclaimed Cynthia.

"Thank you. That's very nice of you," said Candido in a subdued voice.

Odile took Cynthia by the hand and began to pull her toward the kitchen.

"Come with me. You have to see what Candy gave me as an anniversary present."

Candido watched the women depart from the living room. Odile had been very specific about her expectations for her anniversary gift. Candido had only to pay for it and pick it up. The kitchen was now sporting a new Radar-Range microwave oven. It was the latest model and something of a showpiece in a region that was slow to adopt the latest innovations. Microwaves had been gaining in popularity in the United States for ten years already, and Odile was concerned that she might not be the first in her neighborhood to have one.

Louis Salazar strolled over to offer congratulations to his brother-in-law. A widower now for more than a year, Louis found it difficult to participate in anniversary celebrations, but his daughter-in-law Linda had encouraged him to attend. She had said that the Salazars should show up in force, just as the late Fatima would have wanted. Linda had also added, peculiarly, that she would feel more comfortable if her husband's family was well represented at the party. Louis read that as saying that Linda and Manuel would not participate otherwise, and consented to go with them.

"Welcome," said Candido, as he shook Louis's proffered hand. "I'm glad you could come."

"It's good for the family to be together," said Louis. "Fatima always liked gatherings like this. Linda reminded me of that just this morning."

A peculiar expression passed over Candido's face at the mention of Linda's name, but he otherwise remained calm.

"That's very true," agreed Candido. "My sister was a very family-oriented person. I'm sure that's why your family turned out so well."

Louis nodded his head in acknowledgment of Candido's polite exaggeration about the condition of his family.

"*Muito obrigado*, Candido. And I congratulate you on thirty years of marriage. Fatima and I were blessed to have that many plus a few more. A lifelong love is a sweet thing."

Candido suddenly smiled impishly.

"You know, Odile thinks I still love her because I roll toward her in bed."

Candido chuckled at his own wit despite the sour expression on his brother-in-law's face. Louis was not amused by Candido's crass humor, especially in the immediate wake of remarks relating to the devotion of Fatima Francisco Salazar. Louis was offended and let his disapproval show.

Instead of trying to salvage the situation and make as graceful a retreat as he could, Candido laid it on thicker.

"It's gravity, you know. Of course the bed slopes in her direction, but I also think she's big enough to have her own gravity field!"

The volume of Candido's voice had risen as he had been striving to impress Louis with his cleverness, and a wave of silence rippled out from him as guests heard what he was saying and stopped their conversations.

Louis turned slowly and walked casually away from Candido as if nothing had happened. He kept going till he reached the door and left the party. His departure triggered a renewed bustle of activity as Salazars began to say goodbye to their Francisco relatives. Most of them managed to bypass Candido as they streamed after Louis.

Candido saw how his brother was looking at him with disappointment on his face. He gave Paulinho a microscopic shrug and moved toward the kitchen, where party noises could still be heard.

The younger family members were in there, clustered around the microwave, watching in fascination as frankfurters rolled back and forth as they plumped and sizzled.

"Ooh! They look like they're alive!" exclaimed seven-year-old Alex.

Junior and Sofia's four-year-old Filipa was clapping her hands.

"Hot wienies!" she exclaimed.

Candido saw that Paulinho had stepped into the kitchen with him. In a jailhouse whisper he leaned toward his brother and said, "Those are the only wienies getting any warmth in *this* house!"

Paulinho bristled, and whispered back.

"Dammit, Candy, give it a rest! Give it a rest for a change."

"Ha! The only thing it gets around here *is* rest," he said morosely.

But he brightened a bit when he thought of Cindy Parker.

PART VIII

~~~

Paul Takes the Stand

~~~

"Would you please state your name for the record?"

"My name is Paul Francisco."

"Please advise the court of your occupation."

"I am an analyst employed by the State Treasurer's office in Sacramento."

Beatrice Onan seemed nonplussed by the answer.

"Excuse me, Mr. Francisco," she said. "Are you not a professor at Sacramento State University?"

"No, I am not."

The attorney for the petitioners remained puzzled.

"At the University Farm campus?"

"No, Ms. Onan."

Paul finally figured out what was going on. Onan had relied on the fuzzy recollections of his uninterested cousins as to what he was doing in Northern California. Not having done her homework was making her look foolish in the eyes of the jury. Paul could have clarified matters quickly, but he was beginning to see the wisdom of Widener's insistent advice that he volunteer nothing. He would make Onan drag the facts out of him one at a time.

The petitioners' attorney appeared to realize that a war of attrition had begun. She settled down to piecing the puzzle together one bit of information at a time, handicapped by not having foreknowledge of what picture the finished puzzle might display. She was thinking bad thoughts about her clients, whose information had thus far been more misleading than helpful.

"Mr. Francisco, where were you previously employed?"

"Before joining the staff of the treasurer's office, I was employed as a legislative assistant at the state capitol."

"And before that, Mr. Francisco?"

"I was on the instructional staff at the University of California's University Farm campus."

Onan perked up at what she perceived as an opportunity to press the witness.

"Excuse me, Mr. Francisco, did I not ask you about your having been a professor at the University Farm campus?"

The question was innocuous, thought Paul, but Oscar Wilde had warned that answers could be dangerous. Here was an opportunity for him to be his hyper-correct self and simultaneously insult Onan and alienate the jury. It was exactly what Widener had warned him about. He would be carefully correct, but not rub Onan's nose in it.

"Yes, you did. But I am not now nor have I ever been a professor at the UC Farm campus."

"But you said you were on the instructional staff just now, Mr. Francisco."

"That is correct, Ms. Onan. I was on the instructional staff as a graduate student teaching assistant while in the university's graduate program, and I was later on the instructional staff as a faculty associate. I was never a professor. That's a much higher-level appointment and it would be improper to claim something I didn't have."

Onan appeared to be irritated by what seemed to her to be fine distinctions. Paul was mocking her without being overtly rude. She wasn't getting any useful information and she wasn't getting any useful outbursts. She kept plodding onward.

"Thank you for that explanation, Mr. Francisco."

"You're welcome," interpolated Paul, before Onan could frame her next question.

Piqued, she addressed the judge.

"Your honor, I would like the court to note that Mr. Francisco is a hostile witness."

"Yes, Ms. Onan. The court imagines that he would be," said Judge Knight, smiling mildly.

Unassuaged by the judge's token agreement, Onan resumed her questioning.

"Mr. Francisco, what is your relationship to Louis Salazar?"

"Mr. Salazar is my uncle by marriage to my father's sister. He is also my baptismal godfather."

"Portuguese culture takes the role of godparents very seriously, doesn't it?"

"Yes, it does."

"Godparents are thus owed a great deal of respect, aren't they, Mr. Francisco?"

"Yes, they are. Second only to one's parents."

"Mr. Francisco, did you send a threatening letter to your godfather last year?"

"I sent him a *letter*," said Paul, stressing the noun to underscore his omission of the attorney's choice of adjective.

"Are you denying that you threatened him with legal action?"

Paul blinked at Onan in mild surprise at her phrasing.

"No. I pointed out that there were risks in filing legal documents full of falsehoods."

"So you admit you called your godfather a liar."

"I said that he and the petitioners were making false statements about my grandmother and my family."

"Isn't it unseemly for a young person to rebuke his elders, Mr. Francisco?"

Paul recognized that Onan was paraphrasing the text of his letter, perhaps hoping he would disagree with the statement and allow her to catch him in a contradiction.

"Yes, Ms. Onan, it is unseemly for young people to contradict their elders without due cause."

"'Due cause,' Mr. Francisco? What 'due cause' excuses your abuse of your godfather? You've admitted you owe him respect."

"I owe my godfather respect second only to that I owe my father. When they are in opposition, I choose my father's side."

Onan paused to collect her thoughts. She had been considering introducing Paul's letter into evidence and requiring him to read it to the court, but that no longer seemed likely to sway the jury in the direction she wanted. She looked at the serene expressions on the faces of the attorneys for the respondents. One of them had undoubtedly coached Paul to cast any discussion of his attack on his godfather as a defense of his father. Widener smiled at her. She scowled and turned back to the witness.

"Mr. Francisco, I would like to discuss with you the matter of the peculiar letter you are alleged to have received from your grandmother."

Onan's deliberately provocative statement had not been phrased as a question, so Paul did not feel obligated to respond. He did not rise to the bait. Appearing disappointed, Onan went on.

"Is it your contention, Mr. Francisco, that you received a full-page handwritten letter from your grandmother in January 1980?"

"I did receive a full-page handwritten letter from my paternal grandmother in January 1980," said Paul, tweaking the attorney slightly by reminding her that he had *two* grandmothers, so her question had lacked in specificity.

"Isn't it unusual for grandmothers to send their grandsons full-page letters?"

"*Objection*, your honor!" Harold Widener was on his feet and shaking his head as if in bemusement. "The learnèd counsel is asking the witness to make a judgment that is beyond his demonstrated field of expertise. If she would like to prepare the witness for the question by first establishing that he has special knowledge of the epistolary practices of grandmothers with respect to grandsons, then I will withdraw the objection."

Judge Knight was grinning and some of the jurors laughed aloud. The sound of amusement from the jury box reminded the judge to resume a stoic demeanor and he tried to keep a tinge of humor from his voice.

"The objection is sustained. Ms. Onan, do you wish to pursue further questioning along the lines suggested so kindly by Mr. Widener?"

Onan was fingering her collar with one hand in a gesture that Paul had begun to recognize as one of the attorney's nervous tics. She had been scowling at Widener, but softened her features before turning toward Judge Knight.

"No, your honor. We decline to pursue the kind advice of the respondents' counsel. We withdraw the question."

Onan squared her thin shoulders and faced the witness box again.

"Mr. Francisco, was your grandmother in the habit of sending her grandchildren full-page letters?"

"No, Ms. Onan. I don't believe that she was."

"Why, then, did you merit such a distinction as to receive such a letter?"

"I do not know for certain, Ms. Onan."

"Does that mean you suspect a reason, Mr. Francisco?"

"Yes, I have an opinion."

"Are you willing to share that opinion with us, Mr. Francisco?"

"Yes, I am."

Onan waited a few seconds before realizing that Paul was not going to be more forthcoming. She gave him the necessary prompt.

"Please, Mr. Francisco, *tell* the court why you believe your grandmother gave you such special treatment in the form of a full-page personal letter."

Paul turned slightly toward the jury box.

"I believe that my grandmother singled me out because I live over two hundred miles from the Francisco family dairy farm. All of *Avó's* other grandchildren lived within thirty miles of her at the time she wrote me the letter. Only I was relatively far away." Paul decided that the time was ripe to volunteer a nugget of unsolicited information. "I think that it wasn't enough that I called her on the phone every weekend, so she reached out in this way. I was very pleased to receive the letter."

Paul looked back toward Onan and was pleased to see that she looked dyspeptic.

"Mr. Francisco, it was brought to our attention during earlier testimony that the letter you are supposed to have received from your grandmother was signed with her full name. Didn't this strike you as peculiar?"

Onan was trying hard to make Teresa Francisco's letter to her grandson appear suspicious and perhaps even a bit bizarre. She had referred to it as "peculiar" twice.

"No, Ms. Onan. It did not strike me as peculiar."

Onan realized she had no idea what Paul would say if she asked a follow-up question, but she had nowhere else to go.

"Why not, Mr. Francisco? Can you explain?"

"My grandmother had given me a nice sport coat for Christmas. I took the trouble to send her a thank-you note written in Portuguese, which is not a language I write well. It delighted her that I wrote in Portuguese and that is what prompted her to write back. *Avó* was inclined to use the polite language and formality of Old World correspondence, and she honored me by doing that. Formal correspondence, of course, calls for a proper signature at the end, so she signed her full name."

Paul noticed that some of the jurors were nodding slightly. He also noticed that Onan was looking flushed with frustration.

"I presume it must have been a very nice coat if you went to that much trouble to thank your grandmother for it," said Onan in a bitchy voice.

Struggling to avoid answering in kind, Paul mildly said, "You can judge for yourself, Ms. Onan. I am wearing it."

Some of the jurors stifled their chuckles.

Onan sniffed at Paul's two-button navy-blue sport coat and mulled her next move. She wasn't having any luck making the respondents' prime piece of evidence less credible. She wondered if perhaps she could raise doubts in the jurors' minds about Teresa Francisco herself. Could she elicit any answers from Paul Francisco that would make Teresa seem less than competent? He would defend his grandmother, of course, but perhaps she could get him to make statements that would strike the jury as overly protective of her — statements that might raise doubts.

"Mr. Francisco, your grandmother's alleged will goes into great detail, does it not?"

"Yes, Ms. Onan. My grandmother's will goes into great detail."

"Are you willing to state that your grandmother specified all those details in the alleged will and that she was aware of all of the contents of the alleged will?"

Paul thought that the jury was growing restive at Onan's insistence on referring to the "alleged" will every time she mentioned the document. *Good,* he thought. If she was trying the jury's patience, so much the better for the respondents.

"I am willing to state that my grandmother stipulated the contents of the will. That's not the same thing as saying that she was conversant with the details of the legal language that her attorney used to implement her wishes."

Onan realized too late that she had permitted Paul to qualify his answer while she was pondering what to ask him next. He had made a distinction between his grandmother's wishes and the legal language used to execute them. That undercut her effort to raise suspicions in the jurors' minds whether the old lady had known what she was doing.

"Please just answer the question," she said belatedly.

"So, Mr. Francisco," Onan continued. "You would argue that your grandmother was able to make stipulations to her attorney concerning her real property, her holdings in cattle, her possession of homes and other structures, all in full knowledge of the details?"

Paul caught his breath. *Was it possible that Onan had actually said such a thing? How delightfully foolish!*

He leaned forward slightly in the witness box and gave the attorney a smile.

"I would certainly argue that my grandmother knew of her possessions and titles. Unlike some people, Ms. Onan, I don't think my grandmother ever forgot what she owned or what value it had."

Onan went pale as the barb struck home. She was taut with sudden anger and struggling for self-control. On impulse, Paul started counting silently to ten. He carefully avoided smiling when, on his count of ten, he saw Onan exhale profoundly and collect herself. The attorney turned toward the judge.

"No further questions for this witness," she said tightly.

Green Cotton

Cotton Center was little more than a cluster of businesses grouped around the intersection of two roads, but that was enough to make it one of the busiest locations in Tulare County. The tire shop supplied everyone from farmers with monster tractors to ranchers with nimble four-wheel drive Jeeps. The mechanics could handle any kind of internal-combustion engine, whether diesel or gasoline. The truck yard had an array of big rigs and other vehicles for seasonal rentals. The place was an anthill of activity.

In the midst of it all was a rustic coffee shop that was plying early-morning visitors with ham and eggs — and gallons of coffee — and noontime customers with hearty meat-and-potatoes fare — and more coffee. Paulinho Francisco and Dinis Costa were ensconced at a small table in one corner of the coffee shop, shuffling papers and polishing off the remains of a leisurely breakfast.

Paulinho, who was a lifelong believer in hearty breakfasts, had treated himself to an eggs-and-linguiça scramble, cottage-style potatoes on the side. Dinis, who tended to regard breakfast as expendable, had picked at an apple Danish for the duration of the meal. He was also drinking his coffee black, which Paulinho had pretended to take as an affront, pouring large amounts from the cream pitcher into his own coffee.

"You want us poor dairymen to starve, Dinis? Coffee *needs* cream. Use all you want! We've got plenty more to sell."

Although they had moved on to a first-name basis, Dinis didn't think it would be wise to remind Paulinho that he hadn't really been a dairyman in several years — unless "dairyman" was an obscure new slang term for television dealer. Dinis had suggested the breakfast powwow to discuss matters of mutual interest over the receivership of Paulinho's mother's estate. He knew that Paulinho still harbored some reservations over his role as co-executor being overshadowed by the receiver, but he seemed to be a pragmatic man who saw more benefit in cooperation than in resistance.

For his part, Paulinho had originally been outraged at the petition by his sister-in-law Odile to turn the estate over to a court-appointed receiver. He felt like he had suffered collateral damage in the battle between his brother Candido and the estranged Odile. Dinis Costa had, however, eased his dismay significantly when the receiver had chosen Paulinho's son Henry to take over the direction and execution of the farming chores on the estate. That showed that the attorney had at least some smarts when it came to making administrative decisions. Paulinho let go of his resentment.

The papers scattered across their breakfast table related to the arrangements that Dinis was making to deal with the multiple residences on Teresa Francisco's estate. After their marriages, both Paulinho and Candido had built homes on property belonging to their parents Chico and Teresa. Both sons had expected to inherit their homes from the estate at some date in the hopefully remote future. Now that the date had arrived, problems in settling the estate were complicating those long-held expectations. It didn't help that Candido no longer occupied his own house, having abandoned it to Odile when he left to move in with the girlfriend he had been seeing on the side.

The interim solution was obvious to Dinis Costa. Occupants of residences owned by Teresa Francisco would need to pay an appropriate monthly rent to Teresa's estate until the will was probated and the heirs came into their own, bringing Dinis's receivership to an end. One packet of papers documented the comparables that Dinis had researched to establish a fair-market rental rate for Paulinho's home. He had also brought paperwork to permit Paulinho's rent to be accumulated as a lien against his expected inheritance. That would save Teresa's younger son from incurring out-of-pocket rent expenses during the settlement period.

"You know that you nearly drove my sister-in-law crazy when you sent her the schedule of rent payments for her house," said Paulinho.

"I know too well, Paulinho. I had a most interesting conversation with her attorney, Harold Widener. He hadn't had the slightest idea that Odile was living on the estate. Of course, it seems that Odile didn't know it either."

"Yeah," agreed Paulinho. "She is not exactly the shiniest penny in the jar."

"Harold says she nearly fainted when she realized she had successfully put herself under a receivership. He and I quickly worked out a way to save her from rent payments because of her status as one of your mother's heirs. That's the same deal I brought to you this morning. I have to tell you, Paulinho, I've never seen a receivership like this one before."

Paulinho smiled dryly.

"I come from an interesting family."

"That reminds me, Paulinho. Your son Hank said something about 'green cotton' in relation to Candido and suggested I ask you about it sometime."

Paulinho laughed and took a big sip from his coffee cup before saying anything.

"You know anything about growing cotton?" he asked Dinis.

The attorney shrugged.

"Only the obvious stuff. It's a row crop. The plants don't grow very tall. The seed pods are full of fiber. The fiber is harvested and sent to the cotton gin to have the seeds combed out. The fiber is bundled up into bales and shipped off to god-knows-where."

"Not bad," said Paulinho. "That's a perfectly good summary. There's a couple of important details to fill in, though."

Paulinho paused for a few seconds to turn his head and cough into his fist. Not even sixty yet, he was concerned that chest congestion and shortness of breath were to be his middle-aged fate. It seemed an unfair affliction to befall a nonsmoker, but a bout of Valley fever twenty years earlier had left him with scarred lungs.

"Sorry, Dinis. As I was saying. Missing things. One is that the cotton bolls — the seed pods — aren't that crazy about giving up their fiber. They need to ripen, dry up, and pop open before the cotton is hanging out there for us to pick. A second thing is that cotton fields have strict plow-down deadlines. You want to plow your cotton stalks under as soon as possible after harvest to inhibit bollworm growth. A cotton farmer can be assessed big fines for missing the plow-down deadline and risking a future bollworm infestation. It's important to interrupt their life cycles."

"I didn't grow up on a farm that grew cotton, but what you're saying sounds kind of familiar."

"It should. It's all basic farm management. You simply adjust the timing for the life cycle of your particular crop and the pests that go after it. Even so, Candy managed to get it all screwed up. I guess the problem was that he thought he had a brilliant idea."

"Okay . . ."

"It had to do with the ripening phase. Standard practice is to spray your cotton field with a defoliant. You can do it with a spray rig, pulling it down the rows with a tractor, or you can hire a crop duster to buzz over your field and spray the defoliant from his plane. Either way, the cotton plants get the idea. When their leaves fall off, the plants dry up, the cotton bolls crack open, and the cotton fiber pushes out, just waiting to be picked."

"Okay. I'm following you so far."

"Candy decided he didn't like paying a hefty fee to a crop duster to defoliate his cotton fields, so figured he could just be patient and let nature take its course. The cotton bolls were going to ripen anyway. He could wait it out."

"But that might push against the deadline you mentioned," said Dinis.

Paulinho drank some more coffee and smiled.

"Yeah. The 'plow-down' deadline. It could at that. And it did. At first Candy was patting himself on the back pretty hard because he had this pretty cotton field — the prettiest in Tulare County, I'm sure — with white puffs of cotton beginning to peek out in the middle of a forest of bright green leaves. Other farmers had their cotton hanging from stalks that were leafless and all dried out. Cotton on a stick. Candy thought his bright idea had paid off because the cotton bolls were splitting open even without the application of defoliant. And without hiring any crop dusters."

"I'm not exactly sure where this is going, Paulinho, but I have some suspicions. I've been to cotton fields in harvest time. The big cotton-picking machines make a lot of noise, but you can always hear the rustling sound it makes as they go down the rows. It's the dry stalks and twigs being disturbed."

"Yeah. A rustling sound. Candy wasn't getting any of those when he sent his cotton-pickers to his green, green field. Cotton-pickers have arrays of spinning metal spindles. They're covered with little barbs that snag the cotton fiber and tear it out of the boll. The picker has rows of spindles that take turns snagging cotton. When one array is grabbing cotton, the previous array has rotated out of the way to where the cotton is stripped from the spindles and blown into the cotton-picker's big wire-mesh basket. The cleaned-up spindles are then ready to take another turn at picking."

"Uh-huh," nodded Dinis. "I've seen those contraptions at work. You can't miss them during cotton-picking season."

"Candy found out that the spindle barbs are perfectly happy to snag and pull in juicy green cotton leaves. A cotton-picker moving through a defoliated field really sees only cotton to grab. My brother's cotton-pickers were stripping off leaves as well as cotton fiber. The baskets were filling up with a blend of yanked fibers and shredded leaves."

"Sounds like a real mess."

"An expensive mess, too. The white cotton fibers were being stained green by the torn leaves. When Candy took his first trailers of cotton to the cotton gin for processing, the gin manager came out and told him to go the hell away. They wanted cotton fiber, not tossed salad. The manager told Candy that he risked gumming up the gin's machinery if he tried to run the green-stained cotton and leaves through it. Mostly the leaves, I'm sure."

"What happened to the green cotton?"

"Candy had to dump it. And he tore back to the field and made his boys stop the cotton-picking and park the machines. Then he called up the crop-dusting company and ordered a defoliation run over his field."

"In time?"

"In the *nick* of time. The crop duster was retooling for pesticide spraying and was going to leave the area to follow the crop cycles. He worked up and down the state. It cost Candy extra to get the duster to agree to a late cotton job. Then my brother had to wait for the defoliation to take effect and clear the way for picking. He was the last to get to market — so he got the lowest prices — and barely got the cotton field plowed under in time."

"Damn," said Dinis. "That is a hell of a story. Now when did this happen? Were you and Candido still working as partners at that time?"

"Not a chance! It was back almost ten years ago — 1974, I think — not long after Candy and I parted ways. He had suggested it earlier, but I always told him it was crazy. Apparently that discouraged him."

"Too bad he forgot about your warning after he was running the place on his own. That must have been quite a learning experience for him."

"I wouldn't exactly say that, Dinis."

"You wouldn't? Why not?"

"Because if he learned his lesson in 1974, why did the damned fool try it again in 1975?"

The Portuguese Custodian

There was a tentative rap on the office door, which stood ajar.

"Excuse me! Custodian."

"Sure," said Paul Francisco. "Come on in."

He didn't look up from the stack of exams he was grading. He was in his first quarter as a graduate student assistant at the University Farm and he was working into the evening in hopes of returning the corrected exams to the professor-in-charge in the morning. Paul was enjoying the luxury of having his own office, a two-person space on the fourth floor of the university's math building. Since his office partner was seldom around, it was almost like having a private office.

The custodian bustled around with a minimum of fuss, emptying the wastebaskets from next to the two desks and checking that the chalkboard was equipped with chalk. It took him only a minute, but he then paused at the office door.

"Excuse me, but are you Mr. Francisco?"

Paul looked up. The custodian was a slender man approaching middle age, his curly hair streaked with gray.

"Yes, I am," said Paul. "I'm one of the new teaching assistants."

"Pleased to meet you," said the custodian. "Excuse me for bothering you, but I was wondering if your name is Portuguese."

"*Pois sim,*" said Paul, smiling. *Of course.*

A broad grin split the custodian's face.

"Ah, you are from Terceira! I am very pleased to meet you. My name is Ramiro."

Paul was nonplussed.

"You knew my family was from Terceira after hearing me speak two words of Portuguese?"

Ramiro's smile broadened.

"I knew after *one* word. The second just made me sure. I am from the island of Pico. If you were from Pico, then I could tell you which *village* your family is from!"

Paul had no reason to doubt him. He stood up and shook Ramiro's hand.

"I was born in California, Ramiro. I have never been in Terceira."

"That's okay," replied the custodian. "You speak the way your family taught you. It's enough."

"*Não falo muito bem*," said Paul. *I don't speak very well.*

"No, *perfeitamente*," declared Ramiro. *Perfectly.*

"*Muito obrigado*," said Paul, thanking the custodian for his generosity. "Portuguese is my first language, but I don't speak it very much. It's perfect only when I stick to the little I know."

"It is still good," said Ramiro.

The custodian's face darkened a shade.

"I wish my children spoke it as good as you," he said, a hint of disappointment in his voice.

Paul was momentarily at a loss for words. Ramiro broke the silence himself.

"This is how it is," he said. "New land, new language. The old language is for the Old Country. My children are very American."

"I understand," said Paul. "We used Portuguese all the time when I was little, but my baby brother hears mostly English at home. I'm glad I was born early enough to learn Portuguese first."

Ramiro's smile came back.

"*Bom!*" he said. *Good!* "I am glad to see you here and I wish you *boa sorte*."

"*Obrigado, senhor*," said Paul. *Thank you, sir.* "I'm sure I could use some good luck."

The Democratic Process

The absentee ballot was a computer punch card stapled to a Styrofoam backing. Its paper sleeve offered instructions suggesting that an unbent paperclip would make an ideal tool for punching out the numbered chads.

Paul Francisco was sitting on a hassock next to his grandfather's recliner. The sample ballot was open on his lap and he had laid the absentee ballot on the recliner's armrest. It was safe there, as Chico's paralyzed left arm wasn't going to budge on its own.

It was easy to read the voter information in the morning light, which poured in through the large windows in Chico and Teresa's living room. The elderly couple had a multi-paned perspective on their dairy farm. The incapacitated Chico kept watch the entire day, unable to stir from his seat without assistance. Teresa occupied her post at the other end of the room at brief intervals between household chores. She sat there now, attending to some sewing while watching her grandson helping her husband cast his absentee ballot.

Chico was an ambivalent Republican, living in a region with a majority of ambivalent Democrats. He had registered in the same party as the friend who had given him a ride to the county clerk's office. It was more a gesture of appreciation than a sign of political conviction. For the most part, he had supported Franklin Roosevelt's New Deal programs. He liked the public works that created the state's irrigation system and spread rural electrification throughout the nation. He also liked Ike, however, except for Eisenhower's vice president. He had a visceral distrust of Richard Nixon and had not voted for him in the 1950 campaign for U.S. Senate. The recent Watergate debacle had been ample confirmation that his suspicions had been justified.

That simplified Chico's choices for the federal offices on his absentee ballot. In his mind, the accidental presidency of Gerald Ford was discredited by the pardon he had given his predecessor. When asked by his grandson whose number should be punched on the ballot, Chico instructed him to cast a vote for Jimmy Carter. The Democratic nominee was a farmer — certainly a point in his favor. The incumbent U.S. senator was a Harvard-accented ally of the Kennedy family. That still carried weight among the immigrant families who cherished memories of the first Roman Catholic president. The senator got a vote for re-election.

Chico had liked the local Olympic athlete who had served in the U.S. House of Representatives, but he was gone, a Republican who lost his seat in the post-Watergate purge of 1974. The new Democratic incumbent seemed good enough to merit a vote.

Paul turned the page of the voter pamphlet and read the names of the candidates for state offices. Now Chico cast a vote for his own party's candidate, supporting the incumbent assemblyman for another term. He paused, however, when Paul did not give the name of the incumbent state senator, another Republican who would have garnered Chico's vote.

"He's not running," explained Paul. "He is retiring."

Chico frowned and asked his grandson to tell him more about the candidates running to replace the local state senator.

"The Republican is currently representing the adjacent assembly district," said Paul, struggling with his limited Portuguese vocabulary to piece an explanation together. "The Democrat is a rancher."

"Where are they from?" asked Chico.

"The assemblyman is from Fresno County and the rancher is from Tulare County."

The scales were tipping in the Democrat's favor. Chico preferred a rancher who was local to a politician who came from the next county.

"Read me the names again," said Chico.

Paul recited the names and his grandfather's eyebrows went up.

"The rancher is a *woman?*"

"Yes, *Avô*," said Paul.

Across the room, Teresa looked up from her sewing. Her eyebrows were also raised, but she held her tongue.

"A woman should stay at home and take care of her husband," said Chico disapprovingly. He wasn't looking at his wife, so he didn't see Teresa nodding her head in agreement. Both understood a wife's first duty.

"*Ele é solteira*," said Paul. *She is single.*

Chico pursed his lips and pondered. That made a difference. If she didn't have a husband and children to care for, ranching was a permissible profession. He made up his mind.

"I'll vote for the woman," he said. At least she wasn't a career politician.

Somewhat surprised by his grandfather's decision, Paul carefully poked the absentee ballot to record the vote for state senator.

Now they had reached the part that Paul dreaded. The ballot propositions often had deliberately misleading descriptions that would be difficult to translate into neutral Portuguese. Describing the candidates was nothing next to trying to explicate the initiatives that had made it onto the California ballot. He launched into a description of the first one so that his grandfather could decide whether to support or oppose it.

Teresa was still watching the laborious process and began to feel a twinge of sympathy for her grandson. As a rule, she and Chico had never corrected their grandchildren's grammar or vocabulary errors when they spoke Portuguese. They didn't want to discourage them from continuing to use the family's original language. Teresa was now aware that at least some of her grown grandchildren had become self-conscious about speaking Portuguese no better than a youngster might. It was probably too late to do anything about it.

"Oh, Paulinho," she said, using the affectionate diminutive that was usually reserved for Paul's father. "Just finish voting the way you think is right and your grandfather won't mind. You're just tiring him out."

Paul and Chico exchanged glances. The grandson gave the grandfather a mischievous smile.

"Look at that, *Avô*," he said. "That foreign lady is interfering with Americans who are trying to vote!"

Chico grinned at his wife.

"*Tem cuidado, estrangeira!*" he warned. *Be careful, lady foreigner!* "We can put you on the boat back to the islands!"

Teresa smiled indulgently at her husband.

"Just *you* be careful, old man, or I might be ready to go!" she retorted.

Paul sat quietly for a long moment as his grandparents smiled at each other across the room. The sunlight was not the only thing warming the room at that moment.

Eventually Chico chuckled and broke the spell.

"You were saying — ?" he said to his grandson.

Paul resumed his struggle with the descriptions of the ballot propositions. The naturalized citizen listened as attentively as he could while the foreign lady attended to her sewing.

Both still had small smiles on their faces.

Trey's Wedding

The receiving line had been awkward. The wedding guests were eager to express their best wishes to the bride and groom, but a majority of the men fumbled the handshake. Force of habit was difficult to subdue, and only a few of the men thought to thrust out their left hands so that Trey could give them a solid shake with the hand he had left. He endured many awkward clasps of his left hand in guests' right hands.

The women were nearly as bad. Their eyes would drift to his prosthetic shoulder and arm, nonfunctional esthetic devices that gave his tuxedo something to drape over and something to fill its right sleeve. Trey was heartily tired of the poignant pity mixed with their earnest congratulations. Only the comforting presence of his bride Lupita by his side made the ritual endurable.

Trey had lost track of how many people he and Lupita had greeted. Surely they were nearly done with well-wishers and would soon be able to go into the reception hall and sit down.

He had also lost track of his father, who was missing from the spot in the reception line next to his mother. There was no point in worrying about that. Junior Francisco's only rule in life was to do as he pleased. Trey had learned that lesson a long time ago.

Henry and Magdalena Francisco had claimed a table in the reception hall large enough to accommodate ten people. That was enough room for them and their three daughters, along with Henry's parents and his older brother.

"This is quite a show," commented Magdalena. Her daughters chimed in with agreement. Her mother-in-law was regarding the reception hall in approval.

"The decorations are *very* nice," said Carmina.

"They should be!" declared Rebecca, a pretty sixteen-year-old who was Henry and Magdalena's eldest. "They were done by Ferdie and his 'special friend.'"

"Beckie!" said Magdalena in a chastising voice, but Rebecca merely smiled as her younger sisters giggled.

"Does anyone know where Junior is?" asked Paulinho, eager to change the topic.

His son Paul laughed.

"That is *anyone's* guess, Dad. Sometimes I doubt that Junior himself knows where he is."

"He didn't even sit with his wife at the wedding," added Carmina, the disapproval strong in her voice.

"I noticed that, Mom," said Henry. "He was sitting a couple of rows behind her. What was that all about?"

"I can guess," said Magdalena, who had taken the measure of her many in-laws. "Someone told Junior where he was supposed to sit at the nuptial Mass."

"That would do it," agreed Paul. "He'd feel obligated to sit somewhere else, just to prove no one bosses him around."

"Did you see Jojo and Rita?" asked Henry.

Outside of his parents and his siblings' families, Paul seldom saw any of his relatives anymore. Their paths and his had widely diverged since the struggle over Teresa's will.

"Yeah, I did," said Paul. "I haven't talked to them yet, but I saw them. What's happened to Jojo? He looks like a sausage casing stuffed to the point of exploding."

"Same shape, too!" laughed Henry.

"Boys!" said Carmina. "People will hear you!"

Henry lowered his voice and leaned toward his brother.

"You'll notice that Mom didn't say we're *wrong*. She just said we're too *loud*."

The boys laughed while their mother gave their father the long-perfected look of the long-suffering parent. Paulinho reflexively gave her the appropriate sympathetic look in return.

"It's Rita," said Magdalena. "Her husband doesn't think any meal is complete until you put linguiça in it and she indulges him. Linguiça with eggs for breakfast. Linguiça with Portuguese-style beans for lunch. Linguiça in the stew for supper or maybe linguiça pizza instead. Did you know that linguiça makes a good topping for a pepperoni pizza?"

"Instead of, or in addition to?" asked Paul.

"In addition *to*," said his sister-in-law. "How much spicy pork sausage does anyone need? If you're eating pepperoni *and* linguiça on your pizzas, what else should happen to you besides getting fat?"

"A stroke," suggested Rebecca, who had not known her great-grandfather, but knew the family stories. She had tiny glimmers of a memory of her great-grandmother.

"Hush, Beckie!" said her mother, as her sisters giggled anew.

"I guess his Avila genes kicked in with a vengeance," said Paulinho.

"That could be," said Henry. "But at least Jojo doesn't act like he's the world's greatest expert on everything, like his grandfather Alberto Avila did."

"Like his older brother does," added Magdalena.

"Yeah," agreed Henry. "It's a terrible problem to think you're a genius and be totally wrong about it, like Junior is. Jojo has never made that mistake. He and I are the only two successful dairymen in our generation, and that's because Jojo knows enough to let Rita run his operation."

"You mean, like you let Maggie run yours?" said Paul.

"I think I should plead the fifth on that," said Henry carefully, as Magdalena and their daughters laughed.

"Hank, do you know where the restrooms are in this place?" asked Paul.

"Sure," said Henry, pointing across the hall and giving his brother directions.

Paul left the table and headed toward the door his brother had indicated. The hallway on the other side was empty. The reception proper had yet to begin and no one had done a lot of drinking yet. As he walked down the hallway, Paul noticed that a corridor branched off to a small side-entrance lobby. There was no traffic there, either.

On the way back to the reception hall, Paul decided on an impulse to walk down the side corridor. He often lost his bearings inside large buildings and he wanted to peek outside to get oriented again. He was jealous of his father's nearly infallible built-in compass and had learned not to wave his hand as if indicating directions during conversation. Paulinho was highly likely in such instances to correct him. "That's not north. North is *that* way." Taking his bearings was a prudent precaution — as was avoiding directional references while talking in his father's presence.

In addition to deploring his lack of direction sense, Paul also disliked his tendency to be easily startled. It detracted from one's dignity.

As it did now, Paul giving a start upon discovering that someone was unexpectedly loitering in the side-entrance lobby, a tall figure staring out through the glass wall. Fortunately, the man was not looking in his direction, so Paul was able to recover his dignity in the absence of witnesses. And he recognized the lone loiterer.

It was Junior, who turned at the sound of Paul's entrance.

"Hello, Junior," said Paul, wondering what he should say to his cousin, whom he had not seen in years. He decided to try to appeal to Junior's perverse sense of self. "I'd offer you congratulations, but I don't know that I really should."

Junior gave Paul a smile. It looked genuine.

"You're right. There's no reason to congratulate me. People have been trying to do it all day, but I haven't done anything."

The conversation had gotten off to a suitably weird start, given that it was a conversation with Junior. Paul's cousin was engaged by the opportunity to complain about social conventions that he found inconvenient or irritating. But how to continue?

"It's really all Trey's problem now, isn't it?"

"Yeah, he's going to have a problem, all right. Especially from *her*."

Junior hadn't bothered to mention Lupita's name, but apparently he already had some kind of grievance against her.

"So she's a handful?" asked Paul. He had nearly said, "So Trey will have his hands full?" But he caught himself at the last second and amended his question to avoid using an awkward plural in reference to Trey's hand.

"She's got some sass in her," said Junior. "She doesn't show proper respect."

If she doesn't have respect for you, thought Paul, *then she's just a reliable judge of character. It's not very smart of her, however, to let it show.*

"That's too bad," said Paul vaguely.

Junior went off on a seeming tangent.

"Did you see my father at the wedding?"

"Yeah, I did. He was sitting all by himself several rows away from where we were."

"Those were the rules," said Junior, with some satisfaction. "He was allowed to come as long as he left his whore at home and didn't try to sit with the family."

"I see."

"He's not too happy about the wedding, either, but I guess he felt obligated to attend."

The notion of being "obligated" seemed to amuse Junior, who had a smile back on his face.

"Why is he not happy about it?" asked Paul, recognizing a leading statement when Junior laid it right in front of him.

Junior's smile grew broader.

"He doesn't like it that his grandson is marrying a sassy Mexican girl," he said. "The sassy part I don't like that much, but if it gets to my father, maybe I don't mind it that much, either."

"As long as you're happy about his unhappiness, that's the main thing," offered Paul, wondering how Junior would take it.

He took it with a measure of cheerfulness, as if things might work out after all.

"Yeah, I guess maybe that *is* the main thing."

"Well, I didn't congratulate you on the wedding, but maybe it's okay to offer you a little bit of congratulations on the outcome."

Junior wasn't certain he liked coming full circle in the way that Paul appeared to be guiding the conversation, but it still seemed something of a high note. He decided to hang on to that element of happiness that was rare in his life and tentatively conceded the point.

"Maybe you're right about that. Could be."

To avoid the complications of disengaging from a conversation that had appeared to run its course, Junior simply turned his back on Paul and resumed his interrupted vigil.

Paul took the opportunity to return to the table in the reception hall, where he discovered that Mary Carmen and Gerry had claimed the remaining two seats.

"Hey, Paul," said Henry. "What took you so long? We were beginning to think you fell in!"

"Oh, I fell into it, all right," he replied. "I fell into a meeting with Junior. He's hanging out alone in the side lobby."

"What is he doing *there?*" demanded Carmina.

"I'm not sure. Mostly it's just Junior being Junior. But he's also not happy about Lupita. Apparently Trey's new bride doesn't show Junior enough respect."

"It's a wonder she shows him *any* respect," said Paulinho, which sparked a disapproving look from his wife.

"You should always be polite," proclaimed Carmina. "It's not polite for a daughter-in-law to be disrespectful and it's not polite for Junior to ignore the reception."

"I think she's talking to you, honey," said Henry to Magdalena, giving his wife a little nudge.

"She is not!" protested Magdalena, but in the spirit of her husband's teasing. "I am always polite. If you don't agree I'll have to slap you silly."

The younger girls giggled at their parents' mock spat, but Rebecca was rolling her eyes in embarrassment.

A loud noise came from the public-address system as the emcee for the reception turned on the microphone. When he had it adjusted to his satisfaction, he launched the proceedings by welcoming the guests.

"Isn't this the best man's job?" asked Gerry in a whisper to Mary Carmen.

"Ferdie hired a wedding coordinator and they provided a professional emcee. Trey's brother was happy to get out of it. I'm sure he'll do a toast later."

The emcee was introducing the families of the bridal couple and the members of the wedding party.

"Ladies and gentlemen, the mother and father of the groom, Sofia and Candido Francisco, Jr.!"

Heads swiveled to watch Sofia as she did her best to look as if she were unperturbed by walking in alone. Murmurs of sympathy and whispered questions rippled through the room.

The emcee was alternating between members of the bride's family and members of the groom's. When it was time for more members of Trey's family, the emcee caught everyone's attention with his announcement.

"Please welcome the grandmother of the groom, Odile Francisco, her son the uncle of the groom, Ferdinando Francisco, and his friend David Washington."

Odile walked in painfully. Her walking stick was in Ferdie's hand, because he and David had bracketed Odile, each taking an arm to help her walk. The guests watched the trio make its slow progress toward a table near the bridal party's end of the hall. Most eyes were on David, who was the only black man among the attendees. The room was replete with Portuguese and Chicanos, but there was only one African American. Whispered conversations buzzed through the hall.

"I don't think it's right to seat him at the family table," complained Paulinho.

"Honey!" said Carmina, her tone of voice suggesting that Paulinho say no more.

"It's their call, Dad," said Paul. "David is probably in better standing with them than Uncle Candido is."

Paulinho's faced was flushed with disapproval. His granddaughter did not help the situation.

"It's okay, *Avô*. He's Ferdie's 'roommate'!" said Rebecca. Everyone could hear the wry quotes in her voice.

"'Roommate'!" echoed her younger sister, awash again in giggles.

"If you girls keep this up," said Paul to his nieces, "we're all going to need insulin shots!"

The girls tittered in delight at their uncle's admonition.

"Hey, everyone. Look!"

It was Mary Carmen, drawing their attention to the main entrance. A young woman was standing there in a bridesmaid's gown, a tuxedoed escort by her side.

"Please welcome the sister of the groom," said the emcee, "Filipa Francisco, and her escort, Raul Cordero, cousin of the bride."

The guests applauded as Filipa and her escort strolled easily into the room and took their places at the long banquet table reserved for the wedding party.

"Wow," said Paul. "I haven't seen Filly since Junior took the family up to Oregon. She's all grown up."

"She's a bad daughter, too," said Henry.

"According to whom?" asked Paul.

"According to Junior," said Mary Carmen.

"Then I salute her," said Paul. "I think we *all* salute her."

There was a mock raising of goblets and sipping.

"So why is Junior disappointed in his daughter?" asked Paul.

"She stayed behind in Oregon to go to college. Junior said she had to come back down to California with the rest of the family, but she refused," said

Mary Carmen, "Junior was livid, of course. Girls are supposed to obey their dads, you know."

"I agree with that as a general principle," said Paulinho, looking significantly at his daughter, "but I see some leeway if your dad is Junior."

"Anyway, Filly was eighteen then and he couldn't do anything about it," continued Mary Carmen. "She was paying her own way through school anyway, what with Junior being broke after the bankruptcy of his dairy. She got a banking job and a fiancé up in Portland, so she's not going to be coming back down here to let her father boss her around."

"What is Junior doing down here anyway?" asked Paul. "Didn't he open an auto shop?"

"Yeah," said Henry. "That's on its way to the junk heap, too."

"Let me guess," said Paul. "Plenty of mechanical skill, but no customer base. No people skills."

"Exactly," agreed Henry. "He can fix cars and trucks and tractors, but he treats clients as if they're idiots and they never come back. No return business at all. And I'm afraid Trey doesn't help the picture."

"Trey works for his dad?"

"Who else?" said Henry. "Trey is like all of his brothers. Junior told the boys that they don't need school because it's a stupid waste of time. You learn all you need working on the dairy farm. That advice turns out to be pretty bad when the dairy farm is gone. The boys have no educations and no skills outside of following Junior's instructions on farm work. Trey can't get a job as a one-armed farm hand, so he ended up working in his father's auto shop. He's tough and adaptable, but the job is a bad fit for him."

"And it's going away soon, from the sounds of it."

"I'm afraid so. A couple of his brothers are working for their Uncle Jojo and the youngest is still in school, doing badly and thereby pleasing his father. It's the usual perversity where Junior is concerned."

"But Filipa is doing well. What about her sisters?"

"They see Filly as a role model and are aces in school and Junior's second daughter has left for college despite his demands that she not go. It's not like he has purse strings to control them with. They make their own way. Good girls! Bad, though, to Junior."

A hush had come over the reception hall. The family members gathered at Paulinho and Carmina's table fell silent with everyone else. The emcee had made a dramatic pause in the cavalcade of announcements. When the silence was complete, he spoke.

"Ladies and gentlemen, please rise to greet our man and woman of the hour. It gives me great pleasure to introduce to you Candido Francisco the Third and Lupita Cordero Francisco, husband and wife!"

Trey and Lupita walked in, beaming at their guests, Lupita clinging to Trey's good arm. The crowd was on its feet applauding.

There was no sign of Junior, of course.

DECEMBER 1979

Teresa's Cows

Teresa Francisco paused in the midst of writing a letter to her grandson Paul. Candido's pickup truck was leaving the dairy yard by means of the driveway past her house. He was towing the cattle trailer again. It had become quite a habit with him. Every other week or so, Candido would haul up to four cows to the auction. He had become remarkably dedicated to the process of culling the less-productive milk cows from the herd. Or so it seemed.

Was it a good sign that her son had become so diligent in the years since he took over sole management of the Francisco dairy farm? As much as she'd like to think so, Teresa found it difficult to believe that. The pattern had become too clear. Although Candido never let his mother see any of the herd books or the business's financial records — documents that Chico had once freely shared with her — Teresa still had eyes with which to see.

Her eyes watched the flow of familiar cattle to the auction yard and strange cattle into the Francisco corrals. Teresa pondered yet again how best to rein in her older son. She could never bring herself to the point of open confrontation. Even an uneasy tranquility was better than an open dispute within the family. Teresa intended to keep the peace for the undoubtedly meager balance of her life. After that, however, Candido would have to deal with his mother's posthumous wishes.

Soon her revised will would be ready for her signature, prepared in accordance with the exacting specifications she had given her attorney. She would ask Carmina or Ferdie to give her a ride into town when the time came to affix her name to the document.

She wondered if the afterlife really existed. She had assumed so all her life, even when life was so unfair as to steal away her darling daughter and leave less worthy people in good health. If it did exist, would she be able to look down upon her survivors as they moved about on a chessboard whose rules she had created? It made her uncomfortable to entertain any doubts about matters of deeply held faith, so she deliberately pushed such speculations from her mind and turned back to the letter she was trying to write. Her simple note to her grandson would include no religious or philosophical meditations.

But unbidden thoughts continued to intrude.

She was embarrassed to recall how she had scandalized her grandson after Chico's death. Paul had offered completely conventional words of solace, telling her that "*Avô* is in a better place now." Before she could stop herself, she had replied, "Really? Do you really think so? How can we be sure?"

His startled reaction suggested that he wasn't sure at all and was at a loss for further words of comfort. So much for the boy she had groomed for the priesthood. That project had not been one of her spectacular successes.

Nor had she particularly succeeded in building the family unity she had always desired. The dissension was building just below the surface and was likely to erupt once she was no longer present to maintain the peace. She had already seen many instances of her descendants working at cross purposes.

They'll have to work together as a family or there'll be a big fight. Which will it be?

She feared the worst.

Land and houses and cows. They'll fight over the land and houses and cows.

Teresa's pen hovered over the letter. The page was nearly full. She pursed her lips and carefully added her signature, writing out her full name in a formal manner she expected Paul to appreciate.

Teresa sat back and looked out the window toward the barn and the cows wandering in the adjacent corrals.

Cows? I used to have cows, she mused.

~~~

Great-Etcetera-Granddaughters

~~~

Henry Francisco tossed the manila folder on his father's kitchen table.

"One hundred and seventy-nine," he announced.

Paulinho flipped open the folder and began to scan the pages, hand-annotated photocopies of sections from the Francisco dairy-farm herd records. These were the summary pages from the big three-ring binder that had been kept in the workshop office. There were only nine pages, each marked in a fifty-line grid. The first column contained the identification numbers by which the cows were known, followed by columns indicating birthdates, breeding dates, "freshening" dates (when the cows gave birth and began to lactate), and the "dry" dates when they were mustered out of the milking herd to start the process again.

Some of the ID numbers had lines drawn through them in red ink. Others had check marks.

"That many? One hundred and seventy-nine?"

"Yeah, out of a herd of four hundred two."

"I'll be damned."

Henry sat down opposite his father.

"I checked it myself, Dad. Dinis did the first pass and I did the second. We agree that one hundred and seventy-nine of the four hundred two milk cows are in *Avó*'s name. There are calf records, too, that we need to look at, but these are all the cows that graduated into the milk herd.

"Almost half," mused Paulinho. "How is that possible? Candy had plenty of time to turn the herd over entirely, judging from the financials and the auction-yard receipts. How did *Mãe* end up keeping nearly half?"

The court-appointed receiver's inventory of the estate was proving to be eye-opening, but this went contrary to the initial spate of bad news. The first indications had suggested that Candido had alienated Teresa Francisco's holdings in livestock by selling cattle in her name and using the proceeds to buy cattle in his name. But now the receiver and his hand-picked estate manager,

Henry Francisco, had discovered that the first indications were somewhat misleading.

"It's simpler than you think, Dad," said Henry. "The cows still in *Avó*'s name? They're granddaughters. Great-etcetera granddaughters."

"Okay. That makes sense. These are the cows that were born to cows that belonged to your grandmother."

Paulinho paused. Holstein cattle could easily live twenty years or more, but most dairy cows had only half a dozen or so productive years before it was time to cull them. When he had been in charge of the herd records for his father's Paulo C. Francisco & Sons operation, he had taken pride that their cows routinely lasted above the average. Paulinho attributed it to close supervision and care of the livestock, which had no doubt deteriorated under his brother's management during the past decade. All the cows that Paulinho had known were gone from the herd, but their multiply-great granddaughters were still well represented in the dairy's corrals.

"Yeah, they not only belonged to *Avó* — and *Avô* before her — they were the cream of the crop."

Paulinho smiled at Henry's choice of metaphor.

"Yeah?"

"And so Uncle Candy hesitated to cull his highest producers. They brought in the most money. It's your legacy, Dad. Yours and *Avô*'s. Your hand-picked cows were the best cows and Uncle Candy wasn't as good at choosing winners. While your cows had daughters who also hit high production numbers, the offspring from Uncle Candy's new cows tended to trail. Your brother had to choose between turning over the herd versus bringing in the production dollars from the creamery. He often took his own cows to the auction yard in hopes of upgrading. He didn't have your eye for the winners. Or *Avô*'s."

"Well, that's a theory."

"It's a good one, Dad. The numbers in the herd records back it up. So the estate has one hundred seventy-nine cows to deal with."

"What about the two hundred plus in Candy's name? What happens now?"

"They're all mixed together, of course, being milked as one herd for the time being, just the way Uncle Candy did. But do we separate the herds or leave them together until the criminal investigation is over?"

"*Christ!*" exclaimed Paulinho. "This can't go into criminal court. It's the sort of stuff that would have killed your grandmother!"

Henry refrained from making the obvious observation. Paulinho pondered for a while.

"What are our options, Hank? Do we have options here?"

"I've been talking to Dinis, of course. All of *Avó's* heirs have an interest in whether Uncle Candy reduced her estate through fraud. Ironically, that includes Uncle Candy himself, but I assume he won't want to prosecute. And maybe we don't want to, either. It could be costly and would certainly be messy. It could tie up the estate for months. Who knows? Maybe years."

"Candy crossed the line. He crossed *way* over the line. But I don't want *Mãe* looking down on us while we put him in the dock and tear each other apart. If we can handle it quietly, then I want to handle it quietly. Will Dinis let us do that?"

"We can walk a fine line here, Dad. Uncle Candy has to know we have the goods on him. That means he might be willing to be cooperative in dividing up the estate. Strictly speaking, *Avó's* cows belong to Paulo C. Francisco & Sons, a business in which Uncle Candy has a stake. He was trying to go from partial ownership of the cows to full ownership. I think we can squeeze him into signing a quitclaim on his interest in *Avó's* cows. It would be at least a partial offset of his acquisition of cows in the name of his Francisco & Sons business while using money from *Avó's* business. It might be a solution. Kind of a plea bargain for him without the court actually getting involved. If we like his concessions, we let the criminal charges go."

"That doesn't sound like so fine a line, son. Either Candy plays fair or we clap him behind bars."

"Careful there, Dad. If we threaten him like that, we could be charged with extortion. We can't give your brother a chance to accuse us in return."

"Are you kidding me? What kind of legal-nonsense crap is *that*? It's Candy who is the crook here!"

"I'm just telling you what Dinis told me. We have to play it cool, okay? Cool is better anyway. There are fourteen heirs — thirteen, if you set Uncle Candy aside for the moment — and lots of potential for trouble. Cool, Dad. The only way to go."

"'Cool,' huh?"

"*Cool*, Dad. Really."

"Okay. Cool . . . Damn it."

PART IX

The Verdict

"Less than two hours. What does that mean?"

"It means I was right to tell you not to go too far away."

"Yes, I understand that, Harold. But what does it mean in terms of a verdict?"

"There are two schools of thought on that, Paulinho."

"And — ?"

"It means a slam-dunk decision when the jury decides so quickly. I mean, they must have used half of their time in the jury room just getting organized and electing a foreman. The decision was apparently obvious to everyone and quickly agreed to."

"And the two schools of thought?"

"One is that quick decisions favor the accusers — the petitioners in this case — and the other school thinks it favors the defenders — in this case, *you guys*, the respondents."

"What does the Harold Widener school of thought think?"

"Don't answer that, Hare," interrupted Dennis Ramos. "We don't want you to jinx it."

"My distinguished and superstitious colleague here," said Widener, "is afraid that a prediction of victory is presumptuous and is the kind of pride that goeth before a fall. He need not fear that I will make such a rash prediction. I will say only this: When a jury decides a case at the speed of light, as this one did, you need only examine the two sides of the issue and consider whether the ridiculously inept side could possibly be embraced so quickly by twelve sane people."

"My distinguished and optimistic colleague," retorted Ramos, "is forgetting the ample evidence that we are surrounded by crazy people. I would not be surprised if twelve crazy people ended up on the jury. Maybe Onan did such a bad job they'll give her a sympathy vote."

Ryan Bowman came strolling up far faster than his usual measured pace.

"The bailiff has unlocked the courtroom and we can go in. Is this everybody?

It'll have to do. Let's not waste any time. I don't know about all of you, but I can't wait."

Bowman spun on his heel and was heading toward the courtroom.

"The old man has a little life in him, doesn't he?" said Widener.

"Yeah, Hare. Fear him. This case has rejuvenated him. Ryan won't roll over for you when you go after Candido in the divorce suit. I should reserve a seat in the gallery just so I can watch the two of you duel on opposite sides for a change."

"I do not fear him," said Widener coolly.

They reached the double doors to the courtroom. Together, Widener and Ramos held them open for the Franciscos to enter. Their numbers were depleted relative to the earlier session, when Onan and Bowman had delivered their summations and Judge Knight had given the jury his instructions. Some of the Franciscos had then gone home, instead of loitering near the courthouse as Widener had suggested. Paul had departed for Sacramento to avoid missing another day's work while Mary Carmen had gone to her mother-in-law's to collect her two young sons. They would all miss the grand finale.

Candido entered the courtroom and took a seat next to his brother, presenting a temporarily united front. It unnerved him that Widener was smiling in his direction, but he tried to ignore it.

The last of the respondents to arrive were Carmina and Odile, who had been passing time at a nearby restaurant. They had Carmina's youngest son Alex in tow. Carmina saw where Candido was sitting and steered Odile to seats away from their husbands.

The jury filed in just as Beatrice Onan took her place at the petitioners' table. As usual, none of her clients were present.

The bailiff prompted everyone to rise for Judge Knight's entrance.

"Please be seated," said the judge briskly. He turned immediately to the jury.

"Has the jury reached a verdict?"

A middle-aged man with a shock of white hair stood up to address the judge.

"Yes, your honor. We have."

The bailiff collected a slip of paper from the jury foreman and carried it to the judge. The judge unfolded it, glanced at it, and had the bailiff return it to the foreman.

"And what is that verdict?" asked the judge solemnly.

"The jury finds for the respondents," said the foreman, holding the slip of paper up as if he were reading it. A noisy exhalation of air came from the gallery of Franciscos, but the judge ignored the disturbance.

"And so say you all?" asked the judge.

"We do," said the foreman, and sat back down.

"Ms. Onan, do you care to poll the jury?" asked Judge Knight.

"I do, your honor," she said, insisting on playing out the last scene of the opera to its bitter conclusion.

The bailiff called on the jurors in numerical order. Jurors 1 through 12 all replied that they had voted in favor of the respondents. Onan watched the process forlornly, while the Franciscos fidgeted in their seats.

"The jury has found in favor of the respondents. The plea of the petitioners for redress in the matter of the will of Teresa Francisco is denied. The court thanks the jury for its service and dismisses it. The jurors will be exempt from further service in the courthouse for one calendar year, beginning as of this date. Court stands adjourned."

Judge Knight rapped the gavel smartly and rose from the bench. The attorneys rose automatically to their feet as he departed. Freed from further obligation, some of the jurors walked over to congratulate the Franciscos, while others slipped out through the jury door.

The respondents' attorneys were busily shaking hands with their clients when a tight-lipped Beatrice Onan stalked over to confront them. Ryan Bowman let go of Henry Francisco's hand and turned to greet her.

"Thank you, Biddy, for being part of the most interesting case I have ever had the privilege to participate in."

"Then you should be pleased to learn, Ryan, that this case is by no means over. There was ample judicial misbehavior to warrant an appeal. My clients will see justice done, even if it takes longer than we had hoped."

She marched off as concerned murmurs arose in her wake.

"Damn her!" exclaimed Candido. "Is this stupid thing going to go on forever?"

"I don't think you should worry too much about that, Uncle Candy," said Henry Francisco. "In fact, I don't think any of us should worry too much about that."

"What's going on, Hank?" said Paulinho to his son.

Henry found himself suddenly the center of attention. He paused a couple of seconds to savor the moment.

"I had breakfast with Elvis Salazar this morning," he announced. "We got together in Cotton Center for a little chat. It was his idea. He wanted to tell me something."

"Go on," said Ryan Bowman.

"Elvis and Randy have talked to a new attorney. They had a statement drafted that denies Ms. Onan the authority to act on their behalf and disavows any appeal of the original petition. If Uncle Louis wants to spend more money on an appeal, he'll have to do it with Otelo alone. Elvis doesn't think that will happen, because he says Otelo is fed up with the whole thing, too."

"That's excellent news, Henry. You're clear on this? This is really going to happen?"

"I'm certain," declared Henry with great confidence. "I can report that Elvis has definitely left the building."

JUNE 1983

Who Holds the Proxy?

The phone buzzed in the office of Paul Francisco on the fourth floor of State Office Building No. 1.

"Yes?"

"Paul, that's your father on line 2."

"Thanks, Rowena."

Paul punched the button for line 2.

"Dad?"

"Hi, son. I'm calling from the lobby of the county courthouse. The jury just returned a judgment in our favor."

"Already? That was fast!"

"I'm sorry you missed it. The summations didn't take very long and neither did the deliberations. The jury was in and out in less than two hours this afternoon."

"Excellent! Did anyone show up on the petitioners' side?"

"No. Onan was alone, as usual. Your cousins didn't show their faces, although we got some interesting news from Hank."

"Oh? And what did he have to report?"

"Hank said Elvis will refuse to cooperate with any appeal of the judgment. And apparently Randy feels the same. I suppose Otelo could go it alone, but it also depends on whether your *padrinho* wants to keep wasting his money. And ours, too, now that I come to think of it."

"I can't predict what Otelo will do. And I don't know if *padrinho*'s grudge is big enough to make him keep digging into his pocket. But wouldn't he have to get a new attorney? Onan is under investigation for bankruptcy fraud and likely to be put on suspension soon, right?"

"I'll ask the lawyers about that. I hope you're right."

"Me, too, Dad. Too bad I didn't wait one more day. Sounds like I missed a happy occasion. Good luck with the mopping-up operations."

"Yeah. I have a question about that."

"For me? What could I possibly tell you that would have any value? Let Hank handle it."

"That is *exactly* what I wanted to ask you about. We're going to have a settlement meeting next week where the heirs are going to try to divide things up. Hank said he'll vote your proxy if necessary."

"It probably will be. I can't imagine that we're going to have much of a consensus on splitting the spoils." Paul paused. "Sorry, Dad. That's a poor choice of words. It's *Avó*'s estate, not just some prize of war in the battle with the Salazars."

"That's okay, son. But what I wanted to know is — why is Hank holding your proxy? You gave it to your kid brother and not to your dad. I'm not complaining. I'm just curious."

"Oh, Dad. You certainly *are* complaining — or you wouldn't even have brought it up. You know full well why Hank has my proxy. I trust him to do what's right."

"That's harsh, boy. You're saying you don't trust me?"

"Not where Uncle Candy is concerned, Dad. You're too soft on him. You always feel sorry for him. I trust Hank to pin his ears back. That's why he has my proxy, Dad."

"I can't help feeling sorry for Candy. He's had a rough life and a tough wife. I don't condone the things he's done and I never got along with him as a partner, but I can deal with him when I need to."

"Dad, you've been free of your brother for — what? — ten years now. Right? But Hank has had to work as *Tio's* underappreciated farmhand for all that time. He won't give him an inch of slack. Understood?"

"You're a hard one, boy. You know that?"

"Probably not as hard as Hank. In fact, I'm counting on it. Let your middle son take the lead on this. If there's a settlement that Hank likes, I'll like it, too. Besides, Dad, you already have multiple votes. Mom will vote along with you and Alex is a minor and you're his legal guardian. Three votes is pretty good. Hank will have mine and Magdalena's in addition to his own. So he'll have three, too."

The line was silent for a few seconds before Paulinho spoke again.

"Actually, your brother will have *four*. Mary Carmen gave him her proxy as well."

Paul laughed.

"You just made my day, Dad!"

JULY 1983

Candido Meets His Match

"The Candy Man is here," said Magdalena to her husband as she looked out Carmina's kitchen window.

"Thanks, Maggie," said Henry Francisco. "Is he mixing it with love to make the world taste good?"

"I doubt anything your uncle can do will make the bad taste go away."

"That's okay, honey. Everything is under control." Henry raised his voice. "Places, everyone! Maggie just spotted Uncle Candy outside!"

He walked to the side door to admit his uncle.

"Hi. We're all in the family room, *Tio*."

"Okay," said Candido.

As they passed through the kitchen, Carmina and her daughter-in-law were setting coffee mugs out on the table.

"Hello, Candy," said Carmina. "Would you like some coffee?"

"Sure, Carmina. Thanks. Hi, Maggie."

Magdalena poured some coffee into one of the mugs, which Carmina handed to her brother-in-law. Unlike Paulinho, Candido was willing to take his coffee black when he was impatient. He was in a hurry to get down to business. He dumped some sugar into his coffee and followed Henry into the family room.

The couches and chairs in the large family room were usually arranged in an approximate semicircle centered on the television, which sported the largest screen of any that Paulinho carried in his shop. Today, however, a chair had been pulled out of place and set in front of the television. Henry led his uncle to his hot seat, where Candido found himself facing Paulinho, Henry, twelve-year-old Alex, and Dinis Costa.

"What's *he* doing here?" asked Candido, looking at his brother and pointing his chin at the court-appointed receiver. "Isn't his job *done?*"

"Dinis is here for informational purposes," said Paulinho coolly. "He's already approved the plans for the disposition of Mom's estate, but we asked him to be here in case certain questions came up."

Candido tried to hide his confusion and concern behind his coffee mug, sipping the hot brew and wondering what the receiver could do to cause him trouble. *More* trouble, really. He had already caused plenty.

"Dinis, since Candido brought it up," continued Paulinho, "would you mind running down the outlines of the deal?"

"Sure," said the attorney. He pretended to consult his notepad, but the details were all clear in his mind. "Your mother made things interesting by naming fourteen heirs, as all of you know, and all of you are included. Seven are in Candido's family and seven are in Paulinho's. Most of the decisions on dividing the estate were made on an eight-to-six vote."

"Thank you, *Tio*," said Henry.

"You're welcome," said Candido uncomfortably. It wasn't as if he had had any choice. He couldn't broker any deal with his estranged family, so he had to throw in his lot with his younger brother. Paulinho had controlled the entire process, with Henry and Dinis occasionally whispering in his ear. The only joy Candido had taken in the ordeal was the evident anger and misery of his immediate family members, especially Junior, who had walked out in a fulminating rage.

Dinis Costa was continuing his summary.

"The division of the estate assigned the 'home place' with the dairy barn, workshop, two homes, and corrals to Paulinho's controlling bloc, along with Teresa's cows and specified acreage, as set forth in the settlement document. The parcel containing Candido's former residence, still occupied by Odile, was assigned to the minority bloc."

Odile's house was the only building included in the minority bloc's share. In compensation, the majority was ceding the lion's share of the undeveloped land to Odile, her sons, and daughters-in-law. The boys could choose to farm it, rent it out, or try to sell it, but they would have no dairy facilities.

"The dairy cattle on the estate whose title is held by Candido's company, Francisco & Sons, will continue to be maintained and milked by Henry Francisco until such time as Candido and his sons decide how to apportion their interests in those cattle and make arrangements to relocate them. Paperwork has been drawn up to compensate Henry for their care and feeding and to compensate Candido's company for the value of their milk production. That will involve a net payment to Candido from Henry each month. This agreement will be subject to renegotiation if the Francisco & Sons cows are still on the Paulo C. Francisco & Sons dairy farm at the end of six months. That should all be pretty clear from previous discussions. Yes?"

There was general nodding.

"Okay," said Dinis. "And in the delicate matter of the irregularities in the title of ownership for some of the dairy cattle, documents have been executed to clarify that Candido does not lay claim to any interest in the estate's cows. In return, no liens will be placed against the Francisco & Sons cattle, many of which are being allocated to Candido Junior and João José in partial settlement of their dispute with their father. Are we good?"

"We're good," said Henry.

"Yes," said Paulinho.

Alex nodded his head in accord with his father and brother. He wasn't very interested in what was going on, although he was pleased that they were staying in their house. He was also happy that Hank and Maggie would be moving in next door with their little girls. It would be nice to have someone living in *Avó's* house again. Whatever Daddy or Hank said was perfectly fine with him.

Everyone was looking at Candido and waiting for his comment. He drank some more coffee.

"Yeah, fine," he said. "That's the agreement, all right."

He didn't like the dynamic of the current situation, but he had no particular reason to complain about the settlement. No one was making snide remarks about the number of cattle that had not been in his mother's name. That was an enormous relief. He had seized the opportunity to escape from the corner into which he had painted himself. It seemed best to hunker down and ride things out. And the people who made him the most unhappy were the unhappiest over the arrangements. Candido perked up.

"It's a pretty good deal, you know. We saved the dairy from being too split up and that means it can stay in operation."

His mood grew more optimistic as he fell naturally into his old leadership role as senior family member. Candido waxed generous.

"And you know, Hank, you get a lot of credit for keeping things going when Junior and I were having all that trouble." He looked at Dinis Costa. "Maybe you didn't make such a bad decision there."

"Thank you, Mr. Francisco. I did the best I could. As you observed, my job came to its conclusion when the settlement agreement was reached, as much as it displeased some of the parties. We even have Junior's signature on the necessary documents because he's champing at the bit to get his piece and leave town. All the paperwork is done except for the ancillary contracts between you and Henry for the payments you'll be receiving for your cows' milk production. I think the complicated matter of your mother's estate is now concluded."

Dinis Costa slipped his notepad back into his briefcase and closed it with a snap.

"All right, then," said Candido, acting almost as if he were the master of ceremonies. "Then I guess Mr. Costa can go and maybe Hank and I can spend a few minutes talking. It's time to plan the fall crops and do some rebuilding on the dairy."

His words were followed by a long silence as Henry and Paulinho exchanged glances. Henry's eyebrows were raised. Paulinho gave a microscopic nod. Candido watched the exchange with mounting concern.

"Dinis," said Henry to the attorney, "hang on just a minute. We might need you in your professional capacity just a little longer."

Henry turned his attention back to his uncle.

"*Tio*, I think you should know how things are going to go. You know I was managing *Avó*'s estate as a caretaker while it was under receivership. There's no more receiver and I'm not a caretaker anymore." Henry's eyes flickered toward his father, who was listening stoically. "Now I'm the boss. I will continue to operate the home place as its manager, but in my own right."

Candido cleared his throat noisily.

"Hank, that's not how we do things," Candido said, speaking earnestly and with an undertone of long-suffering patience in his voice. Hard eyes were looking at him, but he pressed on. "I'm the senior partner in the business. The *senior*. You need to listen to your elders."

Henry's eyes had not softened.

"*Tio*, you never remembered that elder stuff when *Avó* was still alive. It's a little late to bring it up now. Besides, there's another way to decide how this is going to work. Maggie and I have two votes. I have proxies from Paul and Mary Carmen. That's four votes out of the eight in the majority bloc." Henry turned toward his father. "Dad?"

"Carmina and I will vote with Hank, of course. And I cast Alex's vote as his guardian. Hank has seven out of eight votes, Candy. Hank is the boss."

Numbness suffused Candido's body. He shuddered with a sudden chill.

"You can stay with us, *Tio*," said Henry. "I don't doubt you can be useful. But I will run the dairy farm. I call the shots. You can provide advice, just like Dad has promised to, but I'll decide what's going to be done. Can you live with that?"

Candido set the coffee mug down on the floor next to his chair and stood up.

"No. I've been the boss too long to be bossed by someone else. No deal."

"It's not really a 'deal,' *Tio*. It's a 'take it or leave it' situation."

"Then I 'leave it.'"

"Fine, *Tio*."

To Candido's surprise, Henry walked over to him with his hand out-
stretched. Not knowing what else to do, he submitted to his nephew's handshake. Henry looked back over his shoulder and spoke to the attorney.

"Dinis, we're going to need those separation documents. Uncle Candy and I
have to work out the details of our buying out his interest in the home place."

MAY 1972

The Grand March

Paul Francisco stood stiffly at attention as Maria Anna clung to his arm.
The man with the cassette player pushed a button and a hissy version of
"When the Saints Go Marching In" began to blare from the public-address
speakers.

Lord Almighty, thought Paul, *I do not believe it! Who is responsible for this
sort of nonsense?*

The long line began to move rather tentatively, then began to hit its stride.

Paul's instructions were very simple. He and Maria Anna were to follow
the couple in front of them, preferably without stumbling, until the music
stopped.

Oh, let it be soon! thought Paul.

At least the tempo of the music allowed them to move along rather briskly,
once they got up to speed. It would have been much worse with a dirge-like
tune.

The leaders presumably knew what they were doing as they traced out some
snake-like path through the big room of Tulare's Portuguese Hall. The tables
were all in storage and the folding chairs were confined to the room's margins
for the comfort of the old ladies in attendance. The center of the room had
been left clear to accommodate the young people as they went on maneuvers.

Paul glanced at Maria Anna, who seemed perfectly content to be escorted at her parish's Pentecostal Grand March by a cousin.

I suppose anything is better than showing up alone, mused Paul, *even having a cousin as your escort.*

"Saints" seemed to have more verses than reasonable. Or perhaps the tape was a loop. It kept hissing out of the speakers as the Grand March procession moved back and forth and around the room without quite devolving into chaos.

I wish they'd try a self-intersecting path, thought Paul. *That ought to bring things to a satisfactory conclusion.*

The old ladies sat in clusters against the wall. Most of them were elderly widows encased in black garments that would have passed muster back in the Azores. Their bright eyes peered out appraisingly from under the scarves and hoods they wore.

Paul had read Frank Herbert's *Dune.*

The reverend mothers of the Bene Gesserit are hard at work on their breeding program, thought Paul.

Some of the eyes were tracking him with interest. Paul kept a neutral expression fixed on his face.

I can read your minds, Reverend Mothers! he thought with amusement. *You're wondering who the tall kid is. Who's that stranger?*

The line turned and he and Maria Anna promenaded in front of another gaggle of match-making crones.

Is that Chico Francisco's grandson? he imagined them thinking. *The college boy? He never comes to these events!*

New faces were always a source of excitement for the Portuguese Bene Gesserit.

Who is that on his arm? It's Maria Anna, his cousin! That's okay; they're only third cousins. Sometimes inbreeding can strengthen a bloodline!

Maria Anna noticed that Paul was grinning now and wondered if he was actually beginning to enjoy himself. She had twisted his arm relentlessly to get him to agree to bring her to the Grand March.

I think just about everyone in this room is from the same little island in the Atlantic, he thought. *There sure are a lot of "strengthened" bloodlines here!*

He saw that his cousin had observed him smiling and wiped it from his face. The man with the cassette player took mercy on them at that moment and clicked it off. Everyone began to applaud.

Are we applauding ourselves? thought Paul. *I'm just applauding that it's over.*

"Thanks, Paul," said Maria Anna.

"You're welcome, Maria Anna," replied Paul, with certain mental reservations. "That takes care of that, right?"

"Right. Say hello to your folks for me."

Paulinho and Carmina were Maria Anna's *padrinhos.* That was probably why they had added to their goddaughter's pressure for Paul to agree to go to the Grand March.

"Hi, guys!"

"Hello, Hank," said Paul to his brother.

"Where's Maria Olivia?" asked Maria Anna.

"I don't know where your sister is. She took off as soon as the music ended," replied Henry.

The Francisco brothers stood together as Maria Anna disappeared into the midst of the churning crowd.

"Looks like our job is done. We had the signal honor of escorting our third cousins to the social event of the Portagee season and now we can go."

Henry did not embrace Paul's suggestion.

"Oh, come on, Paul. The only reason I agreed to come was that Maria Olivia said I didn't have to stay with her after the Grand March. I want to meet people and stay for some of the dancing. Come on. Just for a while!"

Damn, thought Paul. They had come in a single vehicle and he couldn't leave until his brother was ready to go. He tried to strike a compromise.

"Okay, Hank. One hour, okay? If I had my choice, I'd leave right this minute."

"Thanks! One hour!"

Now Henry vanished into the crowd.

Paul wandered toward the edge of the room, where he had spotted the parents of Maria Anna and Maria Olivia. Old World courtesy expected that he would at least say hello. If he remembered correctly, it was the father who was second cousins with his own father. No doubt one of the Bene Gesserit could provide details if he were bold enough to ask.

I've really got to get my ass out of here, he thought.

"*Boa tarde,*" he said to the girl's parents. *Good evening.*

They were effusive in their greetings but not cloyingly so. Paul was relieved to discover that they were obviously parties to the alliance of convenience by which the Francisco boys agreed to escort their cousins to the Grand March.

They aren't looking to "strengthen" any bloodlines, he thought.

Having paid his respects, he detached himself and wound his way through the shifting crowd and out the door into the evening air.

A concession stand was swarmed with an infestation of teenagers. Paul looked for any indication of a line and, finding none, decided he would check back later. He was starting to turn away when he heard his brother's voice.

"Hey, Paul! Want a Coke?"

Henry bustled over, several cans hugged to his chest with one arm. With his free hand he tossed a can in Paul's direction. He hated it when Henry did that, but managed to snatch it successfully from the air, fumbling momentarily. Civilized people, he was sure, simply handed things to other people.

"Thanks, Hank," he called after his brother, who hadn't broken stride. Henry merged into a knot of young people who grabbed at the soft drinks Henry had carried to them. They were talking and laughing loudly.

I guess they think they're having a good time, thought Paul. *So I guess they are. Can you ever be wrong about thinking you're having a good time? Probably not.*

He popped open his can and took a sip.

I hope this was a spare and Hank didn't leave any of his friends out.

Paul didn't recognize any of the people talking with his brother. He glanced at his watch. The brief chat with the cousins and the stroll out of the hall had taken only about ten or twelve minutes. The hour he had promised Henry still stretched out before him.

The exterior lighting was all clustered around the Portuguese Hall. By walking farther away from it, Paul could see the night sky. Venus was intensely bright in the west. Paul looked around for Mars, which was much dimmer and more difficult to find. These days the two planets were keeping close company in the sky, although Venus drew the eye away from Mars.

He avoided looking at his watch as long as he could. He traced some constellations in the sky and wished he had a telescope or binoculars with him. Paul found Polaris and noted the locations of its neighboring stars. The sky pivoted fifteen degrees about the Pole Star every hour. He wasn't looking at his watch, but the sky was sending him clues.

The stars eventually signaled that the time was near. When he checked his watch, he was pleased to see that forty minutes of Hank's hour had elapsed. Paul ambled back to the hall and stepped just inside the main doors.

His brother was obviously having a good time on the dance floor with a girl Paul didn't recognize. She was a slender thing with a thick mane of dark, dark hair. Perhaps he should have known some of the attendees, but except for their cousins they all appeared to be strangers. He saw Maria Olivia stroll by in animated conversation with two other girls, but his cousin didn't acknowledge him.

Paul stepped back outside and wandered about until another ten minutes ticked by. When he returned to the hall, the music had stopped. He looked around for Henry and found him chatting with his erstwhile dance partner. As Paul watched, the music struck up again, Henry took the girl's arm, and they headed back onto the dance floor.

Fine, thought Paul, and went outside again to wait a while longer.

To his surprise, Henry appeared at his side as if magically summoned by the expiration of his hour. Paul was impressed by his brother's punctuality.

"Good timing."

"*Please*, Paul. You have got to give me more time! Can I have another half hour? *Please?*"

Of course, thought Paul. *Why am I even surprised?*

"A whole half hour?"

"It's not much. Just another half hour? *Please?*"

Henry's pleading was both pathetic and touching, tinged with a surprising undertone of desperation.

If only my heart were made of stone, thought Paul.

"I can give you another half hour, Hank. But just a half hour, okay? I am bored out of my gourd here."

"Thank you! Thank you! *Thank you!*" cried Henry, pounding Paul on the back with one hand.

"Geez! Try showing your gratitude *without* hitting me, okay?"

But Henry was already gone.

I suppose next he'll be back to ask for fifteen minutes. He's going to nickel-and-dime his way to two hours. At least. Damn.

Maria Anna poked her head out of the Portuguese Hall and saw Paul standing in the yard. She smiled and came over.

"Do you want to know who she is?" asked Maria Anna.

"She?" said Paul.

"Yeah. Hank's pretty friend."

"Sure, *prima*. Who is she?"

"Magdalena Fontes. Her father owns a dairy farm here in Tulare."

"Sounds like a good Portuguese name," observed Paul.

"From the island of Terceira," said Maria Anna. "*Our* island. But they're not related to us."

Yeah, right, thought Paul. *Great. My brother's in love with one of our nth cousins, m times removed.*

"That's good, Maria Anna. Thanks for the news bulletin."

"See? Wasn't it good that you came to the Grand March?"

"Oh, definitely," agreed Paul. "I'm having the time of Hank's life."

NOVEMBER 1982

The Auction Block

Paulinho stood on his porch and watched the vehicles file into the dairy yard. They were on their way to the open field beyond the corrals, where the bank agents had set up their auction stand. He had seen his son Henry go by earlier. His boy had been the dairy farm's manager since the summer, selected by the estate's court-appointed receiver. It was his job to keep an eye on anything that occurred on the grounds.

The caravan of bargain-hunters raised a veil of dust that sparked a coughing fit from Paulinho, but he stood his ground. Like Henry, he wanted to see what was going on. A pickup truck pulled into the driveway to Paulinho's house instead of the driveway to the dairy yard. Darrin MacDonald stuck his head out of the driver-side window.

"Hey, Paulinho! How are you doing?"

With their children grown (except for Alex), the Franciscos and the MacDonalds did not hang out together as much as they once had, but they still dropped in on each other from time to time. Darrin climbed out of his vehicle and ambled over to where Paulinho was standing.

"I'm doing all right, Darrin, except for the damned cough. How about you?"

"Fine. Just fine. What's happening here?"

Paulinho knew that Darrin was just providing him with an opening. Hardly anything happened in Tulare County without Darrin's becoming almost instantly aware of it.

"Candy's raising some cash today. That's what's going on. You doing any shopping yourself?"

Paulinho's question implied that Darrin had known the nature of the event all along, but neither of the long-time friends saw any reason to fuss over details like that.

"Heh!" laughed Darrin. "What would I do with one of Candy's cast-offs?"

"Good question," agreed Paulinho.

The court-appointed receivership had nearly been the death knell for Candido Francisco's operation. Neither Candido nor his sons had had any real appreciation for the degree to which they had been subsidized by his mother Teresa. As long as the matriarch refrained from charging her son and grandsons rent for the use of lands that were in her name, or the use of buildings that were in her name, they had managed to maintain the illusion of prosperity. Her death had knocked the most significant prop out from under their business. The court-appointed receiver had imposed fair-market rent charges. Candido and his boys couldn't afford to pay them.

A deal had been cut with the agricultural accounts managers at the local bank to conduct an equipment auction. Candido's idled tractors and cotton-pickers, plus miscellaneous other items, would go under the auctioneer's hammer. It was one small step short of an everything-must-go bankruptcy auction. A delaying tactic.

"They're going to be disappointed by the take," said Darrin. "Chapter 11 is probably next."

"I'm sure of it," said Paulinho. "But they've run out of options. They were hoping to hang on till the inheritance from Mom's estate was parceled out, but the lawsuit from the Salazars means it's going to stay in its receivership for several months more."

"It's an act of desperation," opined Darrin.

"That would be my conclusion, too." said Paulinho.

"Say, is your son farming the home place now?" said Darrin, asking another question he already knew the answer to.

"Yeah, he is, for the most part. Hank's been taking over more and more of it as Candy pulls out."

"I thought so," said Darrin. "There's actually a crop on it this year."

Paulinho laughed, seeing now why Darrin had asked the question. He appreciated his friend's effort to set up the compliment.

"Nice of you to say so. Hank's going to do us proud, assuming we survive all this legal hassle."

He paused to cough several times, trying to clear his airways, but with limited success.

"Anyway," he continued, "things are as messed up as I've ever seen them. It's a matter of hunkering down and hoping it all goes away."

"I talk to folks who talk to your brother-in-law," said Darrin, meaning Louis Salazar. "He's really out to get you. Louis keeps telling people it's all about you and Candy, but he harps mostly on Candy. A lot of bad blood there. Not sure why."

"Could be a lot of things," said Paulinho. "If you don't know, don't nobody know. It could be just a growing heap of slights that Louis couldn't handle. Candy can be a pain in the ass."

"We certainly have enough people willing to testify to that around here," said Darrin. "In fact, I'll bet some of them are here at the auction just for the chance to enjoy gnawing on Candy's bones."

"Ugh!" exclaimed Paulinho. "But I won't say you're wrong."

They stood awhile, watching the traffic going down the driveway to the auction site. It was tapering off now. Paulinho decided to probe a bit, to see if Darrin knew more than he was saying.

"Darrin, from what you've heard, do you know why Louis is doing this?"

"As best I can tell, Louis thinks he's getting even for something. Maybe you should ask Candy. If anyone knows, he should."

"My brother's almost never around. He lives up in Fresno with his girlfriend and comes down here once a week or so to try to run things. The boys flip him off and do what they please. That's really aggravated their problems."

"There's another factor, too," said Darrin, continuing his answer about Louis Salazar's possible motives. "It was his hotshot lawyer girlfriend who filed the lawsuit. He's bragged to people how smart she is."

Paulinho's face clouded.

"It's because of Fatima. She was the brains in our generation. Sharp as a razor. Louis can't replace her, so he settles for women who remind him of her."

"I hear he's failing, Paulinho. The lady lawyer's not that smart. Everyone says the lawsuit is a farce. And they don't mean funny. They mean stupid.

You'd think these people would be smarter than to try and milk a bull. No happy ending coming from that — except maybe for the bull."

Paulinho laughed.

"Yeah," he said, "Louis ought to be smarter than that. And so should his lawyer friend."

"Like I said. She's smart enough to lead your brother-in-law around like a tame steer, but not smart enough to take this place away from you."

"I hope you're right." Paulinho shook his head. "Stupid Louis. Being taken advantage of and being made a fool of. And making our lives hell, to boot." He looked at Darrin. "What is it with guys and their gals? Is my Carmina the only one who isn't manipulating her man?"

Darrin smiled at him.

"I have my wife's permission to say that she's not manipulating me, either."

PART X

The Divorce Trial

"Hello, tall stranger. So we meet again!"

Ryan Bowman turned his lanky height around and smiled down at his short colleague.

"Hello, Harold. How is my cherished erstwhile ally and my current esteemed opponent?"

Bowman and Widener shook hands.

"I continue to be cherished and esteemed in my fineness," said Widener.

"Good for you. So what do you think? Is this the last act of the opera?"

"I wish I knew," replied Widener. "Does anyone know how many acts there are in this tragedy?"

"Are you tipping your hand? Are you casting Odile as the soprano *abandonatta* who yearns for the return of her lover?"

"You have the advantage of me, Ryan. What opera are we talking about?"

"I'm accustomed to having the advantage of you. How nice of you to acknowledge that. Specifically, however, I'm thinking of the role of Violetta in *La Traviata*. That's where a spherical soprano coughs delicately into a hankie while wasting away from consumption."

"Sounds more like farce than tragedy," said Widener.

"Perhaps farce is really what we're going through."

"Maybe. But we'll see. Who has the tougher task here? I'm supposed to make Candido Francisco look like a bad guy and you have to stop me. Care to place a small wager?"

"It matters not whether Candido is a bad guy or a good guy. It matters only whether the law is on his side."

"Nice phrasing, Ryan. I see we're in for a high-toned debate. You should get a stovepipe hat and a mole if you want to nail that Lincoln impression of yours. And grow a beard."

"And you, my friend, can play the part of Stephen Douglas, Lincoln's famous debating partner — although I admit you're rather more compact than 'The Little Giant.'"

"And I'll thank you to remember that it was Douglas who won the Lincoln-Douglas debates, so brace yourself for the worst."

"It was a miscarriage of justice, Harold. Everyone knows that. Let us go forth and correct that historic injustice today."

"Geez. Lay it on a little thicker. I can still breathe."

Bowman thought it was more dignified to chuckle than to laugh outright, so he favored his colleague with a dry chuckle.

"By the way, it seems Dennis Ramos has gotten plenty of post-trial work on the Francisco case," said Widener.

"He most certainly did. Dennis and I worked out the settlement deal between Candido and his two older boys."

"What was that all about?"

"Simple, Harold. Junior and Jojo wanted to cash out their shares of their grandmother's estate and set up independent of their father. They were going to sue the old man if they didn't like the deal he offered them. Dennis and I brokered a deal before it got too ugly."

"It got too ugly a long time ago," laughed Widener. "Especially when Biddy was involved."

Bowman couldn't help laughing. Chuckling didn't do the situation justice.

"Well, look who's here," said Widener, as they approached the doors to the divorce court. "Hi, Ferdie."

"Hi, Harold," said Ferdinando Francisco. "Mom is inside. I don't see my father, though."

"I have your father in a waiting area," said Bowman. "The bailiff will go get him when the judge is ready to start. I see some benefit in keeping your parents apart."

"Yes, sir," said Ferdinando.

"Go keep your mother company," said Widener. "We'll get going soon, I'm sure."

"Okay," replied Ferdinando. He entered the courtroom, followed by the two attorneys.

Bowman signaled the bailiff, who nodded and went off to fetch the other party in the dispute.

After Candido was in place and the judge had entered, there was a brisk flurry of activity as the opposing attorneys confirmed the stipulations they had filed earlier. Bowman and Widener had reviewed each other's initial filings and counter-filings before coming to court and they had agreed on several items that were not in dispute. These items, such as the date when Candido left Odile, were in the mutually agreed-upon stipulations.

Judge Richard Harmer accepted the stipulations and moved the parties onward toward the matters in contention.

"Mrs. Francisco, I see here that you have filed a proposed settlement order for the court to impose on Mr. Francisco, setting the amounts of alimony and support to which you say you are entitled."

Odile looked toward Widener, who nodded his head.

"Uh, yes. Yes, I did, your honor."

"The court will take your proposed settlement language under advisement, Mrs. Francisco. I am curious, however, concerning the item for medical expenses. Do you have a basis for asking for so large an amount?"

"I'm very sick."

Widener was on his feet.

"If it please the court, your honor, Mrs. Francisco suffers from a number of chronic illnesses which will be considered pre-existing conditions with regard to future medical coverage. We have documentation to present to the court concerning the billings she receives on a regular basis."

Widener approached the bench and provided the judge with a folder. Judge Harmer flipped it open and paged through the photocopies of medical bills that Odile and Ferdie had dug out of their records at home, plus duplicates solicited from the offices of various doctors and clinics.

"Thank you, counselor. Am I to understand the medical costs have been handled out-of-pocket up to this point rather than under a medical coverage plan?"

Widener looked toward Odile.

"Yes, your honor," she said. "I have been paying all my medical bills."

"Excuse me, your honor. May I offer some information?"

"Certainly, Mr. Bowman. If it's relevant to this specific matter at hand."

"It is, your honor. My client would like to inform the court that Mrs. Francisco's out-of-pocket exposure to medical costs during the course of their marriage was precisely *zero*." Bowman approached the bench with a folder of his own. "These bank records show that the bills submitted by Mrs. Francisco and represented by her as having been paid at her own expense are nothing of the sort. A comparison between the bank drafts in this evidence folder and the medical bills in Mrs. Francisco's folder will certainly show that she routinely charged her medical expenses to the family business."

Widener was not looking very happy as he sat back down next to Odile.

"Why did you say you were paying them?" he hissed to his client.

"But I thought I did," said Odile, defensively. "I wrote the checks myself. Or had Ferdie do it."

"*Company* checks, evidently," said Widener sourly.

"Your honor," continued Bowman. "My client would like to bring a further item to the court's attention."

So far, Candido had said not a word in testimony. Bowman returned to his client's position and pulled another file from his briefcase.

"You may proceed, Mr. Bowman," said Judge Harmer.

"It is the contention of my client, your honor, that he was not support-ing Odile Francisco during their marriage. There is no basis, therefore, for determining that he should support her *after* leaving the marriage."

Harold whispered in Odile's ear.

"Do you know what's going on?"

She shrugged. She had no idea.

Bowman gave the new file to the judge.

"As your honor can see, these records demonstrate that Odile Francisco was a salaried employee of the family dairy farm. Not only was she *not* a dependent of Mr. Francisco, she was earning as much money as he was."

Widener felt his face blush hot. He hoped that his cheeks and ears had not turned rosy. He whispered to Odile again.

"Is this true, Odile? You didn't tell me about this."

"No!" she whispered back. "It was money from my husband!"

Ferdie was sitting right behind his mother.

"It was company checks again, Mom. You were a salaried employee."

"Mrs. Francisco," said the judge, "is it true that you worked for a salary on the family dairy farm?"

"I got paid, your honor," Odile said vaguely. "Did that make me salaried?"

The judge seemed irritated.

"Mrs. Francisco, it appears that you were not forthright with either your attorney or this court. May I impress upon you the rashness of such behavior?"

The judge looked down on the evidence folders on the bench.

"Counselors, I would like to speak with the two of you for a few minutes. Court will stand adjourned for a twenty-minute recess."

Judge Harmer rapped his gavel.

"What does all this mean?" asked Candido.

"It means," said Bowman, "that you're not going to be paying a penny of alimony."

"What does this mean?" said Odile to Widener.

Widener let a second tick past before answering.

"It means, Odile, that you're not going to see one red cent of alimony."

JANUARY 1983

Good News for Paulinho

"God damn it, doctor! This is the most outrageous crap I have ever heard!"

"Mr. Francisco, most patients react differently to good news."

"Oh, I am *delighted* at the damned good news! But after a month of holy hell I'm also just a *little* upset!"

Paulinho was hyperventilating. He gradually brought his labored breathing under control and tried to calm himself. The doctor waited patiently, guilt among the mixed emotions that flitted across his face.

"Okay," said Paulinho at length. "You're *sure* this time?"

"Yes, we're sure," replied the doctor. "Let me explain a couple of things."

"No," said Paulinho. "You wait. Carmina gets to hear this right now, right this second. She needs to know immediately."

Paulinho rushed out of the examining room. He returned a minute later with an anxious wife in tow and a concerned receptionist trailing after them.

"Doctor, they just —"

The doctor waved off the receptionist.

"Don't worry about it. I'll see the Franciscos together. It's all right."

The receptionist looked doubtful, but retreated to her post.

"Sit down, sugar," said Paulinho, leading his wife to the pair of chairs in the examining room. They sat down side by side and waited, holding hands, for the doctor to speak.

"Mrs. Francisco, your husband is not as ill as we had thought."

Hope flared in Carmina's eyes as she looked at her husband.

"Is that true?" she asked him, her hand squeezing his tightly.

Paulinho indicated the doctor with a tilt of his head.

"Let him tell you."

"It's a very peculiar thing, Mrs. Francisco. The tumor in your husband's lung is what we call an atypical carcinoid. These strongly resemble more aggressive tumors that spread rapidly, but they are actually slow-growing tumors that rarely spread to other parts of the body. We originally diagnosed your husband as having a quick-spreading carcinoma that was beyond effective treatment. There were enough peculiarities about Mr. Francisco's case, however, that we sent the X-rays and biopsies to Stanford Medical for consultation. One of their oncologists called me to ask if Mr. Francisco had had coccidioidomycosis — Valley fever. When I confirmed that he had, the oncologist explained that residual scarring on the lungs from Valley fever had confused the appearance of the carcinoid on the X-rays and made it appear much more advanced and aggressive."

The doctor paused while Carmina and Paulinho absorbed the good news, but Paulinho was grumbling again.

"I *told* them about the damned Valley fever," he muttered. "I *told* them."

His wife patted his hand comfortingly.

"What happens now, doctor?" she asked.

"Surgery is indicated and is highly effective in the treatment of carcinoids. Your husband will lose the lobe of the lung in which the tumor resides, but his breathing capacity will not be severely impaired. A full recovery without residual impairment can be expected."

The doctor regarded Paulinho for a moment before continuing.

"You have my sincere apologies, Mr. Francisco. I'm not sorry that our diagnosis turned out to be incorrect after the fact, but I am very sorry for having put you and your family through this." He hesitated a bit more. "In partial recompense for your mental anguish and suffering, the clinic is willing to offer you a waiver of the usual fees for surgery and post-operative care."

Another pause. "In return, we would ask you to sign a waiver of any further compensation, if you could see your way clear to doing that."

The doctor waited expectantly for Paulinho's response.

Paulinho looked to his wife, and then at the doctor.

"Doctor, I am not interested in getting tangled up in a malpractice lawsuit or seeking damages for pain and suffering. My family is paying enough money to lawyers as it is. We'll accept your offer and I'll sign the waiver."

The doctor audibly exhaled a sigh of relief.

"Is there anything else right now, doctor?" asked Carmina. "Paulinho and I have a lot of phone calls to make and we need to get home."

"My office will contact you soon about scheduling your husband's surgery. I think matters can proceed on a more routine basis from this point."

"Thank you, doctor."

The Franciscos were quickly out of the room.

MAY 1993

Louis Gets a Greeting

"We have *sopas* from the *festa*," said Carmina as she set out the dinner plates.

"That's great, Mom," said Paul, "but the smell already gave it away."

Henry had brought his parents a large *panela* earlier in the day. He was one of the dairymen who had contributed a side of beef for the Pentecost celebration and was a volunteer in the *festa* kitchen. They got to distribute *sopas* to family members and other *festa* supporters.

Henry's daughter Rebecca was this year's "little queen" in the Pentecost parade. Many people had complimented him on his daughter's regal bearing and dignity during the celebration, qualities often lacking in young girls at the center of attention. Old-timers had been at particular pains to compare Beckie to her late great-aunt Fatima, a woman she had never known.

"She's just like your *Tia* Fatima," they told Henry. "Never seen anyone like her again till your Rebecca. Never!"

Paulinho came in and sat down at the head of the table. Carmina carried over the steaming *panela* and set it down before her husband and eldest son. The aroma had already filled the room, but now it grew stronger. The beef had been stewed in a hearty broth containing red wine, cabbages, and sprigs of *hortelã* (mint). The *sopas* themselves were the slabs of French bread upon which the broth and beef were served. It was hearty religious holiday fare.

"Does anyone need anything else?" asked Carmina.

"No, Mom. Sit down. If I need anything, I can get it for myself," said Paul. He dug into the *sopas*. The beef was extraordinarily tender.

"Nice batch this year."

"Yeah," agreed his father. "Hank does a good job in the *festa* kitchen, just like he does a good job everywhere."

They ate in silence for a while. Miraculously, Paulinho had not yet reached for the remote control to turn on the television that sat in a corner of the kitchen.

"Paul, did you hear the news about your *padrinho*?" asked Carmina.

"Thanks, Mom, but I don't need any news about *Tio* Louis."

It was nearly a mark of disrespect to refer to one's godfather as merely an uncle.

"Now, honey, that's not good. You shouldn't hold a grudge like that," admonished Carmina.

Paul glanced at his father, who was concentrating on demolishing his share of the *sopas* as efficiently as possible. Paulinho was usually the first to leave the table and Paul was usually the last. His father was paying no apparent attention to the conversation.

"Mom, I don't find that holding a grudge is all that difficult."

"But they say it's not good for you, sweetheart."

"Who is 'they,' Mom? Some fake doctor on Oprah or Donahue?"

"Oh, really, Paul!"

"No, Mom. My *padrinho* gets no slack from me. If he wants me to drop my grudge against him, then he can damned well apologize for accusing me and my family of being thieves and forgers. No apology from *padrinho*, then no forgiveness from me."

Paul heard his father mutter, "Good boy!"

Apparently Carmina heard it, too, because she shot a sharp glance at her husband.

"Well, anyway," said Carmina, "I was only trying to tell you the news I heard from your sister."

"And everyone else in the world," said Paulinho, abruptly entering the conversation.

"'Everyone'?" asked Paul.

"Your father's right, sweetheart. Louis has been telling anyone who will listen to him that his niece talked to him."

"Mary Carmen? Why would my sister even acknowledge his existence?"

"She said she was halfway down an aisle at the Thrifty drug store in Tulare when he turned into it right in front of her."

"Then she could have turned right on her heel and gone back the way she came. Or she could have walked right past him as if he were invisible."

Paulinho chuckled.

"Louis Salazar is a little on the big side to just walk past in a store aisle," he said. "But he's no Alberto Avila — rest his soul — so I guess she could have gotten by."

"So what did Mary Carmen do?" asked Paul. His mother answered.

"She told me that she just said, '*Boa tarde, Tio*,' and kept on going. I guess Louis yelled '*Boa tarde*' at her back and has been the happiest man in Tulare County ever since."

"Hmph," muttered Paul. "If *padrinho* thinks Mary Carmen being as polite to him as she would be to a complete stranger is the beginning of a thaw, he's terribly wrong. That man is still on ice. Does Mary Carmen feel any different?"

"No, I don't think she does."

"And neither do I."

A Successful Divorce

"So far, sugar, I would say it's turning out to be a pretty good year."

"What do you mean, honey?"

"I mean that, number one, we survived Y2K. And, number two, we've reached our fiftieth wedding anniversary."

"I agree. Those are both very good things."

"Yeah, it's starting out to be a pretty good new century."

"Don't let your son hear you say that. Paul is very insistent that the twenty-first century doesn't begin until 2001."

"I forgot. Don't tell him. He gives us enough grief as it is."

"'Grief'? Because it's so hard to deal with someone so like yourself?"

"Don't say that, Carmina. That's going a little too far."

"Paul says it, too, honey. He says he's opinionated and stubborn, just like his father."

"Except that we disagree on everything."

"And each insists he is right and the other is wrong. Like I said: completely alike."

Paulinho leaned over and gave Carmina a kiss on the cheek.

"*Not* alike. I am a happily married man and our eldest is the most completely unattached person I know. The boy's not quite right."

"If it's right for him, it's right for him," said Carmina, with her characteristic appreciation of tautology.

"Sounds awful to me!"

"You win that round, honey. Alike, but not *completely* alike."

"I won't complain too much. I like having an educated intellectual in the family. My great-grandfather was considered a wizard back in the islands. We should spawn an occasional smarty-pants just to maintain the tradition. In fact, all of our children are pretty smart. Accomplished, too."

Paulinho gave his wife a little smile.

"Like that Mary Carmen," he said. "She's a sly one. *Just* like her mother!"

Carmina gave her husband's shoulder a playful whack with the back of her hand.

"Absolutely not true!"

"Oh? You can say that even after the 'open house'?"

"Honey, that just proves that Mary Carmen is sly. Not that she's like her mother."

"She has to get it from someone. I'm thinking you. And it was you she was trying to get around."

"I just told her not to make a fuss over our golden anniversary. She was the one who decided to throw a house-warming party. It's not my fault that she and Gerry just moved into a new house."

"It was a nice party," mused Paulinho. "Although most house-warming parties don't include 'happy anniversary' cakes."

"And a guest list a mile long."

Husband and wife fell silent. When Paulinho spoke, Carmina realized they had been thinking about the same thing.

"It was nice to see Candido there," he said, and smiled at her. "Mary Carmen did a good job of staging, that's for sure. Candido and Cindy were out the door and down the road before Odile showed up."

"Ferdie helped with the arrangements. He and David picked up Odile at the retirement home and timed their arrival so that Candido and Cindy would be gone already."

"Well, they pulled off the operation flawlessly." Paulinho paused for a moment. "Poor Candy. I don't think he recognized Paul at first."

"Well, he hardly ever sees him. And your brother can't help it that he has trouble remembering. It happens to everyone, you know."

"Ha!" said Paulinho, without much humor. "Maybe it happens to everyone, but it's worse when you don't have anything to spare. Candy was always a little bit borderline anyway."

Carmina didn't approve of what her husband had said, but chose to remain quiet rather than comment.

"How does Odile like her apartment in the retirement home?" asked Paulinho.

"She likes it. She's not very mobile, but it's got railings and stuff to help her move around. A helper checks on her twice a day and Odile says the meals aren't bad. Just a little skimpy."

Paulinho laughed.

"That sounds like her," he said.

Another silence.

"You know, sugar, Candido and Odile have had a pretty successful divorce." Paulinho looked toward his wife. "You know what I mean?"

Carmina's smile was slightly on the grim side.

"I do. And I have to agree. There's no way that Odile could be dealing with Candido if they were still together. He's become like an overgrown toddler. He's impulsive, easily confused, and too big to discipline. Cindy can handle him — barely. Odile would have been completely defeated."

"And vice versa," added Paulinho. "Candy couldn't give Odile any of the help she needs. He can't drive anymore, so he couldn't take her anywhere. He can't run errands. He's nearly a cipher as company. It would have been a mess."

"Like you said. It's a successful divorce."

Paulinho reached out and took Carmina's hand.

"I really think I prefer a successful marriage," he said.

JANUARY 2006

Legacy

Paulinho let himself out the back door and crossed the yard to the gate. The gate admitted him to the dairy yard. He was going to take his afternoon constitutional.

Carmina had joined him for a walk in the relative coolness of the morning, but Paulinho liked to get in a second hike later in the day. He didn't mind if he sweated a little. He had sweated a lot more for most of his eighty years. A little mild perspiration wasn't going to kill anybody. In fact, it was probably the reason he was so hale for a man his age.

Most men his age were dead.

The heifers in the calf pens bawled noisily at him as he strolled by. Perhaps he should have waited another hour before taking his walk, till after feeding time. The heifers knew that people were associated with food, but they didn't know it wasn't Paulinho's job anymore. They were about forty years too late for that.

The hospital pen was empty, always a good sign. Hank's computerized monitoring system was proving effective in identifying bovine illness at almost the very moment of initial onset. Even the tiniest elevation in the temperature of a cow's fluid milk was tagged and forwarded to Hank's computer screen for immediate attention. Ailing cows were pulled out of the milk herd instantly and quickly given medical treatment. The prompt intervention minimized their downtime and limited their separation in the hospital pen.

Paulinho heartily approved of the innovations. No doubt they were providing Hank with the competitive margin that kept the Francisco dairy farm alive in an era of corporate agriculture. Paulinho wondered how much longer it could continue.

He walked past the barn, which was in the throes of the afternoon milking. Sometimes he liked to pop in and check things out, but he knew the milkers didn't need anyone in their way. These days they were wrangling equipment that Paulinho could scarcely have imagined seventy years ago, when he first started helping out in the barn, but idle sightseers were still considered as much of a nuisance as ever.

Besides, it wasn't really his dairy, was it? It was Hank's.

Sure, Paulinho and Carmina were partners — mostly silent partners — but Hank had been calling the shots since the day he had taken majority control of the old Francisco place. Paulinho took a deeply satisfying pride in the dairy's renaissance under the stewardship of his middle son.

His middle son. Three sons and only one had had the least interest in maintaining the family's heritage. Paulinho accepted that. Frankly, it was impossible to imagine either Paul or Alex trying to run the Francisco dairy operation, but it gave him a pang to think about it. Was this a bad sign for the future?

Paulinho was at one of the corrals containing milk cows. Here was the heart of the dairy, the black-and-white producers who serenely chewed their hay, watched passers-by without interest (unless they were hungry), and moved toward the barn of their own accord twice a day. His vision wasn't what it used to be, but Paulinho could read the herd numbers on the tags of the nearest cows. These days he didn't recognize them all, but in his prime he had carried the detailed herd records of more than two hundred cows in his head at one time.

A nearby bovine flicked her ear and drew his attention. That one he knew.

Her bloodline went all the way back to good old 282, a heifer he had purchased at the auction yard in the sixties. She had been a champion producer. Decades later her many-times-great granddaughters were upholding the family reputation.

Granddaughters.

Hank had only daughters. No sons to carry the Francisco name and take up the job of dairyman. Perhaps it was the end of the line.

There was a grandson, though. Hank's oldest daughter had a one-year-old boy and had already gotten pregnant again. Rebecca joked that she would be a champion breeder if she were in Daddy's herd records. Paulinho smiled at the thought. If Hank could keep his daughter and her husband on the dairy farm, perhaps his grandchildren would produce another dairyman, even if his name would not be Francisco. Or *her* name? Paulinho shook his head. He wasn't sure he was quite ready for the possibility that a great-granddaughter might take over. But if it kept things going . . .

He heard footsteps crunching in the gravel driveway behind him as he leaned against the top rail of the corral and watched 282's legacy amble over to the water trough for a huge and noisy drink of water. Hank eased up alongside him and folded his arms atop the rail next to his father.

"Hey, Dad."

"Hi, Hank. How's it going?"

"Good, good. Did you hear the news?"

Paulinho looked at his son, momentarily marveling that his boy had grown up into this portly middle-aged grandfather.

"I don't much care for news," said Paulinho. "It's usually hype and nonsense."

"Family news, Dad. Not news news."

Paulinho laughed.

"That can be sensationalized, too, son. But what's the news? Good, I hope."

"Well, *I* think so," replied Hank. "Your great-grandson said his first word this morning."

"Really? Good for him. So who won? Was it 'mama' or 'dada'?"

A huge grin split Hank's face.

"It was *neither*. The boy's first word was 'cow.'"

Paulinho gave his son a matching grin.

"No kidding?" Paulinho turned back to the corral and looked out across the herd.

"We have a winner," he murmured.

THE END

Acknowledgments

First, I must thank my extended family: the grandparents, parents, siblings, uncles, aunts, cousins, nieces, and nephews with whom I shared the experiences that formed the background of *Land of Milk and Money*. Second, I warmly acknowledge the dedication and assistance of my friends Gene Weisskopf and Eric Butow, early readers of the manuscript who saw each segment of the book as it was written and were constant sources of encouragement and correction. My colleagues David Viar and Jim Walker at American River College read the entire first draft as soon as it was completed and were generous in their valuable feedback. My old college buddy Dana Reneau and his wife Gail Becker pored over the novel and gave me an invaluable list of plusses and minuses. Dana and Gail's points were reinforced by keen observations by my nephew Christopher Chancellor and his wife Adrienne. Paul Knox at the University of Nevada, Reno, was an indispensable sounding board.

My long-distance cyber-buddy João Paulo Firmino, a Portuguese émigré living in Valencia, Spain, gave the manuscript its first overseas reading and sent me a rave review that I was quick to share with potential publishers—even though João Paulo found ample cause to tease me about my idiosyncratically Azorean use of Portuguese.

A short story based on the adventures of "Mestre" Francisco, alluded to in this novel, was published on-line as "The Voyage to Brazil" by Dr. Irene Maria F. Blayer at *Comunidades*, a website devoted to the Azorean diaspora. Katharine F. Baker kindly brought my work to Professor Blayer's attention and provided yeoman service in manuscript proofing. *Muito obrigado!*

Throughout the writing and publication process I received much support from the "ink-stained wretches" of the Friday lunch group, a circle of retired journalists and journalism instructors that I am fortunate to count among my friends. Ted Fourkas, Walt Wiley, Doug Dempster, Dan O'Neill, Emery "Soap" Dowell, and Barbara Nielsen Dowell all read various versions of the manuscript and provided constructive criticism and advice. I have to single out the late Max Norris, former book review editor of the *Sacramento Bee*, for his encouragement and witty insights—especially his wry remark that my writing revealed a greater fondness for farm life than I was aware of.

Julian Silva (*Move Over, Scopes and Other Writings*) was generous enough to an unknown author to read the penultimate pre-publication version of the manuscript and give me the benefit of his expertise and insight. I am most thankful.

Finally, I am grateful to Reinaldo Silva, author of *Portuguese American Literature* and *Representations of the Portuguese in American Literature*, for suggesting that I share my manuscript with the Center for Portuguese Studies and Culture at the University of Massachusetts, Dartmouth. I followed Professor Silva's advice and have been gratified by the reception I received from Frank F. Sousa, founder of the Center and professor of Portuguese, and Richard J. Larschan, professor of English, who served as manuscript editor for *Land of Milk and Money*. With their gracious assistance, this first-time novelist has been privileged to share a personal perspective on Portuguese immigrant life.

ANTHONY BARCELLOS

Glossary

OF PORTUGUESE WORDS

AND PHRASES

Abença, Avó Bless me, Grandmother

apelido nickname

até logo till later

avô grandfather

avó grandmother

bem feito well done

boa sorte good luck

boa tarde good afternoon

Bom dia, filho Good morning, Son

Bom dia, Mãe Good morning, Mother

branco white

chama-rita a Portuguese dance

credo! heavens!

Deus God

estou aqui I'm here

fantasma ghost (phantom)

festa celebration (Portuguese version of "fiesta")

Festa do Divino Espirito Santo Celebration of the Divine Holy Spirit

jeito knack

madrinha godmother

mãe mother

mestre teacher (master)

muito obrigado thank you very much (much obliged)

nada nothing

não falo muito bem (I) don't speak very well

não sei (I) don't know

Nosso Senhor te abençoe The Lord has blessed you

obrigado thank you

o tolo the fool

padrinho godfather

pai father

panela large pan

patrão/patroa patron/patroness (boss)

perfeitamente perfectly

pois sim of course

primo/prima cousin

querida/querido dear

senhor sir

sim yes

tia aunt

tio uncle

velhinhas old women

Cast of Characters

Paulo "Chico" Francisco, the family patriarch who seeks his fortune in California

Teresa Francisco, the family matriarch who insists on Chico's family accompanying him to the United States

Fatima Francisco Salazar, eldest child of Chico and Teresa; married to Louis Salazar and mother of his seven children

Candido Francisco, the older son of Chico and Teresa; married to Odile

Paulinho Francisco, the younger son of Chico and Teresa; married to Carmina

Louis Salazar, spouse of Fatima and instigator of the lawsuit over his mother-in-law's will

Odile Avila Francisco, spouse of Candido and mother of his three sons

Carmina Soares Francisco, spouse of Paulinho and mother of his four children

Antonio "Tony" Salazar, eldest son of Louis and Fatima

Manuel "Manny" Salazar, second son of Louis and Fatima; married to Linda Fonseca

Otelo Salazar, third son of Louis and Fatima; party to the lawsuit over his grandmother's will

Leonel "Leo" Salazar, fourth son of Louis and Fatima

Catarina "Cat" Salazar, only daughter of Louis and Fatima; married to Kevin Lineman

Elvino "Elvis" Salazar, fifth son of Louis and Fatima; party to the lawsuit over his grandmother's will

Randall "Randy" Salazar, sixth son and youngest child of Louis and Fatima; party to the lawsuit over his grandmother's will

Linda Fonseca Salazar, spouse of Manny and her mother-in-law's successor as matriarch of the Salazar family

Kevin Lineman, spouse of Catarina Salazar

Candido "Junior" Francisco, Jr., eldest son of Candido and Odile; married to Sofia Silveira

João José "Jojo" Francisco, second son of Candido and Odile; married to Rita Branco

Ferdinando "Ferdie" Francisco, third son of Candido and Odile

Sofia Silveira Francisco, spouse of Junior

Rita Branco Francisco, spouse of Jojo

Filipa "Filly" Francisco, eldest daughter of Junior and Sofia

Candido "Trey" Francisco III, eldest son of Junior and Sofia; married to Lupita Cordero

Lupita Cordero Francisco, spouse of Trey Francisco

Paul Francisco, eldest son of Paulinho and Carmina

Mary Carmen Francisco Chamberlain, daughter of Paulinho and Carmina; married to Gerry Chamberlain and mother of his two sons

Henry "Hank" Francisco, second son of Paulinho and Carmina; married to Magdalena Fontes

Alexander "Alex" Francisco, third son of Paulinho and Carmina; a late addition to the family

Gerry Chamberlain, spouse of Mary Carmen Francisco

Magdalena "Maggie" Fontes Francisco, spouse of Henry Francisco and mother of his three daughters

Rebecca "Beckie" Francisco, eldest daughter of Henry and Magdalena

Alberto Avila, Odile Francisco's father

Odolina Avila, Odile Francisco's mother

Odette Avila, Odile Francisco's sister

Cynthia Parker, mistress and second wife of Candido Francisco

David Washington, friend and partner of Ferdinando Francisco

Frank Soares, Carmina Francisco's father

Beatriz Soares, Carmina Francisco's mother

Maria Anna and *Maria Olivia*, third cousins of Paul and Henry Francisco

Ryan Bowman, attorney for Candido Francisco and Paulinho Francisco and Paulinho's family

Harold Widener, attorney for Odile Francisco and Ferdinando Francisco

Dennis Ramos, attorney for Junior Francisco and Jojo Francisco

Beatrice "Biddy" Onan, attorney for Otelo, Elvino, and Randall Salazar; girl-friend of Louis Salazar

John Simoes, attorney for Teresa Francisco

Brevard Knight, presiding judge for the trial over Teresa Francisco's will

Richard Harmer, presiding judge for the divorce trial of Candido and Odile Francisco

Lysistrata Margaret Hunter, self-described handwriting expert for the petition-ers in the lawsuit over Teresa Francisco's will

James Franklin Foster, handwriting expert for the respondents in the lawsuit over Teresa Francisco's will

Dinis Costa, court-appointed receiver for Teresa Francisco's estate

Javier Joaquim, nephew of Beatrice Onan

Darrin MacDonald, farmer and friend of Paulinho Francisco

Bob Challenger, TV shop owner and friend of Paulinho Francisco

George Harper, adult-school electronics instructor

Monsignor Francis X. Pontac, pastor at St. Bartholomew's; founder and prin-cipal of its parochial school

Father Brendan Garrity, pastor at St. Bartholomew's; successor to Msgr. Pontac

Dolores Miller, first-grade teacher at Pleasant Hill Elementary School

Agnes White, fourth-grade teacher at Pleasant Hill Elementary School

Mrs. Knox, teacher for first through fourth grade at St. Bartholomew's Catho-lic School

Mrs. Cruise, teacher for fifth through eighth grade at St. Bartholomew's Catholic School

Giovanni "Gio" Machiavelli, friend and classmate of Paul Francisco's at Tech

Luis, friend and classmate of Paul Francisco's at St. Bartholomew's

Lloyd, third-grader at St. Bartholomew's

Gene, a fourth-grade boy at Pleasant Hill Elementary School

Coral, a fourth-grade girl at Pleasant Hill Elementary School

Ramiro, University Farm custodian; Azorean immigrant from Pico

Bob, auction yard clerk
Vidal, an employee of the Francisco dairy farm
Teofilo Torres, friend of Henry Francisco
Dr. Schein, medical doctor who attended to Teresa Francisco
Jennifer, hospital volunteer and receptionist
Rowena, administrative assistant in the State Treasurer's Office
Marcie, legal assistant to Harold Widener

PORTUGUESE IN THE
AMERICAS SERIES

*Portuguese-Americans and Contemporary
Civic Culture in Massachusetts*
Edited by Clyde W. Barrow

Through a Portagee Gate
Charles Reis Felix

*In Pursuit of Their Dreams: A History of Azorean
Immigration to the United States*
Jerry R. Williams

Sixty Acres and a Barn
Alfred Lewis

Da Gama, Cary Grant, and the Election of 1934
Charles Reis Felix

Distant Music
Julian Silva

Representations of the Portuguese in American Literature
Reinaldo Silva

The Holyoke
Frank X. Gaspar

Two Portuguese-American Plays
Paulo A. Pereira and Patricia A. Thomas
Edited by Patricia A. Thomas